After Rebecca

and Other Mystery Stories

Elizabeth Elwood

First Printing, 2018
Printed in North Charleston, South Carolina
ISBN 978-0-9782724-5-6

Published by Elihu Entertainment
www.elihuentertainment.com
info@elihuentertainment.com

For Jacqollyne

*Elihu
Entertainment*

CONTENTS

Elihu
Entertainment

After Rebecca

Last night I dreamt that Rebecca was alive again. She rose from the lake like some exotic creature of mythology, an undine, graceful, lithe and ravishingly beautiful. As I watched from the shore, she raised her slender arms, and the fluid allure of the water nymph became the sinuous suppleness of a sea serpent, the breathtaking smile transformed into the glittering grin of a sea witch. She glided across the glassy moonlit surface, her gleaming eyes riveted on my trembling form, as I stood paralyzed and helpless at the water's edge. She reached out to touch me; then the frightening spectre vanished, for with the supernatural ease borne of those who wander through the land of dreams, I was rescued from her clutches and transported far from the lake.

Now I was standing on the twisted drive that wound its way through whitened beeches and stunted oaks, meandering east, then west taking me away from Manderley and offering an escape from the vengeful creature who waited for me at the shore. But as I began to walk in the direction that, somehow, in my sleep, I knew led towards the gates, the forest closed in on me. The path narrowed, overgrown with strange and frightening shrubs that I could not recognize, and the pale beeches twined their branches overhead, creating a vault above my head—and suddenly

I realized that I had strayed into the Manderley of fiction; this was the wild and unkempt forest of the novel, not the estate that I knew and loved, where alders, horse chestnuts and walnut trees mingled among towering evergreens. As I tried to find my way through the skeletal branches and ugly, parasitic shrubs, I heard Max's voice in my head reminding me that I should have dressed as Alice in Wonderland, for that's where I belonged, in a land of make-believe.

I stumbled over a gnarled root and clutched at a stump to keep myself upright, but my heart was pounding as I forced my way along the narrowing path. Relief flooded through my soul when I spied the iron gates ahead. As I pushed my way towards them, my nightmare receded. I stepped out from the trees and the ground in front of me was clear again; the gravel restored to the drive, the grass on its verge, smooth and tended.

But then I saw her standing by the gates, the serpent smile etched on her pallid face. I was frozen with terror, unable to take even one step forward, but Rebecca opened the gates and beckoned me through.

"Why don't you go?" she said. "You'll never get the better of me. I'm still mistress here, even if I'm dead. I'm the real Mrs. de Winter, not you."

Mesmerized by her soft voice, I tried to move towards her, but a low wall seemed to block my way. A fog was settling around me, covering the ground and causing Rebecca's figure to become hazy and insubstantial. She appeared to be hovering in the air, and I realized that I was now looking at her through a tall, narrow window. Far below, I could see the lake, a gleaming mirror, reflecting the brilliant moonlight and a purple mackerel sky.

Rebecca's mouth twisted and her eyes became cruel.

"It's you that's the shadow and the ghost," she hissed. "It's you that's not wanted. Why don't you leave Manderley? Why don't you go?"

Someone else had moved behind me, and another voice was whispering in my ear, echoing the voice of the alien spirit beyond the window.

"There's not much for you to live for, is there? Why don't you jump? Go on, don't be afraid."

Then I was hurtling through space, and as I descended, the reflection of the moon became Rebecca's face and the mackerel sky faded into darkness. From the cold, black surface of the lake below, Rebecca reached out to welcome me into her watery grave.

*   *   *

Philippa Beary turned the windshield wipers on high and cursed her decision to continue her journey in spite of the storm warning. She was on her way home from Fort Benton, where she had travelled to sing at a friend's wedding. She had left Montana far later than she intended, but that had been unavoidable. Even though she had set off in early afternoon, she would have been able to reach the Washington border by bedtime if road conditions had been normal. The weather throughout her stay in Montana had been cold, but clear, and she had assumed that the drive back to Vancouver would be every bit as enjoyable as the trip down. Belatedly, she realized that when she stopped for dinner in Missoula, she should have listened to the weather warning issued by the kindly waitress and stopped there for the night. However, the temptation of the cozy bedroom waiting for her at the luxurious home of her parents' friends in Spokane outweighed the practicality of paying for an overnight stop in a motel.

Of course, there was another reason why she was anxious not to delay. After being out of town for the entire spring and summer of 2011, VPD Detective Bob Miller had finally returned to Vancouver. Tomorrow, he was taking a day off to drive across the border and meet her at the Wild Horse Monument in Washington, after which they were planning to enjoy a leisurely day, driving home in convoy, sightseeing en route, and stopping for dinner in Bellingham. Philippa was looking forward to their reunion and had no intention of fouling things up by failing to get there on time. Guiltily, she realized that if she had phoned Miller and told him that she would be late for their rendezvous, he would have told her to play it safe and remain where she was. The young detective tended to worry about her more than her own mother did, which was annoying at times. Still, it was gratifying to know that he cared enough to nag her. She had called her hosts in Spokane to warn them that she'd be coming in late; then, knowing Miller was likely to Google road warnings on her route and text her directives on what she should or should not do, she had deliberately turned off her cellphone. She had paid her restaurant bill, idly scanning the pile of newspapers in the stand by the door while she waited for her card to be approved. Her attention had been caught by a headline—*New Evidence in Death of Actress*—but before she could read further, the transaction was complete. She had tucked the charge slip away and set off again, determined to cover the three-hour drive that evening so as not to cut short the promised pleasures of the following day.

The drive to the summit had been fine, even though the big sky of Montana was rapidly vanishing in the fading light, but the evening had been clear and the traffic on I90 had been light. But once through Lookout Pass and into the Coeur d'Alene National Forest, the rain had started, at first a light sprinkle that only warranted an occasional sweep of the Jeep's wiper blades, and then a deluge, causing streams to race down the glass, rendering the blades as effective as a feather in a monsoon. The Idaho Panhandle, which had been a richly forested scenic panorama on her drive to Montana, was now a black void surrounding a gleaming, treacherous ribbon of road. The scenery she'd enjoyed on the way down—letters carved into mountainsides, picturesque church spires, ancient mines, snow-blanketed ski slopes—all had disappeared into the October night. Somewhere along the way, she had gone by the tiny towns of Smelterville and Wallace—she had noted them on the map before she started—but she had no idea when she had passed them. The wind had started, buffeting the Jeep and hurling the rain in all directions. She was tired, more so than she had realized, and the concentration required to hold the Jeep steady on course was causing her to become exhausted. Every so often, the rumble strips at the side of the highway would growl a warning to let her know she was veering off the road.

She had put on a CD when she'd set off from Missoula. It was one of her favourites, the incomparable Montserrat Caballé singing Puccini arias. The soprano's glorious pianissimos normally thrilled and inspired her, but now the rich tones were battling against the sound of the storm, which distorted the pitches and created an agitating cacophony that jangled Philippa's already taut nerves. She reached out a hand and cut off the music in mid-phrase. The hum of tires on the wet road filled the void and was curiously soothing, in spite of its eerie counterpoint as the wind whistled and gusted around the vehicle.

For a few miles, the rain eased to sporadic drops that were easily swished away, but the wind picked up, and Philippa could feel the tension in her shoulders as she gripped the wheel to keep the Jeep steady. Then a flash of lightning lit the sky, outlining the black mountains so suddenly that they appeared to have sprung up from the earth to surround her. A few seconds later, a distant roll of thunder drowned out the howling wind. Then the deluge began again. Philippa glanced at the clock on the dashboard. It was eight-thirty. Surely she must be approaching Lake Coeur d'Alene by now. Once there, it was little more than another hour to her destination.

The lightning flashed for a second time, and in the glow that momentarily flared across the sky, Philippa saw an exit sign to the right and an iridescent line of blue glittering on the horizon. Almost instantly, the thunder boomed overhead, a deafening roll that growled its way across the mountaintops. There was another flash. The distant line of blue was broader; the lake was getting closer. Then came another lightning crack, but before the giant grizzly in the sky let out its protracted roar, Philippa heard a tiny echo, a snapping sound, and then it was gone, drowned out by the rolling thunder. As the rumbling faded and died, a flapping noise in the engine became audible. The fan belt had broken.

Muttering and cursing—how could everything be going so wrong? —Philippa pulled over onto the verge. Switching on the interior light, she extracted her copy of *Next Exit* from the pile of maps and brochures on the passenger seat. Two sets of headlights flashed by; then the world went black again. Philippa opened the book and searched for I90 in Idaho. If she could locate a service station in the area, an operator could find her the number. Ruefully, she remembered Miller's dismissing comments about her antiquated cellphone and her cheerful rebuttal that she could manage perfectly well without an iPhone. She would be eating her words tomorrow, along with the Black Angus steak dinner that Miller had promised her on their way home from the Wild Horse Monument. She flipped the pages until she pinpointed her location. With a surge of relief, she identified an Exxon that had to be somewhere in the vicinity of Lake Coeur d'Alene, possibly off the next exit, and feeling more optimistic, she pulled out her cellphone and turned it back on. Then her heart sank for the second time that evening. No service. She was in the middle of nowhere with the heavens doing their worst, and she had no way of getting help, short of flagging down the next motorist who came down the highway, and with her current run of luck, that would probably turn out to be a descendent of Jack the Ripper.

She turned off the phone, flicked off the interior light and stared miserably out into the rain. The view in the headlights was dispiriting: a grey expanse of gleaming asphalt, a dull gravel verge, and a black wall of trees. But as she continued to peer into the night, she made out a narrow white oblong a hundred feet ahead. It was the wrong colour for a highway sign, but it might be a billboard. If so, it would be a way she could identify her location once she was able to call for help.

She started the engine again and trundled along the verge. The trees receded to reveal an exit road which matched the number of the Exxon reference in her guide, but there was no gas station in sight. However, the white oblong had expanded into a rectangular sign bearing the single word, *Accommodation*, and a few yards along the dark country road that adjoined the exit, she could see a matching sign with an arrow pointing towards an opening in the trees. Help was at hand.

Philippa decided to risk overheating the Jeep's engine and keep going. She followed the exit ramp onto the country road and pulled up by the second sign. Now she could see a gravel road on her left cutting into the forest. No lights showed through the trees, but the hotel, or whatever it was, could not be far away. She swung the wheel over, and driving slowly, steered the Jeep onto the road.

She had travelled less than half a mile when she came to a pair of wrought-iron gates. They were set between ornamental pillars that seemed out of place in the surrounding terrain. Above the gates, an arch curved from one pillar to the other, its intricate pattern interspersed with leaves and twigs that had blown loose in the storm. Another sign was attached to a tall cedar tree beside the gateway, but although Philippa could make out the words, *Resort Hotel*, and above, in larger print, the letters, *M*, *a*, *n*, *d*, the rest of the word was hidden by a branch that was drooping in the weight of the rain.

The gates were open, so she drove through and found herself on a twisting gravel drive that meandered east, then west, and seemed to go on interminably. The headlights, gliding from corner to corner, illuminated a thick forest where evergreens mingled with horse chestnuts, walnut trees and tall alders whose branches reached towards each other from either side, creating a vaulted canopy for the track below. The shrubs and ground cover were thick, and the ever-moving wall of trees had a magical, yet menacing quality, as if it were gliding towards her, pulling her in and enclosing her in an alien world. The winding track had a familiar air; it reminded her of something—not a place she had been, perhaps, but a place she had read about—something from a storybook.

Manderley, she thought suddenly. That's what it was. She could have been transported to the opening pages of the Daphne du Maurier novel. Manderley had been the epitome of the perfect English country home: a manor house overlooking the water and set in luxurious grounds where cultivated lawns abutted massed rhododendron bushes and thick forests—forests that concealed the twisting, winding drive that must be navigated before reaching the house. Was that what the letters on the iron arch at the gates had spelled? Had someone, seeing the same similarities, whimsically named the estate after the home immortalized in *Rebecca*?

Philippa had read the book as a teenager and been captivated by the story of Maxim, the brooding romantic hero, and his timid second wife who felt haunted by the memories of her glamorous predecessor. Rebecca had been the title character, but she had never appeared in the novel, yet her presence permeated every page. Philippa had loved the book. Young and romantic, she had identified with the nameless second wife, so terrified of the sinister housekeeper, Mrs. Danvers, who was determined to keep Rebecca's memory alive.

As Philippa drove, the story came back to her and she remembered the other characters who had inhabited the book: the dissolute Jack Favell, who hated Maxim and tried to destroy him; Maxim's good-natured sister, Beatrice, so refreshingly normal and down-to-earth; Frank Crawley, the kindly estate manager who offered support and encouragement; Old Ben, the strange old man in the cottage by the water; and Jasper, the spaniel who led the second wife on her explorations about the estate.

Philippa rounded another corner and was drawn from her reverie by a flash of light ahead. The trees glided apart to reveal an expanse of grey storm cloud; then, as the Jeep burst out of the forest, a second bolt of lightning lit the night sky. To the right, an overgrown shrubbery towered above the Jeep. Philippa gasped. Monster rhododendrons? No, impossible. This was ridiculous. She was in Idaho, not England. But beyond was a vista of open space sweeping down to the water, and at the centre, symmetrical and elegant, darkly silhouetted against the glittering lake, was a house with a tier of terraces overlooking the water. *Manderley*, thought Philippa. I've walked into a storybook. I must be dreaming.

Then as quickly as it had flared, the lightning flash faded, and the night was plunged back into darkness. The roll of thunder followed a few seconds later. Uneasily, Philippa saw that only one solitary light gleamed in the window of the building by the water.

*   *   *

When Bertram Beary arrived home after his Monday-night Council meetings, his efficient wife usually had the kettle on, ready for their bedtime cup of tea. However, when he walked through the door at twenty past nine, smugly conscious that he was much earlier than usual and could probably sneak in a glass of Scotch before the tea appeared, he found Edwina looking anxious. Her normally immaculate blonde hair was a little ruffled and her forehead was furrowed with a trio of worry lines that made her look every one of her sixty-five years in spite of her trim figure and impeccable grooming.

"I haven't heard from Philippa all afternoon," she announced.

Beary patted his husky, MacPuff, who had been lying in the hall waiting to greet him. Then he hung up his coat and dumped his briefcase on the hallstand.

"Well, she was starting back today, wasn't she? She'll have been on the road."

"Yes, but she usually texts just to let me know she's arrived safely. But there's been nothing, and look at the time. She should have reached Spokane by now."

Beary was not alarmed.

"She's probably out on the town with the Burleighs." These were the Bearys' friends who lived in Spokane. "As I recall, they took her out for dinner at Milford's Fish House when she stopped on the way down. She's just having a good time and has forgotten to let you know. She's not a child, for heaven's sake."

Beary marched down the hall and headed for the kitchen cupboard where the Scotch bottle was kept. If Edwina was going to fret, he needed that drink.

Edwina was close on his heels.

"I was going to make tea."

"We can have tea, but I'll have this first. If you're really that worried, why don't you phone her?"

"I've tried. I just get her voicemail."

"So call the Burleighs and check to see if she's arrived?"

Edwina glanced at the clock. It was nine-thirty.

"Yes, perhaps I will. You don't think she'll feel I'm being overly interfering?"

"Of course she will, but she's used to that. Just call and stop fussing."

Beary took a sip of Scotch and sighed contentedly. His wife should be worried more often, he thought smugly. Usually, she would be eyeing his glass and commenting acerbically on the size of his paunch, whereas tonight, she had barely noticed. The likelihood of remaining unscathed through a second glass looked infinitely promising.

Edwina started towards the door, but before she could reach it, the phone rang. Beary waved his glass in the direction of the hall.

"There. You see. I told you she was all right."

Beary sat at the kitchen table and put his feet up on the chair opposite his own. He could hear Edwina's voice in the hall, but he was not paying much attention. He picked up the newspaper, still there from the morning, and flipped to the financial pages, but after a moment, he lowered the paper again. Edwina was still on the phone, but her voice had an edge that did not sound like the tone she normally used when talking to their youngest daughter. In fact, thought Beary, it did not sound as if Edwina was talking to Philippa at all.

As he leaned towards the door, trying to hear what was being said, he heard the sound of the phone being returned to the cradle, and a moment later, Edwina appeared in the doorway. Her expression was grim.

"That was Bob Miller," she said. "He's been trying to get hold of Philippa all day. He's been texting her and getting no reply, which is unusual, and what's more, he's been checking the road reports, and evidently there's a horrendous storm where Philippa is travelling. He called to see if we'd heard from her. I'm getting really worried."

"Well," said Beary, trying to process the information calmly, "if there's a storm, the cell service may well be out. That would explain the lack of contact. Look, phone the Burleighs and see if they have any news."

Edwina went back to the phone and flipped through the address book to find the number for their American friends. Beary took his drink out to the hall and watched as his wife made the call. Uneasily, he saw that her expression showed no signs of relief as she listened to the voice on the other end. When she hung up, she turned to him and shook her head.

"No sign of her. She called them shortly before six. She'd stopped for dinner at the Cracker Barrel in Missoula and was just setting off again. She was going to drive straight through and said she'd be there around nine, give or take fifteen minutes or so."

"Well, it's only just nine-thirty. She'll roll in any moment now."

"Yes, I expect you're right. Three hours is a long drive at one sit. She might stop for coffee along the way."

Beary nodded, though remembering the isolated stretch of country through the Idaho Panhandle, he privately doubted it. Still, he had no desire to worry his wife further so he kept his thoughts to himself. Suddenly ill at ease, he noticed that MacPuff, who was lying in his usual spot on the carpet by the kitchen door, was not asleep, but was watching them both intently, as if he sensed that something was not quite right. Minx the Manx had also appeared. She had emerged from the living room and was padding restlessly up and down the hall.

Edwina picked up the phone again.

"Who are you calling now?" Beary asked.

"Bob Miller. I told him I'd let him know if I heard anything."

Judging by the speed with which the call was answered, Miller had been waiting by the phone. Edwina told him what she had heard from the Burleighs, and then, as an afterthought, gave him the Spokane number so he would be able to contact them directly. Then, having done all she could, she returned to the kitchen and put the kettle on.

"I asked Mary Burleigh to phone me as soon as Philippa arrives," she said to Beary. "Just to set our minds at rest."

"Good thought," said Beary, draining his Scotch and putting the glass in the dishwasher. "Now let's enjoy that cup of tea and stop fretting."

But at eleven o'clock, when the phone finally rang, Mary Burleigh was unable to put their minds at rest. Philippa had not arrived. Neither had she called to indicate why she was delayed. Somewhere between Missoula and Spokane, she seemed to have vanished off the face of the earth.

*   *   *

That first summer, Max and Rebecca recreated the Manderley fancy-dress ball. Unlike the ball in the novel, this was not hosted for their friends and neighbours; it was a big-dollar, ticketed fundraiser for the theatre company. Still, everyone entered into the spirit of the occasion and it was a wonderful event.

What was even more wonderful for me was that Rebecca announced she had no intention of wearing the dowdy wig and costume of Maxim's second wife. She was going to the ball as Rebecca; she would dress in the stunning Caroline de Winter costume, the outfit that Maxim's first wife had worn for the final ball of her life. She eyed me up and down, with my mousy hair and pale complexion, and declared that the dowdy blue dress would be perfect for me. I could play the timid wife-number-one for the evening.

What a fabulous night it turned out to be. Max insisted that I should stand with him and Rebecca at the bottom of the stairs as they greeted the guests. It was appropriate: Maxim, the host of Manderley, with both his wives. But unlike the story, Max was not cold and angry, but talked to me kindly and made me feel special. Soon, Rebecca left us to join the dancing, and I remained at his side, still playing my part.

Max, of course, was not in fancy dress, and he looked breathtakingly handsome in his tuxedo. Dear Frank played the part of his namesake well, even to the extent of donning side-whiskers to go with his pirate costume. Danny excelled as Mrs. Danvers, austerely encasing her slender body in drab black linen, while Bea, good-naturedly, put on a peculiar assortment of vaguely Eastern draperies, not caring how silly they made her look. The guests rose to the occasion too, for many were enthusiasts of the du Maurier novel. There was a rouged woman with prominent teeth who wore the salmon-coloured crinoline gown described in the book, and she acted her part, dipping and swaying to the interminable waltz and smiling at me as she went by. There must have been at least four Lady Crowans, some emulating Marie Antoinette and some Nell Gwynn, but all in the compulsory purple. Rebecca had come to life.

The buffet was a fabulous spread, which it should have been, given the exorbitant cost of the tickets. The famous Manderley salmon-and-lobster mayonnaise formed a colourful centrepiece, and every other imaginable treat was laid out on either side. Of course, none of the servers dropped a tray of ices. There were some things in the book that were better forgotten.

At the end of the evening, everyone declared the event a triumph, although I noticed a coolness between Max and Rebecca. She had spent much of the evening dancing with an actor who had performed with them years before when they made a film about Lord Nelson. I pointed out to Max that Rebecca had simply been playing her part, and he gave me a hug and told me I was too sweet for this world and that I should never change.

I could not sleep that night for dreaming. Oh, will I ever experience such an evening again!

* * *

By the time Philippa pulled up on the wide expanse of gravel at the end of the drive, the rain had stopped and the storm was moving away. Sporadic flashes of lightning still lit the horizon, but the thunder followed more slowly and the rumbling was distant and muted. She got out of the car, noticing uneasily that, other than a dilapidated pickup truck, there were no other vehicles in the parking area. She pulled her overnight case out from the back seat and walked towards the house.

As she drew near, Philippa realized that it had only been her imagination that had created the English manor house of the novel. This building did have the grandeur that she associated with Manderley, but it was a product of North American architecture. A glowing lantern beside the huge front door revealed that the walls were red brick, but the white Ionic columns and the inlaid porches and balconies running the width of the house suggested a Colonial revival mansion from the early part of the last century. Philippa glanced up and saw the black silhouette of the eaves outlined sharply against the turbulent night sky. The building towered over her, three, perhaps even four storeys. The one lit window was on the second floor, and yellow light glowed warmly behind lace curtains that were entirely in keeping with the period of the house. The sound of voices, intermingled with music, drifted down from the window. Someone was watching television.

Philippa shivered, suddenly realizing how chilled she had become. She walked up onto the porch and looked for a doorbell. Seeing none, she knocked loudly on the front door. Nothing happened for several seconds. She was about to try again, when she realized that the volume of the television had dropped to a low murmur. Was the watcher coming down, or simply trying to identify the sound that had interrupted the program? Philippa raised her fist and knocked again. After what seemed like an eternity, a woman's voice called out from overhead.

"Who is it?"

Philippa stepped back from the porch and looked up at the window. She could see the outline of the woman. The figure was shadowy against the light, but the voice was clear and strong. Philippa detected a trace of an English accent.

She explained her dilemma, hoping against hope that she sounded genuine and harmless enough for the woman to let her in. After a round of questions, which seemed as interminable as the long, winding driveway, the voice commanded her to wait and the figure disappeared inside the room. A moment later, the fanlight window above the front door was flooded with light.

Then Philippa heard footsteps and the door opened to reveal a tall, thin woman with the kind of ageless beauty that Philippa associated with the elegant theatrical stars who could still play Juliet well into their sixties. She had dramatic bone structure and dark, wiry hair that framed her face like an unruly halo. Her black dressing gown was made from a soft, flowing fabric that hung in well-designed folds around her gaunt frame, and her expression, if not unfriendly, was severe. She stood aside and invited Philippa in.

Philippa stepped forward, uneasily aware that the woman was uncannily reinforcing the *Rebecca* images in her head—Dame Judith Anderson as Mrs. Danvers came to mind. Once inside, Philippa found herself in a hall with parquet flooring underfoot and soaring oak beams overhead. It was as grand as anything the fictitious Manderley had to offer. A sweeping central staircase led to a portrait-lined gallery, while elegant wainscoting lined the walls of the main floor. Above the chair-rails, oil paintings of rural scenes of the English countryside reinforced the sense of old world superimposed on new. On a carved oak cabinet by the entrance, a vibrant arrangement of dahlias brought a startling splash of colour to the room. Beside the flowers was a guest book. Imprinted in embossed gold letters on the soft leather cover were the words, *Welcome to Manderley*.

Philippa's head swam. It was all too much: the winding drive, the rhododendrons, the Mrs. Danvers look-alike, the grand entrance hall. She had stepped into a world where time had stopped. She was Alice fallen down the rabbit hole, Wendy Darling in Neverland, Lucy Pevensie finding Narnia through the wardrobe. Nothing was real. She wondered if she was dreaming.

Her hostess's clipped voice brought Philippa back to earth.

"I can't contact your people or call for help with your car."

The voice was definitely British, but with the precise diction that sometimes indicated a foreigner who had learned English as a second language. Still, *Rebecca* had been translated into many languages and achieved worldwide popularity. Anyone could be a du Maurier junkie, and perhaps this woman was one, fancifully recreating her favourite book. There had to be some logical explanation for the strange setting.

Oblivious to Philippa's thoughts, the woman continued. Her manner was not unkind, though a little detached, as if her mind was elsewhere too. "Our phones have gone out," she said, "but I'm sure they'll be back in the morning. Still, you can sleep here tonight, and at least you'll be safe and warm."

"Is anyone else staying here right now?" Philippa asked. The deserted air of the place was making her feel uneasy.

The woman hesitated before she replied. When she spoke, her voice sounded strained.

"No, we only take guests from May to September. There's only myself and our cook here right now. The rest of the staff has been let go for the winter."

"But it's only October. Don't you have some overlap time? You must have to get things ready for next season?"

"Well, usually, yes. But this year has been a little different. I'm afraid the rooms in the guest wing have been stripped, so other than the private rooms, the only bed made up is in the display suite. I'll have to put you up there."

Philippa followed the woman up to the gallery. She noticed a door marked *private* to her left. Presumably that led to the wing where the owners of the estate lived. The wall of the gallery, like the Manderley of the novel, was lined with portraits of men and women, all similar in feature, wearing costumes from across the ages. Philippa was no longer surprised when she saw the portrait of a dark-haired woman in white at the end of the gallery. Lady Caroline de Winter without a doubt. Whoever had created this strange replica of the fictitious estate had spared none of the important details.

Her hostess disappeared through an opening at the end of the gallery. Realizing the lateness of the hour and the imposition she had put on this woman who had probably been ready to finish her TV program and turn in for the night, Philippa hurried after her. When she turned the corner, she saw a long corridor with doors along the right-hand side. The hardwood flooring was carpeted with a maroon runner edged with gold, and her footsteps made no sound as she followed the dark figure gliding silently ahead.

Halfway along, there was an alcove where a narrow flight of stairs ascended, dimly illuminated by a series of ornamental wall sconces that cast as many shadows as they did light. Her hostess started up the staircase and Philippa followed curiously. At the top was a landing with a tall, narrow window that probably had a fine view of the grounds in daylight. To its left was a white door with gold accents on inlaid panels. The woman opened the door, flicked on the light and stepped aside to let Philippa through.

Philippa entered the room; then she gasped. It was Rebecca's bedroom. Every detail in the novel had been reproduced: the carved bedstead with its quilted coverlet, the curtain hangings, the flowers on the mantelpiece, the brushes and combs on the dressing table, the candlesticks and the clock on the wall. Even the satin dressing gown was there, delicately laid out beside the monogrammed nightdress case.

Unmindful of Philippa's reaction, her hostess bustled forward and whisked away the items on the bed, quickly depositing them in the wardrobe. Then she turned down the bedcovers.

"I expect you're exhausted," she said firmly. She pointed to a door at the far end of the room. "The bathroom is through there, and there's fresh soap and clean towels in the cupboard. You should have everything you need." She stepped back to the doorway as if ready to leave. Philippa realized that any hope she'd had of a drink or bite to eat was not going to materialize. But beggars couldn't be choosers, and she was lucky to have found a sanctuary for the night, even if it was a somewhat peculiar one. The bed looked particularly inviting, and she was suddenly conscious that she ached with fatigue.

"Thank you," she said. "I really appreciate this. You must let me know in the morning what I owe you."

"Don't worry about that. As I told you, we're not officially open at the moment. Consider yourself an invited guest. Sleep well. We'll get you sorted out in the morning. Come down to the kitchen once you're up. It's on the main floor. There's no point in setting up the dining room for just the three of us. Breakfast at nine o'clock."

"Wonderful," Philippa said sincerely. She was about to close the door when she realized that she had not learned the woman's name.

"Oh," she said, embarrassed. "I introduced myself, but I never got your name."

An enigmatic smile came over the woman's face and transformed her sharp features into a strangely disturbing mask. It was impossible to tell whether the gleam in her eyes signified amusement or malice.

"You can call me Danny," she said.

Then, still maintaining her inscrutable air, she stepped into the corridor and closed the door.

Philippa was too tired to react. She was past caring where she was as long as there was a bed to sleep in. As soon as her head hit the pillow, she began to drift off to sleep, but as she hovered briefly in the twilight zone, the vague thought floated into her mind: I don't even care if Mrs. Danvers burns the house down in the night.

Then sleep came, blessedly dreamless. On the floor below, the noise of the television stopped. The light went off and the house was cloaked in darkness.

*   *   *

When Bob Miller learned that Philippa had not shown up at the Burleighs, he put a call in to the state police in Montana, Idaho and Washington, explaining who he was and giving them a description of Philippa, along with the licence number of her Jeep. Then he threw a change of clothes in an overnight bag, hopped in his SUV and set off for the border. If he drove through the night, he could be in Spokane by morning, and from there, if necessary, he would drive the entire route between there and Missoula until he found out what had happened to her. Once across the border, he fortified himself with a meal from Denny's, then drove steadily, only stopping for a short catnap on the way down I5. At each stop, he tried to contact

Philippa and left her another text message. By seven o'clock, he arrived at the Burleighs' house, only to be told that there was still no news.

Calls to the highway patrols in the three states produced no reports of an accident, yet none of the state troopers who had been alerted to her disappearance had found any trace of Philippa or her vehicle. Miller felt sick, knowing well what it could mean when a young woman disappeared while travelling the highway. Still, fretting about the possibility of an abduction was not going to help Philippa. He had to think positively and do something constructive.

There was only one thing for it. He would take a short break at the Burleighs; then he would set off again. One factor was in his favour. Philippa was very distinctive. She was slender and petite, barely five feet tall, but her red curly hair and pert, sharp features gave her a charming elfin appearance that was quite unusual. In spite of her diminutive size, she had excellent posture and great presence, partly natural and partly from her stage training. She was someone that people noticed, and if she had crossed anyone's path, they would remember her. Miller was determined to travel I90, stopping at every town and rest stop until he came across someone who had seen her. She was out there somewhere, and he was going to find her.

*   *   *

Around the time that Miller was arriving at the Burleighs' home in Spokane, Philippa was awakened by the faint glow of light filtering through the window curtains of her bedroom. So far, so good. Nothing sinister had happened in the night. She slid out of bed, padded over to the side window and drew open the curtains. Then she gave a gasp of delight. From the height of her room, she had an unimpeded view of the water. Lake Coeur d'Alene was a vast sheet of metallic grey, gleaming softly in the dawn light and stretching far into the distance, the water's edge jaggedly interrupted by rocky outcrops. The dark mountains on the furthermost shore seemed to lighten to purple, then blue, even as Philippa watched. It was going to be a beautiful day.

She moved to the window in the end wall and opened the drapes. From here, she could make out a strip of lawn between the house and the water. At the lake's edge were two large boathouses. Further to the right, she saw a wooden deck and a series of docks, although no boats appeared to be moored there. Presumably, the rowboats and kayaks had been put away for the winter. Further along the shore was a shadowy wooden structure with a wide deck protruding out onto the lake.

Philippa glanced at her watch. It was only a quarter to eight. She had more than an hour before breakfast, and after the six-hour drive of the previous day, the prospect of fresh air and a walk along the lakeshore was appealing. It was obvious that she had missed her date with Miller, so her sense of urgency had evaporated. But maybe he could come and meet her here, if she could only get hold of him. She turned on her phone to see if there was service, but there was still no signal, so she turned it off again and slipped it back into her bag. Grabbing a change of underwear from her overnight bag, she showered in the luxurious en suite, and then put on the leggings and warm sweater that she had worn the previous day.

By the time she was dressed, the sun had come up and the light was streaming in. The view from the side window was no longer monochromatic; it was now a magical panorama of blues and greens, softened by patches of morning mist and gilded with splashes of gold where the deciduous trees poked out amid the firs and pines. Now that the sun was higher, Philippa could see that a trail followed the lakeshore, curving around to a nearby point where a small cottage, red-roofed and picturesque, huddled among a mass of vibrant perennial shrubs which had weathered the storm of the previous day. The swaths of pink and lavender gave the house a storybook appearance. A thin trail of smoke drifted up from the chimney, dissipating as it joined the mist that rose from the lake and filtered into the trees.

As she watched, a figure emerged from the cottage. It was clearly visible over the colourful bushes, although a toque and bulky coat shrouded the sex of the person beneath. The figure walked around to the back garden; then, like a bobbing cork, the toque began to disappear and reappear as the person bent and straightened, apparently trying to repair the damage of the previous night's storm. The lush garden and the squat stone building obscured the view beyond the point and it was impossible to see whether the trail stopped at the cottage or continued along the shore. It was time to explore. Philippa threw on her coat and hurried downstairs.

When she reached the lower hall, she saw her hostess standing by the reservation desk. Danny was still dressed in black, but now she wore slacks and a cowl-necked sweater, both as stylish as her dressing gown of the previous evening. The light beaming through the fanlight window flashed onto her face, accentuating Magyar eyes that were a startling green. Her expression was disconcerting, and it was impossible to tell her age. She pointed towards the phone and shook her head.

"Still out," she said.

Philippa refused to be daunted by the woman's imposing presence. She decided to tackle her head on.

"You're not really called Mrs. Danvers, are you?"

Danny gave a faint smile as if she was aware of what Philippa was thinking. However, all she replied was, "No. My name is Danuta."

"Danuta? Is that Czechoslovakian? Hungarian?"

Danny shook her head.

"No. Polish, though my grandmother on my father's side was Hungarian."

"How did you acquire that lovely English accent?"

"My parents escaped to England during the Second World War. I grew up in London." Danny's clipped voice delivered the information matter-of-factly. Philippa felt she was concealing as much as she was revealing, but before she could ask any more questions, Danny moved out from the counter and said, "I'll try the phone later. It's bound to be back on soon. Once it is, I'll call the garage and see if someone can come out and look at your car. I'm going to need a mechanic myself because the battery is dead in the pick-up truck so we're stranded too. But in the meantime, make yourself comfortable. Breakfast won't be ready until nine, but you can probably get a cup of coffee if you go down to the kitchen now."

"Actually, I'd like to go for a walk. Are all the paths open to the public?"

"Yes. There's a paved road that leads to the cabins if you go to the right. It runs past the sports pavilion."

"Is that the building on the far side of the docks? The one with the deck that juts out over the water?"

"Yes. We keep our sports equipment there. That deck goes right round the building and it's also used as a dock. No railings, so we can tie up our kayaks and canoes in the summer. It's a lovely spot to sit and relax. The pavilion is locked now, but you can still walk around it and look at the view."

"What about the trail that goes to the cottage on the point? Is that open to the public?"

"Yes. That's where old Sam, our gardener, lives. The trail cuts into the woods by his cottage, and then winds back to the lake and goes on for a long way, but you don't want to go that far. You can make it to the point and back before breakfast. It only takes fifteen minutes to walk round." Danny pointed to an archway behind the stairs. "Go through there and down the steps to the basement. Follow the hall. It'll take you to a door at the back corner of the house. The path starts there."

Philippa thanked her and turned to go. She found her way to the basement and followed the hall, which, as Danny had said, stretched the full length of the house. She passed a laundry room, set opposite a door labelled *storage*, and then went by a large rec room. The door was open and she could see a dartboard and a ping-pong table inside. There was only one other door in the hallway. It was on the opposite side and close to the end. The door was slightly ajar. Philippa peeked in curiously and saw what appeared to be a self-contained suite. It was spotlessly clean. The furnishings were pleasing replicas of Colonial America and the ambience was cozy and welcoming.

Having explored the length of the basement, Philippa reached the back door. She stepped outside and found herself in a concrete stairwell. When she climbed the steps, she saw she was only a few feet from the path by the lake. The air was cold and crisp, in spite of the brightness of the morning, and she pulled her collar up around her neck, tying her scarf snugly to hold it in place. Then she set off on the lake trail.

In the wake of the heavy rainfall, the path was muddy, and covered with wet pine needles and dead leaves which made for slippery walking. Philippa persevered, and fifteen minutes later, the scent of the pine needles became adulterated with the smell of smoke. She rounded a bend and saw the cottage ahead. Old Sam was still outside, tying up the beanpoles that had blown over in the storm.

As Philippa approached, she saw that Danny's description of the trail had been accurate. It clung to the shore until it reached the end of the cottage garden, after which it cut inland, following the border of the property until it disappeared into the woods. Philippa had no desire to venture there, so she stopped when she reached the turn. She peered over the bushes into the garden. Old Sam looked up and nodded a brusque greeting. He was a small, wiry man with piercing blue eyes and skin like wrinkled parchment. His coarse grey hair stuck out in two clumps under his woollen toque, giving him the appearance of an elderly gnome.

In spite of the lateness of the season, the garden was still a mass of colour. The row of shrubs that Philippa had seen from her window bordered the garden on the east side of the point. Close up, the pale pink blossoms stood out sharply against the variegated green of the leaves, which, in turn, contrasted pleasingly with the bright green of the runner beans propped up behind them.

"Those are so pretty," she said. "What are they?"

"Abelia. Stay in bloom late, those do."

"They stood up to the storm well," said Philippa.

"Mebbe did, but not my dahlias," Sam said gloomily.

He pointed to the flowerbed that stretched along the lake side of the property. The tall, proud flowers had been toppled by wind and rain and the once-luxuriant heads were flattened against the dirt. Only one patch of the flowers that had been sheltered against the cottage remained upright.

"Oh, what a shame! They must have been beautiful."

"They bloom late into the fall, but they're no good now. No more for the big house this year."

Philippa suddenly remembered the floral arrangement she had noticed in the hall when she arrived.

"Were those your flowers? The ones in the hall?"

"Aye," said Sam. "She always liked my dahlias. Lush and flashy, just like she was. He used to come by and pick them for her, but not any more. They remind him too much of her. But I always take some up to the house, even though she's gone now."

The uneasy feeling that had haunted Philippa the previous evening returned. She felt an icy grip on her heart that cut deeper than the chill in the October air.

"Who's gone now?" she asked.

Sam looked surprised that she had posed the question.

"Rebecca," he said.

*   *   *

Having slept for an hour in the Burleighs' guest room, Miller made short work of the hearty breakfast that his hostess insisted on providing; then he set off again. He gassed up at the Exxon Station, then headed for the freeway. It was not much past eight-thirty, so he calculated that he could reach Missoula well before noon, and it made more sense to travel the distance to Missoula and work his way back from there. If Philippa had made any stops, they would have been on the north side of the freeway. Besides, the one place he knew she'd visited was the Cracker Barrel in Missoula, so it would be smart to talk to the staff at the restaurant and see if they had any information. His mind drifted darkly, visualizing the alarming scenarios that he knew only too well could be a reality. Had Philippa been talking with anyone in the restaurant? Had anyone approached her in the parking lot? Had anyone actually seen her get into her Jeep and set off?

As he drove, he turned on the radio to hear if there were any accident reports, although he was sure that the state patrol would contact him directly if any new information came in. Idly, he listened to the news as he sped down the highway, overtaking the trucks and slower drivers in the right-hand lane. World news seemed to predominate: more friction in the Middle East—so what else was new—a mass shooting in California, another royal scandal in Britain. He fiddled with the radio, trying to find a local channel, but only succeeded in producing a lot of static and distorted sound. Suddenly, the crackling stopped and a voice came through announcing a new investigation into the death of movie star, Rebecca Vincent. Miller was about to change the channel again when he realized that this news was from an Idaho station. He vaguely recalled hearing about the star's death by drowning, but since he never paid much attention to movie news, particularly items pertaining to the actors of a previous generation, he knew very little about the woman's death. The announcement was frustratingly short of detail, but it did indicate that new evidence had been found on the star's estate at Lake Cœur d'Alene. He wondered what had been unearthed to prompt a new inquiry so long after her death.

$$*   *   *$$

Philippa could glean no other information from Sam, so she gave up and returned to the house. Perhaps the cook would be more forthcoming.

She entered the back door and followed the appetizing smell of frying bacon until she found the kitchen. It was another high-ceilinged room with oaken beams, an old-fashioned sideboard and inlaid cupboard doors that fit the period feel of the rest of the house; however, the steel appliances were spotless and modern. A stout woman was frying eggs at the stove. She had a straight bob of wiry grey hair framing a round face that would have been pleasant if it had not been creased with an anxious frown. She was dressed in a quilted housecoat that reminded Philippa of the dressing gowns her mother used to wear and had abandoned after her father had gleefully referred to them as haute couture oven mitts.

Danny was already eating her breakfast at the sturdy kitchen table, which had been set with cheerful blue and white checked placemats and bone-handled cutlery. She waved Philippa towards the sideboard, where platters of pancakes, bacon and sausages were laid out on a hot plate. No kedgeree or kippers, Philippa noted thankfully. Pancakes were refreshingly American. As she admired the buffet, she sensed eyes upon her. Looking down, she saw a cocker spaniel at her elbow, optimism shining from its soft brown eyes.

"Oh," said Philippa, "please don't tell me his name is Jasper."

The cook managed a faint smile.

"Sorry, but it is—and mine's Bea, but it's short for Betty, not Beatrice," she said, handing Philippa a plate with a perfectly cooked over-easy egg and gesturing towards the sideboard. Philippa filled her plate; curiosity had not diminished her appetite. Then she sat down at the table. She looked at her hostesses and raised her eyebrows. She was not going to budge until one of them explained what was going on.

Danny ignored Philippa's quizzical look. She finished her breakfast and stood up.

"You fill her in," she said to Bea. "I'm going to try the phone again."

Danny rinsed her plate at the sink and placed it in the dishwasher. Then she left the room. Bea washed out the frying pan, and then took her own plate to the sideboard. She piled several strips of bacon on top of her egg and joined Philippa at the table.

"You've read *Rebecca*, then? So many young people haven't."

"Yes, years ago. I loved it." Philippa's response was genuinely enthusiastic. "I've seen the Hitchcock film, too, because it's always popping up on the classic-movie channel."

"What about the BBC version that was made in 1990? It ran out here on PBS."

"No," Philippa said ruefully. "My mother saw it. She said it was fabulous. I keep hoping they'll release it on DVD someday."

Bea's jaw stiffened and her eyes became dark.

"I expect they will soon, thanks to all the publicity," she said. "There'll be money in it now that they're raking up Rebecca's death again."

Philippa stared, open-mouthed, wondering if all the people who inhabited this imitation Manderley were slightly delusional. Then she remembered the headline she had seen in the restaurant, and all of a sudden, the odd disjointed images that had caused her to become so disoriented fell into place.

"Rebecca Vincent!" she cried. "She and her husband starred in the BBC version of *Rebecca*, didn't they? Was this their home?"

Bea sighed and nodded.

"Yes, hers and Maxwell West's. It was Max's idea to name the estate after the house in the book."

Philippa paled.

"Rebecca Vincent drowned, didn't she? Is this where she died?"

"Yes, three years ago. Naming the estate Manderley was tempting providence. Danny and I both told them so at the time, but of course, they didn't listen."

"They met on that production of *Rebecca*, didn't they?"

"Yes. Rebecca in *Rebecca*—that was the publicity-department spiel, though, of course, Rebecca Vincent was playing the nameless second wife. Rebecca doesn't actually appear in the story. It's hard to believe that was over twenty years ago."

"I was only a little girl at the time, but I have vivid memories of both stars," said Philippa. "I've seen TV reruns of the movies they made together, and I remember reading an article about them after she died. Maxwell West was a big stage star in Britain in the sixties, wasn't he?"

Bea nodded.

"Yes, he was the golden-boy of the National Theatre. Everyone thought he was the next Olivier. He had the pick of the roles, both with stage and BBC television. He was happily married and he had two lovely children, so he probably would have spent his life alternating between the National Theatre and the top TV dramas if it hadn't been for Rebecca."

"*Rebecca*, the movie, or Rebecca Vincent?"

"What's the difference?" said Bea, her voice sounding suddenly bitter. "You can't separate the two. Rebecca wasn't a patch on Max when it came to talent or training."

"She was fabulously beautiful, though, wasn't she? Did she start out with stage work too?"

"No. Rebecca was strictly a film star." Bea sniffed dismissively. "She got her first break when she landed a role as a minor James Bond girl. After that, she was cast in a mystery series that lasted three seasons. Then, through her influential friends—" Bea gave the word a special emphasis— "she gravitated to fragile heroines in a couple of Dickensian epics. Very unsuitable really, since in real life she was as robust as the storybook Rebecca. Still, she was very lovely, and she managed to put across that air of fragility on film, which was why she was chosen to play opposite Max when the decision was made to do a remake of *Rebecca*. And that was that. When they met, it was as if they'd been struck by the proverbial bolt of lightning."

"That's probably why my mother thought the film was so magical," said Philippa. "They really were in love."

Her companion sniffed. "It wasn't romance," she said sharply. "It was sexual tension. Rebecca wanted Max, but she wasn't going to settle for an affair. Their on-screen kiss was the first time he got to lay hands on her. No wonder every woman who watched the show was panting with vicarious passion."

"So she broke up his marriage?"

"And hers too. She was married as well. They were both old enough to know better. He was forty and she was thirty-one. They divorced their mates and were married the following year. That was the beginning of the end. All the publicity led to offers from Hollywood. Big money and bad scripts. Hysterical historicals, I call them. Max should have had better judgment, but he was blinded by the money and his obsession with Rebecca." Bea sighed. "He hoped to use the money to make independent productions, but *Coriolanus* nearly bankrupted them, and after that, Rebecca insisted they wrap up their company. Well, he's paid for his folly," she said. "Their relationship was an ongoing roller-coaster ride, which ultimately cost him his career. He held on to his matinee-idol image too long and in the end, there was nothing but bad soap-style TV dramas. After a while even those dried up—and, of course, he'd lost all credibility with the major British companies by then."

"How did he and Rebecca end up here?"

"Max loves outdoor sports, and on one of his fishing trips, he was picking up supplies in Coeur d'Alene and he discovered a beautifully appointed, two-hundred-seat theatre on the outskirts of town. It was inhabited by a struggling rep company, and after talking with the artistic director, Max came up with the idea of mounting *Rebecca* as a stage production with him and his wife playing the leads. They were much too old for the parts by then, but people flocked to see it. The money rolled in, and Max saw a golden opportunity to return to what he really loved."

"Stage work."

"Yes. He ended up taking over the company. His goal was to produce an annual festival similar to Ashcroft or Stratford. He needed a base here, and when he saw this estate advertised, he fell in love with it. He decided to buy it, fix it up and live here for half the year. He noticed the resemblance to the Manderley of the book right away. He felt that he could make money on the investment by capitalizing on his fame and running the place as a resort hotel. In addition to the guest wing in the house, there are six rental cabins along the edge of the lake. He also planned to organize mystery nights with the *Rebecca* theme, using members from the theatre company to round out the various roles."

"Is that how Danny came to be here?"

"No, Danny and Max met years ago. They worked together in London. Danny's father was a tailor, and she learned dressmaking skills from him. Then she married a designer who worked for the British National Theatre. Later, she joined the company and learned all about building stage costumes. Those were the years that Max was at the National and they became good friends."

"Why did Danny leave England?"

"Money. By the time Max received offers from Hollywood, Danny's parents were ailing and she was helping support them. Her husband had died in a car accident the year before and the theatre company was just a reminder of what she had lost. Max valued her talents and got her work on his film productions. She became part of his permanent entourage. She cares for him a great deal. We both do."

Bea finished her breakfast and took her plate to the sink. Using the sprayer, she hosed the plate down vigorously. Her forehead was furrowed and the hand that held the plate trembled slightly.

"You've known him for a long time?"

Bea put the plate in the dishwasher and straightened up.

"I've known Max all his life," she said. "I'm his sister."

Philippa's eyes widened. More strange parallels, she thought. Maxim had a sister too. She wondered if an entire cast of novel characters was going to appear if she stayed much longer.

"No wonder you feel sad about the path he followed," she said. "It must have been hard seeing him wasting his talent, especially if there were problems in the marriage."

Bea sighed again.

"Yes, it was hard, which was why we were all so happy for Max when he remarried after Rebecca's death." Her eyes clouded momentarily. "It was quite a surprise, though," she added, "when he hitched up with The Mouse."

Philippa blinked.

"The Mouse?"

"Elise. She was a props girl with the theatre company. She's a plain little thing, and a lot younger than Max, but she's been a *Rebecca* junkie for years and she's a passionate fan of Max and his films."

"Why was his choice a surprise?"

"Because we all thought that Max would turn to Danny since they'd been friends for so many years. I know for a fact that in the early days when they first met at the National, the naughty boy made a play for her, but of course, she was married at the time, and unlike Rebecca, Danny has a deep sense of morality."

"So why did Max turn to Elise?"

"Male ego, I suppose." Bea shrugged. "Danny is a strong, independent woman, whereas The Mouse worships the ground Max walks on. He'd been humiliated so often during his marriage, so all that unconditional adoration did a lot to restore his confidence. To be fair, Elise has knocked herself out helping him with the resort and making the festival a success. She and Max have been happy together, but we should have realized that Rebecca would never leave them in peace. It's all starting over again."

"What exactly is happening?" said Philippa. "I did see a headline in the paper, but I didn't read the story."

Bea bit her lip, and her hands gripped the edge of the counter so tightly that her knuckles turned white.

"The reason there's no one here but me and Danny," she said tersely, "is that everyone else has been taken into town for questioning. The police have uncovered new evidence regarding Rebecca's death. They're saying that the original verdict was wrong."

"The drowning wasn't accidental?"

"No. It seems Rebecca was deliberately killed by someone who was with her on the sailboat." Bea sat down at the table and sank her face into her hands. "I'm so afraid," she said. "I think they're going to charge Max with her murder."

*   *   *

I love the novel, Rebecca. *I first read it when I was thirteen, and I couldn't put it down. I read long into the night with a flashlight under the bedclothes because I had to find out what happened. Since then, I must have reread the book seven times. I liked the Alfred Hitchcock movie a lot, but the most magical moment of all, other than my original discovery of the book, was seeing the filmed version with Maxwell West and Rebecca Vincent. I think I'd always been in love with the Maxim of the book, but from that moment on, Maxwell West was Maxim for me. It was a dream come true when he and his wife came to perform at our theatre, but it was a disconcerting dream, because I soon realized that however much Maxwell West was the epitome of Maxim, Rebecca*

Vincent was not the sweet devoted wife that she had played on film. She was the embodiment of her namesake in the book. She was Rebecca.

*   *   *

Gently prompted by Philippa, Bea related the whole story. Rebecca had drowned three years before. It had been late September so the resort hotel had been closed. The season had been a success, as had the drama festival, but now the guest wing was empty and the rooms were being cleaned and refurbished for the following year.

Other than Max and Rebecca, only six people were at Manderley that day. Danny and Bea were present, since, as permanent staff, they lived in the second-floor suites in the private wing of the house. Elise was also on site. She had been occupying the staff suite in the basement during the tourist season, but had stayed on to help with the cleaning. Elise had proved invaluable throughout the summer, working as receptionist, maid and general dogsbody. She had even filled in as Maxim's second wife during the mystery-nights, for Rebecca was already sufficiently bored with the project that she had flown back and forth to Los Angeles throughout the summer, never caring if her trips had conflicted with the resort schedule.

Two actors from the rep company were lodged in the cabins and staying on as guests for a couple of weeks. One was Frank Gerber, who, like Max, was a British expatriate whose Hollywood career had ground to a halt. He was also a widower whose obvious interest in Bea provided the rest of the group with a constant source of entertainment. The other was Miles Cottrell, the handsome young man who had alternated between playing Antony to Rebecca's Cleopatra on the festival stage and Jack Favell at the mystery nights. Cottrell's relationship with Rebecca was also a source of gossip, but not the good-natured variety. He was twenty years younger than Rebecca, and the cause of a great deal of friction between her and her husband.

The other remaining guest was Jay Grogan, the Hollywood actor who had played Hardy in an early-nineties epic that had starred Max and Rebecca as Lord Nelson and Lady Hamilton. Grogan's affair with Rebecca at the time had given the tabloids a field day and provided talk-show hosts with a raft of "Kiss me, Hardy" jokes. For Max, this had been the ultimate humiliation. His stiff-upper-lip silence had made him appear weak in the eyes of his public, the picture had bombed, and the studio had failed to renew his contract. Grogan's star had risen as Max's had declined, and he was now a well-established producer. Rebecca was angling for a role in his new TV series, and against Max's wishes, she had invited Grogan to Manderley.

The day Rebecca died had been sunny, and after a late lunch that had included a heavy liquid component and a lot of thinly disguised barbs, Frank Gerber had proposed a game of croquet, noting that the hoops were still set out on the lawn from the last guests who had played there. His intention had been to break the tension in the atmosphere, but his good-natured purpose simply provided Rebecca with another opportunity to play her rivals off against each other. A lively debate followed. Miles Cottrell suggested that they scrap the hoops and set out the cricket stumps, but Jay Grogan pooh-poohed that and voted for baseball. Rebecca decreed that they could use whatever bats they liked. Max was ominously silent.

Bea and Elise opted out of the game. Neither one was feeling well—they were both coming down with colds—and they were alarmed by the look in Max's eye. They preferred to finish cleaning the guest rooms and stay out of the line of fire. Danny also withdrew with the excuse that she wanted to work on the designs for next season. However, the other five trekked outside to play. A drunken session ensued, overtly hilarious, covertly antagonistic, with the participants using a variety of bats and mallets, while Rebecca egged them on to victory. By four o'clock, Max's suppressed fury rose to the surface, and he and Rebecca had a blazing row. The other players by now were in varying states of sobriety, fatigue or indifference, and they made themselves scarce. Leaving their hosts to battle it out, they tossed down their bats and drifted their separate ways.

Bea and Elise were still working upstairs. The noise of the row drifted up from the lawn, but by the time they looked out to see what was happening, the quarrel was over and nobody was in sight. However, they could see the muddle of equipment on the porch of the pavilion. Bea was annoyed, especially since she and Elise had been hard at work in spite of their burgeoning colds. They had finished cleaning the display room and stripped the bed, so Bea determined that they would stop there, clean up the mess created by the inconsiderate actors, and then deal with the laundry. Elise went out to put the bats and balls away, and Bea lugged the linen down to the laundry room.

When Elise came back to help Bea with the laundry, she reported that she'd put everything away, but that one of the baseball bats seemed to have gone astray. Bea could tell that Elise was exhausted— whatever virus she had picked up was really getting a grip on her— and she told her to go and have a rest. Elise said she'd see to the towels and then take a break. Bea went to the kitchen to start the dinner preparations.

The wind came up around five o'clock, and shortly after that, Bea saw Rebecca heading across the lawn towards the boathouse, where her sailing dinghy was moored. A few minutes later, the dinghy headed out onto the lake, and the last Bea saw of it, it was tacking in the direction of the point where old Sam's cottage was located.

Rebecca often went out sailing alone, so no one thought anything of it until dinnertime when she failed to appear.

On checking the boathouse, they saw that the dinghy was still out. However, by now it was eight o'clock and the light had gone, so panic started to set in. Max took Frank out in his motorboat and toured the lake until they saw the dinghy. It was bobbing about, not that far beyond the point where it had disappeared. The mainsheet was loose and the mainsail was flapping in the breeze. Rebecca was nowhere on board.

Four days later, her body washed ashore on the rocks near the rental cabins. She had drowned, but bruising on the side of her head indicated a sharp blow with something round and hard. It appeared that she had let go of the mainsheet and the boom had swung across, cracked her head, and knocked her overboard. Everything pointed to a classic sailing accident, but Jay Grogan thought otherwise. He and Max almost came to blows when Grogan retorted that Max had deliberately got rid of the exotic albatross around his neck so he could exchange it for a comfortably utilitarian sparrow. This, of course, was a reference to Elise, who was slave-like in her devotion to Max. Grogan's attempts to stir up trouble resulted in the police questioning everyone who was on the estate, and their findings refuted Jay Grogan's accusations. The inquest ruling was accidental death and the case was closed.

Max seemed to be hit very hard by Rebecca's death. In spite of their volatile relationship, his friends all agreed that he had loved her. He went back to California for the funeral and remained there for several months. Danny went with him, but then she was called back to London to be with her mother, who was terminally ill. Danny ended up staying there until the following spring. Everyone thought Max would sell the estate and give up on the festival, but Elise quietly continued with the preparations for the upcoming season, and when

Max returned in March, everything was in place to carry on. He was overwhelmed, not just by what she had accomplished, but also by the support of all his friends and colleagues in Idaho. The next season went ahead, and eight months later, Max married Elise. Everything, Bea explained, was perfect until the past summer.

Lake Cœur d'Alene had always attracted divers, due to some Model T Fords from the early 1900s that had sunk when people foolishly tried to drive on the ice. Another draw was the steamboats that had been burned and sunk when their use on the lake had come to an end. Divers were rare off the shore of the Manderley estate, but a group of teenagers, inspired by tales of the professional divers, went snorkeling from the deck of the sports pavilion. On the bottom of the lake, in the vicinity of the boathouse, they found the missing baseball bat.

*   *   *

I hated Rebecca for the way she treated Max. Sometimes I fantasized that she would die and that Max would turn to me, but I knew this was just a dream. I never thought Max would really want me, except as a friend. I knew I could not compete with the passion that he had felt for her. I was plain and shy, and utterly without talent, whereas she was glamorous and sophisticated, a brilliant star adored by millions of fans. But once I saw how she humiliated him by dragging him into projects that were unworthy of his talent, how she shamed him with her flagrant infidelity and emasculated him with taunts about his failing abilities, I realized that simple kindness and genuine admiration were what was needed to heal his embattled spirit. I never believed that he would return my feelings, but I hoped to provide some sort of comfort.

It was wonderful to see how he was strengthened, once away from

Hollywood and without the glaring, intrusive media shining a spotlight on his personal troubles. Back in the world of theatre where he belonged, it was as if the old Maxwell West had returned, invigorated by new challenges and focussed on the work he loved, rather than worn down by the pursuit of fame and fortune. Yet, after Rebecca died, in spite of the way she had treated him, Max was shattered. None of us knew how to bring him back from his dark depression, and when he offered to marry me, at first I thought he was joking. But he really wanted me. He needed the unconditional love and support that only I could give him. It was as if, at thirty years of age, I had only just come to life.

*   *   *

"How did the police become involved?" Philippa asked Bea. "Did someone on the estate start stirring everything up again?"

Bea shook her head.

"Unfortunately for Max, one of the divers was the nephew of the officer who had investigated Rebecca's drowning. The baseball bat put a whole new dimension on her death."

"But you saw Rebecca walk to the boathouse. No one was with her. Why would the police think her husband killed her?"

"Because of the quarrel that took place earlier that afternoon. They're suggesting that Max knew Rebecca was going sailing and waited for her in the boathouse. They think he knocked her unconscious, took her out on the boat and threw her over the side."

"But how would he have got back to shore?"

"No one would have seen him if he'd sailed past the point and come into shore on the far side of the cottage. There's a rocky promontory, so it would have been easy to clamber ashore and shove the boat back onto the lake."

"You saw the boat go out from the boathouse, didn't you? Did you see Rebecca at the helm?"

Bea bit her lip. She hesitated as if uncertain, but when she spoke, her voice was confident.

"I'm sure it was Rebecca, but she was wearing her black hoodie, and by then, she'd pulled the hood up over her hair. The police think the person I saw could have been Max, but by that token, it could have been anyone. Everyone connected with the theatre has black hoodies with our company logo."

"It sounds as if the evidence against your brother is pretty circumstantial."

"Yes, but unfortunately, Max went into town two days after Rebecca's disappearance and purchased a baseball bat to replace the one that had gone missing."

"Oh, my goodness! That's not going to help."

Bea hung her head glumly.

"I know. When Sergeant Krall discovered that, he became convinced that Max was a murderer."

"Well, it is pretty damning," Philippa said frankly. "I'd have thought your brother would have been too upset about his wife to think about replacing missing sports equipment."

"Max was desperate. He was worried sick. We all knew something terrible had happened, but he was just trying to keep himself occupied."

"Where was he when Rebecca set off in the boat?"

"He'd gone for a walk to cool off." Bea paused and bit her lip. "Poor Max. He always felt guilty after he'd lost control and lashed out at Rebecca, and yet he had every cause to be angry with her. She'd been flirting with Miles Cottrell the whole afternoon, and Jay Grogan's presence didn't help. It was as if she was flaunting past and present lovers in his face."

Philippa was appalled.

"Why on earth did Max stick with her? The marriage sounds like a nightmare."

"It wasn't that simple. Rebecca drove Max close to the breaking point many times, but she could always win him back. She knew he'd forgive her, no matter what she'd done. Don't get fooled into thinking that these Rebecca-the-novel trimmings are actually parallel to the lives of the people who live here. Never forget that they're actors. They exploited the fame of the novel, the film and their own reputations, but this Manderley is all smoke and mirrors. Max was only like the Maxim of the novel in that he loved the estate where he lived. My brother was in love with his wife, and he didn't want to lose her to a younger man."

"Where did he go for his walk?"

"He went around the lake trail. Then he stopped at Sam's cottage to pick some dahlias for Rebecca. He'd calmed down, and I suppose that seemed like a way to make up."

"Then surely Sam saw him?"

"No. Sam had gone into town that day. No one was there—which is why the police think Max was able to ditch the boat on the other side of the point and then walk back along the trail. Elise confirmed his story, but the police figured she was lying because she loves him."

"How could she confirm his story? You said she was ill."

Bea nodded.

"She wasn't at all well. Her cold ended up turning to pneumonia and we actually thought we were going to lose her too. But on the day Rebecca died, her cold was just starting. Elise was trying to keep going, and before she went to her room, she folded the towels and took them up to the display suite. That's when she saw Max in Sam's garden. She also saw the boat circling the point."

"Rebecca's sailboat?"

"Yes, and it was definitely under sail, not merely drifting, and Max was down by the water picking the dahlias."

Philippa nodded thoughtfully.

"Yes, she could have seen him in the cottage garden from that room. I had a lovely clear view when I looked out this morning."

"But the police won't believe her. They say that she couldn't have been sure the boat was under sail, and they insist that Max was on his way back, having already killed his wife and abandoned the boat. It's obvious what they're thinking: Elise is Max's wife, so she must be lying. Bloody coppers," Bea said bitterly. "They all have tunnel vision."

"Not all of them," said Philippa, "though some do operate with blinders on. But a good detective will explore every avenue. I know, because my brother is one." And my boyfriend too, she was about to add, but then decided against it. She and Miller weren't quite at that point yet.

Bea looked up hopefully. "Your brother is a detective? Is there any chance he could help us. We have to urge Sergeant Krall to look at the alternatives. There are several people who had very good reason to hate Rebecca."

"Since I can't even get hold of a mechanic to look at my car, I can hardly ask my brother for advice," said Philippa, "but I'd like to help if I can. I know a bit about the detection process and I'm not bad at problem-solving. It's too bad I can't see all the witness statements."

Bea's features suddenly lit up. Even a hint of hope was something to cling to.

"But you can see them!" she cried. "Well, not the current statements, but the ones from three years ago. We were given copies of the original witness statements after the coroner's inquest. I have them in a file in the study."

"Then let's go down there." Philippa pushed her chair back from the table. "I seem to be stuck here indefinitely. That sounds like an excellent way to pass the time."

"Thank you," said Bea. She stood up and looked at Philippa with warm, grateful eyes. "I'll take you there and get you started. Then I'll bring you some coffee. We need all the help we can get," she added. "Maybe your fresh eyes will be able to pick up something we've missed."

Bea ushered Philippa to the door and guided her down the hall.

"Elise will be so grateful too," she said as they walked. "She's absolutely frantic. She's desperate to save Max but, like the rest of us, she doesn't know what to do. Poor girl. She'd do anything for Max."

Philippa looked shrewdly at the bowed shoulders of the woman she was following. Her love for her brother manifested itself in every word and gesture.

And so would you, she thought.

*   *   *

Miller reached Missoula soon after eleven-thirty. He had heard nothing more from the state patrol, so he made his way to the Cracker Barrel where Philippa had stopped before setting off on I90. He decided that he might as well eat while he asked questions. To his disappointment, neither the waitress who had served Philippa nor the cashier who had taken her payment was on duty. However, the cashier was due to start her shift in half an hour, so Miller settled himself in a booth and ordered a hamburger. As he finished the last of his French fries, he noticed the door open and a lanky, sun-wrinkled blonde entered the restaurant. Five minutes later, she had replaced the cashier who had been at the till when Miller arrived.

Miller's waitress appeared with his bill. She flashed him a flirtatious smile and nodded towards the cash desk.

"That's Trudy," she said. "She's the one you want to talk to."

Miller took the bill to the counter and settled up. Close up, he could see that the cashier was definitely on the upper side of fifty, but she had a gleam in her eye that suggested she could make short work of any male who crossed her path. She gave Miller an appreciative look as she rang through his bill and seemed happy to answer his questions. When he described Philippa, Trudy nodded.

"I remember her," she drawled. "Pretty girl with an accent."

She probably thought you were the one with the accent, thought Miller, but refrained from saying it out loud.

"Did you see her leave?" Miller asked. "Did she talk to anyone in the restaurant or the parking lot?"

"No. She ate on her own, paid her bill and went out to her car. I saw her through the window. She made a phone call on her cell. Then she took off. No one was with her."

"And she didn't say where she was heading?"

"No," said Trudy. "While I processed her card, she was too busy reading the newspaper headlines." She bobbed her head towards the stand by the door.

"Really? Any idea what the headline was?"

Trudy peered out from under her blonde bangs and gave Miller a knowing look. "Yes. It was about that movie star who drowned in Lake Coeur d'Alene. The one who was married to Maxwell West."

Miller looked blank. Trudy laughed.

"Before your time," she said. "He was my number-one pin-up boy when I was young. My, but he was gorgeous. Tall, dark, and handsome, just like you," she added with a cougar-like glint in her eye. "Can you imagine, after all these years? Now they're saying his wife was murdered. That's the headline your friend was looking at."

Miller's eyes narrowed.

"Was she now?"

"You betcha," said Trudy. "People are always fascinated to hear that Max West ended up running a theatre company and a resort right here in Idaho. Personally, I don't believe for a minute that he killed his wife. It'll have been one of her boyfriends. Folks round here figure Rebecca Vincent was a tramp and deserved what she got."

Trudy was about to ramble on, but Miller cut in abruptly.

"Where exactly is the resort where Rebecca Vincent drowned?"

"About a two-hour drive back the way you came. It's called Manderley. There's a turn off about ten miles before you reach Coeur d'Alene. Good luck finding your girlfriend," she added.

Trudy turned to the middle-aged couple who were standing behind Miller, waiting to pay. Miller thanked her and went back to his car. He had mixed feelings about what he had learned. On the one hand, he couldn't believe Philippa would break their date and cause everyone to be worried out of their minds, just so she could pursue a mystery, but his gut instinct told him it was just possible. With her incurable thirst for solving puzzles, Philippa had more ability to land herself in trouble than the most headstrong, undisciplined rookies in the force. And if she had somehow become embroiled in a case, it was better than the other unthinkable possibilities that had been dogging his mind.

As he opened the door of his SUV, his cellphone rang. It was the state patrol. A report had come in from a truck driver who was driving the strip of I90 just east of Lake Coeur d'Alene around nine o'clock the previous evening. He had noticed a red Jeep Cherokee parked at the side of the highway.

Miller felt a surge of anxiety and his heart started pounding. Why would she have stopped? If she'd broken down, the car would still be there. And if her car was running all right, why would she not have driven the extra few miles into the town of Coeur d'Alene. He hoped against hope that his gut instinct was right, and that she was simply checking her map and trying to find her way to Manderley. But whatever the reason, her car was in that area. Another two hours of high-speed driving, but at least he knew where to start his search.

*   *   *

As Philippa read over the statements, they seemed to authenticate everything that Bea had told her. Bea and Elise's movements were clearly accounted for, as were Danny's, who had remained working in her own room until six o'clock when she'd come down to give Bea a hand with dinner. Maxwell West's statement was brief and concise. After the lawn game had ended, he had gone for a walk on the lake trail. On the way back, he had stopped to pick some flowers in the cottage garden and had seen Rebecca's sailboat going around the point. He had then returned to the house, set the flowers in the hall so that his wife would see them on her return, and then gone to his room to read a script. He had not emerged until dinnertime, when he discovered that his wife was still out on the lake. He said nothing about the row with his wife, which was hardly surprising.

Frank Gerber's statement was equally circumspect. As Philippa read it, she envisioned a kindly and aging thespian who was loyal to his colleagues—a man who would divulge nothing that would cause them any difficulty or embarrassment. Frank Gerber admitted that the lawn game had been exhausting, but said it was because of Cottrell showing off all the time. Once the game was over, Gerber went to his cabin and had a nap, so he had no idea what the others were doing. He didn't leave his cabin until quarter to seven when he walked down to the main house. Then he went to the kitchen, made Bea and Danny drinks and visited with them until dinner was ready.

While Frank Gerber's statement was neutral and non-committal, the one from Jay Grogan was hostile towards Maxwell West. Grogan had offered Rebecca a role in his upcoming series. He was contemptuous towards Max, and considered the Idaho venture an act of total selfishness. In Grogan's view, Max had dragged Rebecca away from everything she enjoyed and squandered their money on the resort just so he could indulge in a life of outdoor sports and live theatre, the two activities he loved most, neither of which provided a place for her. Rebecca had sacrificed her own career, putting up with the crap they had to perform in so they could make enough money to fund Max's independent film ventures and fork out maintenance payments for the children from his first marriage. According to Grogan, Rebecca was thoroughly fed up, and his statement spared none of the ugly details of the quarrel between her and her husband. As Grogan left, he'd heard Rebecca telling Max that she was going sailing and that he could go fuck himself, since he wasn't capable of doing it to anyone else.

The final statement was even more damning. This was from Miles Cottrell, the young actor who had played Antony to Rebecca's Cleopatra. Philippa quailed as she read it. No wonder the police had taken Maxwell West in for questioning. According to Cottrell, Max had a strong motive for murdering his wife:

After the game, Max started in on Rebecca and there was a hell of a row. I ducked around the back of the pavilion to stay out of the way. I knew Rebecca would join me once she got rid of Max because we'd already agreed to spend the afternoon together. Her talk of going sailing was just a cover. I was standing on the deck at the rear of the pavilion and I could hear everything that was said. Rebecca was taunting the old fart over the fact that he couldn't get it up any more. She told him she was fed up with him throwing away all their assets on pet projects that offered nothing for her other than to keep her shut up in the sticks. She was going to divorce him, and he was going to have to suck it up and sell his precious Manderley to pay for her share of what they owned. Once she'd finished telling him where to get off, Max stormed off into the house and Rebecca came round to the deck. We arranged that she'd come over to my cabin in about an hour. I left her there and went back to my cabin. I waited all afternoon, but she didn't show up. Then around six o'clock, Max stormed in demanding to know where she was. Of course, it was just a big act. He was trying to cover up for the fact that he'd murdered her. The sod killed her just so he didn't have to part with his wretched estate. I hope he fries, or whatever it is you do to killers in Idaho.

As Philippa closed the folder, the door opened and Bea entered the room.

"There's still no cell service," she said, "but the landline is back on. Danny's called the garage, and they're sending a mechanic out later this afternoon, probably around four o'clock. In the meantime, you can call your parents and let them know where you are. Then come on down to the kitchen. I've made some sandwiches for lunch."

Feeling relieved, Philippa hurried to the phone and called her parents to reassure them that she was safe and well. After she rang off, she called Miller's cell. She only got through to his voicemail, so she left a brief message and said she would call again later. Then, remembering Bea's invitation, she went down to the kitchen for lunch.

*   *   *

As Miller got back into his SUV, his cellphone beeped. He had voicemail. He checked the message; then felt a heady rush of relief as he heard Philippa's bell-like voice crisply informing him that she'd had car trouble but that she was perfectly okay and would try calling again later. His eyes glinted as the message continued. Philippa was sorry to have missed their rendezvous at the Wild Horse Monument but wild horses couldn't drag her away from the haven she'd found when her car broke down. She had the most fascinating puzzle to solve. He'd never guess in a million years where she was and she couldn't wait to tell him all about it.

That's what you think, thought Miller. He called the state patrol again. There was no sense in them wasting police time hunting for Philippa, now that he knew she was fine. However, he still felt a twinge of unease knowing she was shoving her nose into something that could be dangerous. Once he'd let the state trooper know that Philippa was safe, he asked about the Rebecca Vincent case. He was relieved to hear that there were no killers lurking at Manderley and that the culprit was already safely in custody. Gratified by Miller's interest in their celebrity murder case, the trooper cheerfully narrated all the details that had led to the reopening of the case and the apprehension of the killer. He also confirmed that the sighting of Philippa's Jeep was in the vicinity of the access road that led to Maxwell West's estate.

Grinning at the thought of Philippa's reaction when he rolled in, Miller drove at speed, flashing by the other cars on the highway. He knew he was tired, but he was re-energized by the knowledge that he had a destination and that Philippa was safe. He had Google-mapped Manderley so he knew where he was going. He estimated that he could reach the resort by two-thirty. What was more, it would be extremely gratifying to arrive unannounced and tell Philippa the solution to her mystery. Much as he enjoyed her bright, able mind, it was about time she realized that the police were perfectly capable of solving their own cases. Feeling smug, he put his foot down and passed a log-laden semi. Less than two hours and he'd be there.

*   *   *

When Philippa reached the kitchen, Bea was slicing vegetables, which appeared to be for the soup that was bubbling on the stove. She gestured to the table where a platter of sandwiches had been laid out. As Philippa helped herself, she saw that Bea had turned from the cutting board and was hovering anxiously.

"Did you finish the statements?" she asked.

Philippa nodded. She looked directly into Bea's eyes. There was no point in avoiding the issue.

"The last two statements look very bad for your brother."

"But they're wrong," Bea insisted. "Rebecca wouldn't have divorced Max. Who else would have tolerated her restlessness? He accepted her affairs, and he let her travel wherever she liked. He didn't try to tie her down. For all their fighting, they were linked by so much history. She would never have left Max for Cottrell, any more than she did for Jay Grogan all those years before."

Philippa was still unconvinced, but she had noted some inconsistencies that supported Bea's point of view. She said, "There is one thing that doesn't ring true in Cottrell's statement. He said that Rebecca had planned to come to his cabin, and that the story about going sailing was just a cover. Yet you saw Rebecca going to the boathouse."

Bea's lips compressed into a thin line.

"Well, that just proves that I was right. Rebecca wasn't going to meet Miles at his cabin. She changed her mind. He and Grogan were delusional if they believed she would ever leave Max."

Bea looked as if she were about to say something else, but then she stopped. She turned away and continued chopping carrots.

Philippa finished her sandwich and left the kitchen. She was still troubled by the discrepancy between what Rebecca had said and what she had actually done. Looking at her watch, she saw that she had three hours to kill before the mechanic arrived, so she decided to go to her room and freshen up. Then she would try calling Miller again.

She walked up to the gallery and strolled its length, staring at the portraits as she went. Now that she knew the history of the house, she recognized the significance of the paintings. They were pictures of Max and Rebecca in their various stage and screen roles. However, the painting of Rebecca as Caroline de Winter was such a perfect representation of the picture from the novel that Philippa decided it was probably the portrait that had been painted for the film production. Rebecca Vincent, with her dramatic good looks, looked exactly right for Lady Caroline. She would have had to drab herself down to play the role of Maxim's second wife, probably covering her glossy black hair with a straight, mouse-brown wig. Philippa wondered how Elise had managed when she had to assume that guise for the mystery nights. In her case, her natural appearance would have been perfect for the timid narrator of the story, but she'd have needed a wig to go with the Caroline costume. Bea might think Maxwell West's Manderley was all smoke and mirrors, but his two wives provided the same study in opposites as the wives in the novel, and Philippa believed that the murder had somehow to be connected with the book.

She left the gallery and walked along the hall until she reached the narrow flight of stairs that led to the display suite. She climbed the stairs and entered the room. In the bright daylight, the suite looked pretty and welcoming, exuding none of the eeriness that had struck her when she first saw it. She walked over to the window that looked out onto the lawn. If Max and Rebecca had been fighting there, their voices would have carried to where Bea and Elise had been working. Bea had to know of the row. She could not have failed to hear.

Crossing to the other window, Philippa looked out towards Sam's cottage. She could see the old man outside, puttering in his front garden. Then he walked around the back and disappeared behind the lushly covered poles of beans that stuck up above the abelia shrubs. As the figure slipped out of view, Philippa realized that there was another anomaly in the statements she had read. There was a question she had to put to Old Sam—and his answer just might provide the solution to the mystery of who had killed Rebecca. Throwing on her coat, she hurried back downstairs.

*   *   *

I know Max didn't kill Rebecca. He's the gentlest, kindest man in the world, and in spite of everything she did, I know he still cared for her. He'd never have been capable of doing her harm, even though she didn't deserve his devotion.

But everyone will be questioned about the fights and her affairs, and the threat of divorce that would have forced Max to sell Manderley. I'm so frightened. I know they'll accuse him. They won't listen to me, a second wife who loves her husband. I told them how I saw him at the cottage picking dahlias for Rebecca. He always picked them for her because he knew she loved them. I was telling them the truth. Max was in Old Sam's garden when the boat was going around the point, but the police simply smile politely and I can tell they're discounting everything I say.

If only there were someone I could turn to, someone who could make them realize there were so many other people who could have killed Rebecca. But the others are anxious to hide their own secrets. None of them will admit how much they wanted her dead. I don't know what to do. She won't let us go. I'm so afraid, and the dream keeps returning. We'll never be free of Rebecca. She's come back to destroy us all.

*   *   *

As Philippa came back down to the gallery, she saw Danny coming up the stairs. Now that she knew Danny's theatrical history, the designer's starkly dramatic appearance made sense. Suddenly the woman seemed human and far less sinister. She was just one more person who had cared for Maxwell West and helped him achieve his goals.

Philippa glanced at the portrait of Max as Lord Nelson. The thin lips and dark eyes were the features of every woman's romantic hero, a man who could take control and sweep his beloved off her feet. But the sad truth was that Max only had the exterior façade of the romantic hero. In reality, he was a clever, soberly creative man who, other than his youthful aberration in falling passionately in love with Rebecca Vincent, was devoted to his work. The womenfolk who made him happy were the ones who created an environment where he could carry out his projects.

Danny followed Philippa's glance.

"He was handsome, wasn't he?" she said.

"Gorgeous." Philippa meant it. She could have easily fallen for the youthful actor. Maxwell West had the same dark good looks that had attracted her to Bob Miller—except that Miller, she thought smugly, really was a man of action.

"Max still has years of good work in him," said Danny, unaware of Philippa's straying thoughts. "The Shakespeare festival will be a triumph, as long as he isn't dragged down again by Rebecca."

"Is that going to happen?"

"I don't know."

"Do you think he murdered his wife?"

Danny shook her head.

"No. I often thought it would have been justifiable homicide if he had, but he would never have harmed her. Killing Rebecca would be like acknowledging that the image he has of himself and his life was all an illusion. You see, Max lives in a world of fantasy, and Rebecca was an integral part of his dream. He relied on her, just as he relies on people like me and Bea and Elise and Frank. We're the ones who have to deal with reality so Max can keep his dream alive."

Danny turned away and went through the door marked *Private*. Philippa continued down the stairs and headed out the front door. She made her way to the back of the house and set off on the lakeshore path.

The afternoon was cold. In spite of the sun sparkling on the water, an icy wind cut across the lake, a hint of winter to come. Philippa hurried along the trail, anxious not to remain outside too long. The last thing she needed was to return from her trip with a raging sinus infection. Opera-chorus rehearsals for *La Bohème* were scheduled to begin next week.

As she drew near to the cottage, she could smell wood-smoke intermingling with the scent of the pine trees. Sam had lit a fire so he must be home. Sure enough, when she knocked on the door, Sam opened it. He was surprised to see her. However, he answered her question about the garden, and when she thanked him and prepared to leave, he seemed sorry that she was going. Telling her to wait, he disappeared inside the house and came back a moment later with a small set of clippers. He had put on a coat and traded his carpet slippers for Wellington boots. Solemnly, he plodded round to the back garden and cut her several of the brightly coloured dahlias from the few remaining flowers by the cottage wall.

Touched, Philippa accepted the bouquet and returned the way she had come. She was not looking forward to telling Bea and Danny what she had discovered. Whichever way the information was interpreted, the result would not be a happy one. As she reached the parking area at the front of the house, she was surprised to see Bea coming out the front door.

"The garage just phoned. Their man should be here any moment now," she said. Then she noticed the anxiety in Philippa's eyes. "You've learned something," she said quietly.

Before Philippa could reply, she was distracted by the sound of an approaching vehicle. Bea looked towards the trees that shielded the driveway.

"That'll be the mechanic," she said.

But the car that emerged from the trees and sailed past the rhododendrons was not the truck from the garage. Philippa was amazed to see Miller's SUV pull up in front of the porch.

As Miller clambered out of the car, she beamed with delight, though her smile froze when she saw his expression.

"Fine bloody chase you've led me," he growled. "Not to mention the highway patrols in three states. I've put over six hundred miles on my car looking for you. Have you any idea how worried everyone has been?"

Philippa apologized, suitably chastened, though secretly she was thrilled that Miller had jumped in his car and driven hundreds of miles to look for her.

Bea interceded. "She really couldn't help it. The storm put the phones out, and then the fan belt went on her car. It's just lucky she was close enough to find refuge here."

Miller was not mollified.

"The cashier at the Cracker Box warned her about the storm and told her she should put up in town for the night." He turned to Philippa. "And then to turn off your phone after you left Missoula! For a bright girl, you can sure do dumb things."

"You've said that before," said Philippa acerbically.

Her first instinctive response to hurl herself into Miller's arms had died an instant death. No one could spoil a potentially romantic moment with the speed of a cop, she thought sourly.

"Well, I'm glad that you're all right," said Miller. "Is someone coming to see to your car? It shouldn't take long to put on a new fan belt."

"Yes. He'll be here any moment."

"Good. Then we'll be able to drive to Spokane in time for dinner. The Burleighs have an extra guest room for me so they've offered to put us both up for the night. We'll still be able to have our planned outing; it'll just be one day later. And this time, I'm going to be behind you all the way."

"Well, that's good." Philippa was still a little cool, but remembering that Bea needed Miller's help, she softened her tone. "There's just one thing we need to see to before we go."

Miller looked guarded.

"And what would that be?"

"We need to stop at the police station in Coeur d'Alene."

"Oh?"

"Yes, it's really important. You see—" Philippa paused. "Why are you grinning?"

"This 'one thing' wouldn't be about the Rebecca Vincent case, would it?"

"Yes. How did you know?"

Miller's smile grew broader.

"How do you think I found you? Anyway, you don't have to poke your nose into this particular mystery. The local detectives have it all wrapped up. They've made an arrest."

Bea paled. Philippa looked urgently at Miller.

"No," she insisted. "We do have to stop. You see, one of the statements in their files is false. I'm sorry," she added, turning back to Bea, "because I know this will upset you, but I know that Elise was lying when she said she looked out the window and saw Max in the cottage garden."

Bea went white.

"No. That's not possible."

Philippa took the trembling woman's arm and looked into her eyes.

"Bea, there is another possible interpretation. However, you did say that Elise would do anything for Max and you have to accept the fact that she may have been lying to protect him."

"There's no way Elise was lying." Bea pulled her arm free and her voice became shrill. "You didn't hear her give her statement. I'd swear on my life that she was telling the truth. She did see Max in Sam's garden."

Philippa sighed.

"That's the other possibility. If she did see Max there, it wasn't from the display suite. Either way, the police have to be told. They'll have to check it out." She turned to face Miller. "That's why we have to stop in at the station on our way. They may have arrested the wrong person."

Miller rolled his eyes.

"I do wish you'd stop thinking you're more capable of figuring out a mystery than the professionals," he said shortly.

"You know as well as I do that the police make mistakes. How can you be sure they've got it right this time?"

Miller's eyes glinted.

"Didn't you just say something about Maxwell West's wife loving him so much she'd do anything for him?"

Bea and Philippa nodded. They looked at Miller, bemused.

"Well, as it happens," said Miller, "she loved him enough to confess."

*   *   *

I never intended to murder Rebecca. If Bea hadn't sent me down to put away the sports equipment, it might never have happened. Of course, we'd heard the terrible row, but neither one of us took any of it seriously. Bea had told me how Rebecca was always making threats, but she never followed through on them. But as I was about to put the last bat back into the rack in the pavilion, I heard Rebecca's voice. She was on the deck with Miles Cottrell. They were kissing each other and making plans to meet at his cabin. I could hear every word they were saying, and I realized that Bea was wrong. Rebecca really was going to divorce Max. She was going to destroy all his plans and dreams, just as she had when they first met.

I stood watching them from the shadows. After a few minutes, Miles left. I was afraid he'd come inside and see me, but he went around to the exit at the far side of the deck. Rebecca watched him go. Then she turned to come through the pavilion. When she saw me standing there, she stopped. She was furious. She accused me of eavesdropping. I went out to the deck to talk with her. I pleaded with her to make up with Max. She wouldn't listen. She said horrible things, awful things about me as well as Max. It was hateful. She wanted to destroy and humiliate every one of us. In that moment, I realized just how evil and cruel she was. She was the Rebecca of the novel, taunting me, goading me, telling me how everyone laughed at me because of my ludicrous devotion to her husband. She told me how even Max had laughed when he heard the nickname that she had coined for me, and that everyone used behind my back. I was The Mouse, plain, stupid and unloved. Suddenly, I couldn't stand it any more. I screamed at her and she stepped back. She looked amazed that I would dare speak out. She was standing at the edge of the deck and in my rage, I swung the bat at her. It struck her on the side of the head. I didn't mean to hit her so hard, but the force knocked her off the deck and into the lake. I looked over, thinking she'd come up and be furious with me, but there was nothing. She'd gone down under the water. I waited and waited, but then, when she didn't come up, I realized what I'd done.

I was terrified. I was too scared even to feel ill any more. I threw the bat out as far as I could. Then I came back to the house and joined Bea in the laundry room. I told her I would take the towels upstairs and then go to my room and lie down, but when I took the towels up, I fetched the dark Lady Caroline wig from the display suite and hurried back to my room. Then I put on the wig and my Manderley hoodie and went out the basement door. It was only a few steps across the grass to the boathouse, but I had to make sure that, if anyone saw me, they would think I was Rebecca.

I took the sailboat out on the lake and sailed it around the point. I did see Max in Sam's garden. He was picking dahlias for Rebecca, and it seemed so pathetic, as if he really could believe that all the terrible things that had been said could be made to disappear with a bunch of flowers. The sight of him there made me weep. I felt chilled to the bone, and weak, as if the adrenalin rush that had allowed me to forget my illness for a while had now caused it to come back far more violently than before. I managed to get the boat in close to shore. There was a projection of rocks just past the point where it was easy to clamber off the boat and shove it back out into the water. Then I ran back along the trail and crept into the house by the basement door. I hid the wig at the back of my closet. Then I undressed and collapsed into bed. The room was spinning. I felt dizzy, and as I lay down, I felt my head starting to pound. All I could see when I closed my eyes was water and sky, sky and water. I was floating, drifting, sinking, and gradually I realized that someone else was floating beside me. It was Rebecca.

And even then, delusional with fever as I was, I knew that Rebecca was never going to let me go.

*   *   *

"It was such a tiny detail," said Philippa, the following evening, as she and Miller sat in the Black Angus restaurant off I5 after an enjoyable day of sightseeing, "but I knew there was a discrepancy once Sam put his beanpoles back up alongside the abelia. They completely block the view of anyone standing at the bedroom window. Elise couldn't have seen Max from there. Either she was lying to protect him, or she was telling the truth about seeing him—in which case, she was the person on the sailboat."

"That was good detective work," said Miller. "You were right on. What a bizarre case, though. There was something very creepy about the whole setup."

"Yes, there certainly was," said Philippa, daintily separating her lobster tail from its shell. "I felt as if I were in a fantasy world the moment I entered that house."

Miller gleefully eyed the steak that their waitress had deposited in front of him.

"I'm not surprised," he said. "Southern antebellum mansion pretending to be a British manor house smack in the middle of the Idaho panhandle. How weird can you get?"

"Well, it made a sort of sense, when you consider that Rebecca Vincent and Max West had met during a production of *Rebecca*. And if you know the Daphne du Maurier book...."

"I don't," said Miller, tackling his steak. "I'd never heard of it until yesterday, and from what you've told me, I wouldn't like it anyway."

"All right, but if you had read it, you would see why that winding drive and the old mansion on the water would have reminded them of the descriptions of Manderley. And until Rebecca died, it sounds as if she and Max did very well capitalizing on their fame from the film. They mounted mystery nights and recreated the fancy-dress ball. People loved it."

"Sort of upper-crust Disneyworld combined with a serviceable fishing lodge? Something to attract the wives as well as the men?"

"Yes, it was a resort that catered to both sports and arts lovers."

Miller swallowed a mouthful of steak and washed it down with beer.

"Okay. So if you figured out the logic of the setup, why complain about the fantasy feel of the place?"

"I'm not explaining this well," said Philippa. "I remember coming into the house and feeling as if I was Alice in Wonderland, but I was really Alice Through the Looking Glass."

"Oh, God, now you're being cleverly obscure."

"Not really. What I mean is, everything was backwards. There were all these bizarre similarities to the book, both with the setting and the people that lived there, but in reality, they were all quite different. Not what I expected at all."

"That's hardly surprising. They were theatre types. You shouldn't talk so much." Miller pointed to Philippa's plate. "Your steak is going to get cold. Come on, eat up. I promised we'd drop in and say hello to your parents on the way back. I think they want to see for themselves that you're fine. They were pretty worried."

Philippa frowned.

"I wonder why they haven't called me," she said.

"They tried, but they didn't get through." Miller smiled an aggravatingly superior smile. "I bet you forgot to turn your phone back on."

Philippa dropped her knife and fork and ferreted in her bag. She pulled out her phone, gave a sigh of exasperation, turned it on and went into the message file.

"Oh, my god!" she said. "There's a ton of them."

"They're all redundant now," said Miller. "You might as well erase the lot. What are you laughing at?" he added.

Philippa was still smiling at her phone.

"I'm reading the last message from you. It says: *Where the hell are you?*"

Miller grinned.

"Right where you belong," he said. "In the real world. Welcome to life after *Rebecca*.

Remembrance Day

Paula Burns felt guilty. It was Remembrance Day and she was too tired to summon up the appropriate degree of respect and gratitude for the men who had served so valiantly. The staff at the Sidley Veterans' Centre would be on the go all day, and Paula quailed at the prospect of the extra work that the commemorative event entailed. She longed for the day to be over; the two-minute silence at eleven o'clock would be merely a welcome respite when she could shut her eyes and enjoy a moment of peace. She must be a very selfish person, or maybe she was simply getting too old. Perhaps her apathetic mood was a sign that early retirement was in the cards.

The day had not seemed so arduous at the old facility where there had been fewer residents and they were housed in pavilions that were set on spacious grounds surrounded by a wide border of woodland and dotted with flowering shrubs and shady maple trees. But in those days, she, like the men, had been twenty-five years younger and filled with the optimism of Perestroika, rather than disheartened by the déjà vu of 9/11, global terrorism and the re-emergence of Russian imperialism. They had all been so much more mobile and energetic.

The men had donned blazers and ties for the ceremony in the auditorium, and afterwards, set off en masse for the legion. A sense of camaraderie infected the day.

But over the years, so many of the men she had befriended had died, and now, even the youngest World War II vets were well over eighty. Many were wheelchair-bound, so getting them down to the assembly hall for the service was a marathon—followed by an equally arduous luncheon. The era of the exodus to the legion was long gone, and what a mish-mash of attitudes the day produced. Those who hated recalling their war service became cantankerous; some put on their medals, barked orders and insisted on military protocol; others were querulous and needy, wanting to participate but needing help every inch of the way. The whole exercise was exhausting—and Paula felt guilty. What those men had experienced had been far more gruelling and traumatic than her duties as a nursing aide. How dare she harbour feelings of resentment!

Paula changed lanes and took the freeway exit that led to East Burnside. Once out of the heavy traffic, her stress level abated and gradually, she coaxed herself into a more positive frame of mind. The weather was conducive to good spirits, for the storm of the previous night had cleansed the air and swept away every trace of grey. The day was bright and clear, even though the temperature had plummeted, and the sky was blue, cloud-free, and perfect for the fly-past.

Paula smiled as she thought of her favourite residents: Scotty, always with a joke to tell or a candy for visiting children, and Billy Bell, his best friend, who was an absolute sweetheart; Stan and Lionel, who never complained about their health or handicaps and still made their way to the crafts room to weave and make pottery; Mr. Davis, a tall, upright charmer in his mid-nineties who was a model of old-world courtesy; Mr. Graham, who loved to paint and had presented her with a picture of a squirrel that hung on the wall of her apartment; Jimmy Henderson, full of high spirits who always greeted her with a song; Joe, the perennial volunteer in spite of his heart condition, and Gerry, a gentle soul who had survived a Japanese POW camp. They were lovely men who deserved every ounce of care that the staff could provide. Now that women had been admitted to the centre, there were a couple of ex-WACs and WAVEs that Paula liked too.

Having counted her blessings and suppressed her earlier feelings of gloom, Paula steered her Toyota up the hill. She passed the low-cost housing estate that had provoked so much recent controversy in the neighbourhood, then turned onto the street that led to the Sidley Centre. The hospital had been built on land adjacent to the original facility, so the road was bordered by tangled blackberry bushes and shaded by tall stands of cedars, cottonwoods and Douglas fir. As she drove along the edge of the wood, she felt sad that the lush greenbelt that had surrounded the original pavilions was about to be developed. The Federal government had donated the land for the new centre, but the deal had stipulated that Council would rezone the old grounds for subsidized housing.

Paula rounded another curve and the Sidley Centre came into view. It was an imposing building, with a domed central core surrounded by two triangular wings, which, from an aerial view, gave the structure the appearance of a large salmon-pink bow. The wings contained individual rooms that were superior to the barrack-style quarters of the original centre, but in spite of its practical advantages, the hospital lacked the charm of the old facility.

Paula slowed as she approached the entrance. To her left, the woods opened up to reveal the road to the former grounds. The opening flashed by, but something caught her eye and she braked and pulled over onto the soft shoulder. Then carefully, she backed up until she could see down the old road.

She had been right to think she had seen something that had no business being there. At the far end of the road, an empty wheelchair had been abandoned in the shade of a towering maple tree.

*   *   *

Bertram and Edwina Beary always attended the Remembrance Day Service at the Sidley Centre. The facility was only a five-minute walk from their home and their visits there had started long before Beary retired from teaching to take up a second career as a city councillor. During their teaching careers, Beary and Edwina had organized field trips to the centre, believing firmly that their students should learn about the sacrifices of an earlier generation and show the appropriate respect due to the men who had fought for their country. Then, when their own children were young, they had made family visits to the Sidley Centre, so over the years, they and their children had got to know a few of the residents well.

The Sidley veterans had influenced the junior Bearys in many ways. It had been a conversation with one medal-covered ex-serviceman that had inspired Richard to join the RCMP. The Bearys' oldest daughter, Sylvia, who was now a lawyer, had discovered her passion for justice at the age of ten, when challenging an autocratic supervisor who had accused a resident of stealing. Sylvia had gathered evidence with the determination of a squirrel storing nuts for the winter, and had proved that the culprit was, in fact, a member of the cleaning staff.

Sylvia's younger sister, Juliette, was particularly fond of the veterans, and during her teenage years, had been a Pets and Friends volunteer, visiting once a week with Circe, the amiable German shepherd who had been the Beary family dog at the time. Philippa, the youngest daughter, had also benefitted, for the veterans had served as a non-threatening audience providing her with valuable performance experience when she sang for them at special events. Now in adulthood, the pattern was set, and if not always at the same venue, the members of the Beary clan continued to honour Remembrance Day.

This year, the Bearys were represented at three different locations. Sylvia and her husband, Norton, lived on the North Shore, so they were taking their children to the memorial in West Vancouver. Juliette and Steven, along with their daughters and their two dogs, had come down from the Sunshine Coast to stay with their parents for the long weekend. Therefore, they were joining Beary and Edwina at the Sidley Centre. The remaining two Bearys were attending the service at the cenotaph in New Westminster: Richard to lay a wreath on behalf of the Force, and Philippa, to watch her brother take part in the ceremony.

Philippa had walked up to the cenotaph from her townhouse at Westminster Quay, and she stood, quietly absorbing the atmosphere as she waited for the service to begin. The crowds had already filled the walkway around the statue of the Unknown Soldier and the latecomers spilled down onto the surrounding lawns. Doggedly ignoring the chatter of the onlookers, a private stood to attention at the statue's base. The gathering was an eclectic mix of old and young, uniformed and civilian, but many from every group were holding wreaths.

Philippa noticed her brother standing on the far side of the circle, his fair hair glinting in the sunlight. He was wearing his navy-blue dress uniform and was talking with two firefighters who were also carrying wreaths. All three men stood a head taller than the people on either side of them. A good-looking trio, thought Philippa, tempted to go round to join them. But the path was too crowded to make navigation easy so she stayed where she was. She and Richard could meet up after the service.

Philippa always found the Remembrance Day ceremony moving. It was a time to contemplate her grandparents and the kindly men she'd met when entertaining at the veterans' home. This year, even more poignantly, she was thinking of the tales Bob Miller had told her about his experiences in Afghanistan. Her relief that he had returned unscathed had been replaced by shock when she realized that one of the casualties he spoke of was a classmate from her high-school days, a quiet, good-natured boy who had always greeted her with a shy but friendly smile. Suddenly feeling a lump in her throat, she let her eyes drift upward to the cloudless sky where the planes would later soar overhead. The murmur of the crowd was a gentle background to her thoughts, and as the reverend took his position and began to speak, she felt a tear forming in her eye.

While Philippa hung on every word of the solemn service, her brother, on the far side of the circle, found his mind wandering. Remembering that his parents were visiting the Sidley Centre, Richard was reminded of a particularly frustrating case that had occurred on the adjacent housing estate, a case that had remained unsolved for the past six months.

For Richard, the murder of Joey Bortolione had become as maddening as the most intricate locked-room puzzle ever devised by the masters of classic mystery fiction. Joey had been known to the police. He had past drug convictions and connections to gangs, which indicated that the murder was most likely a case of one crook disposing of another, especially as there were witnesses who had seen Joey surreptitiously carrying out a deal on the trail behind the estate five days before he died. Joey had been killed by a single, vicious blow to the side of the neck with what was probably his own machete since that article was missing from the corner of the carport that housed his garden implements. The murder had happened mid-afternoon on a bright May day when several residents of the estate had been outside enjoying the sunshine, yet the killer had got away without a single witness spotting him. Joey's wife was home, but had been unable to cast any light on the killing. Anna Bortolione had been in the shower when she heard the doorbell ring. She assumed that her husband had opened the door and brought the visitor inside because, soon afterwards, she heard voices. She could tell that the person talking to her husband was a man, but over the sound of the water, she could not make out what was being said. All of a sudden, she heard a shriek, and then everything went silent. She was terrified. It wasn't until she heard footsteps and the slam of the door that she went out to see what had happened. She found her husband lying in a pool of blood.

At that point, the investigation had stalled. No one had seen Joey's visitor, either arriving or leaving, yet there were people working by the entrance of the estate who would have noticed anyone who had left by the main gate. Therefore, unless the killer lived in one of the housing units, he must have come in from the trail that ran through the Sidley Woods. Joey's townhouse was at the end of the row that ran along the fence, so it was close to the wide space at the corner that contained the dumpsters. Behind the bins was a gate that allowed residents to access the trail. The gate was kept locked to prevent outsiders from coming through, but it could be opened by anyone inside the estate. It was open when the police arrived to answer Anna's hysterical phone call, but in spite of the dog squad's careful searching of the woods, no trace of the killer or the weapon was found. Neither were any drugs or large sums of money discovered anywhere on the property. This, in conjunction with the report of Joey's deal a few days earlier, suggested that he had been killed for something that was in his possession as a result of his transaction in the woods.

Richard's next step had been to instruct his team to take a closer look at Joey's wife. Was the marriage happy? Did she have a boyfriend in the background? Could she have been the perpetrator?

Unlike her husband, Anna Bortolione had no police record. She appeared to be a devoted mother, even to the point of coaching her son's baseball team. However, an in-depth investigation uncovered cracks in the marriage. During Joey's previous time inside, Anna had acquired a friend, a long-haul truck driver and fellow baseball parent who was divorced from his wife. The Bortolione's next-door neighbour gleefully reported that Anna had enjoyed many overnight visits from her friend while Joey was doing time, but further inquiries eliminated the friend as a suspect. He had been on the other side of the country delivering farmed salmon to a wholesaler in Toronto at the time of the murder.

Richard ultimately had to consider the oldest scenario in the book. Anna Bortolione could have fabricated the story of the mysterious visitor. She was capable of delivering the blow that killed Joey. She was used to swinging a baseball bat; she could easily have swung a machete. True, the nosy neighbour confirmed hearing the shower running in the adjacent unit, and the bloodstains on Anna's legs and hands were consistent with her kneeling by the body of her husband. However, the shower was a convenient ploy if Anna were the killer. She could have washed away the original bloodstains, and then come out to "discover" the body. But what had she done with the weapon? She could have hurled it across the fence from her upstairs window, then claimed that the killer had abandoned it in his flight, but if she had done so, the weapon would have been recovered when the constables and dogs scoured the woods. Every scenario resulted in a dead end, thought Richard irritably. The weapon had vanished as completely as the elusive killer. The case had gone cold, but it constantly rankled in the back of Richard's brain.

A nudge at his side brought Richard back to the present. A Legion representative was trying to move past him. With a start, Richard saw that the wreaths were being laid. Guiltily, he realized he had dreamed away the entire service. Pulling himself upright, he set his eyes on the monument and brought his mind back to the business of the day. Remembering the dead, he reminded himself, was not supposed to include drug dealers who had died at the hands of their fellow criminals.

*　　　*　　　*

Edwina was delighted that Juliette was in town for the service at the Sidley Centre. She and Beary were very proud of their middle daughter and her family. Juliette's sylph-like elegance was combined with a sweet and loving nature that generated goodwill in all who met her; her husband, Steven, was talented, industrious and so fit that he could have starred in an advertisement for healthy outdoor living; and their daughters, Jennifer and Laura, were lively preteens, both pretty tintypes of their mother with wide smiles and long brown hair cascading over their shoulders. The girls, having heard tales of their mother's Pets and Friends adventures, had wanted to bring their dogs along too, but that Edwina had vetoed. Purdy and Quasar had to stay home with the Bearys' husky, MacPuff.

However happy she was to have her family well represented for Remembrance Day, Edwina, was not so pleased to see a spattering of other councillors and political candidates hovering around the entrance to the main hall. She was jealous in her guardianship of her husband's council seat.

"You can tell it's an election year," she said acerbically. "They're so determined to squeeze those last few votes that they're bouncing about the lobby like squash balls."

"You watch," said Beary. "Not one of them will be here for the service. They'll glad-hand in the foyer until quarter to ten, then they'll hightail it down to the cenotaph so as not to miss out on the crowd there. They're wasting their time here, though," he added cheerfully. "The Sidley votes are already decided. The residents who follow the issues are ticked off about the low-cost housing estate, so they'll support the right-wingers, and the residents who don't have a clue will support the lefties because the nurses who take them to the polling station are pro-union and will tell them who to vote for."

"Disgraceful," snapped Edwina. "That estate is a disgrace too. You can't take MacPuff through the trails without running into thugs doing drug deals. There was a stabbing last year and a shooting in the spring. It's no longer safe in those woods."

"The stabbing happened in one of the townhouses, not on the trail," Beary pointed out reasonably, "and the corpse in the car was a drive-by shooting, so it had nothing to do with the estate. Still, the veterans are right to be concerned, because if you look at the statistics, this part of Burnside already has more than its fair share of low-cost housing. It would be a mistake to extend the units onto the old grounds and take away the buffer zone that exists now."

Beary suddenly realized he was talking to the air. Edwina had turned away to scrutinize the progress of the competition.

"Who's that?" she demanded, pointing towards a balding, bespectacled man who was hovering by the assembly-hall door and shaking hands with everyone who entered.

Beary followed his wife's glance.

"Him? That's Colin Bell. He's a candidate with the Burnside Citizens' slate. He's run before, but hasn't made it yet. Determined campaigner though."

Edwina sniffed. "Another one with a sudden conscience about the war veterans. He's probably never set foot here before in his life."

"Actually, that's not so. His father is a resident here. Billy Bell, nice old guy. He moved in a couple of years ago."

Edwina was not mollified. "If his father is a resident, what's he doing grandstanding at the door of the assembly hall? Why isn't he looking after his father?" Edwina's lips compressed into a razor line as she watched Colin Bell pumping the chaplain's arm. "I hope he gets carpal tunnel syndrome," she snapped.

A chuckle at her elbow caused Edwina to swing round. A handsome, white-haired gentleman had slapped a hand on Beary's shoulder.

"Ding-Dong Bell never spends time with his father," said the newcomer. "He just trots him out once a year and parades him at the cenotaph. What's more, he's only been doing that since he started running for office. All show and no substance, that one."

Edwina's frosty expression melted as she saw who had spoken.

"Jimmy!" she trilled. Turning to Juliette, she said, "You remember Mr. Henderson?"

"Yes!" cried Juliette, beaming at the smiling man. "I used to see you and your friend, Scotty, in the craft room. You always had candy for me and dog treats for Circe. Is Scotty still alive?"

"He most certainly is. We have adjacent rooms in the west wing. You should come up and visit us some time."

"I'd love to. I'll bring my girls round to meet you. I have my own dogs now, too, so I could bring them along as well. Which end of the wing are you?"

"The northern corner, right by the exit. There's a small fenced patio that you can see from the back road. We're just past that. You wouldn't even have to sign in at the front desk; you could just walk round the building with your dogs and knock on our windows."

"It can't be much of a view looking out over the staff parking lot," said Beary. "Wouldn't you rather have a room at the southern end?"

"No, where we are it's easy to sneak out for a smoke—and don't lecture me about health. We both turned ninety-two this year."

"I don't believe it," said Juliette. "You look wonderful."

Jimmy Henderson did belie his age. His posture was straight, his medals gleamed against his navy blazer and his beret was set at a jaunty angle. He could have easily passed for a man twenty-years younger.

"So where is Scotty?" Beary interjected.

"Glued to his television. He'll be down any minute. Watching the tail end of a movie."

"Battle of the Bulge?"

"No. Harry Potter. Except for the wizards and warlocks, the plots of those films are the same as the stories in our old *Boy's Own Schooldays* annuals. Quite nostalgic. Watch it, lads," he added to two young cadets who were making their way towards the assembly hall and trying to avoid entangling their flags with the passing wheelchairs. "Fine state of affairs we've got to," he said, turning back to the Bearys. "From rolling tanks to rolling chairs. We WWII vets are a dying breed."

"Maybe," said Beary, "but age hasn't dampened your spirits."

"Bloody right," said Jimmy. "You won't find our conversations degenerating into organ recitals. We ignore the aches and pains and take life full speed ahead."

"Literally as well as figuratively? I noticed a sign on the corkboard slapping a speed restriction on wheelchairs."

Jimmy scowled.

"That's Adolf," he said. "Never happy unless she's telling us what we can't do."

"Adolf?"

"Philomena. New administrative head. Proper tartar. Life goal is to get us off nicotine and addicted to yoghurt and rabbit food."

"She's not succeeding on the former," said Beary. "Every other week, we hear the fire trucks go by as another one of you sneaks a fag in your room and sets off the alarms."

"You can't stop our generation from smoking," said Jimmy. "It's ingrained. Puffed our way through the war, and we didn't take on the Nazis in order to wimp out in front of a bunch of bureaucrats. Too many bloody rules in this place, though at least they've brought the ladies in now," he added, waving towards the assembly-hall entrance as a spry-looking elderly woman emerged. She was a tiny, bird-like creature, trim in navy blazer and grey, pleated skirt, and her beret was perched precariously atop a dandelion puff of silver hair. She came over to Jimmy and tucked her arm in his.

"Are you haranguing the councillor over our dinner menus?" she said, cheerfully including Beary in her smile.

"Not at all," said Jimmy, "though I probably ought to. Have you met Flora?" he added to the Bearys. "She and her pal, Olive, are two more members of the Naughty Nineties Brigade. They're the life and soul of the tea dances."

"I remember both charming ladies," said Beary. "We met last Christmas. I haven't seen Olive today, though. Is she already inside?"

"No," said Flora, "she's out for the day with her daughter and son-in-law. Lunch at the Sylvia Hotel. Olive's never been one for ceremony. She'd much rather forget the past and enjoy the present. Besides," she chuckled, readjusting her grip on Jimmy's arm and winking at Juliette, "if she isn't around, it gives me a chance to get this handsome fellow to myself. Now, it's filling up inside," she added, "so you might want to go in and grab yourselves some seats."

"Good idea," said Edwina. "Where have Jennifer and Laura got to?" she asked, noticing the absence of her granddaughters.

"Steven took them down to the craft room," said Juliette.

"They'd better not be late back for the service."

Edwina's eyebrows wrinkled disapprovingly as she peered down the corridor. There was no sign of her grandchildren, but a flicker of recognition crossed her face as she noticed a sweet-faced woman with unruly salt and pepper hair coming down the hall. The woman was pushing a wheelchair that contained a wiry, grizzled gentleman with a crew cut. He was neatly dressed in grey slacks and a navy blazer, and an impressive row of medals gleamed on his chest. Beside his chair, another smartly outfitted veteran limped, heavily leaning on his cane, but clearly determined to manage unassisted.

"Where do I know that woman from?" asked Edwina. "I've seen her somewhere before."

"The dog park," said Beary. "That's Beanie's owner, Millie Jenkins—or rather Millie Burgess, as she is now. She married Maverick's owner. She volunteers here through Pets and Friends, just like you used to," he added to Juliette. "Now, you must remember those men with her. They were here when you were a volunteer."

"I do," cried Juliet. "That's Lionel and Stan."

"That's right," said Jimmy, "more members of the Naughty Nineties Brigade."

Beary hailed the newcomers and introduced Juliette to Millie. The two started to compare notes on their pets and experiences. Edwina, glancing at her watch and looking increasingly irritated, excused herself and set off purposefully in the direction of the craft room. Beary turned to talk with Lionel and Stan. A polite query as to their wellbeing prompted a self-satisfied smile.

"We're fine," said Lionel. He flicked a piece of fluff off his military cross. "Can't say the same for Adolf, though," he added, pointedly directing the remark to Jimmy.

"What's wrong with her?" asked Beary.

Stan grinned as he leaned on his cane. "She's got the staff zooming about like V-bombs. Rumour has it she's got an AWOL."

Beary raised his eyebrows.

"Is that a laughing matter? Someone could be hurt or ill."

Jimmy chuckled.

"Everything's a laughing matter at our age. We've got to go sometime. No use thinking about it and getting depressed. Far better to go flat out until you hit the wall—and all the better if it happens to be at a time that causes the maximum inconvenience to Adolf."

Beary looked at the grinning faces. Old soldiers were a tough breed, but they were also fierce in their loyalties, and he was surprised that they would be cavalier about the possibility of one of their members going missing.

As the thought crossed his mind, an attractive redhead of indeterminate age came down the hall. Her hair was short and stylish, and she was smartly dressed in a green suit, which, in conjunction with her poppy, gave her a festive air. However, her anxious frown was at odds with her cheery outfit. Beary recognized her. It was Mary Stokes, the popular volunteer co-coordinator. As she neared, Beary pulled her aside and asked her what was going on. She paused just long enough to fill him in.

"One of the staff saw an empty wheelchair on the old hospital site," she murmured, "and we've no idea where the owner is. What a worry . . . and what a day for this to happen."

Shaking her head wearily, Mary hurried away. Beary turned back to the veterans who had been hovering nearby. To his surprise, he noticed that the faces looking back at him had lost their cheerful grins. The previous bravado had evaporated and every face registered alarm. The change of mood was disconcerting. Uneasily, Beary noticed the apprehensive glances exchanged amid the group. Why did he have the horrible feeling that something planned had gone horribly wrong?

*   *   *

Paula Burns was smarting. She had been ambivalent about reporting for duty before going down to inspect the abandoned wheelchair but knowing how strict the senior staff were about punctuality, she had decided to check in first. She had told the executive director about the wheelchair and offered to return to look into the situation, but instead of thanking her for her vigilance, Philomena had implied that the abandoned wheelchair was somehow Paula's fault. Furthermore, it was as if Paula had deliberately engineered a crisis to ruin the Remembrance Day service. If Paula had believed there was an emergency, she should have gone down to investigate, but since she chose to sign in for work, she obviously didn't feel there was any urgency to deal with the abandoned chair.

The instructions that followed had been sharply administered and impossible to carry out within an appropriate time frame. Paula was to return to the old grounds to retrieve the chair and look for the owner; however, she was also to distribute the meds that were due at the start of her shift, check her wing to see if anyone was missing, and help with the men who were attending the service.

As Paula hurried about, trying to complete the tasks, she thought resentfully that Philomena had deliberately set her up to be the scapegoat if someone were seriously injured. Not for the first time, Paula cursed the day that Philomena Schmidt had been hired as chief administrator. If only the wretched board of directors could see through her the way everyone else did. It was utterly frustrating and wretchedly unfair, thought Paula angrily as she measured out the doses. The hated Philomena always managed to come out on top.

*   *   *

Beary looked at his watch. It was almost time for the service to start, but Edwina had not yet returned with Steven and the children. Jimmy had gone to the nurses' station to see if he could find out more about the abandoned wheelchair, but he had not come back either. However, there were still lots of people milling about, and guests were continuing to come through the front door. A legless amputee in a wheelchair was handing out programs outside the assembly room, and beside him, another veteran was distributing poppies. Millie had taken Stan and Lionel into the hall, with a promise to save seats for the Bearys, but Flora remained in the lobby, anxious to see if Jimmy would return with any more news about the missing veteran. The grapevine was humming, and the heightened activity of the staff was now evident.

As Juliette looked towards the main entrance, two women came into the foyer. Both were striking brunettes, although one appeared slightly younger and was more casually dressed. She held the hand of a little girl who proudly sported a white lace dress decorated with red bows. The older woman wore a figure-hugging cream suit and a multi-coloured silk scarf, artfully draped so as not to conceal her poppy. Juliette nudged her father's arm.

"Look, there's Alexandra Lacey. I wonder why she's here."

Beary smiled. He had a soft spot for Alexandra, whose mystery novels, much loved by Edwina, provided some peaceful hours in the Beary home when his wife was immersed in a book and too busy to find jobs for him to do.

"I expect she's come with George," he said. "He always makes a point of showing his face on Remembrance Day."

George Lacey had been the riding-association president for the Coquitlam Progressive Conservatives, but when a candidate had been needed for a recent by-election, he had stepped forward and was now the local Member of Parliament.

Flora interjected. "Alex didn't come to accompany her husband. She and her sister are here to visit their grandfather. He's one of our residents. He moved in last year after his wife died. Little Fiona is the apple of his eye," she added, gesturing towards the tot in white lace. "She's three, and quite adorable."

Beary waved and caught Alexandra's attention. Her face broke into a radiant smile and she hurried forward to meet him. She was very fond of the Beary family.

"Hello. Lovely to see you." She beckoned to her sister and introduced her. "This is my sister, Cleo, and this is little Fiona." She attempted to get the attention of the three-year-old, who had spotted the amputee in the wheelchair. The child ignored her aunt and marched over to take a closer look.

"That bad owie," she said, pointing to the veteran's stump. He grinned, nodded agreement and magically produced a candy from his pocket. Cleo rolled her eyes and went to retrieve her daughter.

"I can see she's a star," said Beary.

Alexandra laughed; then she turned to Flora. "Do you know if our grandfather has come down yet?" she asked.

Flora nodded towards the assembly hall.

"He's already inside. He's saving you a seat."

Flora's face grew solemn as she looked past Alexandra and saw Jimmy returning. Beside him walked a short man whose receding hairline and glasses made him look like a benevolent gnome.

"Finally," cried Flora. "Here's Jimmy with Scotty. I'm going to see if they know anything more." Excusing herself, she slipped away. Beary turned to Alexandra.

"Where's George?" he asked.

Alexandra rolled her eyes. "At the cenotaph. He says the Sidley staff are anti-conservative and tell the 'old geezers'—that's his words, not mine—who to vote for so he doesn't bother to come. He knows he gets a few votes here because of me and Grandad, so he goes elsewhere to be visible." Alexandra sighed. "There are times I loathe politics. Self-promotion is so out of place on Remembrance Day."

"Tell that to the Council candidates," said Edwina, materializing at Beary's side, a granddaughter firmly gripped in each hand. "Especially that one," she added, glowering in Colin Bell's direction. "I'm surprised he's still here," she snapped. "I thought he was supposed to take his father down to the cenotaph."

Beary looked towards the assembly hall. Colin Bell was no longer glad-handing the veterans but was engaged in a spirited exchange with a lean, autocratic-looking blonde whom Beary took to be Philomena Schmidt. Shrewdly, Beary noted the tension emanating from both parties.

"Well," said Beary, "it would appear that Colin has been cheated of his chance to show off his father at the cenotaph, and that means they've solved the mystery of the missing veteran. I wonder what has happened to poor old Billy Bell."

*   *   *

Once Paula had seen to the men on her wing, she slipped outside and made her way back to the old grounds. In spite of the good weather, the trees and bushes were still wet from the weekend storm. As she hurried down the slope, she could see the wheelchair, shaded by a towering maple tree that stood at the edge of the parking area in front of the old administration building. The chair nestled against a huge bough that had fallen from the tree. Smaller branches jutted out from the gnarled arm, forming tripping obstacles on the ground and projecting hazards higher up. The bough had torn a section loose from the wire fence and flattened the bushes that grew against the mesh. Through the gap, Paula could see the wooden fence that bounded the housing estate, and above it, the windows of the houses that had been built along the boundary. A shady path ran between the two fences, intended as a sop to the local residents who liked to run their dogs on the trails, though Paula had heard a lot of complaints that the woods were no longer safe for walkers.

Paula became aware of the steady thrum of rap music playing in one of the houses. Closer, persistently mingling with the music, was the tapping of a woodpecker in a nearby cottonwood tree. A strong smell of curry wafted across from the estate, but in spite of the constant noise and the potent aroma, the area was deserted. Paula had been afraid that she would find an injured veteran lying nearby, but although she searched thoroughly, she found no one.

She returned to the wheelchair and examined it. It was an electric model, but there was nothing to indicate who owned it. She noticed that the brake had not been set properly. The ground by the parking area had a slight gradient and there were tracks on the grass verge that were in a direct line with the wheels of the chair. They ran a few feet and then stopped at an overgrown rhododendron bush that had been neatly bisected by one of the wayward branches from the maple tree. Obviously, the chair had been left in a carefully concealed spot. If the brake had been applied properly, it would have remained there. It would not have rolled out into the lot, and it would not have been visible from the road. Someone had deliberately tried to hide it.

Perplexed, Paula tried to think who would have done such a thing. The men who needed wheelchairs were hardly capable of negotiating their way into the bushes and getting away without the chair. On the other hand, she could think of a few of the mobile ones who would consider it a grand joke to take a chair and abandon it in order to create a panic with the staff. But then, why try to hide it so no one would see it? It really didn't make sense at all. She returned to the chair and studied it again, trying to find some detail that would provide a clue to its owner. The arms and seat were covered in dark red leather, and she tried to remember which of the patients had models of this type. Sometimes, the rear side of the backrest would be labelled, so she gripped the armrests, intending to pull the chair clear so she could look for a name. Almost immediately, she recoiled, for the leather on the right armrest felt wet and sticky. Startled, she turned her hand over and stared at her palm. It was covered in blood.

Horrified, Paula stepped away from the chair. She bent down and wiped her hand furiously against the wet grass. Then, with a sick feeling in her stomach, as much from the knowledge of the fury she would unleash in Philomena as from the discovery of the blood, she pulled out her cellphone and dialled 911.

*   *   *

The Remembrance Day service was very touching, all the more so because the passages were read by people with infirmities. Instead of pomp and grandeur, quiet humility was the order of the day. The effort it took for a reader to reach the podium and return to his seat was as meaningful as the text he presented. Beary was profoundly moved, but a nagging concern for the missing veteran hovered at the back of his mind. Billy Bell was a far more amiable character than his son and Beary hated to think that misfortune might have struck the old man. As soon as the ceremony was over, Beary left Edwina to supervise Jennifer and Laura at the tea table and joined the cluster of Naughty Nineties who were huddled near the door. They fell silent as Beary approached.

"Any more news?" he asked.

"Not a dicky bird," said Jimmy. "No idea what's going on."

The group dissolved as if a fairy had sprinkled them with vanishing dust and Beary found himself staring at an empty wall. As

he contemplated the possibility that the onions he had eaten with last
night's dinner were still redolent on his breath, Mary Stokes came
back into the hall. When he posed the same question to her, she
sighed.

"It's Billy Bell," she said. "He's vanished without trace and there
are signs he may be injured." Mary related what Paula Burns had
discovered on her return to the site. "The police have been notified,
but they haven't exactly roared up here with sirens blazing. I guess
when you're over ninety, you're not on their high-priority list."

"Did anyone see Billy leave this morning?" asked Beary.

Mary shook her head.

"No, although Scotty saw him in the corridor. His room is
opposite Billy's. Billy was up early as it was such a lovely morning.
He told Scotty he was going to tour the gardens, and then wait for
his son in the lounge at the end of the hall. It's at the south corner of
the wing—very convenient for the men in that section. It has a coffee
maker and a fridge, and it's a quiet, sunny spot overlooking the
woods. But no one saw Billy there, so I suspect he changed his mind
and went directly from the gardens to the old hospital site. Then
something happened to prevent him returning."

"Why would he have gone down to the old grounds?"

"Billy's nostalgic about the old place. Many of us are. The men
have nicer rooms here and they enjoy their private quarters, but the
facility is crowded and bustling, and the assembly hall—" Mary's
grave expression gave way to a thin smile. "Well, the men call it the
goldfish bowl. It's so inadequate compared to the old auditorium."

"That's true," said Beary, wistfully remembering the tall square-
paned windows and elegant mouldings of the old facility. "You had
a huge hall, complete with a stage, and an adjoining room with six
full-size snooker tables. Now you just have one room, no stage and
one four-by-eight bar table squished into the corner. I can

understand Billy wanting to have another look at his old home before it's pulled apart and redeveloped."

"There's no other reason why he'd go there," said Mary.

"No one else was able to provide any information?"

"Not really. I hoped Olive Grant might be able to help. She's a special friend of Billy's. She's out with her daughter and son-in-law today, but I called her cell as I thought she might have seen Billy before she left."

"And had she?"

"Yes. She'd popped in to check on him, but he was still getting ready to go out. He didn't say anything to her other than grumble about the way his son was using the day to further his political aspirations. Olive helped Billy with his tie, and then she came down to the front entrance. I'd just arrived, and I saw Olive's daughter's Toyota roll in as I was walking up the drive. I chatted with Olive and her family for a few minutes, and I helped her into the car before I came inside. I'd definitely have seen Billy if he'd been wheeling around the pathways by then."

"Could he have gone out the back way?"

"Yes, but he'd still have had to come around the front to get to the old grounds. So, impossible as it seems, he must have slipped out between eight-thirty when I saw Olive off and nine o'clock when Paula arrived. Olive's frantic. She's so fond of Billy. She's worried sick that something bad has happened to him. I had quite a time convincing her not to rush back early. I'm sorry I called her, actually, because she wasn't able to help and I've probably spoiled her day."

Beary shook his head thoughtfully.

"Could Billy have had an accident? Might he have lost control going down the hill?"

"Unlikely in an electric wheelchair, but even if he'd been thrown out, why wouldn't he be lying nearby?"

"I don't know. How mobile is Billy Bell?"

"Not very. He can get around his room without assistance, because he uses the furniture to support himself, but he always needs his chair when he goes out. He had a stroke last year, so it's slowed him down a lot."

"Is he mentally competent?"

Mary sighed. "That's a thorny and debatable point. Unfortunately, his son doesn't think so."

"Why not?"

Mary elaborated. "Billy's quite capable of making decisions about what he wants to do. He's fine interacting with other people, but he can't manage money or keep track of medications, and unfortunately, because of that, he agreed to let his son have power of attorney. The smart thing would have been simply to enact a POA for the bank, but Colin persuaded his father to give him full powers, so Billy is very much under his son's thumb."

"Has that become a problem?"

"It has rather. You see, Colin is on the board of directors, so that, along with the POA gives him a lot of control. He's even used his position to influence staffing. We have an aide here who used to work for him as a cleaner, and I swear Colin had her taken on so she could report back to him on his father's activities."

"How does he get away with that sort of stunt?"

"Because he's like that—" Mary raised two crossed fingers in the air—"with our head administrator, and between the two of them, they have the ability to make Billy's life very difficult."

Beary was puzzled.

"Why would they want to?"

"Don't ever repeat this," said Mary, "and if you do, I'll deny it, but honestly, Philomena lives up to the third syllable in her name. She's an ill-spirited control freak—totally into power."

"No virgin Christian martyr she?" said Beary.

Mary blinked.

"Saint Philomena," explained Beary. "Greek, I believe. She refused to marry and withstood terrible tortures before ultimately being beheaded. As I recall, when they tried to shoot her with arrows, they all bounced back onto the archers."

"Well, that's appropriate," said Mary. "Whatever steps you take to deal with Philomena, it usually comes back on you in spades."

"Interesting. Is your administrative head Greek, by any chance?"

"No," said Mary. "Third-generation Canadian, though there's some sort of European heritage, given that her surname is Schmidt. The men all figure she's German."

"Hence Adolf."

"Yes, exactly," Mary sighed again. "The centre used to be such a friendly place, with people coming and going so that the vets could interact with the surrounding community, but Philomena has put a stop to all that. The local dog walkers used to cut through the grounds and chat with the men, but Philomena sent so many of them off with a flea in their ear that they don't come any more. She's prohibited visiting pets completely unless they're approved through an official program, and she ordered the men to get rid of the resident cat, though they're all wily enough that they still have it, but you can imagine the manoeuvres they go through to keep Philomena from finding out."

"She obviously doesn't like animals."

"No, she doesn't. We nearly lost Millie, our Pets and Friends volunteer, because one of the older men had an accident in the hall— a number two, not a collision—and Philomena insisted that Beanie had to be responsible. What was even worse, she refused to apologize when she was proved wrong? I had to jump through hoops to get Millie to agree to stay on. She was so upset. But it isn't just animals.

Philomena has introduced so many restrictions that the local pre-school teacher has had to give up her annual visit with the four-year-olds. The high-school students don't come any more either, even though we used to have an excellent interactive program."

"So Philomena doesn't just have it in for Billy Bell. She likes making everyone miserable."

"Well, in Billy's case, there's history. Before Billy had his stroke, he was remarkably vigorous for his age, and quite the little romance developed between him and Olive Grant. They'd known each other before. Olive was an actress in her heyday—something of a pin-up girl, from what one hears—and she and Billy actually met during the war when she was in the entertainment corps."

"That must have been quite the reunion."

"It was. It was very sweet, and we even wondered if they'd decide to marry. Well, you can imagine how Colin reacted to that."

"Absolute fury?"

"Yes, he was apoplectic. I suspect that Billy's stroke was brought on by the stress of dealing with his son. Initially, we weren't sure if Billy would recover, and quite honestly, it was Olive's care and attention that pulled him through. She encouraged him to persevere with therapy and wouldn't let him give up. It's really amazing, when you consider how old they are. So much spirit and determination. Anyway, Olive stood up to Colin and told him what's what in no uncertain terms, and because Philomena is Colin's willing lackey, she's done everything she can to obstruct the two spending time together."

"You need a change of administrator," said Beary.

"We've tried," said Mary. "She's created enough problems that a few board members have raised the issue of a new executive director, but Colin's been so solidly behind her that he's always managed to swing the vote in her favour."

"She may not be in favour after today. Not if she's managed to lose his father."

Mary's eyes flashed and her voice took on a waspish tone that was out of character with her gentle nature.

"I doubt if Colin Bell would be upset if the loss were permanent," she said crossly. "His rage at missing the ceremony at the cenotaph will have turned to hope by now. I bet he's counting his inheritance as we speak."

*   *   *

Never one to let the grass grow under his feet, Beary hurried back into the hall and whisked Edwina away from the reception.

"But it's only just started," Edwina protested.

"Things to do," Beary insisted. "Let's hustle home and pick up the dogs. They need a walk and I want to take a look at this wheelchair."

Edwina looked dubious.

"But what if the police have arrived? They'll have the area cordoned off and we won't be able to see anything."

"Given the RCMP response time, that isn't likely, but even if the police are there, they'll seal off the entrance to the grounds, but they won't think to block the trails. And even if they do, MacPuff can't read." Beary smirked. "No one can be faulted for crossing the tape to retrieve a dog."

"All right. You'd better tell the others. They can stay and socialize and we'll text them as we start back. They can meet us at the entrance to the trails."

After a brief word with Juliette, Beary and Edwina left the Sidley Centre. As they walked home, Beary told his wife what he had learned from Mary Stokes.

"Mary thinks Billy must have been ready a good half-hour before his son was due to arrive," he explained. "Her theory is that he went down to the old grounds while he was waiting. She says he feels nostalgic about the old centre. There was obviously some kind of accident once he got there, but nobody has any details. What worries me is the fact that the local thugs use the trails for drug deals. Billy might have had a run-in with one of them."

Edwina nodded gravely.

"Yes, that's true, but what if it's not a question of random violence? I was talking to Alexandra Lacey after the service and she told me that George, with his political connections, knows quite a lot about Colin Bell. Evidently, his financial situation is rocky. George was dead set against Colin's nomination for Council. He doesn't trust him at all."

"That doesn't surprise me."

"No, it didn't surprise me either, but until Alexandra filled me in, I didn't realize how strapped Colin is for funds. Three years ago, his wife divorced him and took him to the cleaners. Now, he's got himself up to his ears in debt over a development scheme that was supposed to set him back on his feet but has actually backfired and made his situation worse. George figures Colin's been using his POA to embezzle money. He must be desperate to get his inheritance."

"He could hardly have abducted his father, though. We all saw Colin at the ceremony. If he is involved, he must have hired someone to do the deed."

"Or have an accomplice." Edwina arched her eyebrows knowingly. "Alexandra says Colin is very cozy with Philomena Schmidt."

"What does she think Adolf has done? Shut Billy Bell in a broom closet? That's a bit far-fetched."

Edwina shrugged.

"Well, Alex is a mystery writer."

"True. Well, who knows? She could be right."

Beary recalled what Mary Stokes had told him about the new aide. If Colin Bell had planted a mole in the hospital, he had put her there for a reason.

Edwina emitted a heavy sigh.

"Do you realize that Alexandra is the same age as our son?" she said. "She's just turned forty, and she has a seventeen-year-old son and a nineteen-year-old daughter."

"So?"

"So, Richard isn't even engaged, let alone married. I'm beginning to lose hope for him. And if Philippa doesn't soon give that nice Constable Miller some encouragement, that'll all go sideways too."

"Our kids are fine," Beary said impatiently. "They can take care of themselves. I'm more concerned about Billy Bell." He glanced at his watch. "Come on, let's hurry. If we don't drag our feet, we may get to the old hospital site ahead of the police."

Conversation ceased as they picked up the pace. Once home, they changed into their walking clothes, leashed the dogs, and set off again, texting Juliette as they went. Five minutes later, they reached the woods. Juliette and her entourage were already gathered at the trail entrance. Purdy and Quasar strained at their leashes when they spotted Juliette, so Beary set them free and they bounded ahead. However, once on the trail, Beary let MacPuff off the leash, and the feisty husky assumed the leader's role. Obediently, the visiting dogs fell back and allowed him to strut in front.

"Pack order," said Beary, falling into step beside his son-in-law. "Fascinating how it kicks in when there's more than two."

Juliette dropped back to stroll with her mother, but Jennifer and Laura darted ahead to run with the dogs. Beary and Steven walked briskly, keeping a watch on the girls and calling back the dogs if they got too far ahead. It was easy to keep moving, for the ground was hard and the leaves underfoot were brown and crisp. The bare branches rendered far better visibility than in the summer months when the paths were tunnels of variegated shades of green. Overhead, crows cawed a protest at the shrill laughter of the children and the antics of the dogs, who were bounding in and out of the skeletal bushes and sending a flurry of twigs into the air as they chased sticks and dashed back to the girls with their trophies.

When the wooden fence of the housing estate came into view, Beary called the dogs back and leashed them. In spite of his quips about dogs and police tape, he had no desire to have a run-in with the constabulary.

"These woods were overrun with police a few weeks ago," he told Steven. "There was a stabbing in the housing estate. Very nasty business." Beary related what he'd heard from Richard and had gleaned from the articles in the local newspaper.

Steven listened attentively.

"Maybe they'll bring the dog squad back to search for Billy Bell," he said, when Beary concluded his tale.

"I doubt it," said Beary as they rounded another corner and came to the gap in the fence that opened onto the old hospital grounds. "Look. There isn't a cop in sight."

"That's pretty slipshod. They haven't even responded to the call."

"Fine with me," said Beary. "This'll give us a chance to look around."

Jennifer and Laura pushed ahead and clambered through the gap. Juliette followed, sharply warning her daughters not to touch the wheelchair, which was still there, nestled against the fallen bough. Steven went through and joined his family on the other side of the fence, but Beary held back. He looked around, noting the distance between the gate of the housing estate and the gap in the wire fence.

He eyed the huge maple tree, towering above the grounds, its branches reaching out over the trail. Then he turned to peer at the tall townhouse on the far side of the estate fence. Finally, pushing aside the brambles that had not been flattened by the falling branches, he stepped through the gap.

"That made a mess," said Steven, nodding towards the massive branch that had bowed the frame of the fence.

"That happened in a windstorm several weeks ago," said Beary, "but the gap has been there much longer. I suspect the local hoodlums ripped a section of the wire loose so they could cut up to the road without having to trek out through the trail." He bent and examined the leather on the wheelchair. Then he took out a handkerchief and dabbed its corner against the arm. "Yes, it definitely looks like blood," he said, "but the stain is only on the one arm. The seat is quite clean, as is the other arm. You'd think there would be a lot more blood if Billy had been attacked."

"The chair has rolled," said Juliette. She pointed to the tracks on the grass between the tarmac and the rhododendron bush at the top of the slope. "There might be bloodstains up there."

"Good point."

Warning his granddaughters to stand clear so as not to disturb the ground, Beary followed the tracks in the grass. He refrained from telling the girls the real reason he wanted them to stay back. Behind the rhododendron bush was an unruly tangle of blackberry brambles and other wild shrubs that could quite easily conceal a corpse.

He was relieved to see no rusty stains on the ground by the bush. He bent down and parted the branches, staring through to the rough dirt, and finding only dead pine needles, stones and the skeletal remains of fallen leaves. He was about to straighten up, but his sleeve caught on a gnarled branch that had landed across the rhododendron bush. As he tried to extricate himself, the harsh winter sun streaked through the opening he had forged, transforming the dull earth into a sepia and orange patchwork quilt. In one corner of the pastiche, there was a sudden, eye-piercing glint of metal. Carefully, Beary pulled his arm free. Then he reached forward until he could clasp his fingers around the object that had caused the blinding flash. Slowly, he drew it out from the bush. His eyes grew wide as he saw what he was holding. Then he laid it gently on the grass and pulled out his cellphone. This time, he was sure the police would not drag their feet getting to the Sidley Wood.

*   *   *

The ceremony at the cenotaph had drawn a considerable crowd. Afterwards, Richard and Philippa stood side by side to watch the fly-past. The precision of the formation flying thrilled Philippa. She knew how much discipline went into any successful performance and she appreciated the skill behind the soaring quartet.

Once the planes had disappeared into the ether, the crowd drifted towards the road. Richard and Philippa looked for a good spot to watch the parade. They had only just settled on a viewpoint when the distant strains of "Colonel Boogie" reached their ears. They turned towards the music and saw a red-jacketed military band turning onto Royal Avenue and beginning its stately progression towards the spectators. As the pipe bands, cadets and scouts marched by, the onlookers cheered, clapped and took photographs.

After the final unit trooped by and turned onto Sixth Street, a few lively souls tagged onto the end of the parade and marched at the rear as the bands proceeded up the hill to the armories. The rest of the crowd began to disperse, but Philippa and Richard took the time to pin their poppies on the tall white cross by the monument before making their way up the hill.

Richard had promised to buy his sister lunch at the Bavaria House, and by the time they reached the restaurant, Philippa was starving. Several people were waiting by the front desk so she hoped that Richard had reserved. As the hostess invited the next group of diners in, the crowd thinned and Philippa had a clear view of the dining room. The area was noisy with the chatter of patrons, many of whom had been wreath-bearing participants during the ceremony. Philippa recognized the city councillor holding court at a table for eight in the centre of the room. Another table was presided over by the president of the Rotary Club. On the far side of the room were the two firefighters who had been standing with Richard at the cenotaph. They were seated at a corner table, along with two equally handsome uniformed reservists.

While she and Richard waited to be seated, Philippa eyed the plates of the diners seated near the doorway and contemplated the merits of chicken schnitzel versus a spinach salad laden with caramelized pecans and goat cheese.

"This is nice," she said. "I like being taken to lunch by a good-looking man in uniform, even if he is only my brother."

Before Richard could comment, a discordant counterpoint intruded into the cacophony of strident voices and clattering china. It was his cellphone.

The call was from their father.

"Has any of your team notified you about the old boy who went AWOL from the veterans' centre?" Beary asked Richard. "Name of Billy Bell."

"They won't call me about a missing veteran," said Richard. "They'll send a constable from the uniformed branch."

"Probably, but I think you'll want to check it out yourself. You see, Billy's wheelchair was abandoned on the old hospital site, and something rather interesting has turned up nearby."

Richard scowled at his phone. He was beginning to be as hungry as his sister.

"Are we talking missing persons or violent crime?" he growled.

"Both. Look, if you want a breakthrough on your cold case at the Sidley housing estate, you'd better hustle over here."

Richard's manner changed instantly. Philippa sighed as she observed the signs. Her brother's narrowed eyes and alert posture could only mean one thing. Another lunch going astray.

"What breakthrough?" demanded Richard.

"I've found your murder weapon," crowed Beary. "A machete. I believe you were looking for one. It's been washed off, but I can still see traces of bloodstains around the handle."

"Where was it?"

"Lying in a rhododendron bush on the old Sidley grounds."

"That's impossible," said Richard. "We had dog teams all through there. We didn't find anything."

"That," said Beary smugly, "is because there was nothing there."

"Stop talking in riddles."

"It's not a riddle. There was nothing there when you searched because the machete wasn't on the ground. I think your theory about Joey Bortolione's wife was right. She must have lobbed it from her upstairs window and the leather loop on the handle caught on the branch of the maple tree. The dogs couldn't sniff it out because it was thirty feet over their heads. Then when the branch came down in the windstorm, the machete landed in the middle of the bush."

Richard's eyes were glowing. "I'll be there in ten minutes," he said. He ended the call and put his phone back in his pocket.

Philippa scowled at her brother.

"It's no wonder you haven't got married," she said acerbically. "No one would put up with you. I was looking forward to our lunch," she added indignantly.

Richard was unrepentant.

"You don't have to miss lunch," he said, glancing across the dining room. "I'll introduce you to my friends. Then you can have lunch with *four* good-looking men in uniform."

He waved across the restaurant to the table where the firefighters sat with the two handsome reservists. Seeing Richard waving and pointing to the petite redhead at his side, the men at the table leapt to their feet and flashed welcoming smiles. Richard propelled his sister across the room and settled her with the broadly grinning quartet. Then he hurried away to meet his father.

And so Remembrance Day proved a day to remember for brother and sister alike. Richard solved his case and Philippa thoroughly enjoyed her lunch.

*   *   *

By the time the RCMP had arrived, taken over the site and finished questioning the Bearys, it was past one o'clock. Beary was anxious to head back to the Sidley Centre to see if there was any news of Billy, but Edwina decreed that the children were hungry and that a proper lunch was needed before any further detection was undertaken— besides which, given Philomena Schmidt's attitude towards animals, they would hardly be welcome if they appeared at the facility with a pack of dogs. Seeing the nodding heads agreeing with his wife, Beary realized he was outnumbered. He retrieved MacPuff, who had been banished to the sidelines with the girls due to his tendency to growl at the uniformed constables, and turned in the direction of home.

Back at the house, Edwina produced steaming bowls of soup and homemade quiche. The dogs, tired from their run, sprawled out on the living-room carpet and went to sleep, and by the time lunch was eaten, the humans felt similarly lethargic. Jennifer and Laura disappeared into the TV room to watch a DVD and visit with Minx the Manx, who had claimed that area as her personal refuge during the invasion of the visiting dogs, and Edwina declared her intention of enjoying a cup of coffee before setting a foot outside again.

"You can't accomplish anything by going back to the Sidley Centre," she pointed out to her husband. "Why don't you just phone and see if there's been a development?"

"We won't get squat from a phone call," said Beary. "I want to quiz the residents. Someone must have seen Billy leave."

Juliette nodded, for she agreed with her father. Therefore, at three o'clock, Beary set off with Juliette and Steven in tow, while Edwina remained at home to supervise the girls.

As they neared the Sidley Centre, Juliette and Steven were immersed in a discussion over which ferry they should take to return to the Sunshine Coast, so they did not notice the Toyota that passed them on the road. However, Beary saw the car and its occupants. He recognized the elderly woman in the back seat, and when the car turned into the driveway and pulled up under the portico of the veterans' hospital, he knew he had been right. It was Olive Grant with her daughter and son-in-law.

By the time the Bearys walked up the driveway, Olive was out of the car and delivering hugs and thanks to her daughter. Judging by the happy farewells, the outing had been a successful one.

However, once the Toyota had left, Olive's mood changed dramatically. Feverishly, she quizzed Beary about what had happened in her absence and reiterated what she had told Mary Stokes earlier in the day. Then she shot through the doors into the lobby, where she collared two of the staff members and, arms whirling like windmills, took up the refrain with them.

"My goodness," said Juliette. "For an old girl, she has an awful lot of pep. What a performance! She's really upset."

"She's very fond of Billy," said Beary, "but the histrionics come naturally. Olive was an actress in her heyday." He waved Juliette ahead of him and followed her through the automatic doors. Steven tailed after them, and the three stood watching as Olive gathered a steadily increasing audience. As Beary observed the spry lady's lavish gestures, Juliette's words echoed in his mind. *What a performance!*

The crowd continued to grow, but a few moments later, a shout penetrated the noise in the lobby. The hubbub of voices was suddenly stilled as everyone turned to see who had called out. Jimmy Henderson was hurrying down the corridor. When he reached the lobby, he stopped to catch his breath. Then he delivered an announcement that knocked the wind out of everyone's sails.

"Ye'll never believe it," he cried triumphantly. "Billy is in his room. He's been there all afternoon!"

*   *   *

Once Billy Bell's safe return had been confirmed, Juliette and Steven hurried away, having decided that they had just enough time to pick up the girls and eat on the six-thirty ferry. Beary chose to remain, for he had more questions to ask.

By the time he walked home, his houseguests had left. Edwina was in the process of feeding Minx and MacPuff, and an appetizing smell emanated from the kitchen where chicken was simmering in the crock-pot.

Edwina was keen to hear the details of Billy's miraculous reappearance, so Beary put on the kettle to make her a Spanish coffee and poured himself what he considered to be a thoroughly well-earned Scotch. "Well," he said, as he measured Kahlua and Grand Marnier into a glass, "the best part of this entire fiasco is that Colin Bell and Philomena have had a major falling out."

"That augurs well for the future." Edwina tossed the parsnips she had trimmed into the pot. "It's time someone clipped that woman's wings. Efficiency is all very well, but it has to be tempered with kindness." Beary refrained from comment. Edwina had earned a few autocratic epithets herself during her years as a high-school administrator, but he had to admit that, however unyielding and authoritarian she had been, she had never been unfair.

Unaware of her husband's train of thought, Edwina continued, "The woman in charge of the crafts room told me that Colin Bell's support was the only reason Philomena Schmidt has not been demoted to a different posting."

"Yes, well hopefully, next time there's a staff review, Adolf's job will be up for grabs."

Beary poured hot water through the coffee filter and finished Edwina's drink. Then he carried it through to the living room.

Edwina settled herself in her favourite armchair, took a leisurely sip and sighed contentedly.

"So how did Billy manage to be missed by all the people who were looking for him?" she asked. "And how did his wheelchair end up on the old hospital grounds? He must have taken it outside at some point."

"I asked Billy every one of those questions," said Beary. "He informed me that he never got out for a tour of the gardens. He went to wait in the lounge as planned, but then he had a call of nature, and rather than go back to his room, he went into the washroom that's just a couple of steps down the hall. He didn't need his chair for that distance, so he went on foot, holding onto the handrail, but when he returned, the chair was gone."

"What?"

"His exact words were, 'Some silly bugger pinched my chair while I was in the loo.'"

"Didn't he tell anyone?"

"He says there was no one around. He sat in the lounge for a bit, thinking whoever took it would bring it back. Then, as it was such a bright day, he took himself out through the door to the garden and sat on the bench by the window. After a while, since no one had come to find him or return his chair, he gave up and headed back to his room, supporting himself on the hallway railings and making a couple of washroom stops en route to get rid of the coffee he'd drunk. He says he was quite happy to miss out on the cenotaph trip, and he tucked up in bed and had a lovely nap."

"But how did everyone manage to miss him?"

"The way Billy tells it, it was like a French farce. Every time someone looked in one spot, he was somewhere else. And by the time he returned to his room, it had been checked by several people and no one thought to look there again."

"That's utterly bizarre," said Edwina.

Beary nodded.

"Yes, I thought so too. But that's the official version, and the goal has been achieved, hasn't it? Philomena is discredited, and Billy managed to avoid another day of being paraded like a prize poodle by his pompous prick of a son."

"That may be, but I still can't fathom why they didn't find him."

"Well," said Beary, "it has something to do with the location of Billy's room. You see, it's in the northwest corner of the building, and that abuts the main road. There's an exit door to a small patio, which is screened from the road by a laurel hedge, but a path runs between it and the sidewalk, so there's easy access to the road."

"I fail to see the connection," said Edwina. "How does that excuse the staff from not finding Billy?"

Beary grinned.

"Let me answer your question by telling you what I asked Billy."

Edwina drained her coffee and looked irritated.

"I'll need another one of these if you're going to go all cryptic on me. All right. Be smug. What did you ask Billy?"

"I asked him how he liked the cream buns at the Sylvia Hotel."

Edwina's eyes widened.

"And what was his response?"

"A huge smile and an affirmative."

"But Olive was distraught over his disappearance."

"You mustn't forget that Olive was an actress. She obviously hasn't lost her touch."

Edwina was still incredulous.

"You said there was no one in that Toyota except Olive, her daughter and her son-in-law."

"When they left, and when they arrived back, yes, but nothing was stopping them from driving round through the housing estate in the morning, opening the gate by the dumpsters and helping Billy through. I bet they had a fold-up wheelchair all ready for him in the trunk of their car."

"So Billy did go down to the old grounds."

"Yes, and much earlier than anyone realized, which was why no one saw him. We only had Olive's word that he was still in his room when she popped by. Scotty made up the bit about seeing him in the corridor, too. Billy was actually down at the old centre before eight o'clock. He tootled around in his wheelchair and toured what was left of the gardens, where, incidentally, he tore his hand on a rose bush, thus the blood on the arm of the chair that put everyone into such a lather."

"How did he explain that to Philomena?"

"With remarkable ease. He'd sliced his finger while cutting up an apple a couple of days ago so he said that he'd banged his hand and the wound had opened up again."

"That was lucky. In fact, they were all extremely lucky to get away with it."

"Not really," said Beary. "Their plan was quite well thought out and should have gone smoothly. It was only derailed when Olive's son-in-law failed to apply the brake properly on the wheelchair and it ran down to the parking lot after they'd left. That's why the Naughty Nineties were so alarmed. Once the chair was discovered, Billy had no way of getting back inside."

"So what did they do?"

"Planned his return like a military operation. Jimmy took charge. He phoned Olive and told her to drop Billy on the main road by the path that led to his wing. Jimmy commandeered another wheelchair and kept in touch by cellphone. Then, when Olive let him know that they were ready to make the drop, he wheeled up to the main road, picked up Billy, and brought him back to his room. All that remained after that was for Olive's son-in-law to drive round the front so that Olive could create a scene until Jimmy appeared to announce that Billy was in his room."

"My goodness," said Edwina. "I really do need another drink. No wonder we won the war. Those old boys certainly haven't lost their initiative, have they?"

"Definitely not."

Edwina pursed her lips.

"I really shouldn't approve such schoolboy tactics," she said. "In my teaching days, I would have given my pupils short shrift for pulling a stunt like that."

"Ah, but they wouldn't have tried because they'd have known you were too smart for them to get away with it."

Beary smirked inwardly at his wife's pleased expression. In his experience, a little flattery always went a long way.

"That's true." Edwina nodded graciously and held out her glass.

"Anyway," she added, "Philomena deserved to be made a fool of, and it served Colin right to miss out on the ceremony. He has no business using his father for political purposes. Still, poor Billy won't get away with it next year, will he? Colin will probably have a quartet of nurses lined up to frogmarch him down to the foyer and stand guard until he's safely in the van."

"With any luck, it won't come to that. Evidently, Olive's son-in-law is a lawyer, and he believes he may be able to challenge the POA and get it reversed."

"That would be excellent, but those sort of things take time, don't they? Billy could still be under his father's thumb this time next year."

Beary took his wife's glass and headed out to make her a refill. But before he left the room, he turned back in the doorway.

"Billy had a comment about that too." Beary smiled happily. "His exact words were, 'No worries. Next year Olive's family is taking her for a weekend in Victoria, including a slap-up lunch at the Empress Hotel. I'll just have to disappear one day earlier.'"

Mimi's Farewell

Carla Raven was the ideal Mimi. Her tiny form and delicate movements gave the appearance of frailty. Her jet-black hair, parted traditionally in the centre, emphasized the pallor of her complexion, and only minimal make-up was needed to make audiences believe that the seeds of consumption lurked within the pretty seamstress's frame. Her voice was metallic, but her technique was superb, and her ability to spin sustained pianissimos compensated for the absence of a pure, ethereal sound. And her acting was legendary. Radiant beauty or hideous crone; grief-stricken maiden or ice-cold princess, fiery temptress or shy virgin—no part was beyond her range. Yet whichever character she inhabited, one common feature was always present—a burning magnetism that dominated the stage. That quality, combined with the steely perfection of her vocal technique and her fanatical determination to succeed at all costs, made her a superstar on the operatic stage, when others with more beautiful voices had only achieved pedestrian careers.

Philippa Beary watched from the wings as Rodolfo took the soprano's hand and began his aria. She was sure the audience would believe that Mimi's tiny hand was frozen, for the soprano looked so fragile. What would they have thought if they had realized that Carla Raven was, in reality, a sinewy, high-powered ball of energy who negotiated contracts with shark-like cunning and clawed her way to the top with ruthless indifference to the feelings of anyone she had to trample on in the course of attaining her goals? She was the only soprano that Philippa had ever met who appeared to be hated by every single one of her colleagues, including her husband, who was sharing the stage with her at that very moment.

Philippa glanced across to the other wing where Rodolfo's fellow artists waited to sing their offstage interjections. Steve Hendry, the young singer who was playing Schaunard, was watching Raven too. Philippa could not see his expression, but she suspected it was full of loathing. A few well-placed words from Carla Raven, and the up-and-coming baritone had lost his opportunity to make his Met debut the following season. Franco Gatti, the basso singing the philosopher, Colline, stood beside Hendry. Gatti hated Carla, and made no attempt to disguise the fact. It was something to do with the iconic designer, Stefan Mauro, who had been Gatti's long-time partner. Mauro had died two years previously, and somehow Franco held Carla responsible.

Philippa could not see John Farrell, the singer playing the painter, Marcello, although she knew he must be hovering there too. Farrell also bore a grudge against the soprano. He had fallen deeply in love with Carla, only to find that she had been merely using him in an endeavor to make her errant husband jealous. By the time he grasped the fact that she was toying with him, he was unable to salvage his own marriage. Now, alienated from his wife and children, he was facing a solitary future crippled by alimony and court appearances.

Rodolfo, the poet, ended his aria and gazed tenderly at his co-star as she began to sing.

"Mi chiamano Mimi . . ."

Philippa mentally translated the words: *They call me Mimi, but my name is Lucia. My story is a brief one . . .*

Not so, she thought wryly. The tale of Carla and her storms and feuds resounded throughout the operatic world, and her volatile relationship with her husband had made headlines on more than one occasion. The tender look that Henri Bouchard was bestowing on her was a masterpiece of acting, judging from the scene that had taken place during the dress rehearsal two days previously. Henri had always had a roving eye, but his current relationship with the spectacular Australian soprano who was singing Musetta was more than a casual affair. Sheila Barber was not only predicted to be the next successor to Melba and Sutherland, she was also a determined young woman who made no secret of the fact that she had set her heart on Henri. For once Carla had met her match.

Philippa glanced towards the pit. Marco Cassini was conducting with a surprising degree of empathy for the soloist, considering the abominable way she treated him. He was a good conductor with a solid reputation. Philippa admired his professionalism but she could not fathom why he put up with Carla's gibes and putdowns. Somehow she intimidated him in a way that no one else could. It was a mystery.

A burst of song from the opposite wing brought her attention back to the stage. Rodolfo's friends sang their few lines, then turned and disappeared into the void beyond the black teaser. The couple onstage began their duet.

The tenor drew his wife forward, and they changed positions so that Philippa had a clear view of Mimi's face as she sang, "Tu sol commandi, amor." One really could believe that love, alone, commanded her. Not a gentle, caring love, perhaps, but a jealous, possessive and demanding passion that refused to be denied. No wonder the soprano was so indifferent to the animosity of the people she treated so badly. She was oblivious to them because they didn't matter. Completely bound by her obsession with one man, she was imprisoned by her emotions and her desperate unhappiness. With a twinge of anxiety, Philippa recalled another rumour about an incident from Raven's past. The soprano had attempted suicide during a performance of *Madam Butterfly*. It had been early in her career, and early in the days of her marriage to Bouchard.

Mimi turned to Rodolfo and uttered the words he professed to want to hear.

"Io t'amo." *I love you.* It sounded like a threat.

They walked slowly out of the door of the garret, but the voices continued to float offstage from the wing. The high C was achieved effortlessly, but its knife-edged purity sent a chill down Philippa's spine.

*   *   *

Norton Barnwell made his way back from the coffee bar and handed his wife the cappuccino that she had requested as the curtain fell on Act One.

"She's very intense, isn't she?" Norton uncapped his bottled water and tucked himself against a pillar to avoid being jostled by the crowd. "You can feel the desperation of a woman whose time is limited."

"She's certainly eaten up with something," said Sylvia shortly, "but I doubt if it's consumption. According to Philippa, the offstage relationship between Rodolfo and Mimi is every bit as bizarre as the onstage one, except that the jealous rages emanate from the female in the partnership, not the male."

"With justification, dear." Milton Lovell fought his way out from the crush at the bar and inserted himself into a vacant space at Sylvia's elbow. "Henri Bouchard gives his wife cause. He has affairs the way you and I take jaunts to the coffee shop. I must say," he added, "it was divinely kind of you to offer me a ticket for tonight."

"You're most welcome," said Sylvia. "My father always gets four council comps, but he and Mother are out of town so the tickets were up for grabs. Philippa hoped Bob Miller could come, but he's working. Norton and I took two—we rarely get to see Philippa in the opera—and Richard was free, but he didn't have a date so Philippa suggested you might want to come. I'm glad you were able to use the spare ticket."

Richard Beary, Scotch in hand, appeared out of the crowd.

"I'm glad they're returning to the traditional way of presenting opera," he said.

"Traditional?" Sylvia looked puzzled.

"Doing the four acts separately. Last time I came, they combined acts and cut intermissions. It didn't improve the production. A couple of drinks along the way definitely enhances the performance."

Sylvia sniffed disapprovingly.

"You sound just like Father."

"Oh, he's quite right." Milton nodded approval. "I mean, I love music, but the bum can only stand so much at once. Besides, the social element is part of the entertainment. One has to see and be seen. Now, take that ritzy-looking set by the far pillar." He pointed towards a well-dressed quartet a few feet away. "That's Carla Raven's entourage. The bald gentleman is Gianni Bruno—that's her voice coach—the dragoness with the flaming hair is her private secretary, and the woman in green lace is her sister who gave up her medical career to tag around after Raven so she could act as her personal physician."

Richard gestured towards the fourth member of the group.

"Who's the brooding greybeard in the tux?"

"I think that's the sister's husband."

"He doesn't look as if he's enjoying his evening."

"No, probably not. Word has it he doesn't like his sister-in-law." Milton pursed his lips. "Well, of course, if one goes by the grapevine, no one likes his sister-in-law. Greatness rarely goes hand in hand with popularity, and Carla Raven has carried the art of antagonism to new heights."

Norton, who was a defence lawyer, always tried to find an excuse for people's behaviour.

"Well, if she's not a happy woman . . . after all, she attempted suicide some years ago."

"Oh, that was simply a ploy to bring her husband back into line. A bid for attention, not to mention an awesome publicity stunt. She graduated from opera star to worldwide tabloid sensation after that."

"No, that isn't the case," protested Norton. "She actually stabbed herself. I read about it in *Opera News*. She was singing *Butterfly*, and she left the retractable dagger on the props table, along with a note to say she was going to end it all. Then she took a real knife onto the stage and performed the hara-kiri scene in deadly earnest."

Milton looked sceptical.

"If she'd really meant to kill herself, she'd have done it. The wound wasn't that serious, but it produced enough blood to scare her husband into submission."

"But she had to be rushed to hospital."

"She did it onstage!" said Milton. "A zillion people were present to save her. Her father, who happens to be a surgeon, was in the audience. She knew he'd be there to treat her, and you can bet your briefs—legally speaking, of course—that having grown up in a doctor's house, she'd know how to avoid any vital organs. Her early life was probably permeated with revolting anatomical detail. Besides, she's a heavy-duty Catholic. Suicide is a no-no. No, she knew what she was doing all right. Hubby has his fun, but he's stuck around. No more talk of divorce. Let's face it," Milton added, peering owlishly over his wire-rimmed glasses, "if he'd left her after that, his own career would have tanked, but as it is, Raven is a superstar and Henri has done very well riding on the back of her reputation."

"Nevertheless," said Richard soberly, "it must be hard to be tied to a brilliant, but neurotic woman. I don't envy him." He paused, and then continued thoughtfully. "She's a strange-looking woman, isn't she? What's her nationality? The name and the face don't really match."

"Italian," said Norton, parroting some more information that he had gleaned from the article in *Opera News*. "Her name is actually Ravenna, but she shortened it to Raven. She's the youngest of a large family—twelve children, I believe—and her voice matured very young. Her mother died of cancer when Raven was only three years old, so she was raised by her oldest sister who recognized her talent very quickly. Raven was already studying voice at age twelve, and other than a serious illness that set her back a few months when she was in her mid-teens, she's spent every moment of her life charting one course—to become an operatic superstar. She married Bouchard when she was in her early twenties, and supposedly, they were blissfully happy and the only blot on the horizon was the fact that they couldn't have children. She has some health issues, including diabetes, but from what I've read, she's overcome them with tremendous fortitude. She's really quite a remarkable woman."

"Media spin with a vengeance," said Milton. "Probably written by some middle-aged lady in a flowery hat who was used to writing for the society columns."

The peal of the chimes reminded them that it was five minutes to Act Two, so they finished their drinks and followed the crowd that was funnelling through the double doors to the lower orchestra. The air felt cooler once they were out of the lobby, and Sylvia drew her stole around her shoulders. They slipped into their seats in the fifth row. Richard noticed the quartet from the lobby moving into the end seats in the front row. Carla Raven's entourage was in place, probably prepared with bouquets for the final curtain. He opened his program to see what was in store for the second act.

"The Café Momus." Milton stabbed his finger at the open page in Richard's lap. "This is the big chorus scene, so now you'll see Philippa. She has a little bit in Act Three as well," he added. "She's one of the peasant girls, not that you'll be able to recognize her at that point. She'll be huddled in an ugly shawl and bonnet and buried under a deluge of fake snow—if, of course, the budget is up to more than a few token flakes. And speaking of token flakes," he added, "there goes Calvin Burton."

"Who's he?" asked Richard.

"Calvin? He must have been on the opera board since the invention of the automobile. He gives his donations, sleeps through the meetings, and occasionally pops awake towards the end and comes up with an idea for someone else to implement. But," said Milton, eyes glinting, "the most astonishing thing happened last year. He morphed from an innocuous waste of table-space to a raging demon. When the general manager hired Raven and Bouchard for this season, Burton threatened to resign unless the engagement was cancelled, and when the manager stood firm, he did just that. I'm actually amazed he's here. He can't stand either of them."

Sylvia, who was sitting on Richard's other side, stuck her head round her program.

"Why ever not?" she asked curiously.

"Ah," said Milton, "that's another dirty story. Six years ago, Raven and Bouchard were here to do *Faust*. Henri's main course for that event was the mezzo singing Siebel, but he also managed a little appetizer on the side in the form of one of the volunteers in the auxiliary. She was a very nice young lady and somewhat naïve, and he managed to get her preggers. She was also Calvin Burton's daughter, and since Calvin is as puritanical as his historical namesake, you can imagine the stir that created."

"Oh, good Lord," said Sylvia. "What a wretched man!" The lights started to dim. Sylvia lowered her voice and leaned towards Milton. "What happened? Did she have the child?"

"No," said Milton. "Raven went berserk when she heard that an opera volunteer was going to have Bouchard's child—well, it would have stung, wouldn't it, considering she hasn't any children of her own—and she threw a screaming fit that could have outdone the Queen of the Night. Needless to say, Calvin's daughter was terrified. She backed away, didn't watch where she was going, fell down the stairs and had a miscarriage. Calvin wanted to sue Raven for assault, but the reality was she never touched his daughter—in fact, she was dreadfully contrite afterwards—and there was nothing Calvin could do."

"I don't blame him for kicking up a fuss," said Richard. "If that's the way Bouchard carries on, I'm surprised he continues to get bookings. Who wants to deal with that kind of garbage when you're trying to put on a show?"

"Raven is a box-office draw, and Bouchard is part of the package. Managers hold their noses and look at the bottom line." Milton shrugged. "It's a tough business."

"Hush," hissed Norton. "Here comes the conductor."

Sylvia sat back and directed her eyes towards the stage. The wide grey curtain swept silently upwards and revealed a colourful crowd of

Parisians, young and old, bustling through the Latin Quarter, buying and selling wares and singing their intentions of having a good time on Christmas Eve. The principals entered and Rodolfo bought Mimi her pink bonnet. Sylvia looked closely at the two stars. From the fifth row, it was easy to see the singers' faces, and having been given so much information about the real nature of their relationship, she expected to catch glimpses of what they were really feeling. Yet she saw nothing untoward; both remained in character. Rodolfo's moments of jealousy were believable, and Mimi's joy seemed genuine. But then, thought Sylvia wryly, perhaps these onstage moments for Carla Raven provided her only moments of happiness, for, within the scene and the character, her husband adored her. In the opera, she achieved the grand passion that she craved. It was only with the return to real life that the dream collapsed.

Parpignol entered with his toys and was immediately surrounded by excited boys and girls. The children's chorus was in good voice, Sylvia thought appreciatively. Perhaps another couple of years and Chelsea might be ready to audition. She liked to sing, and she adored her Aunt Philippa. Sylvia believed in keeping her children healthily occupied.

She drew her attention back to the stage. Mimi was singing. The Italian was simple enough that Sylvia could understand some of the words. *Love is sweeter even than honey.* She couldn't translate Marcello's response, but his delivery was singularly bitter. She glanced up at the surtitles: *It can be honey or poison.* The baritone looked as if he meant it.

A high-pitched shriek of laughter signalled the entrance of Musetta. The Australian soprano made an impressive figure onstage. She was blonde, voluptuous and vibrantly alive. Her voice was breathtakingly beautiful and her vitality was glowing and effervescent, unlike the burning intensity of the other soprano.

Musetta threw a piercing glance Marcello's way, and then settled on a café table and began her aria. As her creamy soprano caressed the glorious phrases of the waltz, Sylvia found her attention drawn back to the table where Rodolfo and his friends were seated. The tenor's eyes, riveted on Musetta, burned with a naked longing that matched the stage ardor emanating from Marcello, but Mimi's joy had been replaced with an anguish so deep that she appeared to have lost her reason.

*   *   *

The second intermission flew by and Philippa just had time to change her costume before the call for the third-act beginners. She trooped upstairs and joined the cluster of choristers in the stage-left wing. They were huddled into as tight a space as they could manage so that their voices would project from behind the tavern wall. John Farrell stood further upstage, waiting for his entrance as Marcello. Then Sheila Barber materialized out of the gloom and took her position in front of the chorus. The reprise of Musetta's solo would be brief, but the melody of the waltz in the lower key, floating from the lit window of the tavern into the snowy night, always provided a moment of magic.

A ripple of applause came from the front of the house. The conductor had entered the pit. A sudden movement to her left caught Philippa's eye. Henri Bouchard had joined the singers in the wing. He moved to the front and stood by Sheila Barber. Embarrassed, Philippa saw his hand come up to caress the soprano's neck. The two murmured together for a brief moment, and then Bouchard drew back. Philippa caught his words as he moved away. "It won't be long now." The soprano gave him a radiant smile and blew him a kiss. Then she turned to face the stage as the two short percussive chords that began the act burst from the orchestra pit. Bouchard melted back into the shadows, and the chorus master took his place and signalled to the singers to get ready.

Onstage, the guards opened the gates for the street-sweepers. Philippa mentally counted out the bars with her eyes glued to the chorus master. Within seconds, the soprano chorus was over and Musetta began her brief lyric solo. Philippa adjusted her bonnet, picked up her basket, and moved upstage, ready to make her entrance as a peasant woman.

She walked onto the wintry set, shivering slightly, for the stage was vast and drafty after the crush in the wing, and the snow filtering down in the blue evening light really did seem to cast a pall on the scene. She sang her lines, offering the customs officers her cheese and butter, then crossed towards the exit that represented the Rue d'Enfer. However, as she approached the shadowy hollow of the wing, she faltered, for it appeared that a ghost with black-ringed eyes hovered there, blocking her way. Philippa moved towards it and the phantom solidified into human form. It was Carla Raven. Her gown blended into the teasers and created the illusion that her ashen face was suspended in space. The prima donna's gaze was mesmerizing; yet she was staring beyond Philippa and she stepped forward as if the younger singer did not exist. Philippa moved aside to make way, and the soprano passed by. Philippa watched the dark figure gliding across the stage, hunched against the winter night and moving as if every step might be her last.

Philippa turned away and walked through the wing, passing the props table as she went. All was in readiness for the final act. She noticed the fur muff, gleaming softly white amid the more utilitarian items on the table. Thank goodness it isn't a dagger, she thought, uneasily remembering the diva's unstable history. She was glad they were doing *Bohème* and not *Butterfly*.

*   *   *

As the curtain came down on the third act, there were bravos from the house. Sylvia was renowned for her cool-headed, rational approach to life, but even she felt shaken by the raw emotion that had erupted from the stage. As the curtains rippled, indicating that the principals were about to appear for their bows, she wondered if the passion that had gripped the stage characters would still be present when the singers emerged. First came Sheila Barber. The Australian soprano had mastered the art of simulated humility. She had left her shawl backstage and she curtseyed low, offering the front rows a generous view of décolletage. Her hands were clasped together as if in a prayer of gratitude, and then she rose, lifting her fingers to her lips, and from there making a grand extension to the audience as if sending an embrace to the very back of the house.

"Not exactly your average jolly outback Sheila," quipped Milton. "A prima donna down to her toes. I predict that one is going straight to the top."

"Nice lungs too," said Richard, clapping enthusiastically.

Musetta mouthed a "thank you" to the house and swept backstage. Marcello strode out next, a cavalier grin splitting his face. He bowed briefly, and with a friendly wave, disappeared behind the curtains. Then came Bouchard and Raven. The tenor was smiling, and he bowed to his wife, acknowledging her as well as the audience, but there was tension in the line of his jaw. Raven made no attempt to interact with her husband. Her demeanour was strange and distant, her lips closed tightly together and stretched into a hint of a smile, but there was no light in her eyes. She looked a little mad, thought Sylvia.

The lights came up, but rather than accompany Norton to the lobby, Sylvia stayed in her seat and browsed through her program.

She noticed a page with translations from Murger's *La Vie de Bohème* and she read the quotations with increasing fascination for they highlighted what she had witnessed on the stage. There was a depth to Rodolfo and Mimi that she had never perceived before. The last line seemed to leap off the page: "It must be admitted that their existence was a veritable hell-upon-earth."

*   *   *

Backstage, the hell-upon-earth was embarrassingly evident. The hysterical scene that Raven threw in the principals' corridor could be heard all the way down to the chorus dressing rooms below. The soprano truly must have chords of steel, Philippa thought, as she came out into the hall and heard Raven shrieking at her husband on the floor above. Philippa could not conceive of abusing the voice to such a degree, let alone during a performance.

"The one battle she can't win," said Christopher Bell, who had come downstairs for a coffee break. "It was just the same when they were here six years ago." Christopher had been stage manager for the opera since the mid-nineties. "Bouchard," said Christopher, "is Raven's Achilles heel. Whether it's a power thing because she can't control him, or whether she really loves him in some jealously obsessive way, her passion for him dominates her existence. But he's had enough now. He's not just threatening divorce this time. He really means it."

"I'm amazed it hasn't happened sooner," said Philippa.

"Bouchard looks out for number one," said Christopher. "He may be so poster-boy handsome that women can't resist him, but he isn't a great tenor, merely a competent one. He's done well out of Raven, and up until now, none of his lady friends have been in the same league, but Sheila Barber is going places. I figure he's planning on trading in Raven on a younger model with a career-expiry date years into the future. Anyway, it hasn't been all *Sturm und Drang*. They used to be very lovey-dovey in between his little flings, and Raven pampered him like a baby when she wasn't yelling at him for having his bits on the side. The first time they were here was in '96, and it was a year after the *Butterfly* fiasco. He was a model of good behaviour, and she was so sweet to him it was nauseating, especially in the light of the fact that she treated everyone else like dirt."

"None of her co-stars like her much, do they?"

"No. Amazing how well they sing, considering that their teeth are clenched."

"I know why Steve Hendry dislikes her," said Philippa. "I gather she put a spoke in his wheel career-wise. And John Farrell is upset because his marriage is on the rocks, but why does Franco Gatti hate her? I'm told that he blames her for Stefan Mauro's death, but how could Raven have been responsible for that?"

Christopher's face grew solemn.

"Franco and Stefan were together for twenty years," he said. "Mauro was a wonderfully innovative designer, probably a bit younger than Franco, and he occasionally had a wandering eye. He was working on a new production of *Traviata* for Raven one summer when Franco was away on tour. Raven brought a particularly beautiful young man on stream to assist him and the inevitable happened. It later turned out that the young man had AIDS."

"That's so sad. But surely she wouldn't have known, and she can hardly be blamed because Mauro chose to be unfaithful to his partner."

Christopher nodded wisely.

"True, but she knew Franco and Stefan well. She should have been mindful of the potential danger. Anyone with any degree of sensitivity would have demonstrated better judgement."

Philippa sighed. "That's her failing, isn't it? She's so obsessed with herself and her own feelings that she's unaware of anyone else's."

"I wouldn't say unaware," said Christopher cynically. "More like cruelly indifferent. One of the reasons she's such a good actress is that she has an artist's analytical eye. I venture to say that she sees other people's feelings with microscopic accuracy. She analyzes their weaknesses, and then she uses that knowledge to control them— witness the way she treats our revered conductor. They go way back. They were in the same choir as teenagers, and she probably knows something about him that he doesn't want made public. Why else would he put up with her insults and put-downs? You're much too sweet, Philippa. You should face the fact that some people who claw their way to the top have no redeeming features whatsoever."

Christopher downed the remainder of his coffee, tossed the cup into the garbage bin, then ambled off in the direction of the stairwell. Philippa looked after him sadly. The stage manager's cynicism was understandable. He had been hurt badly through the actions of another prima donna several years earlier. Philippa pulled off her bonnet and turned towards the women's dressing room. She would have time to change before the final curtain. It would be interesting to hear what her friend, Milton, had to say after the show.

                              *   *   *

From the audience's perspective, the opening of the last act was bland. Richard tried to analyze why he did not feel engaged, and then he identified the missing ingredient. Without the dynamic presence of Carla Raven, the opera fell flat. The mock battle of the artists dragged on interminably, but then it was time for Musetta's entrance, and a moment later, Mimi was ushered in and helped over to the bed. The stage came alive again, but the irony struck Richard right away. The stage might be alive, but Mimi was so obviously dying that it seemed as if every breath was being wrenched from her body.

The friends gathered round her, then, one-by-one, left to trade in their meagre possessions so that they could bring a doctor to the garret. Musetta went in search of a muff, and, at last, Mimi and Rodolfo remained alone together. Softly, Mimi began her farewell.

Richard's eyes glanced up to the surtitles: *Have they gone? I pretended to be asleep because I wanted to be left alone with you.*

It was an unparalleled performance from a superlative actress. I can really believe she's dying, thought Richard. Even her voice sounds frailer. He watched Bouchard's face. He was acting well too. The tenderness and sorrow seemed genuine. The audience was so still it was as if every individual in the house was holding his or her breath. Their quietness hung over the theatre like a shroud.

The others returned. Musetta gave Mimi the muff and retreated a little way off. Rodolfo crept away as Mimi fell asleep. One after the other, Marcello and Schaunard moved to her side. The sound from the pit diminished to nothing. For a transitory moment, the orchestra was poised in silence, and then Schaunard saw that Mimi was gone. As Rodolfo sobbed his last anguished cries over her body, the curtain fell.

The hush that followed the last crashing chords seemed to resonate about the auditorium. Then, gradually, the clapping began, and rose to a crescendo as the audience exploded into cheers. The applause went on and on, and the bravos grew louder and more insistent. But the curtain remained without a ripple and the principals did not appear. Out of the corner of his eye, Richard noticed a flutter of movement in the front row. He turned to see what was happening and caught a glimpse of a woman in green lace being ushered hurriedly through the exit door at the foot of the auditorium.

$*$ $*$ $*$

The demise of Carla Raven made headlines all over the world. Four days into the investigation, when there were no specific answers forthcoming from the RCMP, speculation over her death became a popular pastime and the media became as predatory as a group of Bengal tigers stalking a solitary tethered goat. As the pressure to untangle the cause of the soprano's death mounted, Richard began to develop a chronic headache. He scowled at the press clipping that some insensitive junior had stuck on his notice board.

"'*Mounties fail to keep pace with this musical ride*,'" read Sergeant Martin. "The press is having a field day," he said glumly.

"*They* may be, but we're not. Either we're dealing with the most determined suicide who ever decided to end her life, or we're facing a case of murder—and that," added Richard, "would be an incredible coincidence, given that Raven was in the process of doing herself in." Richard gazed wearily at the pile of statements on his desk.

"If it turns out to be the latter, it's a good job you were on site," said Sergeant Martin. "Can you imagine the mess a theatre full of singers, techies and musicians could have created in a murder scene if your quick-witted sister hadn't called you backstage right away?"

"Actually, it was the doctor—Raven's sister—who said the police should be brought in. She was concerned that something strange was going on. Philippa knew I was out front so she sent the manager round for me."

"So let me get this straight," said Martin. "Carla Raven was unconscious at the final curtain. When she wouldn't wake up, her sister was called backstage. Knowing that Raven was diabetic, the sister's first thought was that she might have missed her insulin injection."

"That's right. Raven kept a supply of syringes in a case in her dressing room. The dresser was told to fetch the case, and when she went to get it, she found a note addressed to Raven's husband. The note said that she had stopped taking her insulin and that she had taken sleeping pills because she did not want to go on living without Bouchard. The sister had the manager call for an ambulance. In the meantime, she opened Raven's insulin case and gave her an injection, but there was no improvement. By the time the ambulance arrived, the singer was dead."

"Surely sleeping pills wouldn't kill a person that quickly? What went wrong?"

"There was a second syringe in the muff. The lab found traces of morphine in it, and the pathologist called me earlier to confirm that this was the cause of death. He was in a hurry so he didn't say much else, except that the autopsy produced a couple of surprises, but he's sending the full report round today. It should be here any time."

"Morphine! Well, I'm damned," said Martin. "No wonder the sister couldn't save her. And you figure it wasn't suicide. You think someone else gave her the morphine, not realizing that she had already taken steps to end her life."

"Oh, lots of people knew there might be a suicide attempt. Raven had been making threats for weeks." Richard stabbed his finger at the pile of statements. "Bouchard says she had become impossible to live with. She complained of headaches and was moody and difficult. He accused her of being an impossible hypochondriac because she was constantly having tests and check-ups, yet nothing was wrong with her physically. Basically, he said she'd deteriorated into a complete nutcase. I can't say that I like the man. He was trying to justify his decision to break up their marriage, but I do think he was telling the truth about her suicide threats. He said there was a terrible scene two days ago. She told him she was going to end it all on the closing night of the production. She even said how she was going to do it. Her sister tried to talk sense into her by appealing to her vanity. She pointed out that Raven might not make it through the performance if she didn't take her insulin."

"That's probably true."

"Actually, Raven's sister admitted to me that this wouldn't have been the case. Raven's technique was so good that she could have sung that last scene on autopilot, even if drugs and a score of health problems were kicking in. I gather she's the kind of trouper who goes on no matter how ill she is and magically manages to grind her way through to the final curtain. She doesn't collapse until it's over."

"Which is exactly what she did."

"True. Anyway, Bouchard claims that, after the big scene with the suicide threats, he overheard his wife telling her sister that she was only pretending, so he realized she'd just been trying to get his attention and he didn't take the threats seriously."

"Was anyone else there when Raven was carrying on about killing herself?"

"Yes. Raven's vocal coach was present, along with the conductor and the singer playing Colline. It wasn't a secret. I suspect every one of the principals knew by closing night."

"But it doesn't make sense," said Martin. "If any of them wanted her dead, why risk a murder rap? Why not just let her get on with it?"

"Because they all knew she didn't intend to die. She'd done something similar once before when she thought she was going to lose her husband. She knew her sister was in the audience and would get her to hospital and pull her through. She was just trying to scare Bouchard. That's why I think the morphine was administered by someone else."

"Any fingerprints?"

"Nothing. The sister's prints are on the insulin vial. She was wearing evening gloves but she took them off to administer the shot. There's nothing on the other syringe."

"If Raven gave herself the shot, her own prints would be on the syringe."

"You would certainly think so."

"I assume the suicide note is genuine?"

"Yes. There doesn't seem to be any doubt about that."

"Wait a minute. Isn't there a bit of a logistical problem?" said Martin. "I can see her struggling through a death scene on an overdose of pills. If she'd taken them just before the act started, they'd not kick in immediately. But a shot of morphine would knock her out right away. It would have to have been inflicted after she sang her last notes."

"Exactly," said Richard. "And each of the soloists went over to the bed during the last few moments of the act. They all had scarves or handkerchiefs. Musetta had the muff. These are all items that could conceal a syringe and protect hands from leaving prints."

"Do any of the singers have a reason to want her dead?"

"Oh, yes." Richard drew the phrase out dramatically and rolled his eyes. "If my sister is to be believed, every single one of the principals had it in for her. Not to mention the conductor and the odd person in the audience."

"How did the husband react to Raven's death?"

"He put on a show of being shocked, but I figure that's exactly what it was."

"A show?"

"Yes. In no time flat, he was huddled in a corner being consoled by Sheila Barber. I'd say he was relieved. The only person who seemed genuinely upset was the doctor—Raven's sister—who, by the way, clearly detests Bouchard."

Martin raised his eyebrows.

"Oh? Why is that?"

"She's a lot older than Raven—a good fifteen years, I should say—and she's been more like a mother than a sister. I get the impression that she's the only person who really loves the soprano, though I suspect Raven took advantage of her kind-heartedness. Still, her sister is the one person who understood Raven and made allowances for her strange temperament. Bouchard's behaviour must have been intolerable to the doctor because she could see how deeply it hurt her sister."

"Did she tell you that?"

"Not in so many words, but her distress was pretty apparent, and unlike the artificial sobs of Raven's spouse, the sister's tears were real. That, by the way, isn't just my personal assessment. When I interviewed the conductor, he confirmed that the relationship between the sisters was a close one. He's known the family since Raven was very young. The Cassinis and the Ravennas were neighbours."

"So," asked Martin, "did he tell you lots about their background?"

"Did he ever. He had a rattling skeleton in his own closet that he was terrified would become public, so knowing that the autopsy would reveal enough to cause awkward questions, he wisely fessed up to a secret from their youth. This will be one of the surprises the pathologist hinted at over the phone."

"And what was this terrible secret?"

"He and Raven had a teenage fling and he got her pregnant. Raven ended up having an abortion, which, by the way, resulted in complications so that she couldn't have children afterwards."

"When did this happen?"

"In 1984."

"Abortion was legal then, even in Italy."

"Yes, but she was underage, so parental consent would have been needed, and her father was a devout Catholic. According to Cassini, Raven was hysterical. She wasn't in love with him and she didn't want a child at that point in her life. All she wanted was to pursue her operatic career. She refused to tell her father because she knew he'd never give permission to terminate the pregnancy."

"So how did she manage the abortion?"

"Cassini says Raven put the heat on her sister, who had just qualified as a doctor. The sister didn't want to do it—she's a devout Catholic too—but Raven threatened to kill herself, and in the end, she broke her sister down."

"An illegal abortion is pretty heavy stuff. Was that why Raven was able to coerce her sister into giving up her career and becoming her personal physician?"

"I asked Cassini that. He said that wasn't the case at all. The sister has always cared for Raven, and she was more than willing to take up the post. He says the love between the two of them is the most genuine thing in the soprano's life. That opinion was reinforced by Philippa, too," said Richard. "She was sufficiently smart to go and have a long chat with Raven's dresser while the rest of us were scouring the stage for clues and preparing to interview suspects, and the dresser said the same thing."

"Did your sister glean any other tidbits from members of the company?"

"She's coming by in a minute. You can ask her yourself. I called her in so we could pick her brains. She may be able to fill in some gaps—all the things we weren't told in the interviews."

"Great idea," said Martin. He was very fond of Philippa. "How is your sister anyway?"

"Still up and down like one of her coloratura scales."

"Torn between career and love life?"

"Pretty much."

"Still that VPD detective? The one who arrested her on her way to a Halloween party?"

"That's the one."

"Maybe that's why she's ambivalent. It might be one way to get a girl, but I'd hardly recommend it to the new recruits."

"No, it's not that. He's taken special assignments and been away for months at a time. She takes that to mean he isn't serious about her. Then she displays her own independence by auditioning for out-of-town gigs, and he probably takes that as a sign that she isn't interested either. So they continue to drift along as casual friends. Her agent has just lined her up with an audition for the Charlottetown Festival. It'll be a coup if she gets it, but hardly conducive to romance. They'll figure it out at some point. I stay out of it and keep my mouth shut."

Martin chortled. "I bet your mother doesn't stay out of it," he said.

Richard rolled his eyes.

"No. She's been on Philippa's case to bring Miller round for Sunday dinner. If Philippa keeps digging her heels in, Mum will simply issue the invitation herself."

"That's the equivalent of a royal decree," said Martin. "Miller won't stand a chance."

"I don't know that he wants to," said Richard. "I think he's seriously interested in Philippa, but she's playing cautious because she's been stung before."

Martin opened his mouth to comment, but a knock at the door ended the conversation. The door opened and Philippa came in. She carried a cardboard tray laden with treats from the coffee shop, and she deposited it on her brother's desk and proceeded to hand out the spoils.

"Non-fat latte and bagel for Richard, caramel macchiato for me, and honey latte and chocolate croissant for you," she concluded, turning to Sergeant Martin. "I figured you'd be here," she added sweetly. "Now, what have you discovered so far?" she asked, turning back to her brother.

"A great deal, but nothing that gets us any further." Richard reviewed the information he had gleaned from the interviews with the members of the company. Philippa listened attentively. Then, while her brother and Sergeant Martin ate their snacks, she told them what she had learned since the night of the singer's death.

"Everything you've said tallies with what I've heard," she said, "but I have come up with something new." She paused and took a sip of her coffee. Then she continued. "Like you, I assumed that everyone onstage went so close to Mimi that any one of them could have delivered the fatal injection. But then I had a long talk with Christopher Bell—he's our stage manager," she added for the benefit of Sergeant Martin, "and he's absolutely positive that only one singer had the opportunity to do it."

"How do you figure?" said Richard. "I watched from the audience. As I recall, every person on the stage went over to the bed."

Philippa shook her head.

"Christopher showed me his blocking notes, and he insisted that no one deviated from the established moves. Musetta does take over the muff, but she moves away to warm the medicine while Mimi is still singing. Marcello goes to Mimi too, but he never touches her or the bed. He simply puts a book on the side table to shade the light of the lamp. Colline comes back onstage after Mimi stops singing, but when he approaches the bed, he puts money on the table, and then crosses directly to the window to help Rodolfo shade the sunlight with Musetta's cloak. Schaunard touches Mimi's hand, but only briefly, and then he goes to alert Marcello that she's passed away."

"So? They were all there."

"Yes, but Christopher was adamant that the contact was so brief that there was no way any of them could have injected her with anything, let alone hidden a syringe in the muff. Chris insists that none of them made physical contact with Raven and none of them had anything in their hands other than their stage props. He followed every move from the wing. He's prepared to swear that in court if necessary. That's how certain he is."

"So it comes back to the husband." Richard tossed his bagel wrapping into the garbage and picked up his coffee. "He was the only one who had the opportunity to administer the shot. It works. He threw himself across Mimi's body as he sobbed her name. He was there for a good minute before the curtain fell."

"Well, it usually is the husband," said Martin philosophically, "and he definitely had a motive, given his wife's horrible temperament and his itch to get away from her and team up with the other soprano."

"Except that he'd already announced his intention of divorcing Raven," said Philippa, "and he was hitching himself to another superstar, so the split wouldn't have hurt his career. In fact, with Raven's increasingly bizarre behaviour, the bookings would probably have started to diminish if they'd stayed together. The situation was quite different from the earlier fiasco. People might have even been sympathetic this time round—so why would he kill her? Something just doesn't ring true."

Before Richard could comment, the door opened and Jean Howe stepped into the room. She handed him a sheet of paper.

"The autopsy results," she said.

As PC Howe left the room, Richard quickly skimmed the report. Philippa and Sergeant Martin leaned in so they could read over his shoulder.

"Good God! Look at that," said Martin, stabbing his finger at a paragraph at the bottom of the page. "No wonder her behaviour was erratic."

"A brain tumour." Richard shook his head incredulously. "Bouchard should have waited a bit longer. He'd have had his freedom within a year."

"Perhaps he didn't know," said Martin.

Philippa caught her breath and she turned to stare at her brother. Richard met her eye, and then, as if by telepathy, they each knew what the other was thinking.

"It's possible Raven didn't know either," said Philippa. "But there's one person who had to have known—"

Sergeant Martin was following the same train of thought.

"Her sister," he interjected.

"Who hates Bouchard for hurting Raven and couldn't care less if he takes the rap for his wife's death," added Richard.

"And who would do anything for her sister," observed Sergeant Martin, "witness the fact that, in spite of her Catholicism, she carried out that abortion all those years ago."

Philippa shook her head in amazement.

"She spared Raven the knowledge that she was dying, and took advantage of the suicide threats to give her the perfect farewell—a mercy killing, downstage centre, at the end of an incredible performance, with the cheers of the audience ringing in her ears."

Richard's face was sombre.

"She probably had the second syringe in her evening bag. While she was examining her sister, it would have been easy for her to administer the morphine and hide the syringe in the muff."

"But Raven was already unconscious," Martin protested. "The sleeping pills couldn't have acted that fast. No one could wake her, and it must have been five minutes before her sister went backstage."

Philippa pointed to the pile of statements on the desk.

"Remember what you told me about Bouchard's statement. He overheard Raven talking to her sister about her suicide threat. He heard her say she was only pretending. I bet he misheard the verb tense. I bet she said, 'I'll only *be* pretending.'"

"Surely she couldn't have pulled off a stunt like that."

"Of course she could," said Philippa. "She was a superb actress. Anyway, I expect the pills were starting to kick in. Think about it. She would have lain back exhausted from the performance. The drugs, and her body relaxing after such extreme exertion, probably resulted in a wave of drowsiness anyway. She knew that if she lay there, apparently lifeless, her sister would be called backstage, and she'd be whisked away to hospital."

"Well, I'm damned," said Richard. He reached for the phone. "I guess it's time to call Raven's sister back in."

Philippa grabbed her coat and slipped it round her shoulders.

"I'll leave you to it," she said.

She picked up her handbag and headed towards the door.

"Keep this to yourself," Richard cautioned her. "I'll let you know what happens."

Philippa nodded. She opened the door, but before she left, she turned back and gave her brother a wistful smile. "The solution was right there in the opera libretto," she said. "The final duet. Mimi tells Rodolfo that she was only pretending to be asleep for she wants the others to leave so the two of them can be alone."

Philippa sighed.

"It's called 'Mimi's Farewell'," she said sadly.

The Feast of Stephen

Good King Wenceslas looked out on the Feast of Stephen,
When the snow lay round about, deep and crisp and even.
Brightly shone the moon that night, though the frost was cruel,
When a poor man came in sight, gathering winter fuel.

B eary looked across the room at the throng of carollers who were diligently working their way through the numerous verses of "Good King Wenceslas" and showing no sign of flagging. Well-fuelled by Christmas spirits, they formed a higgledy-piggledy semi-circle around the grand piano in the living room of Alexandra Lacey's elegant heritage-home.

"Too bad your sister's tied up with *The Messiah*," Beary said to his son. Richard was also attending the Laceys' party. "They could have used Philippa's lyric soprano tonight. If I have to listen to much more of Merve Billings reedy tenor and his wife's wobbly mezzo, I will need a lot more to drink. Mind you," he acknowledged, "I do approve of the Laceys' attitude that one should maintain the festive spirit throughout the full twelve days of Christmas. None of this modern nonsense about Christmas grinding to a halt at midnight on the twenty-fifth and Boxing Day being all about shopping. I always look forward to Alexandra's Feast of Stephen party."

Richard nodded.

"I can see why. It's quite a do. Until Alexandra told me about it, I didn't realize that the Feast of Stephen was celebrated on the same day as Boxing Day."

"We even have 'deep and crisp and even' snow to get us in the holiday mood," said Beary, glancing through the sidelight windows by the fireplace and seeing the white expanse where the lawn used to be. "Perfect Christmas weather. Snow early enough for the roads to be cleared, but cold enough for it to stay on the ground for decoration."

Richard eyed the vaulted window above the carollers' heads.

"Don't tempt providence," he said. "The forecast is for more snow and a long, cold winter. I've already noticed the odd flake drifting down. You may be digging *Arvy* out come morning." *Arvy* was the Bearys' twenty-three-foot motorhome, which was presently sitting in the Laceys' driveway.

Bringing his gaze down to rest on the carollers, Richard said, "Mother's holding her own nicely. She seems to be enjoying herself."

Beary smiled gleefully as he watched his wife clutching her carol sheet and harmonizing robustly between Marge Billings and a tall, dark gentleman with an irritatingly grinding baritone. Edwina, he noted, was unusually flushed in the face.

"Your mother, for once, is letting her hair down—which will ensure that we all have a good time. Juliette and co are staying with us for the week which means MacPuff and Minx are well cared for, so I persuaded your mother that we should come in *Arvy* and kip down overnight. That means she's off the hook as designated driver. Instead of her usual eggnog and non-alcoholic punch, she's already had three glasses of wine."

"I may have to join you and pile into *Arvy's* top bunk," said Richard. "George and Alexandra have given their teenage son the job of bartender, and I made the mistake of accepting one of his cocktails. I'm still not seeing straight. God knows what he put in it."

Beary smiled knowledgeably. "George Junior is working his way alphabetically through the different recipes in his father's bar book. Just be glad you got there early and had a daiquiri. He's really looking forward to getting up to 'p' for petrifier."

"I hate to think," said Richard. "What's in it?"

"Cognac, Cointreau, gin, vodka and triple sec, with a dash of grenadine and ginger ale." Beary glanced towards the bar where the Laceys' son was resisting the urges of a pert under-aged girl who was trying to convince him that he should serve her an alcoholic drink. As Beary noted the interchange, a lithe blonde came out from the kitchen. Her gazelle-like legs looked even more elongated due to the five-inch heels of her silver evening sandals. In spite of her stilt-like shoes, she was gracefully weaving her way through the throng and passing canapés to the guests. "Speaking of different recipes," said Beary, "here comes George Junior's sister. Is that a dress she's wearing or a sequined handkerchief?"

As the pretty blonde reached them, Beary introduced her to Richard. "Alison is in chef's school," he explained. "It's no wonder Alexandra puts on such fabulous parties." Beary helped himself to three of the delectable-looking golden-brown ovals on Alison's tray and added them to the assortment of smoked salmon, cheese and sausage rolls already on his plate. "What have we this time?" he asked.

"Ham and Gruyère cheese in puff pastry. Save some room for the next tray, though. Mom's bringing bacon-wrapped scallops."

Alison waited while Richard sampled the offerings. Then, smiling sweetly, she sashayed neatly through a gap in the crush and moved on.

"It's a bit crowded in here," said Richard. "Didn't Alexandra say something about having a billiard room? Why don't we adjourn there for a bit?"

"No good. It's been taken over by a trio of bossy pre-teen girls who are trying to teach a diminutive blonde angel how not to rip up George's felt."

"There are quite a few children here tonight," observed Richard. "Who do they all belong to?"

"I recognized two of the pool players," offered Beary. "Janet and Judy are daughters of the Ubiquitous Vacillator."

"Who?"

"Merve Billings."

"Oh, right. He's on Council with you, isn't he? Fence-sitter?"

"Definitely. Must have permanent scars from all the pickets on his bum. Good-natured and pliable, though, unlike Mrs. Thatcher, the Sequel." Beary nodded gloomily to a besequinned matron with a Christmas corsage on her bosom and an outdated cocktail hat on her sculpted hairdo. "I suppose George had to invite her. Wouldn't do for the local Member of Parliament to exclude the mayor."

"No, it wouldn't."

A mellow voice broke into the conversation. Beary turned to see his hostess at his elbow. She was carrying a platter that presumably had been laden with the bacon-wrapped scallops that her daughter had promised. However, most of the canapés had been snapped up during her progress across the room. She offered the remaining two to Beary and Richard and fixed her pretty brown eyes on Beary. "You'd better watch yourself, Bertram," she said. "I know how you love to needle Gwendolyn, but it's Christmas, so I expect you to be on your best behaviour."

"I never needle Gwendolyn Pye," said Beary. "I merely keep her on track when she strays into extremist positions that might inconvenience me or our constituents. Madam mayor's problem is that she has no sense of humour and she forgets that political parties don't belong on city councils—unlike myself, who is so well-loved by the hoi polloi that I get elected as an independent and enjoy the prerogative of speaking out against whichever group is getting it wrong at any particular time."

"You're a wicked old anarchist," said Alexandra, "and people only vote for you because they want to see what you'll say next. But I still expect you to behave at my party. Why don't you go play billiards and stay out of trouble?"

"The room is occupied by a bunch of little girls."

"No, it isn't. The children have finished their game. They're trotting off for a sleepover at the Billings' house."

"I thought Marge and Merve lived on the other side of town."

"They used to. They moved to New West last year. They're our neighbours now."

Beary was impressed.

"Don't tell me they live in that spectacular towers and turrets affair next door."

"No, Merve and Marge are next-door-but-one. The house with the turrets belongs to the Grahams."

"The Grahams? Have I met them?"

"Luke and Meryl. They own that adorable moppet who was learning how to play billiards."

"The one who was shorter than her pool cue?"

"Yes. Her name's Beth, and she has two sisters: Rosalie, who was one of the other girls in the billiard room and Emma, the thirteen-year-old who's been trying all evening to get George Junior to give her a Bloody Mary."

Alexandra pointed towards the carol singers. "That's Luke Graham, next to Edwina."

She indicated an affable-looking man with wiry brown hair who was waving his carol sheet in time to the music and nodding conspiratorially to Edwina every time they began a new phrase. "His wife is by the bar remonstrating with Emma."

"Talking of the bar, I need a refill," said Beary. "Besides, I really ought to demonstrate some 'esprit de Council' and get our lady mayor a drink. George Junior must have got to the 'p's by now, and Gwendolyn likes grenadine and ginger ale. She'll think she's drinking a Shirley Temple. Here, let me return that tray for you," he added.

Taking the empty platter from Alexandra, Beary lumbered off to the other side of the room. Richard turned to Alexandra. He was irrationally pleased to detect a mischievous glint in her eye as she watched Beary's retreat. He also noticed that she was looking particularly lovely in a grey silk cocktail dress that showed off her elegant figure and made a softly muted background for her vibrant features and sleek dark hair.

Alexandra pretended she had not noticed the admiring way the handsome detective was looking at her. Deftly, she steered the conversation onto a neutral and impersonal topic.

"I hear you finally sorted out that awful case on the Sidley Estate," she said, "and all because of the war vets."

"That's right. If Billy Bell hadn't gone missing, we might never have found the murder weapon." Richard was curious. "How did you hear about it? Did my father tell you?"

"No, I get the gossip first hand. My grandfather is one of the remaining World War II vets at the Sidley Centre. I was at their Christmas party last week with my sister and my niece. Meryl Graham was there too with little Beth. It's so good for the youngsters to talk to the residents and get a sense of history. The children are a great hit with the men."

"Does Meryl Graham have a relative there too?"

"No, she's a volunteer. Her grandfather was an officer in the Fifth Canadian Armoured Division. They served in Africa. He was killed at the end of the war, but Meryl is very sentimental about him. She feels she's doing the right thing by him when she helps other veterans."

"I can understand that. Where did her grandfather die? At El Alamein?"

Alexandra's eyes twinkled.

"No, right next door." She laughed at Richard's gaping expression. "Yes, this is a story right up your alley. Meryl has a murderess on her family tree. Her grandmother was executed for shooting her grandfather on the very day he returned from the war."

"Good god," said Richard. "You're not having me on?"

"No. Here, you don't particularly like that drink you're holding, do you?"

"Not really. Why?"

"Put it down and come through to the den where it's less crowded. I'll pour you a Scotch from George's decanter and tell you about our neighbourhood mystery."

It was an offer too good to refuse. Richard set down his glass and followed Alexandra through the square-paned glass doors that led out to the hall. Like King Wenceslas's page, he was compelled to follow and he was happy to go wherever his hostess's steps might lead him.

*   *   *

The den was a book-lined room with a cozy, lived-in air. Two overstuffed leather armchairs with matching ottomans were strategically arranged in front of a brick-enclosed gas fireplace whose dancing flames behind the glass emitted golden light and welcoming heat. One of the armchairs was occupied by a folded angora blanket and a large Persian cat. On a corner table stood a set of bar glasses and a crystal decanter, its amber contents gleaming in the flickering firelight. Outside the square-paned window, the sporadic snowflakes were still drifting down and beginning to settle on the sill. To Richard's eye, they appeared larger, fluffier and more frequent. Snow, firelight, and what was guaranteed to be an excellent malt—not to mention a charming narrator with the beauty of the legendary Scheherazade. It was, he thought, the perfect setting for the telling of a mystery story.

Richard smiled at his hostess.

"Won't Meryl Graham mind you airing her family's dirty linen?" he said.

Alexandra shook her head.

"No. She used to be sensitive about it, but Luke is so down to earth, he's made her realize it doesn't reflect on her. Besides, she's always maintained that her grandmother was innocent."

Alexandra waved her guest towards the unoccupied armchair and poured him a glass of Scotch from the decanter.

"Meryl didn't find out the truth about her family history until after her parents' death," she said. "She only discovered what had happened when she inherited the house."

"It must have been hard to keep something like that secret."

Alexandra handed Richard his drink, removed cat and blanket to the ottoman without rearranging either, then sat in the chair opposite him.

"Not really," she said. "Meryl's mother was only six at the time of the murder. Her name was Beth—Beth Robertson—and if you look at photos of her when she was young, it's astounding to see the resemblance to Meryl's Beth. After the murder, Beth Robertson was brought up by an aunt who was canny enough to hold onto the house and divide it into rental suites until her ward was of age and could decide what she wanted to do with it. The aunt lived on Vancouver Island, so Beth was raised there. Beth married a man from the Island, and she and her husband lived there until they were killed in a car crash in 1992. Meryl was their only child. She was twenty at the time of her parents' accident and had just become engaged to Luke. When she and Luke came to view the house that she'd inherited, they fell in love with it."

"That isn't surprising. It's a spectacular house. Four full storeys, turrets and balconies galore, and gingerbread trim to boot."

"It was pretty tatty once it came to Meryl, but she could see beyond the grunge, so when she and Luke married, they evicted the tenants. Then they restored the house to its original glory. It was a big project, but they were able to move in by the end of 1995. Somewhere along the way, her great-aunt, who was still alive, told her the tragic history of the house, but it didn't deter her from living there."

Richard was intrigued.

"So how did the murder come about?"

"It happened in late 1945. It's a tragic but familiar tale. Meryl's grandfather had been away since the start of the war, and his wife— her name was Emily—had an affair in his absence. She took up with a casual labourer, a good-looking man whose eyesight had kept him from active service. His name was Jacques Varney. According to Emily's sister—"

"Sister?" interjected Richard. "Would that be Meryl's great-aunt? The one that raised her mother?"

"Yes. Her name was Gladys. She didn't die until 2003 so Meryl got a great deal of information from her."

"I bet she did. What sort of insights did Great-Aunt Gladys have into her sister's behaviour?"

"Lots. She said that Emily loved and respected her husband, but she was lonely, and she became besotted with Varney, even though he had a somewhat dubious reputation. It was lust, pure and simple. She simply couldn't resist the man. No amount of trying to talk sense could get through to her. She was foolishly indiscreet, hiring the man as a gardener, yet it was blatantly obvious to all her neighbours what was going on. To make a long story short, Emily's husband was due home in November, and with the understanding that she and her husband should have some time with just the two of them together, she had sent young Beth to stay with her sister for a few days."

Richard gave a cynical smile.

"Sounds more like an opportunity to have a last fling with the lover before her husband came back."

Alexandra smiled.

"You do think like a policeman, don't you? Yes, that's what everyone else thought too, although Great-Aunt Gladys believed that Emily would have come to her senses once her husband returned. Anyway, for whatever reason, on November twenty-third, Emily was alone in the house. However, around ten o'clock that night, their next-door neighbours—that would be the people who lived in our house at the time—were awakened by a noise next door. They could hear shouting, and when they went to the window and looked out towards Emily's house, they saw lights and they could hear a man and woman quarreling. As they listened, they recognized the voices and realized that although they had not seen him arrive, Emily's husband had come home. The Robertsons were having a raging fight, and the subject was Emily's infidelity. The quarrel seemed to go on and on, even after the shouting stopped and the voices became a distressing medley of anger and pleas mixed with sobs and recriminations. At last, the voices died to a dull murmur, and thinking that the crisis was over, the neighbours decided to go back to bed. But no sooner had they settled down again than they heard a very loud gunshot. Then everything went silent. They waited a few minutes, but still heard nothing. After some discussion as to whether they should interfere, the husband ran across and knocked on the front door, calling Emily's name and asking if everything was all right. A couple of minutes later, the door opened. Emily stood there. She was white as a sheet and shaking uncontrollably. The neighbour was horrified to see bloodstains on her nightgown. She seemed to have difficulty making herself speak, but finally she whispered, 'It was a burglar. He's killed my husband.'"

"A burglar?"

"That was her story, and she held to it after the police arrived. They found Meryl's grandfather lying dead at the foot of the stairs. It was a grisly sight. The top half of his body had been blasted with a shotgun."

"Whose weapon was it?"

"It was his own shotgun. When he'd gone to war, he'd put it in a cupboard in the bedroom, thinking it would be protection for Emily when she was there alone."

"Then how could a burglar get hold of it?"

"Emily's story was that her husband had arrived home in late afternoon. He had taken off his jacket and hung it in the hall, along with his gun belt and the holster with his army regulation colt."

Richard flinched and rolled his eyes.

"Yes, I know," said Alexandra, "but they weren't as hot on gun control in those days. Anyway, Emily said that she and her husband had dined together and had gone to bed around nine o'clock. About an hour later, they were drifting off to sleep when they were abruptly woken by a noise downstairs. Her husband had thrown on his robe and gone out to the landing to investigate, taking his shotgun with him. She'd slipped out of bed and followed, and she stood watching from the bedroom doorway. Suddenly, her husband called out a warning. He said that there was a man in the bottom hall. What they didn't realize was that the intruder had taken the colt from the holster, and when he saw he was being threatened with a shotgun, he raised the gun and fired, shooting Emily's husband in the chest and causing him to pitch down the stairs. In the process the shotgun went off, creating the mess that the police saw when they arrived and found his body."

"That's feasible," said Richard. "Did the autopsy indicate a separate bullet wound as well as the shotgun damage?"

"Yes."

Richard nodded sagely.

"But her story fell apart because the neighbours had overheard her quarreling with her husband just prior to the shot."

"Exactly. What's more, there was no sign of a forced entry. When she was confronted with those inconsistencies, she changed her story again. She admitted that she had been having an affair—how could she avoid it? Everyone knew—and she told the police that she had arranged a tryst with her lover that night, since her husband was not due to come home until the following evening. However, he turned up one day early and she had no way of letting her lover know not to come by. She said that they went to bed early, and once her husband was asleep, she crept downstairs to wait for her lover and to explain why he couldn't come in."

"And her husband woke up and caught them. Hence the raging quarrel."

"Yes. Emily said that her husband had come out with his shotgun and Varney grabbed the colt to defend himself. He'd fired when her husband raised his own weapon. Then everything else happened as she'd described before. When he saw that her husband was dead, her lover ran away."

Richard was sceptical.

"But the neighbours only heard two voices."

"I know, and there were other things that proved she was lying. The most damning evidence was provided by the fingerprints on the guns."

"Guns? The colt was still there?"

"Yes. Back in its holster yet. She said she put it there because she didn't want it lying around. However, the only prints on it were her own. Also, hers were the only prints on the shotgun, and the police determined that the angle of fire showed that the blast with the shotgun must have been administered by someone standing a few feet away. It could not possibly have happened as an accident during a fall."

"No wonder she was convicted. How did she explain that away?" Alexandra sighed.

"She said her fingerprints were on the colt because she'd picked it up to wipe off her lover's prints. She admitted that she'd fired the shotgun, but she insisted that her husband was already dead."

"How did she justify that?"

"She said she'd done it in an attempt to cover up for the fact that her lover had shot her husband. She told Varney to run away, and she said he'd promised to come back if things went wrong and the police didn't accept her story of the burglary."

Richard frowned and looked thoughtful.

"That's plausible, you know," he said. "It could have happened that way. If the lover had stayed mute, simply watching Emily and her husband quarreling, he might have taken the colt, thinking the quarrel could escalate. If he had shot Meryl's grandfather and then run away, Emily might have taken those steps to cover up for him, thinking she could get away with the burglary story. But why didn't the neighbours hear that first shot?"

"There was a lot of shouting going on. It might have screened the sound."

"And the murmuring voices afterwards could have been Emily talking with Varney after her husband had been shot. Yes, that works. They were planning how to cover up the murder."

"That's what Meryl believes. There's evidence that supports the fact that Emily's lover was present and ran away after the murder. He was never seen again after that night, but a fishing boat was stolen from Westminster Quay, and several months later, wreckage from the boat washed ashore onto one of the Gulf Islands, along with a jacket that had belonged to Varney. It seems pretty definite that he drowned trying to escape by sea."

"So he could have been the killer. Still, I can see why Meryl's grandmother was convicted. Whichever version was the truth, they all pointed to a degree of guilt on her part. Maybe Meryl is right and Emily didn't want her husband dead, but just the fact that she had taken a lover while her husband was fighting for his country would have been enough to prejudice a jury against her."

"Yes, she didn't stand a chance. She was found guilty and executed in June of 1946."

"Did she say anything more before she died?"

"Evidently, she owned up that it was all her fault, but there was one thing she said to the warden that makes Meryl believe it was her lover who fired the deadly shot. Before she was taken for her last walk, she was supposed to have said, 'He promised to return if there was trouble, but he never came back for me. He didn't care that I'm going to die, and I don't care any more either.'"

Richard drained the last dregs from his glass.

"I think your neighbour is right," he said. "At some point, there were three people in that room. One way or another, this was a crime of passion."

"But was Meryl's grandmother innocent?"

"Let's say it's possible her death was merely collateral damage. That's as far as I would go."

Alexandra smiled.

"So the detective inspector doesn't have anything new to add?"

Before Richard could reply, the door of the den opened and a twenty-something redhead with tumbling curls, spider eyelashes and a neckline that barely skimmed her waistline undulated into the room. In tones more saccharine than honeyed, she said: "Oh, there you are, Alex. George wondered where you'd got to. He said to tell you we need more smoked salmon."

"It's in the fridge freezer," Alexandra said coolly. "Perhaps you could get it for him."

The redhead pouted prettily, flashed predatory eyes at Richard, and wiggled out of the room.

Richard raised his eyebrows.

"My husband's aide." Alexandra sighed and stood up. "Still, I should get back to my guests. Can I pour you another Scotch?"

Richard looked at the snowflakes, which seemed even fatter and more abundant that when they had entered. Then he nodded and held out his glass.

"Why not?" he said. "I'm sure my parents have room for one more in *Arvy* tonight."

As he followed Alexandra out of the room, he saw a huddle of little girls clustering in the hall. Meryl Graham appeared to be giving them a key and instructing them that they were to pick up their pajamas and then go straight over to the Billings' house. He moved past the giggling horde and re-entered the living room. His father was at the bar again, talking amiably with Gwendolyn Pye, whose cheeks glowed like twin port lights under her slightly askew cocktail hat. Richard's mother was still trilling with the carollers. Her face had also acquired a suspiciously high colour. Vaguely Richard was aware that the singers had returned to the beginning of the songbook. Still, he thought, looking at the snow drifting past the windowpanes, "Good King Wenceslas" was certainly the most appropriate song for the occasion.

He felt a draft coming through from the hall. The front door had opened to release the group of giggling girls into the night. As they trailed out the door, he heard a little voice piping sweetly in tune with the carollers.

> *Therefore, Christian men be sure, wealth and rank possessing,*
> *Ye who now will bless the poor, shall yourselves find blessing.*

*   *   *

Another blanket of snow had fallen by morning. If it had not been for the tire tracks that marked where the hardy partygoers with four-wheel drive or heavy-duty snow tires had ventured home the night before, the street, with its picturesque heritage homes, could have graced a Dickensian Christmas card. *Arvy*, squatting snugly in the Laceys' driveway, had acquired a thick layer of snow, making it resemble a loaf with marzipan topping. The street was quiet, for most of the residents were sleeping in after the revels of the night before, and even the normal sounds of morning were muffled by the snow.

Alexandra was never able to sleep in, no matter how late she had gone to bed, so by nine o'clock, she had already bathed and dressed, eaten a light breakfast and made considerable headway clearing the debris from the previous evening. Having washed and set aside the platters that belonged to various neighbours, she felt the need to pop out for some fresh air, so she put on her coat and boots, and set off to return the borrowed items.

As she went down the driveway, she heard no sound coming from *Arvy*. The Bearys were enjoying a lie-in. She turned left and walked to the Grahams' property, but as she came up their garden path, she noticed footprints in the snow going back and forth between the house and Dolly's Cottage, the children's playhouse at the far side of the lot. Suddenly anxious in case any of the children had had the crazy idea of camping out, she set the platters on the front porch and went round to investigate. She found herself following three sets of footprints: two human and one obviously belonging to a cat. The human ones were disparate in size. One set was huge, the other, the small prints of a child. Uneasily, Alexandra saw that the large set of prints only went towards the cottage.

Dolly's Cottage had been a labour of love undertaken by Luke when his daughters had expressed a yen for a playhouse that looked like Hansel and Gretel's gingerbread house. It always had something of a storybook appearance, but with its frosting of snow, it seemed positively enchanted—a Christmas-card chalet in pink, white and gold. As Alexandra drew near, she saw that the pink door, although pulled closed, was still slightly ajar.

She bent down and pushed the door open. It gave a couple of inches, and then stopped, lodged against something on the other side. Whatever it was refused to budge. Alexandra put her eye to the gap and peered inside. The morning light beaming through the tiny window on the opposite wall gleamed down on the object that was wedged against the door. Alexandra gasped and stepped back. There was a tramp asleep inside the house.

She stood still, wondering whether to call out to the man and try to wake him, and then, with a growing sense of unease, she realized that if he had not woken up as she was shoving the door against him, he was not likely to wake up at all. She was tossing up whether to call 911 or first notify Meryl of the unexpected visitor on her property, when, kicking herself for being so dim, she remembered that she had the perfect person at hand to deal with the crisis. Richard had declared his intention of kipping down on the top bunk of his parents' motorhome, and as far as she knew, he had done just that. She shoved her phone back in her pocket, hurried to her own driveway and pounded on *Arvy's* door. If the sleeping tramp turned out to be a dead body, the detective inspector could deal with it.

*   *   *

The tramp was dead, although there were no indications of foul play. However, the circumstances demanded an autopsy, and the body was duly brought from the playhouse and dispatched to the morgue. The man appeared to be very old, though living rough could have aged him. However, Richard suspected that the pathologist's findings would confirm that he had died in his sleep, either from old age or hypothermia. If this was the case, the tramp had had an ending that most would envy, for not only had he died peacefully, but he had spent his last night in comfort, tucked on a sleeping bag and wrapped in a voluminous Hudson Bay blanket. He had also been well fed, if the remains in the dishes beside him were anything to go by.

At first, Richard had assumed that the tramp had broken into the Grahams' house and helped himself to these luxuries, but when the children came out from the Billings' house, eager to see what was going on, it turned out that the man had not stolen any of the items. They had been provided for him most unexpectedly.

"It was Beth's idea," said Emma indignantly, when their mother asked if they had anything to do with the food and blankets in the playhouse. "The old man was standing outside our house when we went back to pick up our pjs. He seemed a bit out of it, and we were going to come and tell you to call the police, but Beth said he was poor and old like the man in 'Good King Wenceslas' and we should be nice to him. So we told him he could sleep in the playhouse overnight as long as he took off again in the morning."

"And you brought him our food and blankets?" Meryl looked indignant, but Richard noticed that her husband was grinning. Richard, himself, was amused at the children's enterprise.

"We took him the blanket and sleeping bag," said Rosalie, "and Janet and Judy gave him the bag of chips that we'd brought from the party, because they had lots more at their house."

"But what about the beef patties, the potato salad and the cheesecake?" snapped Meryl. "That was today's lunch."

Emma glowered at her sister.

"That was Beth. We had nothing to do with it."

All eyes turned to the diminutive blonde six-year-old who was watching the debate with wide blue eyes. She was clutching a ginger cat in a vice-like grip that belied her delicate appearance. She seemed unperturbed by her mother's indignation over the pilfered lunch.

"The old man was hungry," she said. "And lonely. He was nice. He was like the people we talked to at the veterans' hospital, and you know how you said we had to be nice to them."

Her mother stared at her, amazed.

"So you took all that food out to him?" She turned to look indignantly at the older girls. "And the rest of you let her?"

"We didn't know," said Rosalie. "Beth went back afterwards. She snuck out when we were watching a movie and we just thought she'd gone to bed 'cos it was late."

Beth nodded.

"I didn't go out for long," she said. "I took the food to Dolly's Cottage, and then I stayed and visited for a little while. Marmalade came out too, which was nice because the man liked cats. I was hungry, so we shared the pie and potato salad. Then the man was tired and needed to go to sleep, so I said goodnight and came back to Judy and Janet's house."

Meryl picked Beth up and gave her a hug.

"Darling, it's wonderful that you wanted to be kind, but you must remember all the things we've told you about talking to strangers. Please, never, ever do anything like that again."

Beth fixed her wide blue eyes on her mother.

"I don't think he was a stranger," she said. "He knew my name." Oblivious to the startled faces of the adults around her, she wriggled out of her mother's arms. Then she fished in her pocket and pulled out a fragile-looking chain.

"See. He gave me this," she said, fiddling with the object for a moment before holding it out to her mother.

Richard saw that the child was offering her mother an open locket. It was an unusual shape, a silver crescent moon that hinged at the centre of the curve. Inside, in a circular frame set between the points of the crescent, was a photograph of a woman. Meryl's eyes flew wide as she took the locket. Then she stared, ashen-faced, at the image inside the frame.

Richard only just had time to step forward and catch her as she fainted.

*   *   *

Ten days later, Richard called Alexandra and let her know that he had arranged to drop by the Grahams' home to tell them what he had discovered about the unexpected Boxing Day guest. He knew she had been eaten up with curiosity ever since the morning following her party and he suspected that she would be eager to hear what he had to say. Given her resourcefulness and her close friendship with her next-door neighbours, he was quite sure she would manage to be present at the interview, if only to offer support for Meryl.

Sure enough, when Meryl Graham led him into her high-ceilinged living room, he saw Alexandra sitting on a peacock-emblazoned loveseat that nestled in a wide bay window overlooking the snow-covered garden. Luke Graham was seated on a matching chesterfield kitty-corner to the loveseat, and a second loveseat formed the third side of a U that extended out from the carved wooden mantel of the fireplace. A square glass coffee table filled the space between the sofas. At the centre of the table was a silver tray with a Royal Albert coffee set. The only other object on the table was a bulky and ancient-looking photograph album.

The aromatic scent of freshly brewed coffee hovered tantalizingly in the air. Alexandra and Luke were already drinking from elegant bone-china mugs, and as Richard settled himself on the loveseat opposite Alexandra, Meryl poured him a cup of the excellent brew that the others were enjoying. Then she sat beside her husband and looked expectantly at their visitor.

"It took a while, but we traced the tramp's background," Richard began. "His name was Donnie Lindstrom and he'd been on the street for the past couple of years, so we managed to get his story from a couple of his cohorts who slept under the same bridge. They told me that Donnie was a bit simple and he'd wandered off from a group home in Sapperton. When we talked to the people at the home, it transpired that Donnie had been in a series of homes ever since the mid-seventies, when his people had died and he had nowhere to go."

"His people?" Meryl raised her eyebrows. Her expression was a mix of surprise and curiosity, but from the nervous tapping of her fingers on the arm of the chesterfield, Richard could tell she was extremely anxious.

Richard continued his explanation.

"Martha and Gunner Lindstrom," he said. "They were a couple who had lived on Gabriola Island since the 1920s. It took a bit of checking and rechecking back through the various contacts, but it appears that Martha and Gunner found Donnie washed ashore on the beach back in November of 1945."

Meryl gasped and bit her lip. Her husband put an arm round her shoulder. Richard watched his hostess thoughtfully. Although he could tell she was upset, he did not think she was surprised. Alexandra finally broke the silence.

"So you think that this Donnie Lindstrom was the man who went missing on the night of the murder all those years ago," she said.

"It seems so," said Richard. "Especially since he was carrying the locket with the photograph of Meryl's grandmother. Obviously, he didn't drown when the boat he stole broke up in the storm, though in a way, he'd have been better off if he had. He had severe brain damage and had no idea who he was. Amnesia and incompetence in one fell swoop."

"Didn't the Lindstroms realize who he was?" demanded Alexandra. "I know the media wasn't as intrusive then as now, but they had newspapers in 1945."

"Not on Gabriola. The Lindstroms were pretty much self-sufficient, living on a smallholding and cut off from the rest of the world. What was left of the fishing boat had washed ashore on De Courcy Island so they weren't aware of the shipwreck. They took Donnie in—they were the ones who gave him his new name—and nursed him back to physical health. He lived with them and helped with the farm. They had no children, so I suppose he became like a son to them. Before they died, they had arranged for him to go into a care home on the mainland, but although Donnie was mentally fragile, he was physically strong, and he lived on long past the time that the money they left had run out. He became a ward of the state, and was moved from place to place, until he ended up in the group home in Sapperton. From there he went walkabout and ended up near Queen's Park, and I suppose something in his confused brain recognized the streets and the heritage houses that he knew when he was young."

Richard had been answering Alexandra's question, but as he turned back towards Meryl, he saw that she was listening intently. Her eyes were moist, and as he watched, a solitary tear slid down her cheek.

"So one day," she whispered, "that sense of recognition led him back to my house?"

Richard nodded.

"Yes," he said quietly. "It's a sad story, isn't it? Judging by what we learned of his last night on earth, though, he had an ending we all could envy. He died from natural causes, with a satisfying meal in his stomach, and with a sweet little girl for company who was the spitting image of the child he knew from his visits to the house all those years before."

Meryl let out a huge sigh.

"So that's why he didn't come back to save her," she said. "It wasn't that he didn't love her. His accident simply made him forget her."

"I suppose so," said Richard. "I think we can say for sure that your grandmother's final version of what happened was the true one. She wasn't a murderer. She was simply trying to cover up for the man she loved."

Meryl smiled sadly. "Yes," she said. "That's exactly what she did."

Richard regarded her shrewdly.

"There is one minor variation though, isn't there?" he said. "A variation that makes the story much more logical."

Meryl remained silent and the others looked at her expectantly. Richard spoke again. "I did hear from the lab that you'd requested a DNA test. You already suspect the truth, don't you?"

Meryl was still for a moment. Then she nodded.

"I know the truth," she said. "My grandmother's death was an act of atonement. She loved my grandfather. The other man was just an insane infatuation, a result of her loneliness. My great-aunt always said that Emily knew in her heart that her lover was a bad lot. She would never have given up her life to protect Jacques Varney."

"You believe it was the husband who shot the lover," said Richard. "A crime of passion. He came home one day early and found Jacques Varney with his wife. What better way for your grandmother to protect her husband than by having him escape in the clothes of the dead man and blasting the corpse with the shotgun so she could pretend that your grandfather was the one who had died."

"It could have been self-defence," said Meryl. "My grandfather may not have shot Varney in cold blood. Perhaps Jacques Varney came out with the shotgun. My grandfather may have been forced to fire."

"Well, that we'll never know," said Richard, "but the DNA test will at least let you know who it was who died in the Dolls' Cottage."

Meryl leaned forward and opened the photograph album on the coffee table.

"The test will be the proof," she said, "but I already know."

She pushed the album across the table and turned it so the others could see. Then she pointed at the photograph on the right-hand page. It was a picture of a smiling officer standing by a tank. He was wearing shorts, and his regulation shirt was open. On his chest hung a locket, the unusual crescent-shape clearly delineated in the harsh desert sunlight.

Richard glanced down at the writing at the bottom of the photograph.

Always with me. My love forever. Stephen.

"I'm so glad," said Meryl, "that Beth was with him. I'm sure he thought she was his own daughter. Just thinking about their midnight feast makes me cry, but they're happy tears." Meryl stopped abruptly and buried her head in her husband's shoulder. Luke cradled her in his arms, and she curled herself into his side. Richard and Alexandra were completely forgotten.

"Well, I'm damned," said Richard, pushing the album away. He looked accusingly at Alexandra, who was smiling mysteriously. "You knew that, didn't you? What's more, you never told me Meryl's grandfather's name, which turned out to be pretty significant, given the occasion."

"That was just an oversight at first," she said sweetly, "and the next morning you were far too preoccupied with your present corpse for me to talk about the one from the past. It was only when I talked with Meryl later that the whole picture started to come together. I knew it was just a matter of time before you figured it out."

Richard laughed.

"Fair enough," he said. "But please, next year, try to manage something a little less amazing for your Boxing Day party."

Instead of replying, Alexandra slid her eyes towards the couple, who remained oblivious to their guests, and inclined her head towards the front door. "Second cup at my place?" she mouthed. Richard nodded and stood up.

Quietly, he followed her to the door and out into the snow, which, he noted whimsically, was still deep and crisp and even. Alexandra waited until they were halfway down the drive before she commented on Richard's observation about her party.

"By the way," she said, "yesterday evening wasn't a Boxing Day party. It was—"

Richard interjected before she could finish. "Yes, I know," he said. He glanced up the snow-covered path to the silvery glade where Dolly's Cottage gleamed in the morning sunlight that was filtering through the bare branches of the maple tree.

Smiling, he turned back to Alexandra.

"You don't have to remind me," he said. "It was the Feast of Stephen."

The Camera Lies

Bertram Beary did not know whether to be pleased or sorry when he received a letter informing him that his cousin was immigrating to Canada. On the one hand, he would no longer hold the questionable title of most politically incorrect Canadian member of the Beary clan, but on the other hand, the chaos that could result from close proximity to Amanda Smythe-Piggott and her daughter, Petunia, was something he could definitely do without. His hopes that Canada could possibly be interpreted to mean Newfoundland, or even Labrador, were dashed when the postscript indicated that the mother-daughter couple would be arriving at Vancouver Airport the following weekend, and that his never-backward-in-coming-forward cousin assumed that the Bearys were prepared to put the two of them up indefinitely while they searched for jobs and a permanent place to live.

Beary sighed. The fallout when he broke the news to Edwina was likely to rival the explosion following the flight of the *Enola Gay*. He was not looking forward to the weeks ahead.

The letter's arrival coincided with the arrival of Juliette and her daughters, who had come down from the Sunshine Coast to stay over the weekend. Beary decided that news of additional houseguests would be untimely, so he took the cowardly course and tucked the letter away for future revelation. Then, in case Edwina's phenomenal radar detected his unease, he resolved to take MacPuff for a walk in the park. The winter had been brutal, but there was a break in the weather, and it would be an opportune time to take advantage of it. Jennifer and Laura announced their intention of accompanying him, and soon he and his granddaughters were approaching the parking lot at the top of Fernie Park. To his dismay, an unusual number of vehicles were parked between the icy pyramids of residual snow.

"Bugger," said Beary, momentarily forgetting who was with him. "They're filming again."

"Cool," said Laura.

"Uncool," countered Beary. "The Parks Commission approves too many of these shoots and they're very disruptive to MacPuff's walks. We'll forget the park. Let's detour through the Sidley Lands."

He referred to the large tract of woodland, wedged between the park and the subsidized housing estate, which had been the site of stately homes and a veterans' hospital in the early part of the previous century but was now overgrown to a natural state, except for the trails where the old roads had been kept clear by the neighbourhood dog-walkers and trail-bikers.

"No way," protested Laura. "We want to see what they're filming." Her eyes bulged with excitement. "Maybe it's *Baying at the Moon!*"

"And what, pray tell, is *Baying at the Moon?*" asked Beary. He had stopped paying attention to the movies the year Sean Connery gave up playing Agent 007. These days, he simply relied on Edwina to tell him which films he would enjoy when they came on television.

Laura was appalled at her grandfather's ignorance.

"It's the sequel to *Blood Fang*."

A vague memory stirred in Beary's brain of a visit to Chapters the previous year. An entire wall had been covered with volumes of that title.

"A book series?" he asked.

"Yes. They're really good," said Jennifer.

"They're about this high-school girl who falls in love with a werewolf." Laura flapped her arms enthusiastically. "His name's Abelard Gray and in the movie, he's played by Darcy Magellan. Omigod! Suppose we get to see him!"

"Is Darcy Magellan the latest teen idol?" Beary continued to expose the unpardonable gaps in his education.

"He's been around for years," said Laura scornfully. "He's the lead singer of Howl. Everyone's in love with him. And now he's acting as well. I'd die if I met him."

"Then let's hope we don't," said Beary.

But he was talking to thin air, for the girls were off, running towards the gate where the park trails began, so sensing defeat, Beary followed. Once on the trail, he unclipped MacPuff's leash, allowing the dog to scamper ahead and run alongside the children. By the time Beary reached the clearing at the middle of the park, Jennifer and Laura were already there, staring bug-eyed at the work crew, some of whom were planting additional shrubs to augment the fir trees, ferns and huckleberry bushes that already abounded throughout the park. The rest were pounding nails into a large structure that had been erected by the stream.

"Good God!" said Beary. "They're building a bloody house."

"Only temporary," the foreman told him cheerily. Film crews were always cheerful, Beary reflected. They couldn't afford complaints from the public.

"It's going to be a derelict cabin in the woods," the foreman elaborated. "We'll have it finished by next weekend, and then it'll only be here a couple of weeks. And all the filming will be at night, so we won't interfere with your walks. Don't worry, we'll put everything back the way it was."

"Hey! What does this dog have against my trees?"

A bellow from the tree-planter caused Beary to swing round. MacPuff was systematically christening all the newly planted shrubs. Beary called him, and the husky came bounding back, pausing on the way to lift his leg against the carpenter's toolkit.

"Sorry," said Beary. "Hazard of the job."

The foreman's smile became a little strained. Beary mentally lauded him for the effort it must have cost to retain his public-relations manner.

"What are you filming?" asked Jennifer eagerly. "Is it *Baying at the Moon*?"

The foreman regarded her amiably.

"Sorry to disappoint you, kiddo. It's a B-movie zombie flic. *Zarostro*. You won't be finding Darcy Magellan on this site."

To Beary's surprise, his granddaughters did not seem disappointed. They continued to survey the scene, avidly taking in every detail of the set-in-progress. MacPuff found a stick to chew and settled himself on the ground, so Beary remained chatting with the foreman while the girls explored.

"Actually," Beary told the man, "if you wanted to keep the site secret and avoid interlopers for the werewolf film, this would have been a good location. No one uses this park except dog-walkers, and we're as anxious as you are to prevent other people coming in because they usually end up complaining about our dogs. We wouldn't breathe a word to anyone else."

"Hadn't thought of that," said the foreman.

He waved to a truck that was driving up the path from the lower parking lot. A second truck was coming in behind the first. Beary's eyes widened.

"You're bringing in a lot of equipment for a B-movie," he commented.

"Hey, we bring in a lot of equipment for a TV commercial. You'd better retrieve your girls," the man added. "We have to unload some heavy gear right where they're standing."

Beary called Jennifer and Laura, and with MacPuff in tow, they set off to complete their walk.

"Well," said Beary, "too bad your hero won't be in the vicinity, but at least you got to visit a film set."

Laura and Jennifer looked smug.

"Honestly, Grampus," said Laura. "You just don't get it. They use code names. That shed they're building is exactly what they'll need for the house where Abelard's grandfather lives, and you heard what that man said. It's all night filming. This is it! We've found one of the main locations for *Baying at the Moon.*" Jennifer turned to her sister triumphantly.

"Now we just have to persuade Mom to let us stay with Grandma and Grampus for the rest of spring break."

The girls charged ahead with MacPuff. Beary sighed again. And he still hadn't broken the news to Edwina of Cousin Amanda's arrival. Life became more and more complicated by the moment.

*   *   *

"I can't wait to see Cousin Amanda again," Philippa told Bob Miller. "My mother can't stand her, but I bet she's going to liven things up around here."

Miller looked apprehensive. He had no qualms about dealing with the gang members and assorted villains that frequented the streets of Vancouver, but Philippa's mother was in a category all of her own. This was his first visit to the Beary home and he wanted the afternoon to go smoothly.

"Is it safe for me to be coming to Sunday dinner?" he asked. "If your mother is going ballistic over houseguests, she won't want another mouth to feed."

"It'll be fine," said Philippa. "My mother approves of you. She's been on at me for months to invite you to dinner. She refers to you as 'that nice young policeman' so as long as you don't do anything to upset me, you'll be in her good books."

Miller raised his eyebrows.

"Is that encouragement or a threat?" he said.

Philippa smiled wickedly.

"You can take it any way you like."

"Right. So tell me about this cousin that's stirring everything up. How can she and her daughter hope to settle in Canada? I thought these days you had to be either a refugee or a millionaire to get landed-immigrant status."

"My cousins have dual citizenship," said Philippa. "Amanda's mother is my Great-Aunt Hermione who, by the way, sang in musicals and operetta on the London stage. She also did minor work in film and had a good career until 1955 when she married an earl and settled down to country life in his stately home. One of Hermione's brothers immigrated to Canada after the war. That's my Great-Uncle Henry. Amanda was born in 1956 during a trip to Montreal when Hermione came out to visit him."

"So she's a Canadian citizen."

"Exactly, but with British parents. She has ties to both countries."

"Convenient. Lucky Amanda."

"Yes. Amanda's led quite the life, but she's very spoiled, having grown up as the only darling daughter of an earl. She's a real anachronism. She was raised on all that 'Britain won the war, King and Country, private box at Ascot' stuff and according to Mum, she has an attitude of entitlement that belongs in the Dark Ages. Anyway, Amanda married a wealthy businessman in the mid-eighties—John Piggott, the Piggott's soap and toiletries baron—and they had a daughter, who's my age, give or take a year. Petunia's actually pretty nice. She came out here on an exchange when we were teenagers. Petunia was born in Canada too."

"On another visit to Great-Uncle Henry?"

"Yes, but this time it was deliberate, because Amanda had learned the value of dual citizenship, and she knew things were going downhill with the business. Her husband went bust in the big crash of '87 and promptly committed suicide, so Amanda lost everything. Her father, the earl, had died the previous year, and the title and estate—what was left after post-war taxes—had reverted to Amanda's younger brother, who had also made a ton of bad investments, so the family was totally strapped. Great-Aunt Hermione amazed everyone by marrying her chauffeur and going back to work in theatre and film, and actually did very well in character parts. I've seen her in several of the BBC dramas that were produced in the eighties and nineties. But Amanda, according to my mother, is averse to anything that resembles real work, so she procured another rich businessman, bought another stately home, and gave Petunia the best education money could buy, including sending her to RADA and film school."

"So you have another actress in the family."

"Actually, no," said Philippa. "Petunia doesn't like acting, but she loves tech work. She and I have kept in touch ever since her visit in '98. We email each other quite often. Pet's already been offered a temporary job here. She's working on the werewolf epic."

Miller groaned. "And what a nightmare that is," he said. "Keeping hordes of lovesick teenagers away from Darcy Magellan. So is that why your relatives have come here? For the film work?"

"Only partly. Amanda's second husband died in 2007. She'd already spent pots of his money, and it turned out he'd invested unwisely too. Amanda lost most of what was left in the big downturn in 2008. She struggled on for a bit, but in the end, she decided to sell up and move to Canada. She and Petunia arrived two days ago and they're already driving Mum crazy."

"She sounds a bit challenging," said Miller. "Are you really sure you want to meet her again?"

"Of course. I have great memories of Amanda because I was three years old when I met her and she was sweet as pie to me. Mum and Dad had taken us all to England to visit our grandparents, and in those days, Amanda was still spending money like a drunken sailor, and she took us to all the fashionable London shops. She was one of the original Sloane Rangers. I still remember her flashy clothes and gorgeous long pink fingernails. I actually thought she was some kind of deity, because everyone was always saying, 'Oh, my God, Amanda.' Of course, she's well over fifty now, but it's going to be very interesting meeting her after all I've heard from everyone else. I wonder if she still has the pink fingernails."

Miller was curious. "If your grandparents are English, why are your parents Canadian?"

"My mother was born here, but Dad came out in 1961 to visit his sister, who had married a Canadian. That's when he met my mother, who, according to him, instantly determined that they had a future together. He went back to England and completed university. Then he came back, married Mum, upgraded his qualifications and acquired a teacher-training certificate through UBC. Turn here," Philippa added. "We're almost there."

Miller turned onto the street that abutted Fernie Park. They passed the thick grove of trees that ran along the edge of the road, and then the view opened up onto a panoramic sweep across to the hills on the far side of Burnside. The pale sky, still wintry even though it was early April, contained only a faint wisp of cloud, hinting that the unusually long winter might be drawing to a close, but here and there, dotted around the grass, were piles of hard, compacted snow. A fleet of mobile dressing rooms filled the top parking lot.

"This weather must be causing the film crews a lot of grief," Philippa observed.

"The film crews are causing VPD a lot of grief," said Miller. "There are four different locations, all of which need top security, and the lunatic who doubles as a werewolf when he isn't playing with his rock group is no angel. He's highly adept at slipping his bodyguards. He's gone missing twice, and we're the ones who get called in to round him up."

"What's he doing? Chasing the local girls?"

"That, and probably drugs, but if we bust him, the media will be all over us. I'll be very happy when they finish shooting, pack up and leave."

Philippa directed Miller onto the road that led to her parents' house, and after three blocks, she pointed to a large white house with brown trim.

"Nice," said Miller. "Heritage home?"

"I guess. It's more than a hundred years old. Look, there's Dad in the front garden. He must be desperate to get out of the house if he's reduced to having a conversation with Ipod."

"Ipod being the miniature goon with the earpiece and the pile of newspapers? His name doesn't fit his equipment."

"Dad gave him the nickname. He's not exactly up to date on technology."

Miller pulled up in front of the house. Beary left Ipod and came over to greet them, but Ipod was clearly in no hurry to complete his rounds. He ambled after Beary, grinned at Philippa and rolled his eyes towards Miller.

"This your cop?" he asked cheekily.

"He's a policeman, yes," said Philippa icily. "Shouldn't you be on your way? People don't like having to wait for their local paper."

Ipod ignored Philippa and focussed on Miller.

"Hey, dude," he said cheerfully, "wait till you see the cougar they've got staying here."

Ipod leered in a manner totally unbecoming his lack of years, then sauntered down the street, shoulders swaying in time to whatever was rhythmically assaulting his ears.

Beary furrowed his brow.

"What in heaven's name is a cougar?" he demanded. "I know he wasn't referring to Minx, the Manx."

Philippa enlightened him.

"It's a geriatric hottie, Dad," she explained.

"Ah," said Beary. "Well, the geriatric hottie is, at present, in the living room working her way through my best Scotch. Dinner will be half an hour, so let's join her before she finishes the lot."

Edwina appeared on the porch. She gave Miller an effusive greeting that implied he was already one of the family and welcomed him inside.

"Sorry about that," whispered Philippa as they slipped into the hall. "I know she's overwhelming. You must feel like you're going into a lion's den."

Miller grinned and winked at Philippa.

"At least she isn't a cougar like your cousin," he chuckled. "Come on, let's go and see if Cousin Amanda still has the bright pink fingernails."

Amanda Piggott-Smythe not only had retained the pink fingernails, but she was clothed in a shocking pink suit to match them. Her streaked blonde hair was drawn back in a French braid, and under the long, artfully tossed bangs, the dark blue eyes emitted the compelling stare with which her ancestors had quelled tribal leaders and junior adjutants in every corner of the British Empire. Miller had occasionally seen the same expression on new recruits who hadn't learned the reality of modern policing. Sheer grit determination over common sense, he thought. He was ready to bet that one of Cousin Amanda's forefathers had led a division in the charge of the Light Brigade.

It also transpired that Amanda, now, went by the shortened form of her name. She engulfed Philippa in an effusive hug, gushed a series of embarrassing reminiscences of how sweet Philippa had been at the age of three, and then turned to Miller and bared an impressive mouthful of whitened teeth.

"Mandy Piggott-Smythe," she barked. The sweet tone she had used on Philippa was no longer in evidence. For all the cougar appearance, concluded Miller, Cousin Mandy wasn't angling for a toy boy. Perhaps two incompetent husbands and an ineffectual brother had jaded her for life. "Philippa says you're a policeman," Mandy continued briskly. She whipped her cellphone out of her purse. It was in a bright pink case that matched her suit. "Give me your contact info," she ordered Miller. "Always handy to have a pet plod on file."

Miller blinked, then seeing Philippa's mortified face, he quietly obliged.

Mandy entered the information, eyed it carefully as if committing it to memory, then put the phone away. She waved her hand towards a thin, bespectacled girl with shoulder-length, mouse-brown hair who sat quietly at the end of the chesterfield.

"This is my daughter, Petunia," she said.

Clearly, Petunia did not share her mother's passion for glamorous clothing. However, Miller noted that, behind the glasses, the same wide blue eyes stared out, except that in Petunia's case, their gaze was one of laid-back resignation.

Philippa flopped down beside Petunia.

"So how's the film business?" she asked.

Before Petunia could answer, Mandy interjected.

"Absolutely marvellous. Did your mother not tell you that I've been taken on as an extra?"

"Did you swing that?" Philippa muttered to Petunia.

Petunia nodded and rolled her eyes upward.

"Have you done any acting before?" Philippa asked curiously, turning back to Mandy.

"God, no, but how hard can it be? Mother is still performing and she's over eighty."

"Grandma took years of voice and dance lessons—*and* drama-school training," Petunia pointed out courageously. "It didn't all come naturally."

"So what. This is film. Any twit can stand in front of a camera. Witness the vapid termite starring in the current *I was a Teenage Werewolf* crap-pic. If that's what's exciting the next generation of young women, we've spawned a breed of tasteless, sexless morons. I'd as soon couple with a stick insect as pair up with Darcy Magellan."

"How did he pick a stage name like Darcy?" Beary asked. "Do you think he might actually be literate?"

"It isn't a stage name," Petunia chimed in. "It's his real name. His mother is Eva Magellan, you know, the soap star. *As the World Turns.*"

Beary didn't know, but Mandy elaborated.

"Eva played Elizabeth Bennett in one of the ubiquitously dreary BBC versions of *Pride and Prejudice*, after which Hollywood nabbed her for anything that required a Brit accent, but she's losing it now—not the accent, of course, but everything else is sagging and deteriorating." Mandy pouted. "The old days were so much kinder, weren't they? What was wrong with filming through gauze or using a bit of tape under the hairline for a temporary lift? Now everyone expects you to have surgery, and then, after you get attacked by some overpriced cosmetic-thingy and look like Mrs. Frankenstein, they ditch you anyway and hire someone new." Mandy took a deep breath and ran her fingers through her tawny bangs. "I could pass for twenty if they filmed me through gauze," she sighed.

"They didn't hire you to look twenty," Petunia pointed out. "The extras will be thirty feet from the camera and you'll be covered in hairy wigs and three-inches of character makeup. Then they'll alter everything digitally, so God knows what you'll look like in the final cut. The only female who'll appear human will be Trinket Rand, and she doesn't want to look twenty because, in her eyes, anything over seventeen is over the hill."

Petunia's mother deviated onto another course without missing a beat.

"Whatever happened to the Grace Kellys and Elizabeth Taylors of the world? Even if their private lives were a bit iffy, at least their public images were the epitome of grace and elegance. Can you imagine having Trinket Rand as a role model for your daughters? If she gets any more photos taken with her tongue sticking out, she'll qualify to be a centerfold for a *National Geographic* colour fold-out on tropical lizards."

Edwina appeared in the doorway to announce dinner. Mandy ignored the summons.

"Still, what do I care if the masses want to idolize a termite and an iguana?" she said, cavalierly reaching for the bottle of Glenlivet to top up her drink. "Pet and I have a job, and we're making a new start. I was pretty down having to leave England and head for the Colonies, but at least we're in British Columbia and not Froggyland on the other side of the country. I don't know how poor Henry can stand it there."

Oblivious to her hostess's comportment, which could have rivalled Lot's wife turning into a pillar of salt, Mandy prattled on.

"We're stashing away our paycheques because we're not having to pay rent or buy food, and with any luck, the filming will happen within walking distance of this house. We won't even need to buy a car. We can borrow the Beary wagon for anything else we want to do. As far as I'm concerned, the longer the gig lasts the better, and with the current awful weather, it's bound to drag on. If we stay until the fall, I'll even be able to help Bertram with his election campaign. I'm very good at that kind of thing."

Mandy stood and waved a hand graciously to the assembled company.

"Now come along, everyone." She gestured across the hall as if she were the person who had toiled in the kitchen all afternoon. "Dinner is served. Do come into the dining room."

Her hosts were stunned into silence. Mutely they watched their visitors file out of the living room. When only he and Edwina remained, Beary found his voice.

"She'll help with my election campaign over my dead body," he muttered mulishly.

"If she's still staying here by election day, it'll be over *her* dead body," his wife replied.

Beary nodded glumly. For once in total harmony, he and Edwina joined their guests for dinner.

*   *   *

Mandy's prediction about the shoot dragging on proved correct, for the weather persisted in its cycle of wind, rain and snow flurries, and the house in the woods became more a source of interest for the dog-walkers than an actual work site. However, it gradually progressed, acquiring a coal chute, a basement entrance, and a sugar-glass window with an inlaid wolf design on the top pane. Before long, the park users were on first-name terms with the techies and security guards, and the film crew became familiar with the names of the local dogs and their assorted quirks and habits. The daily walkers and their pets continued to be entertained by optimistic crewmembers trucking up and down the trails and transforming the park into a wonderland of sandbags, tripods, cables, and banks of floodlights, the scope of which seemed to validate Laura and Jennifer's prediction that the site was indeed a location for *Baying at the Moon*. To Beary's granddaughters' chagrin, Juliette had insisted that they return to their home on the Sunshine Coast, but she promised the girls another weekend in town if and when the set did turn out to be for the werewolf movie and her father notified her that the filming had begun.

To Jennifer and Laura's delight, Beary obliged two weeks later. He had met two teenagers scouting the area while on his morning ramble through the park. The schoolgirls were in touch, via iPhones and Blackberries, with other determined teens all over the Lower Mainland and they were tracking the movements of the stars with military precision. They were remarkably well versed in the filming schedule and they told Beary when his granddaughters would have their best chance of sighting Darcy Magellan. A subsequent call to Petunia, who had been working at the studio where the interior scenes were being shot, corroborated this news. Thus, Juliette, good-natured mother that she was, brought her daughters back the following weekend and took them for an evening foray into the park. There, with Petunia's assistance, the girls managed to sneak through the underbrush and get a photograph of the Werewolf himself, leering lustily at the amply-endowed woman who was touching up his makeup. The girls went back to the Sunshine Coast with their treasure, having informed their grandfather that they were going to Photoshop themselves into the picture to replace the makeup lady and send the results to all their friends.

As the weeks wore on, Edwina, like the werewolf in the movie, felt the urge to bay at the moon, for although Petunia was working on set, Mandy had not yet been called and was, as Beary commented, as restless as a tiger, even if she was only a cougar.

Petunia regaled the family nightly with tales of the film's progress: director, Hank Evergreen, was a nervous wreck; the budget-paring producer was apoplectic over the weather delays; Darcy Magellan spent so much time dissing Trinket Rand that she had quit speaking to him except when she had to deliver dialogue; Trinket had the hots for Jareth Grady, the drummer with Howl, who appeared to have nothing better to do than to hang out on the set and work her up into a sweat; and Darcy's bodyguard was ready to quit, because the teen star was as creative at finding ways to slip his chains as the character he played in the movie.

Petunia was unimpressed by the behaviour of the actors, but she liked the production staff. She blushed very prettily every time she mentioned Will Street, who was head of the camera crew, and she had found a good-natured soul mate in Jane Morgan, the continuity girl. So in spite of the turmoil generated by the stars, Petunia was enjoying her work—until the day that the extras were called on set.

Her hopes that her mother could remain concealed among the massed chorus of werewolves were quickly dashed. In fact, Mandy only managed to last one day before Hank Evergreen fired her. Trinket Rand might remain silent when dealing with the insults of her leading man, but she did not have to hold her peace over an extra who referred to her as The Iguana, even if the words had not been said in her hearing and were only reported after the fact, and with great glee, by Darcy Magellan. The tantrum Trinket threw resulted in Mandy being peremptorily ordered to turn in her costume and leave the set.

What no one was to anticipate was that she would not only leave the film set, but that she would completely disappear.

*   *   *

Never one to apologize or grovel, Mandy had accepted her dismissal with no more than a blazing glare at the unfortunate minion who had been given the task of notifying her why she was off the job. However, she was boiling mad. Once she had tossed her wig and gown and changed into her own clothes, she circled the film set trying to spot Darcy Magellan. Since her job as an extra was history, she had no intention of leaving without giving him a piece of her mind. The park was dark, except for the few eerie green patches that were lit by floodlights, so it was hard to pick people out. A light rain had started to fall, but the crew was preparing to forge on with the scene between Trinket and the Werewolf's grandmother.

Darcy was nowhere on the set, and Mandy wondered if he had been dismissed for the day. She was about to give up and leave the park when she spotted her quarry. He was heading into the small gully that Beary and his granddaughters referred to as Dingle Dell, and if Mandy was not mistaken, Darcy's purpose was a quiet joint. His bodyguard, whom Mandy had assessed as about as useful as a camel with webbed feet, was nowhere in sight.

Darcy stopped at the base of the gulley and sat on a log. There was just enough light spilling from the lamps on the trail for Mandy to see the predicted joint come out. Her blood was up. She marched down and confronted him.

"So this is how you spend your break. Why am I not surprised?"

"Piss off," said Darcy. "I'm through for the day anyway," he added. "They can't shoot in this weather."

"That isn't rain, you little pothead," said Mandy. "It's Jane Austen shedding tears."

"Get lost." With the hand that wasn't holding his joint, Darcy pulled a vial out of his jacket pocket.

"Now what are you taking?" Mandy persisted. "Viagra?"

"None of your bloody business."

Mandy snatched the vial and peered at the label.

"What does a kid like you need with sleeping pills?" she said.

"Give those back. If I don't take one now, I'll never unwind enough to get any sleep. Have you any idea how much stress there is on my job?"

"At least you have one," said Mandy. She popped the vial down the front of her blouse. Then, happily conscious of the rising fury in her companion, she took out her cellphone.

"What the hell do you think you're doing?" demanded Darcy.

"Phoning the police," said Mandy calmly. "Don't you know it's illegal to smoke pot in a public park? Too bad those floodlights aren't beaming on you or I could have taken a photo."

"Now listen, you . . ."

Darcy paused and stared over Mandy's shoulder. She swung round and saw the beam of a flashlight approaching.

"Perfect," said Mandy. "The cops love to have evidence."

She switched her phone to camera and waited for the light to hit Darcy. That would teach the little jerk to get her fired.

Darcy grabbed at the phone and forced Mandy's arm down.

"Okay," he said, "let's negotiate. I don't need any crap from the cops. What do you want?"

Mandy gave a glacial smile. She was beginning to enjoy her evening after all.

* * *

Since the Bearys were attending a party that evening and did not get home until midnight, they did not notice the absence of their houseguest until the next day. Petunia had worked until the early hours of the morning, so she was unaware of her mother's disappearance too.

Darcy Magellan had also faded from sight, but the film company was blissfully unconcerned about their star's absence, for Kevin Prentiss, the Werewolf's bodyguard, had received a text message from his employer's phone shortly after Darcy had left the set. Darcy was heading back to their borrowed West Vancouver oceanfront mansion with the sex-partner-*du-soir* that he had managed to pick up for the night. The message was confirmed by a member of the camera crew who informed Kevin that he had seen Darcy driving away with the middle-aged, but distinctly lush lady who had been fired for insulting Trinket Rand.

Kevin grinned when he received this piece of news. He had a reputation for being lax, and never failed to take advantage of an opportunity to spend an evening at the pub. He had his own car at the park, because Darcy always insisted on driving himself with his entourage following behind, a habit that struck terror into the hearts of the studio heads who regularly bordered on nervous breakdowns over issues of liability. Kevin invited three of the crew members to join him and they drove into Yaletown, doing the rounds of the bars until three the next morning. When he eventually arrived back at the West Vancouver house, he turned in and slept a sound, lager-induced sleep until ten the following morning, when the maid arrived to tidy up and do the rooms. A do-not-disturb sign was hanging on Darcy's door, and since the Werewolf was not needed for the shoot that evening, Kevin told the maid not to worry about his room.

Kevin went out for his usual morning jog along the seawall. At the far end of Dundarave, he stopped to check his messages. A new text message informed him that Darcy had risen and was going to walk to the coffee shop in Ambleside where he intended to hang out and wait for Kevin to join him. Kevin completed his run and wandered into the café. Darcy was nowhere in sight. Kevin ordered coffee and sat down, prepared to wait.

As he sat, drinking his latte and enjoying the easy-listening jazz flowing from the speakers over his head, Kevin heard sirens approaching. The noise grew louder, reached a blaring crescendo on the far side of the plate glass, and abruptly ceased. From the sidewalk outside, the clamour of voices rose to a pitch that drowned out the smooth voice of Diana Krall and brought every patron of the coffee shop to the front window to see what was going on. Kevin went outside and saw two West Vancouver police officers being accosted by an attractive brunette who was waving her arms dramatically and shrieking hysterically.

"It was Darcy Magellan," she cried. "I'd know him anywhere. They snatched him. He was walking on the seawall, and they grabbed him and bundled him into a van. Don't you get it? The Werewolf has been kidnapped!"

*   *   *

Around the time that the police were hearing of Darcy Magellan's abduction, Petunia took a cup of tea up to Mandy's room and found it deserted. The bed had not been slept in. Petunia rushed downstairs to announce that her mother was missing, and in spite of their ambivalence towards their difficult houseguest, Beary and Edwina began to worry. Walking home from Fernie Park in the dark was potentially perilous for a woman alone.

"We'd better call the police." Petunia's voice was trembling.

"The RCMP won't act on a missing-person's report for at least twenty-four hours," Beary told her.

Before Petunia could reply, her cellphone rang. She answered the call and beamed with delight when she heard Will Street's voice on the other end. But the smile faded almost instantly and her face grew ashen as she listened to what he had to tell her. Then she ended the call, sank onto a kitchen chair and burst into tears. When Beary and Edwina managed to calm her sufficiently to elicit information as to what had happened, she wailed, "Darcy Magellan has been kidnapped!"

"Well, that's hardly a loss to the world," said Edwina unsympathetically.

"No! You don't understand." Petunia broke back into sobs. "Will says my mother left the park with Darcy last night. Everyone is accusing her. They're saying it's some kind of revenge thing because he got her fired."

"That's nonsense," scoffed Beary. "Your mother may be a nut bar, but she isn't a criminal."

Edwina looked doubtful.

"You've always said Amanda was a law unto herself. I wouldn't put anything past her."

Petunia's howls grew louder. Beary glowered at Edwina and patted the sobbing girl on the shoulder.

"Brace up, Pet," he said. "I'll get hold of Richard, and I'll phone Philippa too. She can call her friend at VPD. One way or another, we'll find out what's going on."

However, when Beary called Richard, he only connected with his voicemail, so he left a message and tried his daughter's number. Fortunately, Philippa was at home. When she heard about Mandy's disappearance and the rumours that were abounding on the set, she was horrified. She rang off and immediately phoned Bob Miller's cell.

To her surprise, Miller cut her explanation short and told her to come down to the police station right away. He also warned her not to say anything to the other members of her family. He would say nothing more over the phone, so, riddled with curiosity, she drove downtown, found a parking spot and hurried over to the police station. When she was shown in to see Miller, she saw that his face was grave.

"There's already been a ransom demand," he informed her, "and that's not all. Wait till you see this. It was texted to Nathan Bellows from Darcy Magellan's cellphone."

"Who's Nathan Bellows?"

"The studio head who's going to drop a bundle if this film doesn't get made."

Miller clicked an icon on his computer and a picture materialized on the screen.

Philippa gasped. It was an image of Darcy Magellan, terrified and cowering on all fours, while Mandy Piggott-Smythe stood over him holding a revolver to his head.

The expression on Cousin Mandy's face left no doubt that she was prepared to use the weapon.

*   *   *

Earlier that morning, Mandy had woken up with her head feeling groggy. A vague series of pictures floated in front of her eyes. She remembered her confrontation with Darcy in Fernie Park but everything after that was a bewildering tangle of images. Just as she had managed to subdue the little toe-rag to the point where he was ready to help her get her job back, a light had fallen on him and he had risen backwards off his log as if magically levitated. Then the light had gone out and something that felt ominously like the barrel of a gun had been pressed into the small of her back. What had happened next? She had a recollection of a gravelly voice ordering her to keep quiet and march. She and the termite had been taken to the parking lot and forced to get into the front seats of a car, and all the while, the guttural voice kept muttering instructions. No, there had been two voices, and they were both coming from the back seat. When she'd glanced sideways, she had seen a gleaming black gun barrel. With rising fury, she recalled how the termite had obediently driven away. And then nothing. Nothing until she had woken up. But where the hell was she?

She appeared to be lying on a singularly lumpy mattress, and the hardness beneath her, along with the chill that permeated through to her back, indicated that it had been laid out on a cement floor. She struggled to sit up and peered into the gloom. A sliver of light filtered through from a crack below a door, and as her eyes adjusted, she saw that she was in what must be a cellar, for the walls and floor were concrete, and there were no windows. She dimly made out a second door on the side of the room. Stiffly, she rolled onto her knees and stood up. She crossed to the door. It opened, but simply led to a tiny windowless cubicle with toilet and sink. A string hanging from the ceiling hit her face, and when she pulled it, a bare ceiling bulb illuminated the washroom. Her face, pale and distressingly creased around the eyes, stared back at her from a cracked, unframed mirror that hung above the sink, suspended by three rickety-looking screws. She dabbed her face with water and straightened the strands that had escaped from her French braid, then turned back and scanned the room to see if her purse lay anywhere. The light spilled out from the washroom and she could see quite plainly. There was no sign of the handbag. Other than the bedding, the room was completely bare.

A groan emanated from the mattress, and Mandy perceived that the long bundle of blankets on the other side of the makeshift bed was inhabited. She walked across and shoved it with her foot. Darcy Magellan's face, unshaven, unwashed and distinctly unappetizing, emerged from its woollen shroud.

"Where am I?" he moaned.

"No idea." Mandy always cut to the chase. "But I suspect some avaricious sod has decided to use you to augment his bank balance, and I have no intention of letting my life be ruined because a tasteless juvenile public has turned you into a hot commodity."

Darcy looked blank. "Talk English, can't you?" he grunted.

"We've been kidnapped, you twit," snapped Mandy. "Or rather, you've been kidnapped, and I'm the unfortunate innocent bystander."

Darcy's eyes focussed. "Oh, shit, not you again," he said. "What did they bring you for? Just to torture me?"

"Probably," said Mandy, "but that's irrelevant. Come on, Termite, on your feet. We have to figure out a way to get out of here."

"Yeah, right." Darcy's eyes swept around the windowless walls. "We'll get out soon enough. The studio will cough up whatever money these guys want. I'm going back to sleep."

"Don't be ridiculous. How can you be sure they'll pay up? It's not as if you have any real talent, not like Elvis or Paul McCartney. They could replace you in an instant."

"Bullshit," said Darcy. "My fans would tear the studio apart." He grinned languorously. "Even cougars like you have the hots for me. In fact," he added, eyeing Mandy's cleavage, "why don't you stop yapping and get back under the blankets. We don't have anything else to do while we wait."

"Don't be disgusting. Make another suggestion like that and I'll wash your mouth out with the no-brand soap in that rat-hole that passes for a bathroom. You may think you're God's gift, but I don't share your confidence that the world will give its all to have you back. I can't see any Japanese girls leaping into volcanoes over your demise."

"What the hell are you talking about now?"

"Ignorant as well as vapid," sighed Mandy. "I was referring to Rudolph Valentino and all the devastated women who committed suicide when he died."

"Man, are you that old?" said Darcy. "You're not a cougar, you're an elephant."

"And I never forget," Mandy fired back, "so watch what you say while we're stuck in here together." She glanced at her wrist to check the time. Her watch wasn't there. Then she remembered. She had slipped it off and dropped it as their abductors marched them along the trail. Surely someone would have found it by now.

There was a sudden sound of movement on the far side of the door. It opened and a burly man came through. He was dressed in black jeans and a grey sleeveless T-shirt, which exposed the dragon tattoos on both his arms. His head was shaven and a series of gold studs pierced his ear lobes and nostrils. A camera swung from a strap around his neck. He carried a tray with two mugs and two large soup bowls, which he set down on the floor beside the door. Behind him came a smaller man, slight, but somehow tougher-looking, with dark hair and mean, pebble-like eyes. He carried a gun in each hand.

"Enter Thug One and Thug Two," drawled Mandy. She nodded towards the guns. "Isn't that overkill?" she said. "Afraid we might overpower you."

"Shut up," said the man. He waved one gun at Mandy. "Get over here. We're going to do a camera shoot."

"Not with me," said Mandy. "Not unless you give me back my purse. I'm not having any pictures taken without freshening up my makeup."

Pebble-eyes nodded to his partner.

"Go find bigmouth's makeup," he said equably. "We can't have her looking like a dog for the picture." He waved the gun at Darcy. "You, out of your blanket. You're going to be in it too."

"Shouldn't you let him shave first?" suggested Mandy, "or do you actually want that fuzzy lupine aura?"

Pebble-eyes ignored her. The man with the dragon tattoos returned and silently handed Mandy her cosmetic bag. The two men waited patiently while Mandy went to the bathroom and applied her makeup in front of the small mirror. Something about their patience was vaguely unsettling, and glancing in the mirror at the scene behind her, she could tell from Darcy's stance that he was uneasy too. No guts, thought Mandy unsympathetically. She closed her makeup kit and set it on the counter. Then, bracing herself, she turned and stepped back into the room. She pointed imperiously at the bowls on the tray by the door.

"I hope that revolting slop isn't dinner," she sniffed.

Dragon-tattoos looked hurt.

"It's goulash," he said. "It's really good."

"Let me guess. You're the chef."

"Yes—" The man glowered defiantly—"and if you don't want it, I'll eat it."

Pebble-eyes began to look impatient.

"Yeah, well, if we don't do this picture, it'll be cold slop," he snapped. "Then it'll be even more disgusting. Get your camera ready," he ordered his partner. "On your knees," he added sharply to Darcy. "You, doll," he said, turning to Mandy, "take this." He handed her the gun in his left hand. "Point it at his head."

"With pleasure," said Mandy, taking the gun and gluing it to Darcy's temple in one swift movement. "I don't like him anyway. Can I pull the trigger?"

"Got it!" cried Dragon-tattoo.

Pebble-eyes beamed and retrieved the gun.

"It's not loaded, you silly cow."

"Well, obviously," said Mandy. "I knew that."

"Yeah, but he didn't." Her captor pointed gleefully at Darcy who, white-faced, was still quivering on his mattress. "Great shot. He should give randy little Trinket acting lessons. If she could look that petrified when she faces the predator wolf, she'd be up for an Oscar."

*   *   *

"I don't believe it," said Philippa, when she regained her composure. She turned away from the computer screen and faced Bob Miller. "Either Magellan has offered Mandy an insane amount of money to participate in a publicity stunt, or this photo has been doctored in some way. The saying, *the camera never lies*, isn't valid any more. These days, the camera can and does lie."

"Not according to our computer experts. They say this picture hasn't been altered. It's the real thing. Your cousin was seen driving away with Magellan last night and all the evidence leads us to believe that she spent the night with him at the West Vancouver house where he was staying."

"That's ludicrous. Mandy wouldn't touch Darcy Magellan with a bargepole. If she's in league with him, it's purely for money—and if she isn't, there's only one other possibility—that she was forced to pose for that shot."

Miller nodded soberly. "Yes, you're probably right. Even your Cousin Mandy couldn't be so dumb that she'd voluntarily allow that photo to go to the cop shop, but what puzzles me is why she was snatched too. Magellan was taken on the sea wall, and our witness made no mention of seeing anyone else with him. The only thing I can surmise is that Mandy discovered what was about to happen and they took her because she knew too much. There must have been someone at the house who was in on it. The kidnappers must have been tipped off about Magellan's movements."

"Oh, God," moaned Philippa. "If that's the case, Mandy's in more danger than Darcy Magellan because she's of no value to them."

"I don't know," said Miller, trying to be flippant and alleviate Philippa's fears. "After what I saw of her at your family dinner, the kidnappers might be willing to pay for us to take her back. Your cousin struck me as a pretty tough cookie."

"Don't joke about it," said Philippa. "I'm really worried about Mandy. Don't you see? She'll tell them exactly what she thinks of them and they won't think twice about blowing her away."

Miller had already considered that possibility, but had said nothing. He was far more worried than he let on.

"What are the police doing?" Philippa asked. "Have they any leads at all?"

"The woman who saw the abduction didn't get the licence number, but we know it's a blue Econoline van, fairly old and battered, and it took off up Fifteenth Street, so it's a given that it was heading for the Upper Levels Highway. There was one sighting from a motorist who said he saw a similar vehicle on the Squamish Highway, but none of our patrols have turned up anything so far. Still, it has to show up somewhere. Every member of the public is on the alert and hot to help—let's face it, it's the most high-profile case we've had in years—so that van can't hide forever."

"What's happening with the ransom?"

"Bellows has been told not to pay and to leave it to the Force."

"Good luck," said Philippa. "He's not going to hold up his picture while you investigate."

"Actually," said Miller, "amazingly enough, he is. He seems quite happy not to pay. He informed us that he was the one who had made Darcy Magellan, and he could just as easily create a new star from any one of the grimy adolescent rock singers that frequent the planet. He cited Magellan's drummer, Jareth Grady, as a case in point. He's quite prepared to let Magellan go down in history as another James Dean if necessary."

"He's replacing him already?"

"Not quite yet. That would appear too callous. He says he'll reschedule and have the director shoot the scenes that don't involve Magellan, but if push comes to shove, he'll be replaced."

"Well, if it is a publicity stunt, Magellan won't let that happen. He'll manage a miraculous escape before he loses his part. But where does that leave my cousin?"

The door opened and a diminutive blonde entered the room. She was no taller than Philippa, but her slender figure looked wiry and strong, and although she wore a smart green pantsuit, she projected an image of freshness and the great outdoors. She was about to speak, but she stopped when she noticed Philippa.

Miller made the introductions. "This is Detective Constable Tara McGee. My new partner," he told Philippa. "Go ahead, Tara," he added. "Philippa knows what's going on."

The detective seemed mildly taken aback, but she delivered her message.

"We've just had a report," she said. "A van answering the right description has been spotted parked behind a chalet at Whistler. We're checking to see who owns the place right now."

Miller stood up.

"I have to go," he said to Philippa. "Keep this to yourself, and let me know if anyone in the family hears anything about Mandy."

With that, he stood and followed his partner out the door.

*   *   *

Mandy had no idea whether it was morning or evening. The only way to judge the passing of time was by the thrice-daily deposit of the meal tray, but since she and Darcy had been given a steady diet of watery coffee and goulash, breakfast, lunch and dinner had become virtually indistinguishable. Darcy appeared content to drift off to sleep between the indigestible meals, and as Mandy's requests for something to read had been met with three dilapidated back-issues of *People* magazine, she was ready to scream with boredom. She was contemplating emulating Darcy and having a nap when she heard raised voices on the far side of the door.

She walked quietly across the room and glued her ear to the door. Dragon Tattoo and his associate were having an argument. As Mandy listened, her eyes widened, and then narrowed dangerously. A moment later, a door slammed and the voices ceased. Mandy kept her ear to the door panel. She heard shuffling footsteps and the clatter of crockery being set out. Dinner, or lunch, or breakfast was about to be served. She padded back to the mattress, settled herself comfortably, and gave Darcy a vigorous shove with her elbow.

"Wake up, Termite," she said. "Chef Tattoo's *plat du jour* is on the way."

"You woke me up for that?"

Darcy, bleary-eyed, squinted towards the door, which was opening to reveal Dragon Tattoo coming through with a tray, then pulled the blanket around his shoulders and lay back down.

"Don't mind him," said Mandy sweetly. "He's a little discouraged. I'm sure he'll eat in a minute, and if he doesn't want it, I'll call you and you can have it."

"Do that," grunted the man with the tattoo. He set the tray on the floor and left the room.

"Oh dear," said Mandy. "He's stressed. It must be because Mr. Bellows has refused to pay the ransom."

The blanket beside her twitched and Darcy's head emerged.

"What did you just say?"

"Your precious studio head. He's decided you're not worth it. I just overheard them talking out there."

Darcy sat bolt upright.

"Shit! You're kidding. You're just trying to upset me, right?"

"Wrong. We have to get ourselves out of here. No one else is going to do it."

Darcy stared wild-eyed at Mandy. The arrogant superstar had vanished and in its place was a frightened teenager.

"How do we have a hope in hell of doing that?"

"Well, for starters, we'll have to put Dragon Tattoo out of commission." Mandy reached into her cleavage and pulled out the vial she had confiscated from Darcy in the park.

"Those are my sleeping pills!"

"Exactly, and since I overheard Thug One telling his buddy that he was going into town, we only have one body to deal with on the other side of that door." As she talked, Mandy pulled off her silk scarf, placed it on the cement floor and poured the contents of the vial onto it. "Give me your shoe," she demanded. Darcy obliged, and, using the heel, she ground the pills into powder. Then she picked up the scarf and emptied the contents into Darcy's bowl of goulash.

"Hey, that's *my* dinner," grumbled Darcy.

"You said you didn't want it." Mandy hopped up and went to the bathroom, extracted her tail comb from her makeup kit, and returned to give the contents of the goulash bowl a vigorous stir. "Now, lie back down and pretend to be asleep," she ordered.

"Why?"

"I'm going to call greedy-guts back in and tell him you don't want your dinner. Haven't you noticed? He always finishes off anything we don't eat. In about an hour from now, he should be having a really good nap."

"Good nap! You might kill him."

"No, I won't. Haven't you noticed the size of the man? Anyway, there were only four pills left. Just enough to knock him out. All I have to do is use my irresistible charm to keep him in here for long enough for the stuff to take effect and then we'll be off and away."

Darcy snorted rudely. "And what charm would that be? There's a side of you I haven't seen yet?"

"Just shut up and lie down."

Darcy did as he was told. Mandy picked up the bowl of goulash and stepped over to the door. She knocked loudly and called out, "Darcy really doesn't feel like eating. He hasn't touched this, so you might as well have it. Seems a pity to waste good food, and it really is quite tasty. It's growing on me."

In more ways than one, she added mentally.

There was the sound of a chair scraping back, and a moment later the door opened. Dragon Tattoo loomed in the opening. Mandy held out the bowl and gave him a seductive smile.

"Why don't you eat in here while I have mine," she simpered. "I hate dining alone."

Dragon Tattoo took the bowl from her outstretched hands.

"Yeah, me too," he said. "But it sure as hell beats eating with a stuck-up English broad with a big mouth and an attitude."

The door slammed shut in Mandy's face. There was the unmistakable rasping as the key turned in the lock. Darcy's face popped out from the blanket.

"So what's plan number two?" he said.

*   *   *

By the weekend, the police investigation had stalled. The blue van at Whistler turned out to belong to a retired teacher who was supplementing his pension with a small carpentry business, and no further leads had materialized. Petunia had become a shadow of her former self, consumed with anxiety, and ridden with guilt over every flippant quip about her mother that had ever escaped her lips. Mandy might be aggravating, but Petunia loved her all the same.

The weather had finally warmed up and the filming in Fernie Park was finished. By Saturday morning, the only remaining workmen were the cleanup crew who had the daunting task of returning the park to normal and removing every miniscule item that might create a hazard for the regular walkers. Knowing that the park would be busy, Beary decided to take his morning walk in the adjacent Sidley Lands. As he was leashing MacPuff in the front garden, Philippa's Jeep pulled into the driveway. She hopped out, and seeing that her father was setting off for a walk, offered to accompany him. MacPuff greeted Philippa exuberantly. He was always happy to see another member of the family, but after a moment, she pushed him away.

"Persistent, isn't he?" commented Beary.

"It's my scarf," said Philippa. "It's Mandy's. She gave it to me because it matched my jacket. MacPuff must have picked up her scent. He's the only family member that loves her without any reservations."

Beary nodded. "Mandy's good with dogs," he acknowledged. "She often walked with us. If she talked to humans the way she talks to canines, she'd be a lot more popular."

Philippa sighed. "Poor Mandy. I know she's infuriating, but I'm still fond of her. I hate to think what she's going through."

She bent to stroke Minx the Manx who had prowled around from the back garden to see what was going on. Then she followed her father up the driveway, and they set off with MacPuff eagerly leading the way. They walked through the lanes, where a riot of buttercups, dandelions and bluebells bordered the back fences of the adjacent lots. Soon, they reached the entrance to the woods, which was framed in a tangle of blackberry bushes and morning glory, the pink flowers of the blackberries thrusting up valiantly amid the white bell-shaped blossoms of the invasive vines.

Once in the woods, Beary unleashed MacPuff and the dog trotted ahead. They walked a short distance on the main trail, then cut into a narrow path by a massive hemlock that Philippa had loved from childhood because of its strategically placed knotholes and plate mushrooms that made it resemble a storybook talking tree. The trail was a favourite route for dog-walkers. It descended through a series of ravines before rising again and coming back to a wide gravel path that connected the top trail with the power line by the freeway. The circuit provided lots of freedom for the dogs and a good workout for the owners.

MacPuff raced back and forth while Beary and Philippa negotiated the twists and turns, but as they climbed out of the last ravine, a high-pitched yelp cut the air. MacPuff's head jerked up. Eyes glittering, he bolted forward and shot through the bushes at the top of the rise. Beary bellowed at him to stop, but the dog did not return. Swearing profusely, Beary broke into a trot. Philippa sprinted ahead of him, but by the time she broke through the bushes and reached the gravel path, MacPuff was bounding down the hill towards the power line.

Philippa sighed. Dog walks with the family's various ill-trained pets had always been an adventure when her father was in—or more appropriately—not in control. Beary burst out of the bushes, huffing, red-faced and fully justifying the nickname of Grampus that Jennifer had given him at age two. He hollered again, but MacPuff ignored the command and loped onto the power line.

But then, miraculously, the dog stopped and shoved his nose vigorously into a clump of ferns at the side of the path. Beary puffed down the bank and clipped the leash back onto the dog's collar.

"Obstinate animal," he growled.

Philippa caught up to her father. "What set him off?" she asked. "Coyotes?"

"Yes." Beary scowled. "Last time Jennifer and Laura were here, he took off for three quarters of an hour and came back stinking of dead fish that he'd stolen from their lair. God knows what distracted him this time, but I'm glad something caught his attention. If I have too many more runs like that, I'm going to have a heart attack."

"How are Jennifer and Laura?" asked Philippa, tactfully changing the subject and slowing the pace to give her father a chance to recover. "Did they ever get their photograph of Darcy Magellan?"

"Yes, they did." Beary's breathing was gradually returning to normal. "They emailed the picture to us a couple of days ago—both the original and the Photoshopped one."

"Photoshopped?"

"They blanked out the woman with Magellan and stuck their own faces on. Very resourceful," said Beary proudly. "There were some other people in the background too, and they replaced them with trees. The end result is Darcy Magellan posing in the forest with both of my granddaughters. No idea how they did it."

"It's not that hard," said Philippa. "These days, the camera lies. Why don't we walk back via the park," she suggested. We're practically there. Let's go see what the film crew is doing."

"There's no more filming," said Beary. "It's just the reconstruction crew, running around on their gators and cleaning up the mess. But we can go that way if you like."

Still keeping MacPuff leashed, they walked along the power line until it came out on the road that led to Fernie Park. Philippa raised her eyebrows when she saw the tangled, overgrown gardens at the end of the cul-de-sac.

"These properties have deteriorated since the last time I was here."

"Only the two end houses. They've been unoccupied for three years now. The homes at the top of the hill are well-maintained."

MacPuff veered to the right and tried to go up the driveway of the property that abutted the power line, but Beary pulled him away and dragged the reluctant dog past. Then he and Philippa continued up the hill and into the park.

The clean-up crew had done a remarkable job. If one had not known about the filming, it would have been impossible to guess that the shoot had taken place. All the equipment had been removed and no trace remained of the cottage. One solitary worker stood in the glade. He was eyeing the ground carefully.

"That's the stuff," said Beary. "Make sure there aren't any sharp objects to cut the dogs' paws."

"No worries," said the crewman, who had a marked Australian accent. "We use giant magnets and metal detectors to make certain we get all our gear . . . along with a few extras we didn't drop," he added with a grin, holding up a silver Rolex watch and a cellphone in a bright pink case. "Can't imagine why someone hasn't come back to claim these little gems," he said.

He paused, surprised and gratified at the reaction from his audience, for Philippa and Beary's jaws dropped and, in unison, they chorused, "Those belong to Mandy!"

*   *   *

Mandy had her ear to the door.

"He's snoring like a buzz saw," she said. "This is our chance. We have to get out of here before his buddy gets back."

"You keep saying that," said Darcy. "You tell me how we're going to do it. That door is solid as a fu—bloody tank," Darcy amended, wilting under Mandy's steely-eyed gaze, "and even if we could break it down, dough-brain out there wouldn't sleep through that. What's more, the hinges are on the outside, not to mention the key for that double-cylinder lock, so you tell me what miracle you've got planned."

Mandy eyed the lock. Seeing it was attached with Philips screws, she glanced down and fingered the buttons on her jacket.

"Oh, great," groaned Darcy. "As if anyone cares what you look like right now."

"Don't be stupid," snapped Mandy. "I need something hard and thin. We'll unscrew the lock and take it right out."

Darcy's expression changed to one of interest.

"Now, that's not such a bad idea. What did they leave you in that makeup kit? A nail file would be perfect?"

Mandy shook her head.

"No. All they left me was the plastic comb and the makeup."

Mandy's eyes peered at Darcy's rear end. "Don't you have one of those plate-thingys on your overpriced designer jeans? Damn. Why couldn't you be wearing a belt like a normal person?"

"Why couldn't you?" Darcy retorted.

"I know. The clasp on your zipper. Take your jeans off. We'll try and detach it."

"Use your own bloody zip."

"I don't have one. This skirt has elastic. Come on, I won't tell anyone I've seen the Werewolf in his shorts."

"I don't need to take my jeans off." Darcy went red in the face as he heaved on the top of the zipper. With a triumphant grin, he wrenched it free and held it up. "Okay, now what?"

"Undo the screws."

Darcy slid the top of the zipper into the slot. It fit neatly but after an attempt to turn the screw, he frowned and stepped back.

"I can't get enough leverage."

"Let me try. My fingers are smaller."

"It won't work," said Darcy. "You need something long for a handle. Crap." He scowled at the lock.

Mandy's eyes widened. She reached into the back of her French braid and triumphantly pulled out a steel hairpin. Darcy grabbed it and slid the zipper head back into the slot. Then he threaded the steel hairpin through the hole in the zipper head and twisted it to the right.

"Not that way, idiot," snapped Mandy. "Righty tighty, lefty loosey. God, I wish I were holed up with a techie or a proper juvenile delinquent instead of someone who just twiddles guitars and makes goo-eyes at pubescent girls."

Darcy ignored the slur and exerted pressure the other way. The screw shifted slightly, and with a beam of delight that made him suddenly appear the kid he really was, he tackled the task until, at last, the plate gave way and he could pull it free. He peered into the hole. There were two more screws inside, so with an industry that his film directors had never witnessed, he attacked the second set of screws until, with a loud clunk, the entire lock disintegrated. There was a thump on the far side of the door as the outer plate fell. Darcy and Mandy froze. The rumbling snore beyond the door erupted into a snort. Then, after a moment, the rhythmic breathing began again.

Darcy turned to Mandy with a grin. She held a finger to her lips and quietly turned the door handle. Darcy gently lowered the inside section of the lock to the floor, then followed Mandy through the open doorway. Mandy slid the pieces of broken lock back inside the room and gently closed the door.

They found themselves in a drab kitchen with ancient appliances and chipped Arborite counters. Dragon Tattoo was slumped at the table, his right arm tucked pillow-like under his head and his face turned sideways. Two empty bowls stood at the centre of the table, and Darcy's Blackberry lay near his right hand.

Darcy reached for his Blackberry, but Mandy snatched it up and took a picture of the comatose man. Having saved the photograph, she punched in Miller's number and pressed send. Then she handed Darcy his Blackberry and they tiptoed out the door.

The kitchen door opened onto a neglected garden, which was a mass of long grass and overgrown brambles. It was bordered by a high hedge and surrounded by an ominously thick and impenetrable stand of evergreen trees. The sky was still bright overhead, but the light was fading, and in the shadow of the trees, the visibility was poor. The only apparent way out was a path around the side of the house.

"Hold on a sec," muttered Darcy. "I have to send a message, too."

"Do it later. Come on, we've got to get out of here."

"This can't wait. It's to Nathan."

Darcy tapped out a message, a twisted smile on his face. As he pressed *send*, Mandy grabbed his wrist and held her finger to her lips.

"Sssh," she hissed. "There's a car coming."

Darcy's eyes widened as he heard the hum of a car engine approaching. There was a momentary glare of lights on the other side of the building. He shoved the Blackberry into his pocket and drew back against the rear wall of the house. Mandy froze too.

A car door opened and closed, and then footsteps were heard coming along the path.

"Quick, round here," hissed Mandy. She tugged Darcy's sleeve, and he followed her around to the other side of the house.

"Damn," said Mandy. The narrow space between the house and the hedge had been used to pile bricks and lumber. The route was completely impassable. "We'll have to run for it when he goes into the house."

"But he's going to see dough-brain the minute he opens that door."

"We'll have a couple of seconds. He'll just think his pal is having a nap and he won't realize we've escaped until he sees the broken lock on the inner door. Get ready. He's coming round the back."

The footsteps stopped. The back door creaked open and then slammed shut.

"Now," hissed Mandy, shoving Darcy back round the corner.

Rising on tiptoe, they ran across the back of the house and onto the side path. It led to a gravel drive that curved through the trees so that it was impossible to see what lay beyond. Dodging around the Dodge Ram pickup truck parked by the house, they crept down the drive. It came out onto a cul-de-sac that ended at a concrete barrier. On the other side of the concrete blocks, a path led into the woods. Mandy stared at the entrance to the cul-de-sac. The road rose up a hill towards another high bank of trees.

Mandy gasped. "My God!" she said. "I know where we are. We're back at the park."

"Look," said Darcy. "There's a car coming. Wave them down before that asshole discovers that we're out of there."

But before Mandy could respond, the headlights of the car illuminated the ground in front of them. The car stopped and the driver's door opened. A man stepped out onto the road, but from where they stood, he was no more than a silhouette.

All at once, a voice shouted out from the driveway.

"Stop them. Don't let them get away!"

"Oh shit," said Darcy. "Here we go again."

"No, we don't," snapped Mandy. "This way."

"You're kidding. That won't take us anywhere except into a bloody jungle."

Mandy yanked Darcy's arm and pulled him across the concrete barrier. Then she took off along the power line.

"Trust me," she bellowed, as she vanished into the blackening woods. Darcy saw the silhouette on the road accelerating towards him and he heard the pounding of footsteps on the drive to his left. With no other choice available, he turned and raced after Mandy.

As the black forest closed in around him, a thought flashed into his mind. *Just like my stupid bloody werewolf movie, except I don't have any techies to give me bionic powers to get me out of the mess. Real life is the pits.*

*   *   *

Philippa called Miller to report their find, but she only reached his voicemail. Rather than leave a message or talk with a dispatcher who would send a minion to collect the items, she and Beary went downtown to talk to Miller directly. He was in his office, but when they deposited Mandy's possessions on his desk, he was not as surprised as they had anticipated.

"The girl who reported the abduction has vanished," he said. "She's never lived at the address she gave us. The story of the Econoline van was a set up to create the impression that Magellan was snatched the following day. We were searching for a vehicle that didn't exist. When Magellan drove your cousin away from the park, I'd say there was someone in the back seat with a gun pointed at his head. The kidnapping happened in the park. Whoever took them was using Magellan's Blackberry to send the messages to the bodyguard to make him think Darcy had gone back to the house. So that makes me wonder who on the film set was trying to give themselves an alibi for the time Darcy was taken."

The door opened and DC McGee came into the room. Without preamble, she said, "There's another message from Magellan's Blackberry. It's a photograph. Bring it up. It's on your email."

"What the hell is this supposed to be?" said Miller, staring at the recumbent figure in the picture on the screen.

"Wait a minute," said Beary. "I know that face. I'm sure I've seen it before."

"What about the tattoo?" said Miller. "That's distinctive."

"No," said Beary. "It's the face I recognize, not the tattoo. That square, shaven head and the thick features." He peered closely at the picture. "There's something else as well," he muttered. "That blacked-out window with the peeling yellow frame . . . I've seen that somewhere too."

As he continued to scrutinize the photograph, a uniformed constable popped his head around the door.

"Nathan Bellows just called in. He's received another text message."

"Another ransom demand?"

"No." The constable shook his head and rolled his eyes. "It just said, 'Eff you, cheapskate!'"

"What is going on?" said Miller.

"Got it!" cried Beary.

Every eye in the room swung round to stare at him.

"I know who that man is." Beary tapped the computer screen and turned to Philippa. "Remember, I told you there were other people in the background of Jennifer's photograph. Well, that's one of them, and unless I'm much mistaken, he was having a cozy conversation with Darcy Magellan's bodyguard. I'll lay you odds that the incompetent bodyguard who couldn't keep track of his charge has known where the missing movie star was every step of the way. The text message telling him to take the night off and go pubbing was just to set him up with an alibi while his underlings carried out the abduction." He looked knowingly at Miller. "If you search hard enough, I bet you'll find a connection between the bodyguard and the woman who reported the kidnapping." Beary's face became smug. "What's more," he added, "I can tell you where Mandy and the Werewolf are being held. They never left Burnside. They're in the empty house at the edge of the Sidley woods. That's why MacPuff stopped and tried to go down that driveway. He knew Mandy was there."

"But they were seen driving away from the park," protested Miller. "They left the area."

"Yes, but it was dark. The house I'm talking about is just a skip and a hop from the freeway. All the kidnappers had to do was force Darcy to drive to the freeway and turn back towards Vancouver. They would have pulled over just below the Sidley Lands, walked up the bank, and hey presto, they'd be almost back where they started from. Then, once Darcy and Mandy were shut up in the house, one of the abductors could have driven the car over to the West Vancouver home, knowing everyone would assume that Darcy had taken it there himself. They knew that the last place anyone would search would be next to the park, but that's where you'll find them. I know the paintwork on that window. It's the house at the end of the cul-de-sac where the power line begins. Call my son," he added. "Richard knows where it is. He can get an RCMP unit there within minutes."

"We'll contact him right away," said DC McGee. "Actually," she added, "you come with me and speak to him. That'll facilitate matters." She hurried Beary out of the room. Miller rose to his feet. Philippa stood up.

"We'll get out of your way," she said. "I'll drive Dad home and wait there." She looked anxiously at Miller. "Please call me as soon as you get some news."

Miller's steady gaze was warm and reassuring. He took her hands and held them firmly in his own.

"Don't worry," he said, "we'll get your cousin back. I'll let you know the minute she's out."

Then with a comforting arm round her shoulder, he ushered her into the hall and returned to join his colleagues.

Feeling bemused, Philippa went down to the main entrance to wait for her father. Her tangled emotions were wound as tautly as a Gordian knot. She was deeply worried about her cousin, but she was also comforted by the obvious concern that Miller felt for her. While she stood there, guiltily aware that this was not the time to be thinking of the attraction between herself and the young detective, Beary came down the hall.

"Solving the world's problems?" he said.

Philippa blinked. "What?"

"You were lost in thought," said Beary. "Penny for 'em?"

Philippa shook her head.

"Nothing worth paying for," she said firmly. "What's the word on Mandy?"

"They're sending out the full kit and caboodle," said Beary. "Swat team, negotiators, dog squad—you name it. They'll have Mandy out in no time. Tonight's news should be exciting. A TV dinner will definitely be in order. You'd better stay and watch with us."

But as it happened, when the police arrived at the Sidley lands, they drew a blank. The kidnappers were easily apprehended, but the negotiators that had been brought in to secure the release of the victims had a wasted trip, for Mandy and Darcy had once again disappeared. Dogs were taken in to search the woods, but they returned without finding their quarry.

However, when Philippa drove her father home, they saw a grim-faced Edwina standing on the front porch. One glance at her thundercloud visage told Beary that his cousin had reappeared. Edwina frostily confirmed what her husband was thinking.

"Our houseguest is back," she snapped, "and she's brought a singularly uncouth youth with her, whom I gather is the film star everyone has been searching for. I have notified the police," she added, "so presumably we will get rid of the loutish young man fairly soon, but if you want your usual glass of Glenlivet this evening, you'd better run by the liquor store, since your cousin is working her way steadily through the last of your current supply."

Beary looked glum.

"I'm too tired to go out again," he grumbled. "I'll just have a beer, or has the werewolf depleted those supplies too?"

"Certainly not," sniffed Edwina. "He's underage. I told him he could have juice or milk, and not even that until he went upstairs to clean up. He obviously hasn't washed the entire time he was in captivity. He is now upstairs in the shower, and hopefully he'll stay there until his minders come to take him back to his billet."

Edwina swept back into the house. Philippa grinned at her father as they followed her inside. The Werewolf had finally met his match.

*   *   *

To Edwina and Beary's delight, Mandy's stay proved far briefer than they had anticipated. Three days after her reappearance, she blithely informed them that she had regained her job on set, and added, with a coyly insincere blush, that she had even been assigned a tiny cameo part. Within two weeks, she had acquired a condo in False Creek, and shortly afterwards, she and Petunia vacated the Beary premises.

Around this time, all thoughts of her British relatives sailed from Philippa's mind, for a call came informing her that she had been cast as Anne of Green Gables in the Charlottetown Festival. The news should have made her euphoric, but she found herself tormented by a strange reluctance at the prospect of being away for so many months, especially since Bob Miller was now teamed with an attractive female partner. Still, she reflected philosophically, he had spent enough time away himself during the past year, and she was curious to see how he reacted to the prospect of *her* absence for such a lengthy period. Selfishly, she hoped he would express horror at the idea of her going, but to her chagrin, Miller took the news calmly and told her in no uncertain terms that she should take the job. So hardening her heart and firmly squashing any romantic dreams that had started to blossom in her breast, she focussed on career-advancement, signed the contract, and made plans for her trip to the East Coast. She would combine work with play, and enjoy a visit with her cousins in Halifax before she headed to Prince Edward Island, then spend the summer there as the star of the festival. Who knows what was in the future, but if nothing else, it would be a test of how much she and Miller would miss each other.

Two weeks before she was due to leave, Petunia called and invited her over for coffee. Philippa was glad to take the opportunity to catch up on her cousin's news. When she arrived at the condo, she was astounded. Mandy's new residence was lavishly upscale and furnished with sufficient style to qualify it for a full-colour spread in an interior-design magazine.

Petunia took Philippa out to the deck, where a mosaic-topped café table was arrayed with coffee pot, mugs and a plate of appetizing pastries from the bakery on Granville Island. The island could be seen from the deck. From that height, it resembled a storybook illustration of Peter Pan's Neverland, with paths, jetties and buildings standing out clearly in the morning sunlight. All around, the sparkling blue water was dotted with yachts and motorboats, and periodically, tiny aquabuses threaded their way back and forth between the island and the high-rises on the far shore.

"How on earth is Mandy paying for all this?" Philippa asked. "The film work can't be that lucrative."

Petunia grinned.

"It's not," she admitted. "Mum is writing a book: *My Three Nights with the Werewolf.* She has a whopping great advance from the publisher, plus a huge payoff from Darcy to make it a total fabrication. It'll sell millions. We'll be rolling in lovely lucre by this time next year."

Philippa's jaw dropped.

"Trust Mandy to land on her feet," she laughed. "Just wait until I tell my mother. But why does she have to make it a total fabrication? Isn't the truth exciting enough?"

Petunia chuckled. "Oh, it's exciting enough," she said, "but it's not overly flattering for Darcy. How do you think Mum convinced him to cough up money and get her a part in the film? She pointed out that if she described everything verbatim, he would seem a pretty wimpy werewolf, but she could be persuaded to use a bit of artistic licence and come up with a mutually agreeable version if he were really nice to her."

"That may be," said Philippa, "but nothing can stop him looking like a wimpy werewolf once that photograph of him in captivity is made public."

"Well," said Petunia, "since that photo was taken with Darcy's Blackberry and the only other image is in a confidential police file, there isn't really a problem. They're simply going to doctor it and superimpose a more acceptable picture of Darcy's face on top—you know, something bravely defiant. It'll work like a charm."

Petunia's eyes twinkled.

"After all," she chuckled, "these days—"

Philippa smiled and finished the sentence for her.

"The camera lies."

Too Late the Verdict

The phone rang as Beary came through the back door. He hung up MacPuff's leash, hastily wiped his feet, and hurried in to answer the call. When he picked up the receiver, he was surprised to hear the authoritative tones of his oldest daughter's voice. Sylvia never wasted time on pleasantries. She came straight to the point.

"I'm glad I caught you in, Dad," she said briskly. "I need your help."

This was unusual. After her mother, Sylvia was the most self-sufficient individual Beary knew.

"Glad to do whatever I can, my dear." Beary was intrigued. "What do you need help with?"

"A sexual assault."

Beary paused.

"You know," he said, after a moment's deliberation, "every comment that comes to mind will probably result in you making an acerbic remark about my lack of political correctness."

"Oh, for heaven's sake, it's a case." Sylvia also shared her mother's impatience with facetiousness, especially when it resulted in any deviation from the job at hand.

"Ah," said her father. "Proceed." He tucked the phone between ear and shoulder and filled the kettle as he listened. He suspected that his daughter's problem would require several cups of tea.

"You were teaching at Carnarvon High when I was a little girl," Sylvia went on. "How long had you been there?"

"Let me see." Beary struggled to remember. "I put in a few years at that school. I must have started there in '79. Yes, that's right, because that was the year your mother first applied to be a department head."

"That's not quite as early as I needed, but close. Do you still have your old Carnarvon annuals?" The school annuals, with candid shots of their parents in various poses of indignity in the classroom or on field trips, had been a great source of entertainment when the Beary children were young.

"Yes, they'll be tucked away on a bookshelf somewhere."

"Good. I'll pop round after lunch and pick them up."

"I vaguely recall that your mother intends to drag me around Costco tomorrow afternoon. We're stocking up for a trip to the cottage next week. Could you come by later?"

"No, I'm tied up all day. Just dig them out for me and leave them on the porch."

"Right," said Beary, recognizing a royal command when he heard one. Edwina had trained him well. "So fill me in," he continued curiously. "How does my old school annual relate to your new case?" But he was talking to dead air. Sylvia had already hung up—and the kettle had not even boiled yet.

*   *   *

Beary's curiosity was not satisfied until the following day. Once again, he was alone in the kitchen, except for MacPuff and Minx the

Manx. Edwina was at an opera-guild meeting, so Beary was taking advantage of her absence to indulge in a fry-up for dinner. As he flipped his sausages, each one watched by the eagle eye of MacPuff, the phone rang.

Beary instantly recognized the cultured tones of his caller.

"Philby, good to hear from you," he boomed. "It must be ten years. How are you?"

"Impressed," said Gordon Philby flatly. "How do you do it? Is it your political training—or do you have a microchip with records of voices and faces embedded in your brain?"

"God, no. I'm hopeless remembering people. Edwina nags me about it constantly. But having heard you declaim Shakespeare across the hall for twelve years or so, I couldn't forget you if I tried. Are you still in harness?"

"Yes, unfortunately. Two more years until I retire. I see you're keeping busy. It must be nice having council income to augment your pension."

"It helps." Beary adjusted the telephone to speakerphone, transferred his sausages to a plate that was already covered with a generous pile of hash browns, onions, fried eggs and bacon, all of which were forbidden when Edwina was home, and sat down at the kitchen table. MacPuff shifted from his position by the stove and hovered at Beary's elbow. Minx, also aware of her mistress's absence, leapt onto the table and stared, vulture-like, at the rashers of bacon.

"I called," said Philby, "because I'm very worried about Frampton. I thought you'd have some inside knowledge, seeing as your daughter is involved in the case."

"Inside knowledge? I have no idea what you're talking about."

Beary cut a sausage in two, popped one half into his mouth and tossed the other half to MacPuff. Conscious of a glare from his cat, he broke off a sliver of bacon and passed it to Minx.

"You must remember John Frampton," Philby prompted him. "He joined the English department the same year I came to Carnarvon."

"Yes, I know who you mean. I run into him now and then at the library. He was a pretty pedestrian English teacher, as I recall. Taught Drama too. I don't think he's at Carnarvon now."

"No, he's at Meadowbrook High. He's been there two years."

"So what's the problem?"

"He's been accused of rape."

"Good God! Is he Sylvia's sexual assault?"

"Sort of. Your daughter is acting on behalf of one of the girls."

"One! You mean he's accused of molesting an entire classful?"

"Not exactly. There's another teacher involved. Ian Reese. The RCMP have charged—"

"Hold on," said Beary. "Are we on the same page here? Sylvia is a civil lawyer. She doesn't deal with criminal cases."

"No, no. I know that. Frampton and Reese are fighting a civil suit launched by the girls, but they're also facing criminal charges as a result of the complaint. Your daughter is representing Reese's accuser in the civil suit, so she's following the criminal case like a hawk. If the teachers are found guilty, her work will be virtually done for her. It'll just be a case of deciding how many of their assets they'll be deprived of while they're serving time."

"They won't have any assets left if they're having to hire lawyers to fight both a criminal and civil case."

"Yes, even if they're innocent, it'll cost them big time."

"So fill me in." Beary was intrigued. "What exactly are the charges against them?"

"That they took advantage of a field trip to influence and seduce two of their students—though in Frampton's case, the charge also includes violent assault."

"I don't believe it," said Beary. "The man's a perfect gentleman, and he's much too old to 'influence and seduce' anyone. He must be nearing retirement age, and he's such a dry old stick, no girl would ever look twice at him without dissolving into giggles."

"Ah," said Philby. "You obviously don't know anything about it. I forgot to explain."

"Explain what?"

"The rape occurred forty-three years ago."

*   *   *

Sylvia sighed inwardly as she stared across the table at her client. She was not enamoured of punk-rock haircuts and leather jackets even on the very young, and this woman, with her painted leatherette face, looked far older than her fifty-seven years.

"Why did you wait until now to lay charges?" Sylvia asked pointedly. "Why did you not report the incident at the time?"

Tracy Keane blinked and opened her green eyes sufficiently wide that the folds and creases temporarily disappeared.

"We were embarrassed," she said. "You see, neither of us realized that the other was in the same boat. It was only when we got together at the school reunion that we realized what had happened."

"How did that come about?"

"Donna's husband, Roy—he's a real piss-tank—was drunk and coming on at me. He was reminiscing about our high-school band trip and saying how dumb I was to have been chasing after Ian Reese when I could have had a much better time hanging out with him and getting properly laid. I've never been able to stand Roy because I'd always assumed he was the one who raped Donna all those years ago. Anyway, I'd had enough of his crap so I told him where to get off and I told him that I'd got laid very nicely that night, thank you, and that Reese was more of a man that he'd ever be since Roy had to beat his women up to get them to comply. I guess I made some reference to the fact that I knew about what had happened to Donna on the last night of the band trip. You should have seen him. He went ballistic. Donna nearly had a fit, and that's when she told me the truth. It had been her drama teacher, John Frampton, who had raped her, not Roy. It was a good job Frampton wasn't at the reunion because Roy would have punched him out. Anyway, Roy told Donna right out that we should launch a lawsuit. I'd never really thought about it, but when he started in about how we'd been taken advantage of, it made me think we should bring it out in the open."

"All right," said Sylvia. "You'd better start at the beginning. Tell me about Donna Harmon . . . or Urquhart as she was then."

Tracy looked surprised, but she complied with Sylvia's request.

"Donna was a mousy little thing," she said. "Quite pretty, but she didn't do anything with herself. She didn't have much confidence because her father pounded it out of her. Rotten bastard he was. Donna's mom never stood up to him so Donna had a crappy home life. I took her under my wing. Smartened her up a bit."

"You say she was quiet. Did she have any boyfriends in school, or was she too shy?"

"Roy was her only boyfriend. They started going together in Grade 8 and she never went with anyone else. Roy's another mean sod, just like her father, and she never should've married him, but they do say, don't they, that women go for the same type? Donna's spent her whole life being downtrodden, poor little bitch."

Sylvia suppressed her distaste and continued with her questions.

"Was she a good student?"

"Average. Didn't come easy, but she plodded along and did okay. Teachers liked her. Not like me—I was always in detention or on a trip to the office."

"Go back to Donna for a moment. Why was she singled out by the Drama teacher—" Sylvia consulted her notes again—"this John Frampton? Was she a good actress?"

"Donna? You must be joking. She couldn't act to save her life, but she volunteered to help with school productions. She just liked being a part of it all. She'd do anything—prompting, lights, props—whatever was needed. So when Frampton came along on the band trip, it was natural for him and Donna to hang out. They were so used to being together at school."

"Yes, the fatal band trip—the spring of 1969. This is when the assaults took place?"

Tracy looked Sylvia straight in the eye.

"Yes," she said. Sylvia returned Tracy's stare, amazed that this woman who was fifteen years her senior still had the air of a defiant teenager. Very few people failed to wilt under one of Sylvia's stern looks, but Tracy held her gaze for several seconds. Then she raised her eyebrows, folded her arms and sat back.

"So what else do you want to know?" she said.

"You both liked band?"

Tracy shrugged.

"I didn't particularly," she said, "but I took it because it was about the only way to travel in those days. I wanted to go to London, so I practised hard and sold chocolate bars and made all the right moves."

"The right moves?"

"Well, you know. Made sure I was the teacher's pet."

Sylvia flinched. "I don't think we need to use that term," she said. "Let's say you were cooperative and helpful. Now tell me," she went on hastily before Tracy could interject, "what was this band teacher like? Describe him to me."

"Ian Reese? He looked like a young Michael Caine. Sexy. Wore great clothes. Drove a Jag."

"On a teacher's salary?"

"His wife was loaded—or at least her parents were. Reese had it laid on for him. At the time we thought he was really cool, but looking back, I realize he was just a jerk on a big ego trip. He liked being surrounded by a bunch of girls who were nuts about him."

"Did he ever make advances to you prior to the band trip?"

"He was pretty nice to me. He made me feel I was special."

"Did he ever take any action that could be construed as being in conflict with his professional code of conduct?" Seeing the blank look on Tracy's face, Sylvia rephrased the question. "Did Mr. Reese ever have any physical contact with you prior to the night of the assault?"

"Well no . . . I mean, he never actually touched me . . . but you can say a lot with your eyes. I could tell he thought I was attractive. I was a flashy little thing." Tracy smoothed her mini-skirt and tossed her head so her earrings swivelled like miniature hula-hoops. She fixed Sylvia with a direct stare as if challenging her to comment. "I flirted with him a lot. You know what girls are like. He was a good-looking man and the attention was flattering."

"Did he single you out during the band tour?"

"Oh yes. He often sat with me when we were travelling, or ate with me if we were at a café."

"Whereabouts in London were you staying? Were you all at the same hotel?"

"No. Only the teachers stayed in the hotel. The students were billeted. And we weren't actually in London. We were in Harrow, but it was only a half-hour ride on the tube into London so we went on a bunch of field trips in town."

"I see. Did you and Donna share the same billet?"

"Sort of. We teamed up with Belinda Gordon. Her mom is from England, so she came along as a chaperone so she could visit with her sister. Belinda's aunt and uncle had this fabulous house up on the hill. They were loaded—fantastic car, riding stables, swimming pool and guest suites over the pool-house. That's where we got to stay. We didn't even have to share rooms. The location was perfect because the big event of the tour was a joint-school concert at Wembley, which was only a couple of stations up the line."

"Let's go to the night of the assaults." Sylvia glanced down and checked her notes. "Try to give me a precise chronological account of what happened."

"Right." Tracy wrinkled her brow and thought for a moment. She swivelled her chair and stared towards the plate glass window at the side of Sylvia's office, but the look of intense concentration on her face made it clear she was not taking in the view of the Vancouver skyline or the North Shore mountains.

"It was the last night of the tour," she said. "Belinda's aunt had offered to host a farewell party."

"Was everyone there?"

"Not until later on. Ian Reese had wangled four tickets for a play in town. He and Frampton were going, and they offered to take two students with them. Well, naturally Donna and I leapt at the opportunity. The party paled by comparison."

"What did they take you to see?"

"Some mystery show that had been on since the Stone Age."

"*The Mousetrap*," Sylvia said crisply. She had seen the play during a trip to London in the eighties. "That would have been running at the Ambassador in '69. So you'd have been around the Leicester Square area."

Tracy gawped at Sylvia as if she had magical powers.

"Go on," Sylvia continued. "So you went to the theatre with your teachers that evening."

"It wasn't evening—well, not when we started out. It was a five o'clock show."

"Did you travel up to town together?"

"No, like I told you, the teachers were staying in town. Reese and Frampton had taken three of the boys sightseeing during the day, so once they ditched the boys, they walked up to the theatre and met us there. Donna and me were in town early too, because Belinda's mom and aunt wanted to spend the afternoon shopping, so they drove us up—along with Belinda, of course—and we had lunch together and went to Harrods and Harvey Nichols. Then Donna and I headed off to the theatre."

"What about your friend, Belinda?"

"She went back to Harrow with her mom and aunt. They had to get organized for the party."

"They drove back and left you and Donna in town?"

"No. Belinda's aunt left the car for Reese to drive us back after the show. The traffic was really bad at five o'clock, so she figured they'd be faster on the tube."

"They parked the car in town?"

"Yeah. Belinda's uncle's office was only a couple of blocks from the theatre, so they left the car in his private parking space. Belinda's mom had given Reese a spare set of keys the day before."

"All right. Tell me the events of the rest of the evening, and try to give me some approximate times."

"The show was over a bit after seven. I wanted to hang out in town for a while, but Donna was anxious to get back to the party, so Frampton took her back on the train."

"You split up?" Sylvia's voice dripped disapproval.

Tracy stared at Sylvia defiantly.

"Yeah. So? Me and Reese stayed and had something to eat. We went to Ivy's. It was across the road from the theatre. We stayed there until . . . well, I guess it would have been around quarter past eight."

"And after that?"

"We started back to the car, but when we got there, Reese realized he'd left the keys in his other jacket which was back in his hotel room, so we had to go and get them."

"You went to his hotel room? Is this where the assault took place?"

"Yeah. Let me go on."

"No, this is important. Where was he staying?"

"The Charing Cross. It was one of those British transport hotels. It was pretty nice, actually . . . fancy, old-style décor. I could see why Reese liked it. Some of the parents were staying there as well."

Sylvia steered the conversation back to the point at hand.

"Whose idea was it for you to go to Mr. Reese's room?" she asked. "Did he invite you up?"

"Well, not exactly. I didn't want to wait on the street so I followed him into the hotel. Then, when we were in the lobby, I saw Miss Phillips by the reception desk, and the last thing I wanted was a lecture from her—"

"She was one of the teachers?"

"Yeah. A real stuffy one. Dried-up old maid. Got on our case about everything, so I didn't want to stick around."

"Did she see you in the lobby?"

"No idea, and we can't ask her anyway because she was killed in a bus crash a few years back."

"Was anyone else in the lobby? Did anyone see you there?"

"No. The place was deserted. Anyway, I went up with Reese to get the keys."

"And?"

"And that's when it happened."

"He assaulted you. Was he violent?"

"Of course he wasn't violent. He just grabbed me and kissed me, and the next thing I know, his hand's up my skirt and we went on from there."

"Did you try to fight him off?"

Tracy stared at Sylvia defiantly.

"No. Haven't you heard a thing I said? Like I told you . . . I was crazy about him. I wanted it as much as he did . . . but that's not the point, is it? He was my teacher, wasn't he, and he abused that trust. I was fourteen, and that makes it rape."

Tracy's green eyes glittered with greedy anticipation.

"I expect you to help me take the bastard to the cleaners," she said.

*　　　*　　　*

Between her father's old high-school annuals, Facebook and the services of a private detective, Sylvia managed to track down several former pupils and teachers who had been on the band tour in 1969. Sylvia was particularly anxious to trace the ex-classmate with the British relatives who had provided the billets for Tracy Keane and Donna Urquhart. Fortunately, Belinda Stevens, née Gordon, was easy to find as she was married to a lawyer who was a partner in another prestigious Vancouver firm. She was quite willing to come downtown for an interview, insisting on an eleven-thirty appointment so that she could meet her husband for lunch afterwards. She sailed into Sylvia's office punctually at half past eleven, slipped off her Gucci sunglasses and glanced at her watch as she sat down, as if to make clear that her time was every bit as valuable as Sylvia's.

Belinda Stevens was a strikingly attractive woman. She looked twenty years less than her fifty-seven years. Her gleaming hair was short and elegantly styled and her expensive suit exuded wealth and sex appeal. This one, decided Sylvia, was probably the belle of the high school. She wouldn't have been wasting her time hankering after any of the teachers; she probably had her pick of the football team.

Mrs. Steven's manner was as cool and assured as her looks. Her recollection of the last day of the London trip was clear and her narration was concise.

"Tracy and Donna were over the moon about the theatre trip, and they spent all morning fixing themselves up and deciding what to wear."

"You were all staying in your aunt's guest suites?"

"No. I had a room in my aunt's house, but Tracy and Donna each had a guest suite on the top floor of the pool house."

"So that was a separate building from the main house?"

"Yes. I went over there to lend Donna a blouse and Tracy a pair of mesh tights. Tracy and I also spent quite a lot of time helping Donna with her make-up. It was amazing what a difference it made when we back-combed her hair and gave her Liz Taylor eyes."

"So there was an air of anticipation?"

"Absolutely."

"I gather your mother and aunt drove the three of you up to London that day. Did you see the girls meet the two teachers?"

"No. My mother and aunt hadn't finished their shopping. We were still in Harvey Nicks when Tracy and Donna left for the theatre, so when I next saw them, it was much later in the evening."

"How much later?"

"Donna came back first. She must have arrived around eight, because almost the moment she and Mr. Frampton arrived, there was an awful scene with her boyfriend. Roy Harmon actually took a swing at Mr. Frampton and one of the other boys knocked him cold. Between the booze he'd drunk and the sock on the jaw, Roy was out of commission for the best part of an hour. I distinctly remember the grandfather clock booming nine o'clock and bringing him back to consciousness. By then, Donna and Mr. Frampton had long since left the party. Poor Donna was dreadfully upset."

"She and Mr. Frampton left together?"

"I assume so. He took her out of the room. He was trying to settle her down. I didn't actually see him take her up to the guest suite, but I know he was there an hour later because I saw him leave the pool house and slip out through the back-garden gate."

"You were in the garden?"

"Yes. I told you, the noise of the clock brought Roy round, and the next thing we knew, he was in the garden bellowing insults under Donna's window. We all flocked outside to watch the entertainment, but my mother came out and told us to stay away and let her deal with it. She managed to usher the others inside, but I slipped away and ambled down the garden for a cigarette—in those days we didn't dare smoke in front of our parents—and that's when I saw Mr. Frampton leaving the pool house. By the time I returned, Roy had calmed down. He was still by Donna's window, but he was just calling up to her quietly and saying he was sorry."

"Did you speak to him?"

"Yes. I told him he was an idiot and that he should grow up. He said he'd put things right with Donna later, but he'd had it for the night and was going to head back to his billet."

"Was he billeted nearby?"

"Down the other end of town. There were some big houses on Marlborough Hill and several of the kids were put up there. It was only a half-hour walk down Station Road and it was a lovely June evening. It was still fairly light."

"Did you see him leave?"

"No. I went back to the party and I was there when Ian Reese dropped Tracy off."

"Dropped her? He didn't stay?"

"No. He didn't even come in. My mother had offered to drive him back to his hotel. She'd arranged to have a drink in town with one of her old friends, and I think she was anxious to get going as it was so late. One of the other teachers came in with Tracy though. Mr. Rowell . . . he was coming to take the last shift supervising at the party. I think my mother had arranged for him to stay over that night, even though he was booked into a hotel in town. Reese had seen him near the tube station and offered him a ride."

"So what time did Tracy and this other teacher arrive?"

"Some time between ten and ten-thirty, I think."

"Did you talk with Tracy?"

"Not really. She was in a sulk about losing her charm bracelet. She didn't stay long at the party either. After she heard about the row between Roy and Mr. Frampton, she went to hang out with Donna."

"She didn't return to the party?"

"No. I didn't see her until the next morning."

"Did you notice anything unusual about her manner?"

"She was a bit subdued, but then we all were. Sheer fatigue finally hit us. I think Tracy was concerned about Donna, too."

"Why?"

"Well, everyone was. Poor Donna had a massive shiner and her lip was split down the middle. She had to wear dark glasses for the next two weeks. She told us she'd been crying so hard she missed her footing and fell onto the arm of the chair in her room. It was one of those Danish modern things with a knobbly bit sticking up which could have whacked her in the eye. At the time, we believed her. It never occurred to us that she had been beaten up."

Sylvia leaned back in her chair and fixed her eyes on Belinda Stevens.

"What was your opinion of the two teachers?" she asked.

"Frampton and Reese? They were as different as chalk and cheese. The only thing they had in common was a love of theatre. But they were young and male, so naturally, we were all interested in them.

Reese had blonde hair and sleepy eyes, and you just knew he was a bit of a tomcat—an Alfie—he even looked like Michael Caine. Frampton was dull by comparison. He was nice enough to look at— an early George Harrison type—but he was pretty aloof. He appealed to the quiet girls who read Brontë novels and dreamed of brooding, angst-ridden heroes. Donna was that sort, so I can see why she liked Frampton, and Tracy was a ball of fire, so naturally she gravitated to Reese. Both girls were totally infatuated, which was why they were so determined to have their night on the town with their idols."

"Did either girl talk about the evening at any later date?"

"Donna never did. She clammed up whenever it was mentioned. But Tracy crowed incessantly about what a great night it had been."

"Did she ever give any indication that intimacy had occurred between her and Ian Reese?"

"Oh, hints and rolled eyeballs, that sort of thing, but Tracy did that all the time. However, I do remember an occasion two years later when a group of us were having coffee together. It was a giggly girls session with a lot of talk about sex, and Tracy announced that she'd 'done it' with Mr. Reese. Of course, none of us believed her. She was always a terrible liar, so we thought she was boasting in her usual fashion. But now we know better, don't we?"

*   *   *

Later that evening, while Mai Ling, the Barnwells' nanny, put Chelsea to bed, Sylvia talked over the case with Norton. She had rarely represented a client whom she disliked so intensely, and she felt the need for her husband's calming presence and balanced point of view. Norton was never a fire-eater in the courtroom, but he was meticulous when it came to analysing evidence and she was eager to hear his perspective on the case.

Norton poured Sylvia a glass of wine and listened patiently while she recounted her client's story.

"Tracy Keane asked for it, of course," Sylvia concluded, "but it doesn't make Reese any less accountable. I don't see how he can wriggle out of it if they left the restaurant soon after eight and it was past nine-thirty when they picked up the car."

"How can you know that for sure?"

"One of the other teachers ran into them outside Reginald Gordon's office. This teacher—Rowell is his name—was heading for the tube station. He was going to Harrow to do his shift supervising at the party. Reese offered him a ride."

Norton nodded sagely. "Pretty hard to account for a gap of an hour and a half. Does Reese have an explanation?"

"A thin one. He says Tracy wanted to go sightseeing so they strolled through Soho and along the embankment, which is why they were so late going back to his hotel. He swears they were only in his room for the few seconds it took him to pick up the keys and insists that one of the other teachers saw them there, but as the teacher in question has since died, that doesn't give him much of an out. What is certain is that Tracy got to the party around ten-fifteen, and several witnesses attest that she was thoroughly out of sorts when she got there. To me, that suggests there was definitely some sort of incident with Reese. I don't like my client but I think she's telling the truth."

Sylvia fell silent. Norton eyed his wife shrewdly.

"So why are you picking at your thumbs as if you want to exterminate them? There's something you're not satisfied with."

Sylvia sighed.

"It's the situation with the other couple. It doesn't fit. Because it's so unlikely, it could undermine my case. A seduction in a hotel room is one thing, but it's harder to pin misconduct on the couple that dutifully got on the tube and headed back to Harrow."

"And if one scenario sounds dodgy, the other becomes questionable too?"

"Yes. John Frampton is a vastly different character from Ian Reese, and because of that, Donna Harmon's story doesn't ring true."

"Where was Frampton supposed to have attacked her? On the train?"

"No, it was during the party."

"Oh, so they did return?"

"Yes, but when they arrived, there was an ugly scene with Donna's boyfriend, who, by the way, is now her husband. Word is that Roy Harmon is extremely obnoxious, often violent, and I gather he's determined that they're going to win this case."

"So there's history between him and Frampton."

"Yes. It sounds as if he was hostile to the drama teacher even before the London trip. He was jealous of the time Donna spent helping with the school plays, so the outing to see *The Mousetrap* was the last straw. Evidently, when Donna and Frampton arrived at the party, Roy Harmon was so drunk and abusive that he actually tried to assault Frampton. The other boys had to restrain him and one of them ended up knocking him cold. By then, Donna was hysterical, so Frampton took her outside and calmed her down. It appears they went up to her room, which was in the pool-house."

"A separate building?"

Sylvia nodded.

"How can you know for certain that Frampton went up to the girl's room?"

"There's a witness who saw him leaving the building shortly after nine o'clock. I don't think there's any doubt about it."

"He tried to comfort her and the inevitable happened?"

"Not according to Donna Harmon. She says Frampton raped her, and violently too. She had a split lip and a black eye the next day."

"Sounds unlikely," said Norton. "Are you sure the boyfriend didn't beat her up?"

"That's what Tracy Keane assumed at the time. She went to Donna's room and found her in a terrible state. She looked like she'd been punched in the face. Tracy took her into the bathroom to put some ointment on her lip, and she saw a mass of bloody towels, not to mention a bed-sheet that had been rather ineptly washed out. She noticed the careful way her friend was walking, and she knew that Donna had been a virgin—so she guessed right away that she'd been forced to have sex. Donna wouldn't talk about it at all and she made Tracy swear not to say anything. She insisted that she'd fallen on the arm of the chair. Amazingly enough, Tracy went along with Donna's wishes and kept her mouth shut. It wasn't until the high-school reunion that it all came out into the open. Once she realized that her friend hadn't been assaulted by Roy Harmon, but that she'd been raped by a teacher on the same night that Reese had seduced her, Tracy decided it was time to go public."

"It's a cash grab, of course," said Norton. "From what you've told me, your client couldn't care less about the fact that her teacher slept with her."

"Definitely. Donna's story simply provided a golden opportunity. With the second accusation, a case can be made that the teachers set out deliberately to isolate and seduce the girls."

"The joint suit will certainly be easier to prove than a solitary one."

"I know. Tracy is anticipating cleaning up big time. I don't like the woman at all, but legally she has right on her side, so despite my reservations about her friend's story, I have to go all out to win."

"Hard to round up witnesses after all this time."

"Actually, I've had a real stroke of luck from the London end. The maître d' who worked at Ivy's in the sixties was originally from

Vancouver and he returned to Canada after he retired. He lives in Port Moody now. I've passed his name on to the crown prosecutor so she'll be able to bring him into court for the criminal case."

"Who is prosecuting?"

"Roberta Hacker."

"That'll help your case. Hacker's as persistent as a terrier and as tough as a pit bull. She'll chip away at the defence until she's demolished every piece of evidence that might help Reese. He's doomed, especially if you intend to feed the prosecution every negative detail that you unearth."

"Of course I do," said Sylvia. "If Roberta Hacker wins the criminal case, my job will be easy."

The telephone rang in the adjacent room, and a moment later, Mai Ling bobbed through the doorway. She handed the phone to Norton and slipped silently out of the room. His expression grew serious as he answered the call.

"Yes . . . yes," said Norton. "Good heavens! Yes, I see . . . Yes, of course. Look, this is tricky for me." Norton gave Sylvia a sidelong glance. Then he fell silent and listened to the voice on the other end of the line. After a few moments, he said, "All right. I'll see you in the morning."

"That sounded rather fraught," said Sylvia as Norton ended the call. "Has something come up?"

"It has rather," said Norton. "That was John Kirkpatrick."

"John? Isn't he defending Frampton on the criminal charge? What on earth did he want?"

"Me, actually. It turns out he's having to drop the case. Heart acting up again. He's been ordered complete rest."

"And?" said Sylvia dangerously.

"He's asked me to step in," Norton finished apologetically.

"You won't!"

"Well, I think I will," Norton said bravely. "After all, everyone is entitled to a defence, and from what you've told me about Donna Harmon's injuries, I think it's far from certain that the teacher is responsible. Furthermore, according to Kirkpatrick, Roy Harmon is a litigious type who will sue anyone and everyone at the drop of a hat. I gather he's wangled two large settlements from ICBC and a tidy sum from a dispute with a neighbour over property damage. The first smell of money, and he launches a lawsuit. Your case may be cut and dried, but the other one isn't."

"And, of course," said Sylvia, her voice dripping with sarcasm, "you already have a mass of details at your fingertips since I just gave you a first-class briefing."

"Well, yes, you did," said Norton sheepishly. "Thank you, darling. Much appreciated."

*   *   *

Beary put down his book and stretched his legs, eliciting an indignant protest from Minx the Manx who was sleeping in his lap. Beary was sitting in his favourite cottage armchair, amply stuffed and appropriately upholstered in a sturdy fabric with sailboat designs, but he could not concentrate on reading. The dilemma of his former colleague kept intruding into his thoughts.

"The late sixties," he sighed, rearranging Minx into a tightly knit ball. "The age when skirts got shorter and movies got longer—and neither legs nor films seemed any more exciting because of it. Do you realize that the same individuals who triggered the Swinging Sixties now actually *are* the swinging sixties? We could have geriatric hysteria on our hands."

"Dishes, Bertram," Edwina reminded him. "It's your turn. You can philosophize from the sink."

"Can you imagine it?" Beary lifted Minx carefully, stood, and deposited her back on the chair. "Hordes of osteoarthritic Twiggies in Carnaby Street fashions, all eligible for government pensions, and ready to stage sit-ins at the drop of a toupee if any bureaucrat dares so much as intimate that money is running out. No wonder euthanasia is becoming a hot topic."

Edwina looked up from her crossword.

"What are you rambling on about? Why this preoccupation with the sixties?"

Beary stepped over MacPuff's recumbent form and took the few short steps to the cottage kitchen.

"I'm trying to remember what it was like," he said. "The attitudes . . . the atmosphere. It's easy to say now that two male teachers were acting inappropriately squiring young female students about London, but it was a very different climate from the current era where people cry sexual harassment if you so much as pat someone on the shoulder. Look at what's happening in the entertainment industry. Retroactive rape charges flying in all directions, but they date back to a period of time when sexual liberation was practically foisted on the public as a new religion."

"Don't be silly, Bertram," said Edwina. "Professional ethics are professional ethics, no matter what other foolish nonsense is going on in society."

Beary picked up the dish-soap and splashed a generous portion of liquid into the sink.

"Yes, but I'm trying to visualize the ambience of an uninhibited age. Could so much talk of freedom have affected John Frampton to the point where he would have lost all sense of right and wrong?"

"He was a hard one to read," mused Edwina. "He was a very serious young man, though I often felt his quietness was simply an absence of substance. No gumption at all. He never spoke out in staff meetings, even if there was something on the agenda that affected him directly."

Beary stared wide-eyed at his wife. "Did you know Frampton early in his career?"

"Yes. Don't you remember? I did a four-month stint at Carnarvon right after I graduated from UBC."

"Good Lord," said Beary. "I'd forgotten. You were subbing in those days."

"That's right. I didn't get on permanent contract until 1973."

"How did Frampton behave with you? You were pretty sharp-looking back then—and still are, of course," Beary added hastily. "Did he show any interest in you or the other women on staff?"

"No, none at all. He was politely standoffish, and, as I recall, I thought him rather immature."

"So what's your analysis of the accusations against him?"

"Probably true," said Edwina. "I suspect he made the fatal mistake of falling for a student and let things get out of hand. She probably led him on, and then became frightened of going the whole way, so he forced himself on her. Either that, or they were having a full-blown affair and now that retrospective rape charges are fashionable, she's decided to call him to account." Edwina tapped her pencil on her puzzle. "What's a six-letter word for despoil?" she added. "It has a 'v' in the middle."

"Ravage," said Beary. "So if you were at Carnarvon for four months," he persisted, "you must have known Ian Reese too?"

"Of course."

"Edwina, you sly old dog, you knew I was interested in the case. Why didn't you say something?"

"You never asked me. You've just been gossiping with the old-boy network, all of whom are only interested in proving those two young women liars."

"I'm interested in the truth. There is a phenomena called false memory syndrome, you know."

"Only for the very young. These women were teenagers. Personally I think it's outrageous when teachers disgrace our profession by taking advantage of the impressionable creatures they work with. I hope they both go to jail."

Beary rinsed the suds off a plate and plopped it into the rack.

"Did you have any inkling at the time that there was anything going on?"

"No, of course not. But I do remember how the Urquhart girl used to tag around after Frampton. She used to help him with the school plays. It was quite a close friendship. I suppose that's why I thought Frampton was immature. Like us, he was in his early twenties, and I remember thinking it was rather pathetic that he had to rely on a student for a friend."

"What about Ian Reese and Tracy Keane? Do you remember them?"

"Ah, well, in retrospect, I realize that was a very likely case for abuse. Reese was flashy. He'd married right out of university but he didn't get along with his wife, and he was always involved in some activity or other with a host of young girls. He was quite flirtatious with them. I always thought him rather an idiot, but I didn't realize that he was actually preying on those girls physically. Mind you, a girl like Tracy Keane was asking for it, but then, so many of them do. It's up to the teachers to ignore all those raging hormones and flattering crushes."

"Yes," Beary said slowly. "I'm afraid you're right about Reese. I worked with him at Redfern High. He was older then, but he still liked the girls. What puzzles me though is why others haven't come forward. I mean, if he is a classic case of an abuser, why haven't there been accusations before?"

"As this case becomes public, others may come forward," said Edwina. "I must say I'm extremely disappointed in our son-in-law for agreeing to defend Frampton. Sylvia must be furious."

"Very wise of Norton," muttered Beary. "Professional ethics will prevent him and Sylvia from discussing anything about the case, so he'll be spared months of listening to her haranguing him about how disgusting men are. You know," Beary added thoughtfully, "I may go and listen when Frampton's case comes before the court. I'm very curious to see how it goes."

"Good idea," said Edwina. "It'll get you out of my hair for a few days." She peered back at her crossword and frowned. "An invaluable kitchen appliance? Ten letters. Now, let me think. What could that be?"

"Dishwasher," said Beary, slapping down the tea towel. "We should get one for the cottage."

*   *   *

Norton looked across his desk and sighed. The man sitting opposite him was slumped in his chair, his very posture screaming defeat. John Frampton was a thin, neurotic-looking individual with shaggy grey hair and a face that made Norton think of engravings of medieval monks—a monk who had taken a vow of silence, too, reflected Norton irritably. So far he had managed to squeeze exactly two sentences out of his client: "I didn't rape Donna. I would never have harmed her."

"But you did go to her room?"

"I took her there, yes. The poor kid was upset. Her boyfriend had gone crazy when we arrived at the party."

Frampton's eyes glazed over as if he were trying to visualize the scene. For a moment Norton thought he was going to say something else, but then his mouth twisted bitterly and he compressed his lips tightly together.

Norton sighed and persevered.

"You were there a long time," he said. "At least forty minutes. You were seen leaving the pool house just after nine o'clock. What happened during that period you were in Donna's room?"

"We talked. I calmed her down. I tried to comfort her. She . . . she was a very sensitive girl. She didn't deserve the abuse she got from that ape she ended up marrying. I felt badly for her . . . I still feel badly about her."

"Did it not occur to you that being alone with her for that length of time might be misconstrued or considered inappropriate?"

Frampton shook his head miserably.

"I didn't even think about it. I . . . I was fond of Donna. She was upset. I just wanted her to stop crying. I wanted her to calm down."

"And did she calm down?"

"Yes, until Harmon came out and started bellowing under her window. Then she got really agitated again."

"What did you do?"

"I left. There was a side door at the end of the garden. Donna begged me to go out that way so that Harmon wouldn't know I'd been there with her. She was afraid of what he would do."

"So you simply left her there to cope on her own."

Frampton had the grace to look ashamed.

"I had to. I . . . I'd have only made things worse. There were other adults present. I heard Belinda Gordon's mother telling Harmon to smarten up. I figured Donna would be okay."

"Yet the next day, she had a split lip and a black eye. How do you explain that?"

Frampton's face flushed.

"I can't," he muttered.

"According to all the witnesses, Donna explained it by saying she fell on a chair. Now she's accusing you of hitting her. How did she explain her injuries to you at the time?"

Frampton looked shamefaced again.

"She didn't. I think we were both so embarrassed about the big public blow-up that we steered clear of each other. I didn't want to cause any more rows between her and Harmon, so I kept my distance. I suppose it's possible she fell and hurt herself. She was in a state of panic with that brute yelling under the window."

"Isn't it also possible that Harmon beat her up?"

Frampton looked bitter.

"Well, whether Donna fell or whether Harmon beat her up, he's terrorized her into saying that I'm the one who hurt her. Donna is lying, but she would never have pulled a stunt like this on her own. She's doing as she's told because she's scared of him."

*   *   *

Beary was particularly curious about the charges that had been laid against John Frampton, but it was Ian Reese's trial that first came to court. Since the two cases were so closely related, Beary decided to go downtown and monitor the proceedings. When he entered the courthouse, he had barely started down the hall before he heard a shrill cry from behind him.

"Mr. Beary!"

He turned to see a stout woman making her way towards him. She had a motherly air and her face was vaguely familiar. When she reached him, she smiled and shook his hand vigorously.

"Mary Bryant," she said. "Remember me? I was in your Grade Twelve English class."

"Of course," lied Beary. He often found himself in this dilemma. "What are you doing here?" he asked.

"I've been called as a witness. Isn't it awful, this business about Mr. Reese and Mr. Frampton? I find it so hard to believe."

As Mary Bryant's plump lips stretched around her elongated vowels, a younger version of the woman's face swam into Beary's mental eye. "I remember," he said triumphantly. "You transferred over from Carnarvon just before your final year. Don't tell me you were on the infamous band trip."

Mary nodded. "I certainly was. Not that I know anything, but I suppose they're calling as many of us as they can lay their hands on."

"So what do you think?" Beary asked curiously. "What's your view of Ian Reese? Did he really come on strong to you girls?"

"I thought he was more jolly than flirtatious," said Mary. "He was full of vitality. It was fun to be around him."

"So you never felt his behaviour was inappropriate?"

"No. Not at all. Mind you, I was one of the shy, underdeveloped ones. None of the boys gave me so much as a glance until after I graduated."

"Did any of your friends talk about his treatment of them?"

"Well, he was quite a source of gossip. You know what girls that age are like. His wife was never at school functions, and he seemed very friendly with the women on staff. We were all sure he was a terrible ladies man, and I think, because of that reputation, some of the girls tended to read more into his behaviour than was warranted."

"Did Tracy Keane ever talk to you about Mr. Reese?"

"Yes. She'd often brag to the other girls about how much he liked her, but I personally thought it was all wishful thinking. He was involved in a lot of extracurricular activities with students. I don't think she received any special treatment from him."

"Wouldn't a trip to the theatre constitute special treatment?"

"Not from Mr. Reese. He was a great theatregoer and he often took students to see plays. He was like a good-natured uncle."

"But not a funny uncle? That's what the prosecution will put forward. You can bet they'll say that Reese taking Tracy to a post-show dinner was rather unusual."

Mary sighed. "I suppose it was," she said, "but Mr. Reese was always ready to eat. I can well believe that he would have gone to a restaurant rather than have to face pizza and chips at a teenage party. Besides, according to Donna Urquhart, Tracy had made a big fuss about how starving she was and how she was dying to go to a fancy London restaurant."

"It's too bad the other two didn't go with them. Their splitting up is what makes it look so suspicious. How did the theatre outing come about anyway? Have you any idea?"

"Of course. We were all told about it. Mr. Reese was quite apologetic that he and Mr. Frampton could only get two extra tickets. He said he'd hoped to take a whole group of us. He suggested we draw lots to decide who would go."

"Is that how Tracy Keane and Donna Urquhart got to go?"

"Not exactly. The two of them wanted to go so desperately that they pretty well bribed and bullied the rest of us into agreeing."

"Why were they so eager to attend the event?"

"I'd have thought that was obvious. They both had wild crushes on the two teachers involved."

Beary shook his head sadly. "Oh, the folly of youth."

He said goodbye to Mary and made his way to the courtroom where Ian Reese's trial was underway. He noticed Sylvia sitting in the back row, so he shuffled his way along the bench and sat down beside her.

"Watching the criminal set doing your job for you?" hissed Beary. Sylvia nodded.

"Of course. The outcome of this trial will govern what happens in the civil suit." Sylvia kept her eyes on the front of the room. "That's Daniel Clarke," she added, nodding towards a dapper-looking man seated next to Ian Reese. "He's top notch, according to Norton. Reese has got himself a first-class counsel. Not that he'll stand a chance against Roberta Hacker."

"Which one is she?"

Sylvia pointed to a paper-thin, beige-suited woman at the front of the courtroom. Beary looked at her curiously. Roberta Hacker had light brown hair and a pale olive complexion. With her faded, one-colour appearance, she could have disappeared into the oak panelling on the walls, except that her heavily framed spectacles could not conceal the laser intensity of her icy blue eyes. Not an adversary he would like to face, Beary decided. He glanced towards the bench where the judge sat, gaunt-faced and stiff-necked. A hanging judge if Beary had ever seen one. He looked as if he should have retired years ago. Reese would not get any quarter there. Beary turned his attention back to the witness box.

A middle-aged woman with facial features that mirrored the judge's austere expression had seated herself and taken the oath. Hacker moved forward and addressed her.

"Ms. Morgan—" she began politely.

"Mrs. Morgan." The reply came like a rifle shot and the snapdragon mouth closed into a tight line.

The prosecutor's face remained impassive.

"Mrs. Morgan," she continued, "you were a student at Carnarvon High School in 1969? I believe you were in the same band class as Tracy Keane."

"Yes, that is correct." Althea Morgan shifted her broad frame and glowered at the lawyer through steel-rimmed glasses. "I was in the class for three years."

"I know that woman," Beary hissed suddenly. "She's on the Burnside Community Standards Committee. When it comes to morality, she could out-rant John Knox. She must call Council at least once a week to complain about some grievance or other."

Sylvia glared at her father and he dutifully fell silent. He turned his attention to the front of the room. Roberta Hacker was asking what, in Beary's view, was a leading question.

"Did you ever notice any unusual interactions between the band teacher and Tracy Keane?"

Althea Morgan obliged with an equally leading answer.

"It depends what you mean by unusual. The man was an outrageous flirt. It was utterly inappropriate, the way he carried on."

"At any point did Mr. Reese begin to single out Tracy Keane?"

"Yes, the year of the band trip. Tracy was always hanging around his room. Once we were travelling, it was even more obvious. Often as not, she would be sitting next to him. When he got those theatre tickets and offered to take a student to the play, it was a given that she'd be the one picked to go."

"Can you explain to the court where you were staying during your time in London?"

"My mother was on the trip as a chaperone and she'd booked a double room at the Charing Cross Hotel, so I stayed with her. Our room was on the same floor as Mr. Reese's."

"So you saw quite a bit of Mr. Reese during the trip?"

"Yes. Well, coming and going."

"Did you see Mr. Reese with Tracy Keane on the evening of their theatre outing?"

"Yes."

"How did that come about?"

"I hadn't wanted to go to the Gordons' party, so my mother took me to the ballet that afternoon. Then we went out to dinner. We got back to the hotel around quarter past nine and headed up to our room. When we came out of the elevator, we saw Mr. Reese and Tracy. They were coming out of his hotel room."

"You're quite sure you saw them both coming out of the room? Could Tracy have been waiting in the hall? You might have merely seen Mr. Reese coming out to join her?"

"Oh, no." The rattrap mouth managed a smirk. "The door flew open and she came out as if the hounds of hell were pursuing her. Then he came out, looking very smug and self-satisfied, and calmly shut the door. You could see something had been going on, just by the way they were looking at each other. I mean the atmosphere was electric. It was pretty obvious what had happened."

Daniel Clarke rose to his feet. He bore a look of pained indignation, but before he could object, the judge gently rebuked the witness.

"We must not speculate, Mrs. Morgan. You may have been right in your conjectures, but what happened inside that room is for the jury to decide."

Roberta Hacker's mouth relaxed into a satisfied smile and she turned the witness over to Daniel Burke.

"That was a back-handed reprimand," muttered Beary. "Obvious whose side the judge is on."

Sylvia nodded complacently. "Yes," she said. "Judge Logg is a great ally if you're prosecuting."

"Log? You're kidding."

"Two *g*'s," hissed Sylvia. "Shhh."

She nudged Beary and pointed to the front of the court. Daniel Clarke was beginning his questioning.

"Mrs. Morgan," he said, "am I to understand that you saw a fellow student coming out of a hotel room with a member of the school staff? If you had thought there was something improper going on, would you not have said something to your mother or to one of the teachers who was present? After what you said about Mr. Reese earlier, were you not concerned about your classmate?"

Althea Morgan sniffed.

"Why should I be? Tracy Keane was no better than she should be. There wasn't much point in protecting a girl like that. I mean, she'd done it all before and was quite proud of the fact. She was a nasty piece of goods and I had no intention of interfering."

"So you considered her fair game."

"Yes."

"I see. Mr. Reese has been teaching now for thirty-eight years, a long career in which to prey on his students. How many other complaints are you aware of that have been laid against him?"

"Lots of us have grumbled about—"

"Formal complaints, Mrs. Morgan."

"That's not the point, is it? If we'd been aware of the issue of sexual harassment the way we are now, I'm quite sure he'd have been pulled up short years ago."

"Mr. Reese is still teaching, Mrs. Morgan, and I repeat my question. Do you know of any complaints that have been laid against him other than the present case we are dealing with here?"

Althea Morgan growled her answer in a low voice.

"Could you repeat that, Mrs. Morgan? I don't believe the members of the jury heard you."

"No," snapped the woman in the witness box. "I don't."

Judge Logg leaned forward as Daniel Clarke sat down.

"Prior complaints, or the absence of them is not the issue," he soberly informed the jury. "You are here to address the charge that is before us today."

Leaning back complacently, he called the break for lunch.

*   *   *

"Judge Logg is aptly named—wood between the ears and plate mushrooms covering the eyes." Beary hacked at his pork chops in an attempt to free the meat from the bone. The courthouse restaurant where he and Sylvia had adjourned for lunch was not renowned for its haute cuisine. "Reese doesn't stand a chance if this keeps up," he continued thoughtfully. He gave his daughter a cynical glance. "I suppose you're already gleefully totting up your damages."

Sylvia nodded.

"Yes, but if he's guilty, he deserves what he gets," she said. "The girl was only fourteen, and that constitutes rape, whatever sort of character she was. I'm sure the jury feels she asked for it, but that's irrelevant, especially given that the man was a teacher and the situation is one of duty of care. I'm quite sure we'll win."

"Yes," sighed Beary. "Professional ethics have to be observed. You shouldn't teach high school unless you are mature enough to maintain the appropriate relationship between teacher and pupil. At that age, young people can be a delight, but they also have the potential to be horny, romantic, moody and mischievous. Even I, with my ugly mug, remember in my early days of teaching having a nubile young thing leaning over my shoulder as I marked her essay. She actually rubbed her bosom against my shoulder. I wonder," he added pensively, "if I could track her down after all these years and sue her for sexual harassment."

Sylvia looked appalled.

"Don't be absurd," she said. "Nobody would believe you, anyway."

"Ah, there you are," said Beary. "The whole issue of credibility. You know what's so awful about these cases," he added. "It's one person's word against the other, and how can one prove with absolute certainty who is telling the truth? The present case could be nothing but a tissue of lies."

Sylvia took a sip of coffee and shook her head.

"I doubt it," she said. "I'm quite sure that Tracy Keane, abhorrent as she is, had sexual relations with Reese. He had no business taking advantage of a female student in hormonal overdrive."

"These chops have the consistency of filing folders," said Beary, scowling at his plate. "No wonder Judge Logg is so sour and dyspeptic." He put down his knife and fork and picked up the glass of Scotch he had ordered in spite of his daughter's disapproving eye. "You know what I find hard to reconcile," he continued. "It's the fact that there are two incidents on the same day. Either there is an amazing coincidence at work, or else there's conspiracy involved— but whose conspiracy? Is it a case of trumped up charges by two women who got together at a high-school reunion, or was there deliberate conniving by two teachers to separate and seduce two young girls who had obvious crushes on them and were easy game?"

"I suspect it's the latter. Reese doesn't want Daniel Clarke to call Frampton as a witness, so that tells me he's afraid Frampton will break down under pressure. Frampton's case is puzzling, though. He sounds an entirely different type of person."

"He is," said Beary. "Donna Harmon would never have come forward if it hadn't been for her husband and Tracy Keane. But is she being urged to bring the truth into the open, or coerced into lying by a husband who sees an opportunity to cash in on Tracy's lawsuit? I wouldn't like to make the call on this one."

"You won't have to," said Sylvia crisply. "That's up to the jury." She lay down her fork, gathered up her purse and beckoned the waiter. As she did so, her cellphone rang. She answered the call and listened briefly, then returned the phone to her bag. Her face held a satisfied smirk.

"What was that about?" her father asked. "Another nail in Reese's coffin?"

"Could be. I hired a private detective to trace hotel staff from the relevant period and he just called to say he's located the maid who serviced Reese's room. What's more, Roberta Hacker's crew beat us to it and the woman has already sworn an affidavit which is going to be introduced during the criminal case."

"What could the maid possibly remember after all these years?" said Beary.

"I don't know," said Sylvia, "but if it wasn't incriminating, Hacker wouldn't have gone to the trouble of getting a sworn statement. I venture to say we have Reese right where we want him. No," she added, forestalling her father's attempt to order a second glass of Scotch, "you don't have time for another drink, and even if you did, I have no intention of having you fall asleep and snore all through the afternoon session. Let's go."

"You don't want me sawing Loggs or sleeping like a Logg?" quipped Beary.

But his words drifted into the air for Sylvia was already halfway across the room. Beary lumbered to his feet and obediently followed his daughter out of the restaurant. Sylvia, he thought glumly, grew more like her mother every day.

*   *   *

Beary recognized the first witness of the afternoon session. Mary Bryant looked more serious than when she had greeted Beary in the hallway. She also seemed nervous, and she watched anxiously as the prosecuting counsel approached.

"Did you see Tracy Keane at any time during the day of the theatre trip?" Roberta Hacker asked Mary.

"Not during the daytime. Our English teacher, Miss Phillips, took several of us sightseeing. We started early in the morning and we wound up at the Tower of London at six o'clock. By the time we got back to our billets to change for the party, it was eight-thirty, and we didn't get to the party until half past nine. Tracy wasn't there yet, so I didn't see her until Mr. Reese dropped her off."

"When did they arrive?"

"Around quarter past ten, I think. There was a big grandfather clock in the house and Tracy came in a bit after it had chimed ten o'clock. I didn't see Mr. Reese but someone said Belinda's mother was driving him back to London so I guess he just waited in the car."

"So Tracy arrived at the party on her own?"

Mary Bryant nodded.

"What was her frame of mind when she came in?"

"She was pretty irritable. I remember us all feeling indignant that she snapped at us when we'd been so accommodating letting her have the theatre ticket."

"Did she indicate why she was in an ill humour?"

"No. Well, we didn't know, but actually, we assumed it was because she'd lost her charm bracelet."

"Her charm bracelet?"

"Yes. It was an incredibly gaudy thing—once seen, never forgotten, typical of Tracy—but it had a loose catch. It had probably slipped off in the car, because she did get it back. I saw her wearing it again on the trip home."

"Did she recover her good humour during the party?"

"Oh, yes. In fact, as soon as we commented on her sulky face, she did an about-face and started boasting about what a fabulous time she'd had."

"What about the rest of the trip? Did you notice any change in her behaviour?"

"She seemed the same exuberant Tracy . . . though . . ."

Mary Bryant paused and looked thoughtful.

"Yes?" prompted Roberta Hacker. "There was a change?"

"Well, I did notice that her attitude towards Mr. Reese was different."

"In what way? Anger? Increased familiarity?"

Daniel Clarke rose and objected. Judge Logg shook his head and allowed the question to stand.

"She's leading the witness," muttered Beary. He glowered at the lady in front of him who had turned to raise a finger to her lips, then sat back to hear the witness's response.

"She wasn't angry," Mary Bryant was saying, "and she certainly wasn't any more familiar with Mr. Reese. Rather the reverse if anything. She just didn't seem as interested in him. If anyone brought the subject up, she was every bit as insistent that he liked her, but I think her crush had cooled."

"Did you get the impression that Mr. Reese had upset her?"

Mary Bryant looked puzzled and rather distressed.

"Well, yes, but—"

"So she *was* upset after the trip to London?"

"Yes, I suppose she was."

"And she never told you why?"

"No. She didn't say anything, but I thought—"

"We can't deal in conjecture. The reality is you really don't know the reason why she had this change of heart towards her teacher."

Mary Bryant bit her lip and glanced down at her lap.

"No. I didn't know why she'd changed."

With a look of triumph, Roberta Hacker withdrew and Daniel Clarke came forward. He asked only two questions.

"Until these charges were laid against Ian Reese, what did you think caused Tracy Keane's change of attitude towards him?"

Mary Bryant looked relieved to be allowed to speak.

"At the time, I took it to mean that her nose was out of joint because Mr. Reese had continued to treat her like a student throughout their so-called date."

Daniel Clarke nodded with satisfaction.

"You concluded that she felt slighted?"

"Yes."

Sylvia's eyes narrowed. Beary leaned towards his daughter and muttered in her ear. "It's logical," he said, "and quite possible. You better not count your damages yet."

He looked up to see that Mary Bryant had left the stand and an elderly, silver-haired man was being sworn in. The newcomer wore an expensive-looking suit and carried himself with dignity.

"That's William Aird," Sylvia hissed. "The maître d' at Ivy's."

Beary looked at the man curiously. The former restaurateur radiated good humour and poise, and Beary could easily imagine him working a dining room and charming the occupants with light-hearted repartee.

"I spent twenty-three years at Ivy's," the witness was saying. "Over the years, I met many people. Some stand out in one's mind, and some fade from memory. Of course, a good maître d'hôtel is trained to remember people, and it is surprising how many clients one can recall."

"Do you remember the defendant in this case?" asked Roberta Hacker.

"Yes, I remember him because he returned for several other visits to London over the years. Mr. Reese is an enthusiastic theatre-goer. He often dined at our restaurant, before or after shows."

"Were you on duty the night he brought Tracy Keane to dine in your restaurant?"

"Yes. I remember the occasion."

"Did you talk to them at all?"

"Yes. I always stopped by the tables to see if everything was all right. But I also greeted them as they arrived. I remember Mr. Reese introducing Miss Keane as his student. He was in a very jocular mood. He said she was ravenously hungry and to make sure she had double portions of everything she ordered."

"Do you recall what time they arrived?"

"They had been to the afternoon performance at the theatre across the street, so it would have been soon after seven o'clock."

"Did they stay long?"

"Long enough to eat. Probably about an hour. I don't recall them lingering after they had finished their meal."

"Did you overhear any part of their conversation?"

"It's so long ago. I can't remember anything specific. They appeared to be having a good time. The atmosphere was cheery, I think. In my job, it is rather like listening to music all day long. You only sit up and notice if someone strikes a wrong note. I don't remember anything unusual about the occasion."

"Did you sense any aura of romance?"

"I remember thinking that the girl was rather sweet on him . . . well, not exactly sweet. She wasn't that sort of girl. But she was rather seductive in her behaviour for one so young."

"Thank you. No further questions."

William Aird blinked as Roberta Hacker returned to her chair. The dismissal had been abrupt.

"I wonder what Aird knows that Hacker doesn't want made public," muttered Beary.

Daniel Clarke was smiling as he rose to question the witness.

"You seem to think Tracy Keane had a crush on her teacher?"

"Yes."

"Did you have any sense that her feelings were reciprocated?"

"Not really. I don't think Mr. Reese was leading her on at all. It wasn't like the other occasions."

"What other occasions?"

"Well, on two of his subsequent trips to London, he had lady friends travelling with him, and even when he travelled alone, he often met up with women and dined with them."

"Did you ever see him with a woman during the tour of 1969?"

"No. Not on that occasion. But then, it was a school trip . . . an event that called for discretion, I think."

Judge Logg leaned forward ominously.

"Am I to understand that Mr. Reese visited your restaurant with a different escort every time he made a trip to London?"

The retired maître d'hôtel shrugged.

"He was quite a ladies' man, Your Honour. One could see that the liaisons were romantic in nature, but his companions were always grown women. I never saw him with young girls."

"How long has Mr. Reese been married to his present wife?" Judge Logg asked Daniel Clarke.

"Forty-six years, Your Honour."

"I see." The judge nodded sourly and made a note on his pad.

Daniel Clarke ignored the judge's disapproving tone and reiterated the witness's statement.

"So it is correct to say that when you saw the defendant in situations of a romantic nature, he was always with adult women, never with young girls."

He nodded towards the jury and indicated that he was through with the witness. Beary glanced towards his daughter. Her frown had deepened and she was starting to look worried. The case was becoming more ambiguous by the moment.

*   *   *

Anxious to beat the rush-hour traffic, Beary abandoned Sylvia at three o'clock and left the courtroom. He had parked at Pacific Centre, so he had a few blocks to walk. As he cut up past the Vancouver Art Gallery and crossed the open square that led to Georgia Street, he noticed a heavy-set man smoking a cigarette by the fountain. Seeing the large bald dome on the man's head and the much larger, covered dome around his midriff, Beary felt less guilty about his own indulgence at lunch. Beary was a sylph by comparison. To his surprise, the man waved and called out to him.

"Hey, Beary! It is Bertram Beary, isn't it?"

Beary stopped in his tracks as the man approached. He had no idea who had accosted him. Seeing Beary's blank expression, the man jogged his memory.

"Jack Jones," he said. "I came to Carnarvon the year you left."

"Right," said Beary, identifying a familiar countenance amid the excess pounds of flesh. "In those days you had hair and a waistline."

Jones was unoffended.

"Exactly," he said. "You were over at the trial earlier, weren't you? I thought it was you on the other side of the courtroom. A lot of us old-timers are coming to see how Reese is doing."

Beary nodded.

"So what's your assessment?" said Jones.

"I never knew him that well," said Beary, "so I don't know what to think. One thing is certain: Reese's extra-marital flings will work against him. The judge's voice dripped censure once that came out."

Jones bit his lip.

"Reese did have affairs," he said soberly, "but his wife was just as bad. The two of them were a mismatch from the word *go*. They agreed to go their separate ways."

"You knew him well, did you?"

"Yes. We used to go pubbing together on Friday nights. He often talked about his women friends, but I never had the feeling that he was into young girls. I mean, he liked them. We all did. It's quite a boost to the ego to have nubile young things sighing about you and offering to run your errands, but one takes it for what it is. Teenage hormones. We didn't refer to them as jailbait for nothing."

"Did Ian Reese talk to you about his students?"

"Well, of course he did. I don't need to tell you that. All teachers talk about their students."

"True," acknowledged Beary. "Usually the best ones or the ones that drove us round the bend. Which did Reese talk about?"

"Mostly his fan club, as he called them, but I never thought he took their moony eyes seriously. I still have trouble believing he'd have done anything improper. If only Rowena Phillips hadn't died in that bus crash in Mexico last year. She could have established what time Reese and Tracy got to the hotel."

"How so?"

"She was in the lobby when they arrived."

"Did she tell you that?"

Jack Jones looked blank.

"Well, no. She never mentioned it, but I was talking with Mary McFee last week. She was rooming with Rowena Phillips on the London trip. Poor old Reese was so bloody desperate he asked Mary if she'd pretend that she'd been with Rowena in the lobby when he arrived."

Beary blinked.

"He asked her to perjure herself."

"Like I said, he was desperate. Mary was sympathetic, but of course, she wouldn't play ball. She was quite upset about it though. I met her at the retired-teachers' luncheon, and she asked me if I thought she'd done the right thing. She said she'd have given way if

Rowena had said anything about it to her, but the reality was she knew nothing about it. Which doesn't mean a thing, of course. Rowena Phillips kept everything close to that flat chest of hers. Reese could be telling the truth."

"Did you go on the band trip to London?" Beary asked.

Jones shuddered.

"No. I avoided that sort of extra-curricular outing like the plague. I enjoyed my students during school hours, but ten days straight on a school package tour would have been about as enjoyable as going on holiday with my mother-in-law."

"But Ian Reese was more gregarious, wasn't he?"

"Yes, and given his propensity for extra-marital flings, any time away from home provided him with opportunities. He always managed to line-up a bit on the side, no matter where he travelled."

"Did he talk about the trip on his return?"

"A bit. The usual tales of calamities with luggage, lost instruments and problems with billets."

"Nothing about the 'bit on the side' he lined up in London?"

"No." Jones paused. "He was close-lipped after the band trip."

"And that's what's bothering you, isn't it?" said Beary. "No stories for the boys about his latest conquest."

Jones nodded ruefully.

"Did Reese say anything about Tracy Keane?" Beary asked.

"He mentioned taking the girls to the theatre," Jones said reluctantly.

"Was that all?"

Jones' brow clouded over.

"No. I asked him how he coped with Tracy panting after him all through the band trip."

"And what was his reply?"

Jones sighed and shook his head despairingly.

"He laughed, and said not to worry because he'd fixed Tracy Keane."

Jones looked at Beary, as if hoping for reassurance, or failing that, absolution for having misgivings about his friend. When Beary remained silent, Jones continued wearily. "I took it to mean he'd put her in her place, but now I can't help wondering just what he did do to her. What a bloody mess. Everything can be interpreted two ways."

Beary nodded gravely.

"Sadly, it can," he said. "I don't know what to think either. The jury is still out."

*   *   *

As Beary was having breakfast the following morning, the phone rang. It was Norton. He sounded perplexed.

"Sylvia says you came down to the courthouse yesterday. Are you going back today?"

"Yes, I thought I might."

"Could you give me a call if you hear anything significant? I trust your judgement, especially since you're a teacher and you knew the men involved."

"Stuck, are you?" said Beary sympathetically. "Can't figure your client out?"

"Honestly, no. The man's a puzzle. He's facing a jail term and the loss of his professional status, and yet he only seems concerned about not hurting the woman who has laid the charges against him. He says she's lying but he doesn't want to say anything that will cause her trouble. I'm beginning to think it was a mistake to get him out on bail. Being stuck inside might have scared him into opening up. As it is, I don't know what to do with him."

"Frampton always marched to a different drummer. I could never make him out, either. But your case doesn't depend on the outcome of Reese's trial. The circumstances are totally different. Frampton took Donna back to the party and was only alone with her because she'd been upset by her boyfriend."

"I know," said Norton. "I think I could convince a jury that Roy Harmon latched onto the fact that Tracy went to bed with Reese on the last night of the band trip, then persuaded her to sue, figuring he could bully Donna into accusing Frampton and creating a bogus suit on the back of the other case."

"You can't assume that Reese will be convicted," said Beary. "The last two witnesses weakened the prosecution's case. There's no hard evidence as yet."

But Beary spoke too soon. When he arrived at the courthouse, he was met by a jubilant Sylvia coming out the main entrance. She was wearing her coat and carrying her briefcase.

"Leaving already?" he asked her.

"I am," she trilled. "They're on a break, but I have everything I need so I'm heading back to the office. Remember the maid I told you about. They just played the video with her testimony. It was incredible. She just put the last nail in Reese's coffin."

Beary looked sceptical.

"How on earth could she accurately remember a hotel guest after so many years?"

"Oh, she remembers," said Sylvia. "Don't forget, Reese visited London often and always stayed at that hotel. But leaving that aside, it was her first job. She was hired the very day the Canadians arrived. She was young and naïve, and she was intrigued by the people in the school group. In those days, she was a good-looking seventeen-year-old, and Reese made a point of letting her know how attractive she was. Every tip came with a flirtatious conversation. If she'd encouraged him, we might not have this case today. Anyway, she changed the bed in his room the next morning, and not only were there indications from the sheets that sex had taken place, there were condoms in the waste-bin and a woman's charm bracelet on the floor beside the bed. From her description, there's no doubt that it was the one that Tracy Keane lost. And when she picked it up and set in on the night table, Reese winked at her and said, 'Shh, not a word,' and gave her an extra-large tip."

Sylvia flashed a triumphant smile and trotted away in the direction of Georgia Street.

Beary shook his head wearily. Natural pride in his former profession had made him hope for a different outcome, but that hope was gone now. Disillusionment was a bitter pill to swallow. He paused, suddenly reluctant to enter the courthouse. While he was contemplating buying himself a coffee, he saw a couple coming along the street. The man was Daniel Burke, and he was engaged in earnest conversation with an attractive woman. Beary could not remember seeing her before. Her clothes were casually expensive and her hair was dyed a soft brown and smartly styled, but in spite of her youthful air, there was a gauntness about the neck and cheekbones that no degree of makeup and superficial elegance could disguise. Beary decided she must be in her seventies, though she had worn extremely well. The defence lawyer continued to talk earnestly as he opened the door at the entrance of the courthouse. As he held the door for his companion, Beary caught a glimpse of his face. Burke looked serious, but he did not look downcast. In fact, his expression seemed surprisingly smug. Feeling exceedingly curious, Beary abandoned the idea of coffee and followed the couple into the courthouse.

As he made his way down the hall, he saw a familiar face coming towards him. It was Althea Morgan. Not in the mood for a lecture on community standards, Beary started to detour to the other side of the hall, but then a sudden thought occurred to him and he held his course.

Althea Morgan did not looked surprised to see Beary.

"Good morning, Councillor Beary." Her tone was supercilious. "Teachers sticking together? I suppose you're here to support your colleague."

Beary refused to rise to the bait. He adopted a grave pose and spoke with unctuous insincerity.

"I heard your evidence yesterday, Mrs. Morgan, and I must say I was shocked at what was going on during that trip. I'm surprised that one of the other teachers didn't step in to rectify the situation. I gather one of the English teachers actually saw Ian Reese and his student come into the hotel, so she should have spoken out when she saw them going upstairs together."

"She might not have noticed," said Althea Morgan. "I'm sure Miss Phillips would have acted if she'd seen anything questionable going on. But the front desk was tucked around a corner so she wouldn't have been able to see the elevators. Anyway, whatever she saw or did is immaterial because the poor woman was killed in an accident, so she can't tell us anything."

"Reese probably used her name for that very reason," Beary said innocently. "He knew she couldn't counter his story. She might not have even been at the hotel that evening."

Althea Morgan fell right into his trap.

"Oh no, she was there. She was in the lobby when my mother and I came back."

"From the ballet and your late dinner?"

"That's right. She was on the phone as we came through the lobby."

"Well, what do you know?" said Beary. He smiled smugly and was about to continue on his way when another thought occurred to him. He pointed towards the double doors that led to courtroom number three. Daniel Burke and his companion were about to go inside.

"Do you know who that woman is?" Beary asked.

"The one with Reese's lawyer?" Althea Morgan looked surprised at the question. "Yes, of course I do. That's Belinda Gordon's mother. She was one of our chaperones. Not that she spent much time supervising the students," she said with a sniff. "She was much too busy having a good time visiting old friends or running up to town to see shows."

Althea Morgan tossed her head and walked away. Thoughtfully reviewing what he had learned, Beary continued down the hall. He was about to enter the courtroom when he noticed a solitary man sitting on a bench further along the hall. With a start, Beary recognized him. It was John Frampton. His face was ashen, and the lines around his eyes were indicative of strain rather than age. He did not notice Beary, but was staring past him further along the hall. Beary turned to see two people coming down the corridor. One was a heavily built man with a surly expression. His companion was a pale-looking woman with long, salt-and-pepper hair tied back at her neck. She wore an ill-cut, unadorned navy blue pantsuit. Beary walked over to John Frampton.

"Is that Donna Harmon?" he asked quietly.

Frampton glanced up and nodded briefly. He expressed no surprise at finding Beary beside him. Beary had the feeling that the man was in a dream world where people could appear or disappear without causing him the least surprise. Whoever materialized was simply part of the progress of his bizarre nightmare.

"You'd already left before she came to the school," Frampton said softly. "You didn't know her, did you?"

"No. Was she a good student?"

"The best. Not in the academic way, but a good girl. A kind girl. She . . . was special. I thought the world of her . . . and she used to think the world of me. But now she hates me. Why else would she do this? Why else would she want to destroy me?"

"She hasn't destroyed you yet," said Beary. He watched Donna Harmon and her escort as they reached the courtroom doors. She had not looked their way, yet Beary was sure she was aware of Frampton's presence. As the couple disappeared inside the courtroom, Beary turned back to Frampton. "Are you sitting here because you may be called as a witness?" he asked.

"No, I don't have to testify."

"Then come with me into the courtroom," said Beary. "I think the next witness may prove to be the most revealing of all."

*   *   *

Amelia Gordon stood serenely in the witness box, apparently unperturbed as she stated her evidence. She was now widowed after a long and happy marriage, but she admitted that in the early years, she and her husband had gone through some difficult times, and during the band trip to London, she had had an affair with Ian Reese. On the final night of the trip, she had not really been meeting a friend in town. When she drove Reese back to London, she went with him to his hotel room and remained there until the early hours of the morning, after which she drove back to her sister's house in Harrow. She also enlightened the court as to how Ian Reese had "fixed" Tracy Keane, for Reese had told her all about the earlier incident and they had shared a laugh together, along with a bottle of champagne, while tucked between the sheets.

On returning for the keys, Reese had told Tracy to remain in the lobby but she had forged ahead into the elevator and come up to the third floor. She had followed him down the hall, and once he unlocked his room, had shot inside and sprawled out on the bed. She had flatly refused to move, and when Reese went to pull her up, she tried to pull him down on top of her. In the struggle, her bracelet came off, but Reese did not notice. Realizing that the situation was getting out of hand, he went to the telephone and dialled down to the lobby. Sure enough, Miss Phillips was still there chatting with the girl on the desk, who happily put the older teacher on the line. As soon as Tracy heard Reese asking the English teacher to come up and help him deal with a difficult situation, she got off the bed like a rocket and flounced out the door. Once she had left, Reese told Miss Phillips that the emergency was over, hung up and followed the sulking student outside.

Neither one of them had noticed the bracelet, which had fallen on the floor beside the bed, and it was not found until the maid picked it up the following morning. When the maid held up the bracelet, Reese had assumed it belonged to Amelia Gordon—he was the sort of man who noticed women's natural attributes but rarely paid attention to what they wore—and he handed it over to her when they met at the airport. She realized immediately whose bracelet it was and she returned it to Tracy, saying tactfully that it had been dropped in the car during the journey back from town.

Beary looked long and hard at the faces of the jury as Amelia Gordon came out of the witness box. Their expressions were as clear as if the words "not guilty" had been printed on their foreheads. As the judge began his summing up, it was clear that his attitude had switched from contempt for the accused to outrageous condemnation for the woman who had put him in the dock. As Judge Logg continued his diatribe on the subject of false accusations and abuse of the court system, Beary nodded to himself with satisfaction. There would be no difficulty in getting Frampton off now, he was certain. He glanced across the room to where Tracy Keane sat, alongside Roy and Donna Harmon. He was not surprised to see that Tracy Keane's features were distorted with rage, her eyes glittering and her mouth twisted with spite; neither was he taken aback at Roy Harmon's surly countenance, suffused a dark red from the bitter mixture of disappointment, anger and humiliation, but Donna Harmon's reaction took him by surprise, for the woman looked stricken with terror. Her eyes roved wildly around the courtroom, but when she saw Frampton at the back of the room, her glance froze, fixed on his face. She stared beseechingly at her former teacher, and as Frampton's eyes met hers, his shoulders sagged with defeat. Beary took his elbow and guided him gently from the courtroom.

*   *   *

"I'm not going to fight the charges. It's over."

Frampton stared into the cup of coffee that Beary had bought him but he made no attempt to drink it.

Beary could not believe what he was hearing.

"Are you out of your mind? The prosecution's case won't hold now. It's obvious that the girls made up the whole story."

Frampton looked up from the table and his eyes drifted off into space. He looked tired and utterly miserable.

"Didn't you see her face?" he said. "She's terrified of him."

Beary felt exasperated. He wanted to reach across the table and shake Frampton. However, he kept his voice level and tried to impart some sense into the apathetic man.

"You can't throw your entire life and career away because Donna Harmon is scared of her husband. For heaven's sake, man, you're being charged with beating her up and forcing yourself on her. You're not telling me you did that, are you?"

"No, of course I didn't, but—"

"Well, then, what are you thinking of?"

A strange expression came into Frampton's eyes, although he still evaded Beary's gaze. There was resignation, and another quality that Beary couldn't pin down.

"I'm thinking of a debt that has to be settled, albeit far too late," he said. "I owe it to Donna. I can protect her. It's the only thing I can do for her now."

"Why do you owe her? What do you owe her?" Beary felt utterly bewildered.

At last, Frampton looked Beary in the face.

"Justice," he said simply.

An icy wave of comprehension rolled through Beary's veins. All at once, he saw that his dismissal of John Frampton as too timid to stray from the rules was naïve and irrational. He should have listened to Edwina's assessment of her colleague. Guilt did not have to stem from evil intent; it could also be borne of weakness and immaturity.

"What really did happen that night?" he asked, dreading the answer that he knew was coming.

Frampton sighed.

"We made love. She was so upset, and I wanted to comfort her— and it just happened. You see, we really were in love with each other, though of course we'd never admitted it, because we knew it was impossible—not just because she was underage, but with me being her teacher. And yet, when you consider that she was fourteen and I was only just twenty-one—I was fresh out of university and teacher training, for God's sake. People marry all the time with age differences far greater than that."

He stared at Beary as if hoping for some sign of compassion, but, met with only a blank stare, he continued: "I really cared about her," he said sadly, "but it wasn't the way I expected. She ... she was inexperienced, and I suppose I hurt her. It was her first time. It wouldn't have mattered except, well, I suppose I was a bit shocked because . . . well, she had been so eager. And then we heard Harmon bellowing below the window. Donna was terrified. So was I. Suddenly I realized the situation I was in. I hurried to get my clothes back on and Donna ran to the window to stall Harmon, but she tripped and fell on the arm of the chair."

"You mean the black eye and the split lip really were from the fall?"

"Yes, she told the truth about that, the first time, anyway. I wanted to stay and make sure she was all right, but she begged me to go . . . and . . ."

"And you did."

"Yes. What else could I do? If I'd stayed it would have meant disgrace . . . the loss of my job . . . the loss of my profession. And that Gordon woman was there. She was dealing with Harmon. I thought everything would be all right."

"You were afraid for your own skin, so you ran and left her to cope on her own."

Frampton hung his head.

"I know it was contemptible and you probably despise me. I was immature and weak. But now you know why I can't fight the charges. I'm ready to face the consequences."

Beary nodded.

"Yes, you're going to have to, but you'd better approach this realistically. Talk with Norton and let him guide you. Donna was fourteen so it will still be a rape charge, but statutory rape if you didn't force her—and you didn't hit her, so that will help when it comes to the final sentencing. You have to speak up and tell the truth."

Frampton shook his head.

"No," he said sadly. "I can't tell the truth. I destroyed her once. I can't do it again. Didn't you see how she looked at me in the courtroom? She didn't want to hurt me. She was just terrified of what Harmon would do if he realized that she'd slept with me of her own free will. That's why she accused me of rape. Once Tracy Keane blabbed about what she'd seen that night, Donna was backed into a corner. This is the only way I can keep her safe. It's the only way I can atone for the way I ruined her life."

Beary shook his head in bewilderment.

"Look, get things into perspective. Yes, you were in the wrong. You were in a position of trust and you abused it, but you said yourself that she was keen and willing. Admit to what you did wrong, but you don't have to take the weight of everything that happened for the rest of her life on your shoulders."

"But I do," said Harmon. "Making love to her that night wasn't what hurt her so deeply. It was the fact that I abandoned her afterwards that destroyed her. You see, the next day, I was so shocked at what had happened—at what a close escape I'd had from total ruin—that I ignored her. From that moment on, I treated her like all the other students, with total impartiality, never allowing us to be alone together. It must have devastated her. For the rest of the time she was at the school she was utterly withdrawn. She was completely dominated by Harmon and she didn't resist. She'd never been a confident girl, but she had begun to blossom throughout the time I'd encouraged her and made her feel special, and in one blow, I destroyed everything that she had gained—her confidence, her self-image and her hope for a better future. I continued my career and retired with a full pension, while she spent forty-five years in a marriage with a domineering bully who took away any last shreds of self-worth she had left. Now, if I tell the truth, her life will become a nightmare."

Beary fixed Frampton with a stern stare. "You'll go to prison, you know," he said. "The judge won't show you any mercy. The police could be warned about Harmon. They could take steps to ensure Donna's safety."

"I doubt it," said Frampton. "I wouldn't want to risk it."

Beary sighed.

"What a bloody mess," he said. "There's absolutely nothing to be gained if you proceed on this course."

Frampton looked up and his face reflected the glimmer of a smile.

"Oh, but you're wrong," he said quietly. "Donna knows the truth. If I stand up in court and admit to all the charges against me, even though it means that I'll be going to prison, she will know I'm doing it to protect her. When the judge delivers the verdict of guilty, she'll know that I really care about her."

"It's a meaningless gesture," said Beary. "More than half her life is over. It's too late to restore what's she's lost."

Frampton stood up and slid his chair into the table. As he slipped on his coat, he looked down at Beary and smiled wryly.

"Donna is the only one who can decide that," he said. "Too late the verdict? I'm prepared to take the chance that it's not."

The Boat Chain

Judith Canning was born in 1961, the only daughter of an Alberta oil baron who ruled his large family with a rod of iron. Jack Canning was industrious, disciplined, and tough on anyone who failed to meet his standards. He was smart with money, but extremely frugal, except when it came to his passion for outdoor sports and extra-marital adventures. He didn't care what his family thought about his philandering, but he did expect his children to step up to the corporate mark and share his enthusiasm for hunting and fishing. However, in the seventies, the world was undergoing many philosophical changes, and to Canning's fury, none of his sons displayed an aptitude for business or an interest in blood sports.

Judith was the daughter who made up for the apathetic sons. She shunned the pot-smoking, psychedelic world indulged in by so many of her contemporaries and grew into a business-oriented, lean, mean outdoor girl who could manage money, dictate to employees and hunt and shoot with the best. Bent on emulating her father, she intended to make a massive fortune and have a large family that she could rule with the same narcissistic inflexibility she had experienced at his hand; so, when at eighteen, she met a handsome young man who was the scion of a wealthy Vancouver family and an enthusiastic hunter and fisherman to boot, she set her sights on him and brought him down as neatly as if he had been an elk standing in an open field.

As it happened, Harold Fairlie was willing to be snared. He was a thirty-six-year-old bachelor and an only child, so his parents were anxious for him to marry. Grandchildren were needed to inherit the Fairlie fortune and carry on the family name. Judith, with her desire for children and her shared enthusiasm for Harold's hobbies, seemed the perfect choice. She also had one other advantage. With her tiny boyish figure and her lack of feminine wiles, she was far more appealing to him than the voluptuous daughters of his parents' friends who were regularly presented as marital prospects. Harold was willing and able to do his duty, but when it came to bedroom sports, he infinitely preferred the company of his men friends. Since coming out of the closet was not an option, marriage to Judith was the next best thing. His life would simply have to be compartmentalized to accommodate both lifestyles.

What Harold did not take into account was the effect such a marriage would have on Judith, who turned out to be as lustily enthusiastic about sex as her father. Although frustrated at Harold's lack of interest, Judith coped during the early years, since she was pregnant most of the time and produced three children in rapid succession. However, in 1985, she caught Harold in flagrante with the skipper of their Grand Banks trawler yacht, and the realization of the reason for her husband's lassitude struck her as if she had been pole-axed. When her hysterics, rage and subsequent depression subsided, Judith remembered one of her father's favourite pieces of advice: Never get angry; just get even. Divorce was out of the question. She was younger and far healthier than Harold and was determined not to settle for a mere portion of his assets. Besides, she now had a sword to hold over his head, which she cannily used to make him re-write his will.

Having ensured that she was now her husband's sole beneficiary and that their children's futures were placed securely in her hands, Judith affirmed that she and Harold would carry on as usual. They would still take their hunting and fishing trips together, not to mention the annual family cruise—the difference being that Judith would now hire the guides and skippers, and she would select healthy macho males who would meet her needs rather than cater to her husband's. Harold could find his entertainment elsewhere. Judith Fairlie had always been tough. Now she became hard as the drill bits that bored into her father's oil wells. No one was ever going to put anything over on her again—and no one did, until twenty-seven years later.

*   *   *

June, 2012

The watcher in the woods raised his binoculars to his eyes and studied the boats anchored off the shore of the marine park. He could understand why the park was so popular with boaters. The horseshoe-shaped cove offered sheltered anchorage for yachts, and at the eastern point, a small dock protruded from the rocks, allowing an easy landing for smaller craft bringing people and pets to shore.

In the course of his vigil, the watcher had become so familiar with the park that he could have drawn a map of the forested network of trails. The longest trail followed the curve of the rocky shoreline all the way around to the Pool Bay Pub, but within the park, a rough track looped round the horseshoe cove, linking the long pebble beach on the far side of the eastern point with a secluded cove at the western point. The watcher had seen lots of swimmers enjoying the safety of the shallow beach on the east side of the park, but his main viewing post had been the western point, with its view of the tiny cove that provided a private refuge for sunbathers who sought some moments of solitude. What he was looking for was far more likely to happen there.

At present, the cove was deserted so he continued to study the anchored boats. An elegant sailboat rode the tide a hundred yards off the eastern point, and a clinker-built converted fishing boat bobbed gently nearby. Near the western point, closer to shore, was a custom-built cabin cruiser with generous above-deck accommodation. Beyond it, half a mile across the glittering expanse of water, the watcher could see the red roof of the Pool Bay Pub standing out brightly in the sunlight.

He brought his binoculars down and trained them on his target. This was the group of five linked boats within the horseshoe cove. The *Ocean Princess*, a forty-foot Grand Banks trawler yacht, was first in the chain. Next came the *Helena*, a slightly smaller Bayliner, and beside it was the *Osprey*, a thirty-foot Tollycraft. An expensive-looking Carver called *Kingfisher* was linked to the Tollycraft, and last in the chain was a twenty-four-foot Trophy, the *Klahowya*. With the outer vessels secured by lines to the trees on shore, and the ones between lashed together at the cleats, the line of boats resembled a floating hotel. A large yellow dog hopped back and forth along the swim grids, following two young children who appeared to enjoy the freedom of all the boats. The adults occasionally followed suit or passed food dishes to their sailing companions. Occasionally, a bark or a raised voice would carry across to the watcher on the shore, but otherwise, he felt as if he were watching a silent movie.

Even at a distance, he could pick out the members of the Fairlie family. The Grand Banks belonged to the wealthy matriarch and was skippered by her current toy-boy. Judith Fairlie had been widowed for five years. She had inherited fortunes from both her father and her late husband and was rich enough to indulge her every whim, one of which involved hiring a new hunk each year to run the *Ocean Princess* for her summer cruise. The widow was certainly not reticent about flaunting her latest flame. This one's name was Barry King, and at present, he was reclining on the deck looking for all the world like a young Robert Redford. Looking pleased with himself too, and why not? The Widow Fairlie was not only rich; she was quite the eyeful. She had obviously married young, because it was difficult to tell the difference between her and her thirty-year-old daughter who was sunbathing on the deck of the Tollycraft further down the chain. Christine Spence, née Fairlie, could have been her mother's twin. Both women were petite with toned, tanned bodies and short blonde hair. The widow could still fit into her daughter's clothes, and often did, if only to make the point that she could, and in doing so, needle her younger daughter who was built on much more generous lines.

Christine's sister, Robin, looked nothing like her mother or siblings, all of whom were lean and fair. Referred to as The Afterthought, Robin, at nineteen, was a decade younger than the other Fairlie offspring. She had the lush, dark beauty of a young Raquel Welch, and her statuesque figure and dark hair had given rise to much conjecture. Some said her colouring and build had been inherited from a yachtsman from Tofino; others speculated that the father was a hardy moose hunter from Prince George. Still, all the gossips agreed that her sweet nature did not come from her self-centered mother. At present, Robin was standing at the stern of the Bayliner that was lashed between her mother's boat and the Tollycraft. It was owned by the oldest Fairlie son, Jordan, and named after his wife, Helena. They were the parents of the two young children who were jumping from boat to boat and playing with the dog. Presumably, Jordan and his wife were in the cabin or below deck. Robin seemed to be the only person keeping an eye on the boisterous antics of the youngsters.

A sudden movement on the Tollycraft caught the watcher's eye. A man had come out from the cabin and joined the look-alike daughter on the deck. The watcher scrutinized the couple with particular care. Christine and Godfrey Spence made an unusual pair: she, so tiny and fair, and he, a former NFL star, six-foot-four and black as coal. A mismatch if there ever was one, emotionally as well as visually. The marriage was in trouble, but given Judith Fairlie's attitude towards divorce, splitting up could prove expensive. The threat of being cut from her mother's will would keep Christine in bondage, but not, perhaps, be enough to keep her from straying from her obsessively jealous husband.

Still, she was no worse off than her siblings. They all had to dance to the widow's tune. If Harold Fairlie had not left his assets to his wife and allowed her the final distribution of their estate, it was unlikely that any of the younger generation would have taken part in the annual cruise. Two weeks with an autocrat who controlled them with the same cold-blooded skill she used to play a twenty-pound salmon was the holiday from Hell. Whatever was willed to her heirs in the future, they were earning in the present.

A man came out of the cabin of the fourth boat in the chain. With his lean figure and blonde good looks, Lee Fairlie was even more handsome than the widow's toy-boy. Lee was only one year younger than his brother, Jordan, but he had a youthful air that spoke of his unencumbered bachelor life—which was soon to end, since he was engaged to the exotic South Asian beauty who was lolling on the bow of the Carver. Lee clambered up to the bow and bent to kiss his fiancée, who responded enthusiastically. Lucky Lee, the watcher thought. Nazeem Murji was gorgeous, and brave enough to defy her parents who were opposed to the match. That was one thing that could be said in the widow's favour. She might be narcissistic and power-hungry, but she was definitely not racist and she didn't care about people's religion. An Afro-American Muslim son-in-law and a Sikh for a prospective daughter-in-law, neither had created a ripple in her smoothly Botoxed complexion. It seemed that good looks were the only passport necessary for entry into the Fairlie clan.

The watcher turned his attention to the final boat in the chain. It was a far humbler craft than the rest. The *Klahowya* was more of a runabout fishing boat than a cruiser. It was manned by a darkly handsome stud who appeared to be a friend of Lee Fairlie, although the majority of his time was spent with Lee's youngest sister, Robin. The watcher lowered the binoculars and pulled out his iPhone. The man's name was on the notepad. Jake Seagrove—he was a film actor—and a girl-magnet, too, judging by the way he behaved with the women on the cruise. Probably hoping to be the next James Bond, the watcher thought cynically.

He slipped away his iPhone and looked back at the boat chain. Jordan and Helena Fairlie had come onto the deck of the Bayliner and were now looking after their children. Robin Fairlie had gone over to the *Kingfisher* and was standing at the aft rail with Nazeem. They were watching Lee and Jake. Egged on by the girls, the two young men had taken spear guns and were scuba diving off the Trophy.

A high-pitched screeching erupted overhead. An eagle was bringing food to her greedy young. There was a nest perched at the top of a nearby Douglas fir and the eagle had been flying back and forth for the past few days. The cries increased in volume, and the watcher glanced upward. Two large, black wingspans soared above the treetops. The eagle was chasing off a turkey vulture. The shrieks were ear-piercing, but gradually, the noise faded as the predatory birds retreated across the water. Relieved, the watcher turned his attention back to the occupants of the boat chain.

The screeching had caught the attention of the boaters, for they were looking up, trying to pinpoint the location of the nest. The watcher stepped back into the trees and lowered the binoculars. If the sun caught the lenses, the glint could alert the boaters that they were being observed. But after a moment, they lost interest in the eagles. Jordan Fairlie joined the scuba divers in the water and an impromptu competition began between the three men. Soon, the children were hanging over the stern of the Tollycraft, cheering on the divers, and the big yellow dog was barking excitedly. The noise brought the widow to the rail of the *Ocean Princess* and she stared down silently at the aquatic display. Curiously, the watcher trained his binoculars on her face, for her body language revealed nothing of her thoughts, but all he could detect was a faint, enigmatic smile that could carry a thousand different interpretations.

A shout brought the watcher's attention back to the water. Jake Seagrove had emerged from the deep and was holding aloft a large lingcod. He tried to pass his catch up to Robin, but she squealed and backed away. Suddenly, all heads turned the other way. The watcher had heard no one speak, for the eagle had returned and the young in the nest were screaming to be fed. However, he knew a command must have been issued from the *Ocean Princess*, for everyone was looking towards Judith Fairlie. Her eyes were fixed on her son's muscular shipmate. Silently, Jake slid back into the water, glided across to the trawler yacht and slipped the fish into the net that she held down to him. The watcher could not see their expressions, but he could tell that their eyes were riveted on each other. The moment seemed to freeze time, but then Jake pushed himself away from the boat and swam vigorously back towards the Trophy.

Curious to see the reaction from the other boaters, the watcher let the binoculars sweep the length of the boat chain. At first, he thought none of them had noticed anything unusual about the exchange between the widow and her son's friend, but when the binoculars landed on the Trophy, the still figure of Robin Fairlie made him realize that he had not imagined the unspoken message that had passed between the man in the water and the woman on the boat. Robin was not speaking; however, her body language was eloquent. It was a silent scream, as heart-rending as the shrieks of the eaglets overhead.

*   *   *

Alexandra Lacey looked up from her laptop and stared out at the sparkling waters of Pool Bay. The view from her cottage deck could have graced a jigsaw puzzle: the picturesque pub to the left, the moss-covered rocks following the curve of the bay, clear blue sky above and ocean, smooth as glass, below. In spite of the heat wave, it was lovely where she sat, shaded by the awning and cooled by the breeze from the fan inside the French doors. Alexandra sighed. In theory, the cottage was a wonderful place to work on her books. There were so many distractions in town, and she had been sure that she would be able to finish her manuscript in no time if she could just have two weeks of solitary time on the Sunshine Coast. She had no feelings of guilt about leaving her family, for George had been so busy with work during the past year that she hardly ever saw him unless she was entertaining his friends or accompanying him to political functions. Motherhood had also ceased to make demands on her time. Their son was hitching his way around Europe, and their daughter was enrolled in a summer program at the Cordon Bleu school in Paris. But in spite of this freedom from responsibility, Alexandra's story kept stalling like a car with a plugged fuel filter. What's more, she was still distracted. Every conversation from the deck of the pub floated up to where she was sitting. The chatter of people at the yacht club carried clearly across the water too, and most intrusive were the casual exchanges of those who walked the pub path that followed the shoreline below the rocky boundary of her property. Worse still, every one of these dialogues seemed to be more interesting than her plot.

It was her own fault, she thought wryly. She should be writing a sun-drenched story set in the harbour, with outdoor action to make use of the glorious setting, and a plot that utilized the offbeat characters that inhabited the area. Instead, she was struggling with a scenario that took place in a dingy theatre filled with temperamental actors who were making as much of a botch of their production of *Othello* as she was in creating her mystery. She had spent the last twenty minutes trying to think up a suitable metaphor to describe the leading actor, who was as fanatically jealous and mistrustful as the character he was portraying. Wasn't there anything other than a black panther for an analogy to suggest stealth, power and ferocity? Her mind continued to be stuck in the one groove. Time to quit and take a coffee break. Sometimes the combination of movement and caffeine served as a stimulant.

She was about to get up when she heard a woman's voice. It sounded close by, as if the speaker was standing on the pub path right below her deck. Usually Alexandra could hear the murmur of voices as people approached, but she soon realized why there had been no preliminary chatter. The woman had stopped to make a call on her cellphone. Curiously, Alexandra stayed in her chair and listened. There was an urgency about the woman's tone that had caught her attention. Even though the caller's manner was furtive and she kept her voice low, the words still carried clearly.

"We have to be careful," the woman was saying. "I'm certain he doesn't know about us, but he's suspicious. I thought I'd be able to slip away while we're anchored here, but he's as watchful as a bloody cat. It's like being caged with a black panther. Those gleaming eyes track my every movement. Yes, I know, it's driving me crazy too, but it's not just my husband. My mother would go ballistic if she found out. Yes, yes, I know you're prepared to bring things out into the open, but I can't. Not yet. I told you how jealous he is. I'm afraid of what he might do. Look, tomorrow may be okay. He's going hiking on the mountain, so there will be a good three hours . . ."

There was a sudden intake of breath, and abruptly, the woman's voice dropped in volume. "I can hear someone coming," she muttered. "I have to go. I'll call you later."

A moment later, Alexandra heard a cheerful exchange of greetings, presumably from the walkers coming along the path. But although she waited to see if the call would be resumed, the air was silent. Inquisitively, she wondered if the caller's husband really was black and a real-life Othello. The woman was hardly a paragon like the virtuous Desdemona, though. Clearly her husband had good reason for his jealousy.

Alexandra glanced down at her laptop. Oh, to hell with it, she thought, rapidly typing a couple of sentences and pressing save. If a real-life Desdemona felt that a black panther was an appropriate symbol for her husband, the wretched animal might as well serve for the story. Sometimes the obvious was the best solution. It was time for that cup of coffee.

*   *   *

Judith Fairlie emerged from the cabin of the Bayliner. Her tanned skin glowed with sun lotion, contrasting dramatically with her short, pale blonde hair and her bright yellow sundress. It was hard to imagine that she was over fifty for she was an exceptionally alluring woman, but at this point in time, her bearing was too haughty to be seductive. She came to the rail as if preparing to announce a royal edict.

"Barry says the V-belt on the *Ocean Princess*'s engine is worn and it has to be replaced before we go further up the coast. Now that he has me worried about it, I've asked him to check all the engines. He doesn't need people running interference, so I suggest you make yourselves scarce for a few hours. Today's going to be a scorcher so I'm going to relax on the beach at the marine park. The rest of you can take Lee's Zodiac over to Pool Bay for the afternoon."

"Great idea," agreed her son. He turned to his siblings and their mates. "We can walk up to the lake for a swim, then go back to the pub. There's entertainment on Sundays, starting at one and going right through into the evening."

His older brother rolled his eyes.

"We had dinner there yesterday. We're supposed to be on a cruise, not a pub crawl."

"So what? There'll be nothing but fishing and camp cooking once we go further up the coast. We should make the most of civilization while we can."

Jordan shrugged. "Fine. Go ahead. But count me and Helena out. We're going to take the kids ashore for a picnic. Sam needs a hike around the trails. He's been boat-bound too long."

The yellow mongrel looked up and wagged his tail when he heard his name. Judith, however, did not look pleased.

"I want to sunbathe and read in peace. Grandchildren popping by to show me their beach treasures aren't part of the plan."

"It's a big park," said Jordan, clambering over to the stern of the *Ocean Princess* so he didn't have to shout to his mother. "Where are you going to be?"

"In the western cove. It's a nice private spot, and I intend it to stay that way."

Jordan ignored the edge on his mother's voice.

"So we'll be on the eastern side. There's more than a mile of woods between our beach and your cove. We'll have no problem keeping the kids out of your hair."

"Good, that's settled," said Lee. "So are the rest of us for the lake and the pub?"

Nazeem, who was tucked in the crook of his arm, smiled and nodded. Robin was sitting with Jake on the Trophy. She hesitated, but Jake grinned and answered for her.

"Of course we'll come. Right, Robin?" He slid behind her, put his arms around her and pulled her back against him. Robin relaxed against his chest and smiled happily.

A pathetically grateful smile, thought her sister, watching with narrowed eyes from the stern of the *Osprey*. Christine had seen the look exchanged between Jake Seagrove and her mother the previous day. Robin was deluding herself if she thought Jake was going to be the Prince Charming who would marry her and sweep her off into the sunset. Jake had made a play for every woman in the party, including herself, and Christine didn't trust him an inch. Neither did she trust her mother, who was ruthless enough to encourage Jake as a future mate for her daughter, simply because she fancied him as a lover.

Sometimes Christine thought that the breakdown in her and Godfrey's relationship had begun because of the signals her mother had given to her son-in-law. From that moment on, the question in the forefront of Godfrey's mind had been: "Like mother, like daughter?" She had sensed his doubt, and in time, after four years of suspicion and jealousy, his lack of trust had become a self-fulfilling prophecy. All the love she'd originally felt for him had died. All that remained was fear and the desire to escape. She was afraid of what he might do if she filed for divorce, and she knew she would get no support from her mother, but her marriage was stifling her. She was trapped . . . suffocated . . . and her despair was making her reckless. Godfrey had gone off for the day and she knew he would be away all afternoon. She was going to grab her chance, whatever the cost.

She came out of her reverie, suddenly aware that someone was calling her name. She looked up to see Jake flashing his film-star smile at her.

"What about you, Christine? Coming? Godfrey's gone hiking so you're off the leash."

Christine stared back at him frostily.

"It's too hot for me. Besides, I have a headache. I'm going to stay on board and rest."

Helena emerged onto the deck of the boat that bore her name. She was carrying a large picnic basket, which she passed over to Jordan. He placed it in the Zodiac that was tied to the stern of his mother's boat. Judith looked annoyed.

"What are you doing?"

"Our outboard is acting up," said Jordan. "Barry's going to have a look at it this afternoon, but I figured we could use your Zodiac today."

"Godfrey has taken the outboard from the *Osprey*." Judith's knife-edge enunciation signalled trouble. "If Lee's Zodiac goes over to the pub and *Helena*'s outboard is out of commission, how am I supposed to go ashore?"

"We'll take you over," said Jordan. "There's no use having two boats at the marine park."

"Oh, for heaven's sake. Didn't you hear what I said? I want peace and quiet. Not a hectic ride balanced between picnic baskets and screaming children."

"Keep cool, Judith." Jake extracted himself from Robin and stepped across to the Carver. Then he jumped over to the Tollycraft and smiled up at the widow. "I can row you ashore in my dinghy and hike up to join the others at the lake. You can phone me when you're ready to head back and I'll run across from the pub in the Zodiac. We can tow the dinghy back. You don't mind if we borrow your beach mattress, do you, Christine?" he added, tossing it across to the Trophy.

"Borrow what you like," said Christine shortly. "Mother's already wearing one of my sundresses."

Jake grinned cheekily.

"In that case, we'll take this too," he said, picking Christine's red sunhat off her head. You won't need it if you're going to sleep all afternoon."

He winked at Judith and her features relaxed into a smile.

"All right," she said. "Be ready in fifteen minutes." With that, she turned and swept back into the cabin of the *Ocean Princess*.

Jake hopped back over the gunwales and pulled Robin to her feet. "Peace in the family," he said, and planted a kiss on her upturned lips. "I'll be round at the pub before you know it."

Christine watched her sister melt in his arms. Robin might believe it, she thought, but she certainly didn't. The little scene that had just played out was as slick as a carefully rehearsed Broadway play. She knew perfectly well what her mother had in mind.

* * *

Alexandra was stuck. Her cast of characters refused to come to life. Frustrated, she closed her laptop and stood up. It was a glorious day. A walk would free up her mind, and, with any luck, kick-start her creative juices. The circular route around the pub path and lagoon was not long, but it was pleasantly scenic since it went past the heritage inn that overlooked Loon Bay, across the footbridge that spanned the channel, and back around the pretty stretch of water that lay between the two bays. Plopping a cap on her head, she grabbed her sunglasses and headed out the door.

As she strolled around the pub path, she gazed at the boats anchored in the bay and idly wondered which one belonged to the woman she had overheard the previous day. Perhaps, even now, she was enjoying her assignation with her lover while her husband hiked on the shore. The jealous spouse had certainly picked a beast of a day to go tramping up the mountain. The day was hotter than she had realized when sitting on her shady covered deck, and she was relieved once she entered the cool tunnel of vine maples that arched over the last section of the path.

The path ended with a short flight of steps which led to the pub's parking lot. As Alexandra reached the top, she noticed a man coming out from the marine-park trail. He was a turbaned Sikh, an unusual presence on the Sunshine Coast. Japanese tourists were often seen on the peninsula, but the South Asian community had not been attracted to the area so far. This man did not look as if he was enjoying his visit. His lips were set in a tight line and his eyes darted wildly about the parking lot. He appeared to be looking for someone, and he brushed past Alexandra, turned abruptly and went into the pub.

Alexandra left the parking lot and followed the road round to the Hampton House Inn. It seemed as if the temperature had risen several degrees in the short time she had been out. The sun was baking the tarmac and she could feel the heat coming up through her sandals. She stopped to wipe the sweat from her forehead and contemplated walking up to the lake for a swim. If she went for a dip in her shorts and T-shirt she would dry off in the ten-minute walk back to the bay. Perhaps if she cooled off, her brain would work better.

Before she could make a decision, she heard the sound of laughter and high-pitched voices. She glanced towards the lagoon and saw two young girls running across the footbridge in the direction of the general store. Behind them loped a chocolate Lab and a large, black German shepherd. Alexandra recognized the girls. They were the daughters of her neighbour, Juliette Ayers. At the end of the bridge, the girls paused and waved to someone down at the docks. Alexandra looked over to the marina. Immediately, she noticed a familiar boat at the dock. It was the *Optimist*, the clinker-built fishing boat that belonged to Juliette's parents. It was moored in town during the winter, but she knew that the Bearys brought it up the coast during the summer months when they came to visit their daughter.

Alexandra abandoned the idea of a swim and walked towards the docks. The lane to the marina wound between ocean on one side and a colourful bank of wildflowers on the other, although the delicate pink blooms of the wild roses had now been replaced with purple snapdragons and yellow St John's Wort, all prettily framing the bobbing boats and sparkling water of the marina.

Juliette was standing on the dock and she waved when she saw Alexandra. "We're going out to set the crab traps," she called. "Then we're heading to the marine park for a picnic. Do you want to come along and take a break from that manuscript? There's lots of food. It'll be fun if you don't mind being crammed into the stern with Quasar and Purdy. They get a bit puffy in the heat."

Alexandra made her way down the ramp and joined Juliette on the dock.

"I'd love to," she said. "I'm getting nowhere with the book. The change might be just what I need. Where's your Dad?"

"Not here this time. Richard brought the boat up, but he'll go back in our old Tracker, so the *Optimist* will be here through the summer for everyone to enjoy. We have a great system—car and boat alternate with the seasons."

"That sounds very efficient."

"It is, especially as Richard has a few days off, so he'll be able to spend them visiting with us before he goes back to town."

"Oh, just the ticket," said Alexandra. "A real-life detective to help plan my crime."

"Did I hear my name?"

Richard's head bobbed out from the cabin.

"Yes," said Juliette. "You remember Alexandra. She's suffering from writer's block so I've invited her to come with us."

Richard smiled approval.

"Excellent," he said to Alexandra. "You can run your plots by me while we bait the traps. Where are my little gremlin nieces?" he added to Juliette. "They were supposed to be picking up pop from the store."

"Probably buying out the candy section," said Juliette.

"Pop and candy?" Alexandra laughed. "Just like when my two were young. Most mothers these days go around with packs of protein drinks and Nutribars."

"Ah, but they're a different breed on the Sunshine Coast," said Richard.

"Yes, I'm beginning to realize that," said Alexandra. "You've no idea the things I hear from my cottage deck."

Excited shrieks from the bridge signalled the approach of Jennifer and Laura.

"Here they come." Juliette rolled her eyes at the size of the bags the girls were carrying. She gave her brother an apologetic look. "I hope you're not expecting any change."

The girls raced along the lane and down the ramp. Quasar and Purdy bounded ahead of them. While Juliette settled the dogs in the stern, the girls handed their purchases to their uncle and he stowed them in the cabin. Then they hopped on board and clambered up onto the bow.

"No Stephen today?" said Alexandra, suddenly realizing that Juliette's husband was nowhere in evidence.

"No. School is still in for the teachers."

Richard came back out of the cabin and set up two deckchairs beside the crab traps.

"There you are, ladies," he said gallantly. "Climb aboard. Time to get underway."

Alexandra settled herself in the stern of the *Optimist* and sighed contentedly. This was so much better than staring at her computer screen. On days like this, she didn't care if she never wrote another word.

*   *   *

Helena Fairlie looked up from her book as she heard the crack of a twig from somewhere behind her. She twisted round to see Jake Seagrove emerging from the trees. He loped down the rocks with athletic ease. Seeing she was alone, he flashed his movie-star smile. It bordered on a leer. Helena was not impressed.

"What's happened to Jordan?" Jake asked.

"He's taken Sam for a walk."

"Left you in charge?" Jake nodded towards the two children who were playing at the edge of the water.

"I don't mind," said Helena coolly.

"Foolish fellow." Jake squatted down on the rocks beside her. He let his eyes slip down to Helena's cleavage, then rise again to meet her eyes. "I wouldn't leave a gorgeous girl like you unattended."

Helena met his gaze with an icy stare.

"Shouldn't you be going to meet the others?"

Jake shifted his weight onto his buttocks and stretched his bare legs out in front of him. He leaned back, cradling his head in his arms, and his open shirt fell back to expose even more flesh. He smiled complacently, aware of the discomfort he was causing.

"There's no hurry now that I've had to trek over here. They'll be packing up by the time I get to the lake. I'll just walk round and meet them at the pub."

"That's a long walk." Helena sat up stiffly and slid sideways to put more distance between them. "It'll take you at least an hour. Don't let me keep you. I'm perfectly happy reading my book."

Jake laughed and languidly got to his feet. His expression was sardonic as he looked down at Helena. "Your wish is my command, ma'am." He unzipped the fanny pack at his waist and pulled a tube out of the centre compartment. "By the way, you should cut the deep freeze because I'm doing you a favour. I brought you this. It's the non-allergenic sun lotion you use for your kids. Somehow it ended up in Judith's bag."

Embarrassed, Helena moderated her tone. "I wondered where that had gone. I must have left it on the *Ocean Princess* when we were there for dinner. Thank you," she said awkwardly.

"Don't thank me. Thank your mother. She's the one who told me to run it over to you."

"Yes, I will."

Jake grinned. "I'd call and thank her now if I were you. Queen Judith never expects any delays when acknowledging her good deeds, even if they are carried out at someone else's inconvenience."

Helena sighed and nodded. She dug her cellphone out of her bag and punched in her mother-in-law's number. After a brief conversation, she ended the call. Then she picked up her book and pointedly began to read. She could sense Jake watching her, but resolutely she kept her eyes on the page and continued to ignore him.

Jake shrugged and climbed back over the rocks. Haughty bitch, he thought. But what did he care? The widow had proved every bit the hottie he'd anticipated when he'd chauffeured her to the cove so he didn't give a damn what Jordan's whey-faced wife thought of him. It actually blew his mind that Judith Fairlie figured it was fine for him to marry her youngest daughter and be available for the occasional romp with his mother-in-law. Jake considered himself pretty ruthless, but Judith's cold-blooded approach to life was incredible. If his inclinations had leaned towards spending his life with a wealthy older woman, he'd have married her himself. But that was definitely not in the cards—and it didn't matter, because the widow had made it clear to all and sundry that he was a favoured suitor for Robin. Everything was going nicely as planned. The Fairlies were going to be his passport to fortune, and he was thoroughly enjoying the trip.

As he reached the top of the rocks, his cellphone rang. It was Lee saying that the others were ready to leave the lake. Jake asked him to explain his delay to Robin and said he would meet them at the pub.

Helena heard the phone ring and the sound of Jake's voice as he answered the call. Once his voice faded and she was sure he was out of sight, she set her book aside. She had not read a word since he had appeared. She found his presence disturbing and wished that Jordan would hurry back. She looked out across the water. A boatload of holidaymakers setting crab traps had provided a sense of security for the past half hour, but it looked as if they were now on the move. The boat was heading towards the horseshoe cove. Helena knew there was a dock on the other side of the promontory, and she hoped the boaters were coming ashore there. She did not like being alone. She felt vulnerable, and marvelled that her mother-in-law could be so cavalier about spending a solitary afternoon in a deserted cove that was hidden from the water and isolated from the other areas of the park. But Judith was tough, and her arrogance seemed to provide her with a shield against the world. It would take a very strong-minded person to take her on. Either that, or a raving lunatic.

Helena called the children over. Mia and Michael had been in the water long enough. It was time to give them something to drink and reapply their sunblock, now that she had the brand that she preferred to use on them. As they finished their snack and she collected the cups, she heard voices. She looked round to see a group of people coming over the top of the rocks. It was the party from the crab boat. Two young girls and two large dogs came loping down to the beach. Coming more slowly behind was a tall, handsome man with fair hair who carried a picnic basket. Two pretty brunettes walked beside him, one carrying a knapsack, and the other deftly toting folding chairs.

Helena smiled a welcome and gestured to a flat spot beside her blanket. The adults settled themselves at her side, and in a flash, Mia and Michael claimed the girls and dragged them down to play at the water's edge. Quasar and Purdy loped after them. After the strain of dealing with her husband's family and their cruise-mates, Helena was happy to enjoy a pleasant interlude with friendly people who appeared to have no agenda other than to have a good time in congenial company.

It was another half an hour before Jordan returned with Sam, but Helena no longer cared. Sam bounded down the rocks and headed for his water bowl. Jordan followed more slowly.

"You look like you haven't been lonely," he said, when he reached his wife.

"Not a bit. These lovely people have been keeping me company. This is Juliette Ayers, and those—" she nodded towards the girls playing with her children at the water's edge—"are her daughters,

Jennifer and Laura. They live in the house beside the fish and chip shop." Helena gestured to Alexandra. "And this is Alexandra Lacey who owns the cottage above the pub path. She's a mystery writer, and she comes up here to work on her novels. Last, but definitely not least, Juliette's brother, Richard. He's here to enjoy a fishing holiday."

Richard had deliberately avoided disclosing the fact that he was a policeman. When people discovered his profession, they either became guarded and reserved, or else bored him to tears with questions about his job. Alexandra Lacey was one of the few exceptions to this rule. With her bright and clever mind, she had provided the odd tip that had helped with his work and he enjoyed trying to find the hitches in her book scenarios.

"Who are these guys?" asked Jordan. Quasar and Purdy had come up from the water and were nose to nose with Sam. Juliette introduced her dogs, and Jordan opened a bottle of water and emptied it into Sam's bowl to accommodate the newcomers. Then he plopped down beside his wife and pulled a beer out of their cooler. As he opened it, the children came running up from the water. They seemed excited.

"Why are the birds making so much noise?" asked Laura.

"There's an eagles' nest further along the shore," said Jordan. "They're feeding their young."

"There are other birds besides eagles," said Jennifer, "and they're going crazy. Look at them."

Helena peered upwards. There were three large turkey vultures circling the sky.

"You know, we've been chattering so much, I hadn't really noticed," she said, "but the children are right. The birds are noisier than usual. Let's walk up to the top of the rocks. We'll be able to see from there."

Sam leapt up when he saw his people climbing the rocks. Eager for another walk, he bounded after them. Quasar and Purdy followed. Richard strode ahead and reached the top of the promontory first. From there, he could see a mass of turkey vultures and seagulls swooping towards the shore of the western cove.

"Bullying another bird," said Juliette, coming up behind him. "I can hear crows as well. Nasty creatures. They're probably chasing an owl or a raven."

In Richard's opinion, the amount of activity from the birds was abnormal. It was possible that a dead deer or some other mammal had attracted them, but he was curious to find out what was causing the commotion.

"I wonder what's attracting them," said Jordan. "My mother must be going ballistic. So much for her peaceful afternoon."

"Let's walk over and see what's set them off," said Richard.

"It takes forever to walk round the other side," wailed Jennifer. "Won't it be faster to take the boat across?"

"Yes, but the *Optimist* is too big to land on the shingle and I don't have a dinghy. Besides, you children are going to remain here with Juliette and Helena."

Jennifer and Laura started to protest but their uncle cut them short. "No. You stay with your mother, and keep the dogs here with you. We'll be back in a moment."

Jordan played the peacemaker. He undid the band on his wrist and handed it to Jennifer. "Here," he said. "You girls can have fun with this."

Jennifer looked scornful.

"A watch! What's the big deal?"

"It isn't a watch. It's an underwater compass. There are snorkels in the basket by Helena's beach blanket. I'm leaving you girls in charge. Make sure my two little ones don't come to harm."

Having mollified, Jennifer and Laura, Jordan turned back to Richard. "Let's go," he said.

Alexandra fell into step behind them.

"I'm coming too," she said firmly.

Richard was about to protest, but realizing he had no authority to order her back, he shrugged and set off at a brisk pace. Jordan and Alexandra followed more slowly. The path led to a clearing at the top of the horseshoe cove. From there, another trail branched off into a forest where the ground was covered with salal, sword ferns and Oregon grape. Richard started towards the gap in the trees but Jordan called him back.

"Not that one," he said. "It goes to the lake and the Pool Bay pub. There's another path at the far end of the clearing. That's the one that goes to the western cove."

Richard moved on. Soon he saw another opening in the bushes. He turned onto the trail and the others followed. Halfway down, the path emerged from the trees and the track became steep and rocky, winding through jagged crevices and bordered here and there by a solitary arbutus. They clambered down, and as they approached the cove, the shrieking of the birds became deafening. Richard raced down the last few yards and jumped onto the sand. A sheer wall of rocks still screened the cove, but he could hear another sound, an eerie low counterpoint below the screaming of the birds. Someone was crying.

He followed the curve of the rocks until the cove came into view. Then he stopped, stunned. Alexandra and Jordan came up behind him, but he was unaware of their presence. All his attention was riveted on the bizarre scene before him.

A muscular black giant was kneeling on the sand. He clutched a red sun hat, and his clenched hands were wringing the straw to a pulp. His head was bowed and his body was wracked with convulsive sobs. Before him, a woman lay on her back, sprawled out as if sunbathing, but the leisurely impression was shattered by the bolt that stuck out from her chest.

The man looked up as he heard Richard approach. His tear-streaked face was contorted into an anguished mask.

"I thought it was Christine," he gasped. "I thought it was Christine."

*   *   *

Detective Sergeant Klein of the Sunshine Coast RCMP detachment was well acquainted with the soap-opera existence of the Fairlie family, and he was surprised that Judith Fairlie had lasted as long as she had. What amazed him was the fact that she had been killed in place of her daughter. Judith, thought Klein, should have been murdered in her own right. Still, on the plus side, it looked like an easy case. Godfrey Spence's confusion over the identity of the victim and his presence at the scene implied a straightforward crime of passion and a speedy conviction, especially since the witness who discovered him with the body was a detective inspector from Vancouver. Klein looked forward to a voluntary confession and an early lunch at Colonel Flounder's. However, to his great disappointment, neither the confession nor the three-piece cod and chips was forthcoming. Instead, he faced an investigation that became mired in the tangled morass of the Fairlie family's tawdry affairs. In life, Judith's shenanigans on her annual cruise had caused annoying ripples in the smooth surface of coastal life; in death, it appeared she was to be equally aggravating.

Judith's murder had been a particularly brutal one. She had been shot at close range with a spear gun. The line attaching the gun to the spear had been cut and the gun itself appeared to be missing. A comprehensive search of the area failed to produce it, but when the tide went out the following morning, the gun was discovered lying in a rock pool. The sea had washed away all trace of fingerprints and DNA, but there was no doubt that the murder weapon had come from the boat chain. Three spear guns had been kept in the Zodiac at the stern of Lee Fairlie's Carver, and one of these was missing.

Godfrey Spence vigorously denied killing his mother-in-law and insisted that she had already been dead when he arrived at the beach, but beyond that, he refused to say anything. Since the prime suspect had fallen infuriatingly silent, Klein's first task was to pin down who had access to the murder weapon.

He set up his incident room at the community police station at Madeira Park. It was on the other side of the harbour, but still convenient for the boaters since they could come across by Zodiac and moor at the government dock. He decided first to tackle the men who had been using the spear guns the previous day, starting with Judith Fairlie's younger son, Lee. However, he had barely begun his interrogation when there was a tap at the door. It opened to reveal Detective Constable Adrian Wright. Her eyes were sparkling. It was obvious she had something significant to impart.

"Could I have a word, sir?"

Klein suspended his interview and joined Adrian in the hall. She was a bright young detective who had just graduated from the uniformed branch. Klein had been impressed with her work in the past and considered her an asset to the team.

"A man named Gary Quartermain just phoned in," Adrian announced triumphantly. "He's a private detective. Evidently, Godfrey Spence was convinced his wife was having an affair and he hired the PI to keep an eye on her. Would you believe Quartermain's been stationed on shore, observing the people on the boat chain ever since they arrived in the harbour!"

Klein's craggy face split into a broad grin.

"Has he, indeed?"

"Yes. He's staying at the Hampton House Inn. He said he'd have come round to the station sooner but he's had a dose of summer tummy so only just heard what happened. Do you want him to come in or should I tell him to wait and we'll interview him there?"

"Let's not waste time. You go over and talk with him now. Depending on what he has to say, we can bring him in later. I'll carry on here. When you get back, we can compare his story with those I get from the members of the family." Klein rubbed his hands gleefully. "This could be a piece of cake after all."

He turned to go back to the interview room but Adrian called him back.

"There's one other thing, sir," she said. "That witness . . . the man who discovered Godfrey Spence with the body—"

"A detective inspector from Vancouver. Yes, I know."

"He also happens to be my cousin," said Adrian.

Klein blinked.

"How many cousins do you have? Wasn't that opera singer your cousin too? The one who helped with the oyster case last May?"

"Yes. That was Philippa. Richard is her older brother. He's in the lobby. He said to tell you he's willing to help if you're short-handed."

"That's very kind of him, but far be it from me to interfere with his fishing holiday," said Klein, who much preferred an afternoon on the water pursuing salmon to a day on land pursuing criminals.

"He won't mind," said Adrian. "I think he'd like to help, and he won't step on any toes."

"All right. Send him in. Off you go."

Klein nodded briskly and headed back into the interview room. Adrian went to retrieve her cousin from the waiting area by the front desk. She sent Richard to join Klein, then called the Hampton House

Inn and left a message that she would be there to interview Gary Quartermain in half an hour. She couldn't wait to hear what he had to say.

*   *   *

When Richard entered the interview room, Lee Fairlie was sitting at the table. He gave Richard an inquisitive look, which was far from unfriendly, and nodded pleasantly when Klein introduced him as a fellow detective working on the case. Richard sat quietly at the side of the room and listened while DS Klein interviewed Lee, and he remained in the background throughout the afternoon as the other members of the Fairlie family took their turn to be questioned. Richard noticed a consistency to the evidence that suggested the Fairlies had managed to consult with each other before being rounded up to give formal statements. Lee Fairlie acknowledged that he, his brother, Jordan, and his friend, Jake Seagrove, had been using the spear guns the previous afternoon, after which, they had tossed them into the Zodiac, along with the scuba diving equipment. He had no idea when the third gun went missing, but he insisted that all three guns had been present when he and Jake said goodnight to the girls and went back to the Trophy. Jordan agreed that the guns had been returned to the Zodiac, but could not swear that all three were there at the end of the day since, by then, he was on the Bayliner, which was on the other side of his sister's Tollycraft.

When describing their movements on the day of the murder, the boaters were clear and concise. Everyone agreed that Godfrey Spence had been the first to go ashore. At nine-thirty that morning, he had tossed a backpack into the Tollycraft's outboard and set off for the government dock in Loon Bay. His stated intention had been to hike up the mountain that overlooked the bay.

Lee Fairlie had set off an hour later with his younger sister, Robin, and his fiancée, Nazeem. They had taken his Zodiac across to Pool Bay, moored at the pub's marina, and walked up to the lake for a swim. At twenty-five to one, Lee had called Jake to tell him they were leaving the lake—Lee could give precise times as his calls were recorded on his cellphone—and he and the girls had strolled down to the bay. Lee went directly to the pub to reserve a table, but Robin and Nazeem continued down to the lagoon and went over to the store so they could check out the local books. At ten to one, Jake called Lee to say he was on the trail and should be able to make it by one-thirty if they wanted to go ahead and order. Lee called the girls to let them know, and, around quarter past one, they came back to the pub and went inside. Lee remained outside smoking a cigarette. Soon after that, Jake had arrived. The group stayed throughout the afternoon, only leaving when the police came to inform them of Judith's death.

Jordan and Helena Fairlie had been the next people to leave the boat chain. They had packed a picnic and taken their children ashore in the *Ocean Princess* Zodiac. They had set off shortly after eleven, around the same time that Jake Seagrove had rowed Judith Fairlie to the other side of the park. They had spent the afternoon on the beach, but Jordan had taken their dog for a walk and had been away for the best part of an hour. Helena had stayed with the children. Helena recounted Jake Seagrove's visit to the eastern cove, and she handed over her phone, which verified the fact that her call to Judith Fairlie had been made at twelve thirty-one. This tallied with the record of calls on Judith's cellphone. Forensics had already reported that Judith's fingerprints were clearly marked on her phone—not that there was any question about who received the call as Helena said that her mother-in-law's distinctive voice was unmistakable.

Helena's sister-in-law, Christine, the tiny blonde who looked so like her mother, claimed to have stayed on board, as did Barry King, Judith's pilot-cum-toy boy. Christine said that a migraine headache had kept her in her cabin all afternoon. She had only emerged when Barry called her cell to tell her that there was a police boat in the bay. She and Barry had changed quickly and swam ashore to see what was going on. She had been afraid that something had happened to her young niece and nephew. When asked if she had not been worried about her mother, since she'd been alone in the park, Christine had laughed. Her mother, she informed them acerbically, had not been alone. Christine was quite sure that Judith had been in the company of Jake Seagrove, and if the police had any sense, they would be pulling him in for questioning instead of harassing the members of Judith's family.

Barry King blandly confirmed Christine's statement and explained why he had spent the afternoon on the boats. He had needed to change the V-belt on the engine of the Grand Banks and had intended to check the other engines as well. By the time the hubbub started in the bay, he had only just finished the job on Judith's trawler yacht.

Klein was unconvinced.

"Those two are lying," he said, after the pair had left the room.

Richard nodded. "I agree, but it doesn't necessarily mean they're guilty of murder. Barry King may be the lover that Godfrey was trying to identify. Pretty convenient, the two making excuses to stay on board while the others went ashore. Mind you, Barry King would be taking a chance, starting an affair with Judith Fairlie's daughter, given that he was supposed to be her resident toy boy for the voyage."

"Maybe he figured he was off the hook once the widow started eyeing Seagrove," said Klein, "assuming, of course, that Christine Spence is right that her old lady had her eye on the youngest daughter's beau."

"God! What a family," said Richard.

Klein's eyes grew crafty.

"You know," he said, "if Barry King and Christine Spence were carrying on, they had a pretty good motive for getting rid of the widow. Judith Fairlie was a great one for double standards. She did whatever the hell she pleased, but her children had to toe the line. Divorce was a no-no. Once they'd made their beds, they had to lie on them. The last thing the widow wanted was exes trying to winkle out a share of the Fairlie fortune. No aberrational behaviour either. She couldn't stand gays, and I often think her marriage might have had something to do with that. I suspect her husband had batted for the other side, or at least swung both ways, and if that was the case, it could explain why she was such an embittered woman."

"Any foundation for that?"

"There were a few rumours, even before the marriage. Judith Fairlie was young and naïve when she got hitched and Harold Fairlie was seventeen years her senior. Judith was wildly in love when she married, so something must have happened to sour things. Besides, the youngest child looks nothing like Harold Fairlie. Everyone figures she's a sprig off the toy-boy tree."

Richard thoughtfully steepled his fingers.

"Let me get this straight," he said. "Godfrey Spence figures his wife is having an affair. If he hired a PI, that means he's ready to see a lawyer if his suspicions prove correct. Christine Spence may not mind a divorce but doesn't want to be cut out of her mother's will, so getting rid of her mother would leave her home free."

"Exactly."

"But even if she and Barry King were in it together, how did they do it? There were no boats left to take them ashore, other than the one with the gimped outboard, and if they'd rowed across in that, Spence's PI up on the hillside would have seen them."

"One of them could have swum over to the cove. If they'd slipped in off the bow, the PI wouldn't have seen them. They both swam ashore when the police boats appeared," Klein reminded him. "Hell of a good way to cover the fact that they were already wet and in their swimsuits."

Richard nodded. "Yes, and Christine Spence's boat was tied next to the Carver, so she could easily have taken one of the spear guns."

Klein pulled out a handkerchief and mopped his brow. The room was becoming uncomfortably warm.

"She could have," he agreed, "but since no one noticed that one of the guns was missing, anyone could have taken it during the night and hidden it on the shore. Or taken it with them when they left the boat chain the next morning. Jordan and Helena Fairlie had a huge picnic basket, and Godfrey Spence's backpack was large enough to conceal a spear gun. The whole thing could have been premeditated."

"Only if someone knew that Judith Fairlie was planning to spend the afternoon in the cove."

"Judith Fairlie had some predictable habits, one of which was to get rid of her entourage and arrange some solitary quiet time when she had a new man in her sights. If anyone on those boats had sized up what was developing between her and Seagrove, they'd have known an opportunity to get her alone was imminent."

"Malice aforethought in preparation for the opportunistic moment? Interesting theory."

"It is. So we'd better get Seagrove in to hear what he has to say. Whether or not he and the widow were an item, he was the one who rowed her ashore and he was probably the last person to see her alive."

Without waiting for Richard to reply, Klein directed the constable who was taking notes to bring Jake Seagrove into the interview room. A moment later, the darkly handsome actor was led in and seated at the table opposite Klein. Jake Seagrove looked anxious—understandably so, thought Richard—but it quickly became apparent that he had no intention of hiding the truth about his relationship with Judith Fairlie. Seagrove admitted that he and the widow had indulged in a vigorous interlude of highly enjoyable sex as soon as they reached the cove. He insisted that the tryst had been tacitly understood between them, and that the widow had been hot to trot the minute they landed. He also shame-facedly acknowledged that the liaison was purely physical and that he hoped the widow's youngest daughter didn't have to find out, because she was the one he really cared about. Klein refrained from comment, but Richard could tell that the detective sergeant was biting his tongue.

Oblivious to the distaste felt by his audience, Jake continued with his story. After making love, he and Judith had gone for a skinny dip. Once back on the beach, Judith had discovered that she had a tube of sun-block in her bag that had been bought for her grandchildren, so she told him to take it to Helena on his way out of the park. Yes, the side trip was out of his way and held him up sufficiently that he missed joining the others at the lake, but one did not disobey commands from Judith. The last he had seen of her, she had put on her dress and applied her sun-block. She had then placed her sunhat over her face and lain back on the beach mattress to tan her arms and legs.

Klein nodded. This statement rang true. Judith had cruised the coast for more than thirty years and she was renowned for her acerbic comments about boat women with faces like contour maps from overexposure to the sun.

Jake had left Judith and walked over to the eastern beach where he delivered the sun-block to Helena. After that, he headed for the pub trail because Lee had called to tell him the others were leaving the lake. No, he couldn't remember what time he'd arrived at the pub. It must have been around one-thirty. The band had not started playing yet but they began soon after he got there. Lee had been outside smoking a cigarette, and they'd chatted on the steps until they heard the music begin. Then they went inside to join the girls.

After Jake left the interview room, Klein looked sour.

"What a slime-ball," he said. "I'd love to pin the murder on him but there's no way we can. If he was still in the eastern cove at twelve-thirty, he must have hoofed it at speed to get to the pub by half past one. A detour back to the western cove would have taken him an extra half-hour."

Richard frowned thoughtfully.

"What if he'd swum across to the other point? It's a long way round the horseshoe cove, but it would only take a strong swimmer five minutes to swim across at the entrance. It can't be more than a couple of hundred yards. Seagrove's fanny pack looked like it was waterproof, and it was big enough to cram a pair of sandals into it. He was only wearing swimming shorts and a lightweight shirt. In this heat, he'd have dried off pretty quickly."

"It doesn't work," said Klein. "It'd take him more than five minutes. He'd be bucking the currents in the harbour. He could do it at speed with fins and scuba gear, but none of that equipment was missing. I had my men check. The scuba gear was kept in Lee Fairlie's Zodiac, and it was all present and correct. The only item that was missing was the spear gun. Anyway, even if Seagrove did swim to the western cove, it's still an hour's hike to get to the pub because he'd have to get up to the trail at the top of the horseshoe. There's no way he could have done it."

Richard grinned wryly.

"Leaving aside the fact that he doesn't have a motive. Sounds like he and the widow were two of a kind. Still, his liaison with her provided a powerful motive for Godfrey Spence if he was under the illusion that it was his wife with Seagrove. If the PI saw what they were up to and passed the information on to Spence, I'd say your case was wrapped up."

Klein sighed and tapped his fingers rhythmically on the top of the table. "Probably, but there's one thing that doesn't ring true. Judith Fairlie was a formidable woman. None of her brood will mourn her. She was hard on them all. There was no unconditional love for the Fairlie children. It had to be earned. Approval was rationed out according to how they lived up to expectations, and if they blotted their copybooks, they were just as likely to have been cut out of her will. Every one of them was under threat at one time or another, but now they're out from under the yoke. They'll all breathe a sigh of relief now she's gone."

"So what are you trying to say?" asked Richard.

Klein's forehead was pleated as tightly as a folded accordion.

"I still can't believe she was murdered in place of someone else." he said.

*   *   *

When Adrian reached the Hampton House Inn, the sweat was pouring off her forehead. The sky, so clear and blue in past weeks, had become a white, gauzy veil, and the sun, beating through the haze, added humidity to heat and rendered the day oppressive. Inside the inn was no less uncomfortable in spite of the whirring ceiling fans. Adrian was certain that a storm was coming.

She found Gary Quartermain seated in the public lounge that doubled as a local artists' gallery. The high-ceilinged room overlooked Loon Bay, and the hard white light from the window cast a blinding glare onto an abstract painting of geese in flight, washing out the vivid colour scheme that the artist had so meticulously created. The private detective was still recovering from his digestive upset and was nursing a mug of herbal tea. Adrian eyed and rejected the coffee urn that was kept on hand for guests. She would make do with her bottle of water. She joined Quartermain in his corner. With a thrill of excitement, she noticed a video camera on the table beside his chair.

Since Adrian had not been present to hear Jake Seagrove's interview, she was astounded at Quartermain's evidence. The detective had seen the tryst between the widow and the actor. What's more, he had the photographs to prove it. Gary Quartermain was nothing if not thorough. His assignment had been to watch Christine Spence in her husband's absence, and after three days of getting nowhere, he had thought the decisive moment had arrived. Just as he reached his lookout in the marine park, he saw what he thought was his client's wife going ashore with Jake Seagrove. Quartermain had hurried down from his rock and forged his way through the bushes until he found a spot where he could see into the most secluded corner of the cove. He was a hundred yards off, hidden in the trees, but he had a clear view as the couple landed. No sooner were they ashore, he reported, than they threw down the beach mattress, sprawled onto it and started going at it like a couple of cats in heat. He had whipped out his camera and, using the zoom lens, videotaped the action.

Unfortunately, he did not remain long enough to witness the murder. He videotaped the skinny dip and waited a bit longer because he thought the couple might have gone for a second round. However, after the widow had put her dress back on, he saw Jake kiss her goodbye and set off onto the trail. He confirmed that the widow had settled down to sunbathe with her hat over her face. At that point, he packed away his camera and hot-footed it back up to the road, from where he had phoned Godfrey Spence and reported what he had seen. He had been very uneasy at Godfrey's response. He had assumed the man really was hiking on Mount Daniel, but it transpired that Godfrey had stayed in the vicinity of the park so that he could take immediate action if his suspicions were proved correct. Hearing Quartermain's report, Godfrey had gone ballistic. He had pinned Quartermain down as to where the adulterous interlude had occurred, and then rung off. Quartermain had hurried down the road, hoping to head Godfrey off and talk sense into him. However, Godfrey came into the park from the other end of the trail so Quartermain missed him.

Adrian thanked the detective for his help. Then, taking the video camera with its graphic record of Judith Fairlie's last moments on earth, she left the inn. As she crossed the parking lot, she looked up at the pale sky. The day had acquired an unearthly stillness, which, in Adrian's experience, was the precursor to turbulent weather. Adrian wiped her brow and got into her car. With the windows wide open, she transported her precious cargo back to headquarters.

When she arrived, Klein and Richard had finished their interviews and were sitting under the ceiling fan, reviewing their notes while finishing off the remains of a pizza. Klein's forehead was gleaming with sweat, and as he looked up to greet Adrian, a tiny stream flowed down onto the end of his nose. Undeterred, he mopped the drops from his face and turned to hear what Adrian had to say.

Once he had listened to her report and been told about the contents of Quartermain's video camera, Klein decided that his original instincts about Godfrey Spence had been correct. Most likely, he had killed Judith in the mistaken belief that she was his wife.

"We'll bring him back in tomorrow," he said. "He's bound to talk once he realizes we know about Quartermain."

"What if he doesn't?" Richard foresaw problems in proving the case. "Getting a guilty verdict would be touch and go. Quartermain's evidence indicates anger, but not premeditation, and you'd still have to link Godfrey to the murder weapon. A good lawyer would point out that Judith Fairlie made a lot of enemies throughout her life. It wouldn't be that hard to show reasonable doubt. There's always the chance that she was killed by someone outside the family group."

"Unlikely," said Klein. "If Spence isn't guilty, the killer will be one of her kids. Every one of them will inherit a bundle. But we need to cover all the bases."

He turned to Adrian. "You like going out in the Zodiac. Go around the harbour tomorrow and talk to the occupants of the other boats that were moored in the area. They're all potential witnesses. Maybe one of them had binoculars trained on shore. They're not likely to move on tonight as there's a storm brewing."

Adrian nodded.

"Yes, sir. Speaking of the storm, it feels like it could break any time." She looked at her cousin. "If you came over in the *Optimist*, you'd better not wait around too long."

"Not a problem," said Richard. "I drove round."

"Good," said Adrian. "It's going to be a nasty night." She turned back to Klein. "Is there anything else I can do now?"

"No, you've done enough for one day. Off you go. We need to look at this film before we leave and we don't need a demure young lady breathing over our shoulders."

Adrian rolled her eyes as she left the room, but Richard sensed she did not mind being dismissed. It had been a long day and the heat was brutal. Richard was ready to go home too. However, Klein seemed impervious to the weather. He pulled the camera out of the case as the door closed behind Adrian.

"Well, let's see what we have here, and then we'll call it a night."

He switched on the camera and replayed the film, turning the camera so that the small screen was visible to Richard too. Richard noticed that the timer on the video was consistent with the evidence given by Jake Seagrove and Helena Fairlie. No surprises there. When the film ended, Klein switched off the camera.

"Pretty hot stuff," he said as he returned the camera to its case. "That young man was sure sticking his neck out if he wanted to marry the widow's daughter."

"He struck me as very arrogant," said Richard. "I wouldn't put it past him thinking he could marry Judith Fairlie herself."

"Well, if he did, he'd have been in for a disappointment. The widow was a tough nut. The locals called her the Three-F Queen."

"What was that supposed to mean?"

Klein stood up and headed for the door. He turned back and grinned as he answered Richard's question.

"She could out-fish, out-finance and out-fuck everybody. Jake Seagrove was over-estimating his talents if he thought one piece of tail was enough to win Judith Fairlie."

*   *   *

Richard was pleased to find a refreshing breeze as he walked out to the parking lot, but by the time he turned onto the highway, the wind was buffeting the car violently. The remainder of the drive to the other side of the harbour was a tiring struggle against sudden bursts of air. When he got out of the Tracker in Juliette's driveway, a strong gust hit and forced him to brace himself. He wondered how the occupants of the boat chain were coping with the squall. Inside the cove, their vessels were probably secure, especially as they were tied to the trees on shore. However, it was not the best time to be on the water and Richard was glad he had a snug berth on land for the night. In spite of the wind, the heat was still oppressive, but the earlier haze of the day had cleared and the distant mountainside gleamed pale green against a pigeon blue sky. One wisp of white cloud floated high overhead.

He looked towards Loon Bay and wondered how his father's boat would fare in the storm. Juliette came outside to greet him and correctly interpreted his worried frown.

"I've checked on the *Optimist*," she said. "She's okay."

"Are you sure?"

"Yes. We're fairly well sheltered here, but they're having a tough time in Pool Bay. The squall has all the boats dragging their anchors. It's so bad that a couple of the sailboats have come round to stay at the government dock for the night. It's a good evening to hunker down at home. Come on in. I bet you're dying for a drink."

Richard was. He followed his sister inside, and a few minutes later, he was settled in a chaise longue on her glassed-in deck, a tumbler of Scotch at his side. Strangely, the drink did not help him relax. He was overtired, and something in the back of his mind kept niggling at him. Restlessly, he looked across to Loon Bay and saw that there were more clouds hovering in the sky. As the sun crept lower, the wisps of cloud turned from white to gold, then gradually became streaked with gleaming layers of pink. On the far side of the lagoon, the flag above the store fluttered like a frightened bird, then thrashed wildly against the pole as another gust whipped across the roof of the store.

The air was muggy, and Richard found himself breaking out in a sweat. He was troubled, aware of an item overlooked. It was something his sister had said. It should have registered with him, but whatever it was would not come to the fore. The oppressive heat was affecting his brain. He got up and opened the door to the outer deck. Immediately, he found respite in a burst of cooling breeze.

As he stared towards Loon Bay, the sun sank behind the mountains. Within moments, the sky was aflame. It was a spectacular sunset—smooth and red like the Technicolor burning of Atlanta. Awed, Richard went outside and stood at the deck rail. From there he could turn to the right or left and see each of the bays and the lagoon in between. The solitary cloud over Pool Bay had turned a brilliant, bloody red, reflecting the blaze of colour on the other side of the lagoon. As the glow faded, the lagoon dimmed to a shadowy green, then darkened to black, but an opalescent patch of pale blue appeared magically at the centre as the streetlight by the store came on and cast its light across the water. Against the gleaming circle, the black branches of bushes tossed and danced in the breeze.

The air seemed cooler now, and Richard finally grasped the thought that had been eluding him. Juliette had said that a sailboat had come around from the other bay. What had he been thinking of? The occupants could be the witnesses that Adrian had been told to find. Richard tossed back the rest of his drink and went inside. Telling Juliette that he was going out to check on the *Optimist*, he headed out the door.

The sky above Loon Bay was now a rich crimson, and everything against it looked black, although the Hampton House Inn and the curve of the road glowed dimly in the light of the street lamp. At the marina, the dock lights and white masts of the sailboats stood out distinctly against the shadowy sea and the dark mountains across the bay. Richard quickly identified the sailboat that had come round from the marine park, but other than a dog barking inside the cabin, no one was on board.

The occupant of the adjacent motor cruiser bobbed out onto his deck.

"They're round at the pub," he said. "Young couple. Big tough bruiser with a crew cut and a cute little redhead."

Richard thanked him and set off again.

It was black as pitch walking alongside the lagoon, but once he reached the pub path, he could see clearly. The walkway had taken on a fairy-tale aspect, gleaming golden where the halogen light at the corner lit the dry grass and dead pine needles that lined the trail. A string of lanterns dangled from the eaves of the pub and the glowing lights were mirrored in the black water below. Tiny lamps lit the wooden bridges at the creeks and glowed within the risers of the stairs leading up to the pub.

As Richard reached the entrance, the door opened and a couple came out. They matched the description given by the boater at the marina, so Richard introduced himself and pulled them aside. They had heard about the murder and were avidly interested, but had seen nothing to indicate who was responsible. It was another dead end. Richard thanked them and turned to go, but the redhead called him back.

"This is probably nothing," she said apologetically, "but I did hear someone quarrelling when I took our dog ashore the following evening. It was around eight o'clock so it was still light. As I tied our dinghy up at the dock, I heard angry voices coming from the direction of the eastern cove."

Richard was curious.

"What did you overhear?"

"Not a lot. There was a man and a woman. She was going on at him about someone's disgusting behaviour."

"Did you hear any names?"

"I think I heard her say Jack."

"Could it have been Jake?"

The woman nodded.

"Yes, that could have been it."

"Did you see the man?"

"No, but when I got further up onto the trail, a woman came blazing past me, and it must have been the one that I overheard because she looked very upset."

"Very young, pretty brunette? Gorgeous statuesque figure?"

The redhead looked surprised.

"Gorgeous brunette, yes. But she wasn't statuesque. She was tiny. South Asian, I think."

Richard thanked the couple and said goodnight. As he walked back round the pub path, he reflected on what he had been told. So Nazeem had discovered what her fiancé's friend had been up to with her future mother-in-law. But when had she learned about the rendezvous? Before or after the murder? The timing could be critical. Nothing about the case seemed straightforward, but then, he thought dryly, all the detours were probably red herrings and the obvious solution would prove to be the right one after all.

Still vivid in Richard's mind was the image of the distraught black man sobbing over what he thought was the body of his wife. Godfrey Spence was a modern-day Othello—a king in the world of athletics, feted and honoured for his prowess, but vulnerable and insecure in his private life. Was it his obsessive jealousy that had driven his wife away, or was Christine Spence as ruthlessly immoral as her mother?

As Richard pondered the tumultuous emotions that had driven the tormented man to despair, a flash lit up the sky. He stopped at the turn and waited for the roll of thunder, but no sound followed. He looked across the water and saw white sheet lightning flashing soundlessly above the mountains. Another squall hit the shore, buffeting the arbutus trees and tossing more leaves onto the path, but the electric storm was as eerily silent as the grief-stricken man who was about to be arrested for the murder of Judith Fairlie.

*   *   *

The following day, Godfrey Spence was brought across to the station and formally charged. At last, he broke his silence, but only to indicate that he would not say anything more until his lawyer was present. Since the Fairlie family's legal affairs were handled by a firm based in Vancouver, it was mid-afternoon before Godfrey's lawyer made it to the Coast. Once again, Richard was present during the interview, but after two hours of questioning, neither he nor Sergeant Klein learned anything that they did not already know. Godfrey admitted hiring the private detective. However, he still denied killing Judith Fairlie, and no amount of questioning could shake him from that position.

Tired and frustrated, Klein put the interview on hold. He and Richard left the police station and went in search of coffee. The day was calm and the air was pleasantly cool. All that remained of the previous night's turbulence were the twigs and leaves littering the parking area and lining the road. The two detectives walked across the road and bought lattes from the coffee shop, but as they were bringing their drinks back to the station, Klein's phone rang. He handed his coffee to Richard and answered the call. Immediately, he looked alert. Richard could not hear what was being said, but he thought he recognized Adrian's voice. Klein ended the call quickly and took back his coffee.

"That was your cousin," he said. "Bright girl. She's turned up another suspect."

"So Godfrey Spence might be telling the truth when he says his mother-in-law was dead when he arrived at the beach."

"Could be. Adrian's had quite a day tracking down the boats that were anchored by the marine park because many had left due to the storm. However, she's discovered a link between the Fairlies and the skipper of a custom-built cabin cruiser called the *Seagull*. It had been anchored off the marine park for three days but left the area right after the police boat came into the bay. Adrian went round the marinas to find out if anyone could identify the owner or knew where he'd gone, and when she got to Whisky Slough, she struck gold. The *Seagull* was moored there." Klein smiled a foxlike smile. "The owner," he said gleefully, "was not on board, but ten minutes after Adrian docked, he appeared at the top of the ramp, saw her by his boat, and came down to speak with her. According to your cousin, the skipper is a drop-dead gorgeous man, probably in his early forties. His name is Brian Maltravers."

Richard raised his eyebrows.

"Adrian must have told you more than that to prompt that Cheshire Cat grin. What links this man to the Fairlies?"

Klein's grin settled into a satisfied smirk.

"Before the owner showed up, Adrian slipped on board and had a look around," he said. "And she found a very interesting picture in the cabin. It was a photograph of Maltravers with his arm tucked around an attractive blonde. They're standing on the bow of a ritzy-looking Chris Craft named the *Oriole*. Adrian identified the woman as Christine Spence."

Richard whistled admiringly.

"So Barry King isn't Christine Spence's boyfriend. He was just covering for her. She probably swam over to meet this Maltravers fellow. His boat wasn't anchored that far from her Tollycraft. I remember noticing it when we came in on the *Optimist*."

"Hold on," said Klein. "I said Adrian identified the woman as Christine Spence. I didn't say she was right." Klein leaned back in his chair and grinned broadly. "You see, the *Oriole* was Harold Fairlie's first boat, but there was a fire in 1990 and the damage was so great that the boat was scrapped. Christine Spence was only nine years old at the time."

Richard stared blankly at the sergeant, and then the light dawned. "Well, I'm damned," he said. "The woman in the photograph—"

"—has to be Judith Fairlie, not her daughter." Klein nodded smugly.

"But given the family's record," Richard pointed out, "mother and daughter could have shared the same lover."

"You'd better believe it," said Klein. "First thing tomorrow, I'm going to bring in Maltravers and find out what he has to say for himself."

*   *   *

Richard was glad to head back to Juliette's house and enjoy what was left of the evening. He was looking forward to his sister's home cooking followed by a quiet read with his feet up. However, when he arrived at the house, he found that Steven had taken the girls to Sechelt for dinner and a movie, and Juliette and Alexandra were getting ready to go to the pub for prime rib. Laughingly, Juliette informed him that it wasn't a girls' night out and he was welcome to come along, so he left his jacket on and walked with them round to the pub.

The moment they entered the building, Richard saw three familiar figures seated at a table in the corner. It was Lee Fairlie, his sister, Robin, and his friend, Jake Seagrove. Lee and Jake looked uncharacteristically solemn, and Robin's face was suspiciously damp. Richard deliberately led Alexandra and Juliette to a table on the far side of the restaurant, but as they crossed the floor, Jake Seagrove looked up and noticed him. The actor nudged his companions and nodded towards Richard, and they all looked round and stared. Richard sighed. He wanted to enjoy his dinner, not sit uncomfortably, knowing he was spoiling someone else's. He went over to Jake's table and looked him in the eye.

"Look, I'm not following you around. I'm here for dinner. Don't let my presence give you indigestion. I'm very sorry about your mother," he added sincerely to Lee and Robin, whose tear-stained face portrayed a very unhappy girl.

To his surprise and embarrassment, Robin broke down into sobs. Jake put his arm around her shoulder and tried to comfort her. Lee hung his head ruefully. "It's not just my mother's death," he said. "My engagement has become collateral damage." He paused and looked up at Richard. "Nazeem has broken up with me," he said. "Her father is here. He came up with the express purpose of persuading her to come home. He's been hovering in the area for the past few days, just waiting for the right opportunity to get her alone and put the heat on. The murder gave him the perfect justification to demand that she abandon the cruise—and me too."

Richard personally thought Nazeem had made the right decision, but he kept his tone neutral.

"Nazeem's ethnic background makes it hard for her to go against her family," he said. "She may be afraid of the consequences if she doesn't obey her parents."

Lee shook his head. He seemed determined to make an effort to be open and charming, something that always made Richard wary when he was conducting an investigation. However, Lee appeared sincere in his efforts to be friendly, so Richard squashed his cynical thoughts and heard the young man out.

"That isn't the case with Nazeem," said Lee. "She always stood up to her family in the past. She was never afraid. But now, she's given in meekly and gone home. Robin is upset, because she and Nazeem have been friends for years. They were at school together. That's how I met Nazeem in the first place. The rotten thing is, she's not only broken our engagement, she's told Robin she will have nothing more to do with our family. Given what's happened to our mother, the last thing Robin needed was to have her best friend turn on her."

"I'm sorry to hear that." Richard eyed the girl who was nestled onto Jake Seagrove's shoulder. Inwardly, he winced. Some comfort that Lothario would be, he thought. He hoped sincerely that Robin would only use Jake as a shoulder to cry on, and wise up to his true nature before she suffered any more heartache. He nodded politely to Lee and returned to his own table.

Juliette and Alexandra looked at him expectantly.

"Well," said his sister, "can't you tell our ears are flapping?"

"Could we at least order?" grumbled Richard. "I'm starving. Let's get a drink. Then I'll fill you in. Get your mystery-writer brain in gear," he added to Alexandra.

He opened his menu and read over the selections. Once the waiter had served drinks and taken their order, Richard related everything he had learned over the course of the day. Juliette had already heard some of the details, but to Alexandra, it was all new. When Richard finished his account, Alexandra nodded wisely.

"You're quite right about the older daughter," she said, keeping her voice low. "This explains the conversation I overheard when I was sitting on my deck."

She told the others about the call, trying to remember word for word what had been said.

"That had to have been Christine Spence," agreed Richard. "Her husband is a black ex-football player and jealous as hell. Klein will be able to use what you heard to break her down. Christine Spence may or may not be guilty of murder, but she was definitely meeting someone that afternoon. Her lover is either the widow's toy boy or the man who was on the *Seagull*."

"She said her mother would be furious," pointed out Alexandra. "It's more likely she was having an affair with Barry King. The other man may well prove to be an ex-flame of Judith Fairlie, but why would she care if her daughter was seeing someone from her past?"

"She was a dog in the manger," said Juliette, who was apt to use canines for metaphors. "It sounds to me as if Judith Fairlie had a mean streak the size of the Highland Valley copper mine. I bet the show of grief in that far corner is all about the loss of Lee Fairlie's fiancée. Inwardly, they're cheering to be free of their mother."

Richard glanced back towards the other table. He agreed with Juliette, and he found the loss of Lee Fairlie's fiancée particularly interesting. Had Nazeem broken her engagement because she was shocked at Judith Fairlie's behaviour with Jake Seagrove, or had her father seen something else that had enabled him to persuade his daughter to return home? One thing was certain: the private eye had not been the only person watching the boat chain. Nazeem's father had also been in the area and Klein might have one more valuable witness that he knew nothing about.

*   *   *

Richard had to return to town the next day. The temperature had plummeted and the morning air was cold as he loaded his gear into the Tracker. The sky was overcast, changing the sea to a starkly dramatic shade, somewhere between royal blue and indigo, and the mountains were streaked with green and gold. The scene appeared painted by a surreal hand that scorned the conventional colours of nature.

There was very little traffic as Richard drove round to Madeira Park. He had left early to allow a stop at the police station since he wanted to tell Klein about the phone conversation that Alexandra had overheard. He also wanted to pass on what Lee Fairlie had told him.

Klein looked annoyed when he heard about the broken engagement. "I knew Adesh Murji was in the harbour," he said. "He came in with his daughter to make a statement. They confirmed Lee Fairlie's alibi—Murji was able to back up Seagrove's, too—but neither one of them said anything about Nazeem breaking up with Lee. Her father wanted to take her home once they'd answered my questions. If I'd known they were holding back information, I wouldn't have agreed," he snapped.

"Where do they live?" asked Richard. "If they're in town, I could drop by and speak with them."

Klein seemed happy to take Richard up on the offer.

"They're on the North Shore, right on your way home, so it won't be much of a detour once you're off the ferry. Call me as soon as you find out what caused the rift. It may be nothing to do with the case, but I'd still like to know."

Richard nodded. He took the address of the Murji home and asked Klein to phone and let them know he would be coming by.

As he left the office, Richard saw a powerful-looking man coming into the police station. There was something familiar about him, yet Richard could not place him. The man was tall, dark, and ruggedly handsome. Richard listened to hear his name as he gave it to the desk sergeant. It was Brian Maltravers, the boater who had left the bay so quickly after the murder.

As Maltravers was taken through to the interview room, Richard struggled to remember where he had seen the boater before. But try as he could, he drew a blank. The inability to pinpoint where he had met Maltravers nagged at him throughout his drive to the ferry, but finally, out of sheer frustration, he thrust the puzzle to the back of his mind and concentrated on the task ahead. Klein could deal with

Maltravers and Christine Spence. Richard had other things to do. He was very curious to know why Nazeem Murji had given way to her father's pleading and ended her relationship with Lee Fairlie, but he also wanted to find out what Adesh Murji had witnessed during his time on the coast. Someone, somewhere, had to have the key piece of information that would explain why Judith Fairlie had been murdered.

*   *   *

Klein's expression was inscrutable as he listened to Brian Maltravers' statement. Maltravers admitted that he had known Judith Fairlie many years ago. She had hired him as skipper of the *Oriole* in 1992. It had been a very enjoyable summer. Her children had been twelve, eleven and ten, respectively—the fun ages before teen troubles began—and all had been very harmonious. Yes, Judith had made it quite clear that she was available for some extra-curricular activities, and her husband had not seemed to mind. However, after the cruise, she had terminated his contract and he had never heard from her again. No, there were no ill feelings. This was her usual practice, and he had been happy to go back to his regular life. He moved to Ontario and worked on the lake boats for five years, but then he met a Vancouver Island girl who was holidaying there, and after they married, they came back to British Columbia and set up a charter business out of Port Hardy. He lost his wife to cancer in 2008. They had no children, something that had been a source of sorrow to them both, but their marriage had been a happy one. He and his wife had taken summer cruises together, and he had continued to do so after she died. It was pure coincidence that he had been anchored off the marine park at the same time as Judith Fairlie. He had no idea that she had been there with her family.

When asked to hand over his cellphone, he smiled and apologized. It had fallen overboard two days ago. Was that all, and could he go?

Klein smiled his foxy smile.

"Interesting," he said. "So why did Christine Spence phone you on her cell two days ago and tell you that you had to be careful because her husband was jealous?"

Klein nodded towards the one-way glass of the interview room and a moment later, the door opened and Christine Spence was ushered into the room. She looked at Maltravers with sad, desperate eyes.

"We don't have to lie any more," she said. "They know."

Maltravers looked stunned. He started to rise in an attempt to go to Christine, but Klein signalled him back to his seat.

"So," said Klein, jabbing the statement with his forefinger, "I expect you'd like to start again."

Maltravers eyed him soberly.

"We didn't kill Judith," he said. "All we're guilty of is having an affair."

Klein narrowed his eyes.

"You had an affair with her mother in 1992. You make a habit of this with the Fairlie family? Trying for the youngest daughter next?"

Maltravers face darkened dangerously.

"Don't be disgusting. It's not the way you think."

"What way is it then? I'd love to hear an explanation."

Maltravers and Christine exchanged glances. Surprised, Klein noticed the look that passed between them. It wasn't what he'd expected. There was genuine affection there.

"My affair with Judith was the one-summer fling I told you about," said Maltravers, "except it meant more to me than it did to her. At the time, I was very young, only twenty, and dazzled, if you want to know. She was twenty-eight, not that much older than me. She was beautiful and rich, and she had a fabulous boat. Her husband seemed indifferent to her, and I fell for her big time. I also loved her kids. They were a great little trio. Lee was nine and Jordan was ten. Chris here was the youngest. She was eight, and the sweetest little kid you could hope to meet. She was vulnerable too, more upset by the obvious coldness between her parents than the other two, and I tried to make up for that. Believe it or not, I had dreams of Judith leaving her husband and marrying me. I had no idea that I was just one in a constant stream of gigolos, and when I found out I was nothing more than a summer adventure, I was devastated. She was one of the reasons I left Vancouver. But the reality was, I got over her in no time—I felt worse about losing touch with the kids than not seeing her—and I was married and happily settled back here within five years."

"So when did you run into Judith Fairlie again?"

"I didn't. I met Chris. She was in Victoria."

Klein turned to Christine.

"What were you doing there?"

"Visiting my old nanny," she said. "She moved there after she retired, so I used to go over once a year and stay with her for a weekend. Every visit, I'd take her to tea at the Empress Hotel. She loved the old-world atmosphere there. That's where I ran into Brian."

"I was there with my wife," said Maltravers. "I saw Chris and it was like seeing her mother all over again. I actually tried to avoid speaking to her, but she spotted me and called out, so my wife and I had to go over and say hello. Almost immediately, I realized that the resemblance to Judith was purely physical. Chris was still the same sweet kid, even though she'd grown up. She was twenty-five and engaged to be married. I wished her well, and that was it. I didn't see her again for another three years. She was in Victoria again for the weekend with her nanny. She phoned to see how I was doing. She also had something to—well, that's not relevant. By then my wife had died, and Chris's marriage had turned out badly. I had to come down to Victoria on business anyway, so we arranged to meet for coffee. Neither of us had any intention of starting an affair. We were just affectionate friends who kept in touch via calls and texts to cheer each other up. It wasn't until last year that we realized that we were in love. If I'd had my way, Chris would have brought it out into the open. Her marriage has been torture, and I wanted her to divorce Godfrey and marry me. She didn't because she was scared of him—still is, come to that—so she may be running to you lot for protection once he finds out."

Klein cut in abruptly.

"There was another good reason for keeping your relationship secret," he said. "Judith Fairlie had a thing about divorce, didn't she? Not to mention the fact that she wouldn't be impressed by one of her ex-flames taking up with her daughter. Christine could have ended up losing a pretty big inheritance. In my book, that gives you both a motive for murder."

Maltravers shook his head.

"You can't pin this on us. We were together on the *Seagull*. Chris swam over once the others had left. Barry King knew, and agreed to cover up for us if anyone came back. When he saw the police boat coming into the bay, he called Chris and warned her to hustle back fast. He'll confirm that that's true."

"I'm sure he will. But he doesn't know what you got up to during that hour on your boat. There was nothing to stop you swimming ashore. You were anchored no more than a hundred yards from the cove where Judith Fairlie was sunbathing." Klein leaned back and eyed the couple sternly. "Everything you've told me puts you right in the frame."

*   *   *

Richard caught the two-thirty ferry back to town. The Murjis lived in British Properties, so when he reached Taylor Way, he branched off the Upper Levels Highway and headed for the enclave of expensive homes on the West Vancouver hillside.

Nazeem's house was a multi-level dwelling with pink stucco siding and vast plate-glass windows. Adesh Murji opened the door and greeted Richard courteously. He led Richard into an expensively furnished living room and invited him to sit down. Clearly, Richard had to talk with the father before the daughter was going to be produced.

Adesh answered Richard's questions frankly. He admitted that he had come to Pender Harbour to check up on his daughter. He had been staying at the Hampton House Inn and taking frequent walks to the marine park in order to watch the boaters and to see what Nazeem was up to.

He was appalled at the idea that his daughter was cruising unchaperoned on the same boat as her fiancé, even though she had insisted that the sleeping arrangements were entirely proper, with her and her friend, Robin, sleeping in the cabin of the Carver and her fiancé dutifully kipping down on his friend's Trophy at night. Adesh assured Richard that Nazeem was a well-brought-up young lady, and he believed her intentions were good. However, as everyone knew, propinquity could weaken young people's morals. He suspected that this had been the reason for the breakup, and that Nazeem's silence was due to her feelings of shame. He understood that Robin Fairlie was in love with her brother's friend, and suspected that Robin and Lee had tried to persuade Nazeem to change the sleeping arrangements so that the men could have their women with them overnight.

Adesh freely acknowledged that he was glad the engagement had been ended, but insisted that he did not know why his daughter had changed her mind. All he knew was that he had called her cellphone to let her know he was in the harbour. She agreed to meet him at the Hampton House Inn, and when she arrived, she had her bags with her and informed him that she wanted to go home. Adesh could cast no light on Judith Fairlie's murder, and was confident that his daughter was equally in the dark about the cause of the widow's death.

When Adesh called Nazeem down to the living room, she answered Richard's questions with the same quiet courtesy that her father had displayed. She was a breathtakingly lovely girl, thought Richard, with a gracious air that was all too rare in modern young women. He could understand why she was so precious to her family, and he felt a twinge of sympathy for Lee Fairlie having lost such a prize.

However, Nazeem's evidence gave Richard no further insights into the murder. When he came to the subject of her fiancé, Nazeem simply said that she had been very much in love, but she now realized that her parents had been right. The differences between their way of life and that of the Fairlie family was impossible to reconcile. The marriage would never have worked. No matter how hard Richard urged, she gave nothing more away.

Adesh Murji saw Richard out and apologized for being unable to offer more assistance. He was anxious to avoid casting blame on the Fairlie family.

"I hope you understand that I have nothing personally against Lee Fairlie," he said firmly. "My reluctance for Nazeem to marry him was because of cultural differences, not because I disliked him. I know he is innocent of this terrible crime, so I wouldn't want you to misinterpret Nazeem's change of heart."

Richard raised his eyebrows.

"I wasn't going to," he said. "I'm curious, though. Why are you so sure Lee is innocent? Klein told me that you backed up his alibi. How were you able to do that?"

Adesh looked surprised.

"I saw him at the pub."

"You were in the pub?"

"Yes. I'd been watching the boats from the marine park, but once I saw Lee take my daughter and her friend out in his Zodiac, I walked back to Pool Bay. I saw the Zodiac tied at the end of the dock, but I had no idea where Nazeem was, so I decided to have lunch on the deck of the pub where I could watch for her to come back to the boat. I'd just finished eating when I saw Lee enter the pub. He came out onto the deck to have a cigarette, so I thought I'd take the opportunity to have a talk with him, but as I approached him, his cellphone rang."

Richard nodded. "That would have been Jake Seagrove."

"It could have been. It sounded like a man's voice but it was a very short call. Lee looked at his watch and said, 'Twenty minutes, okay.' Then he noticed me and rang off."

Richard blinked. Something did not ring true. Jake Seagrove's call to Lee Fairlie had been made at ten to one.

"You're sure it was twenty minutes? Could it have been forty?"

Adesh looked surprised.

"No. My hearing is very good. It was definitely twenty. Why do you ask?"

Richard fell silent. What he had just been told did not make sense. Jake's alibi depended on the fact that the walk from the park to the pub took an hour. If somehow he had arrived in less time, he must have come by another route—and that meant he'd lied to the police. And so had Lee Fairlie.

Richard became aware that Adesh was scrutinizing him curiously. He turned back and asked, "Was Lee surprised to see you at the pub?"

"Yes, but we spoke civilly to one another. He was hoping I would come to accept his relationship with Nazeem. He was very courteous, though I think, rather nervous, which I suppose was understandable."

"In what way nervous?"

"He kept looking at his watch and glancing away. After a few minutes, he noticed a group of people congregating at the end of the dock. It was a trio of young people who'd just returned their kayaks to the rental dock. I think Lee was worried that they were hanging around his Zodiac, because he made his excuses and slipped away. Then, a moment later, I saw him going down on the dock and talking with them."

"What time was that?" Richard asked.

"It was a quarter past one. I looked at my watch because I was trying to decide whether to return to the marine park or stay in Pool Bay."

"So what did you do?"

"I had an hour to pass while the young people had lunch, so I finished my coffee, paid my bill and decided to go back to the inn. As I came out of the pub, I saw Lee in the parking lot. He'd come up from the dock, but he was still smoking. A moment later, his friend, Jake, came out from the marine park trail and the two of them went into the pub together. The band had just started playing so I was glad that I had left. Inside, it would have been very noisy."

"Then Jake did arrive at one-thirty," Richard said thoughtfully.

Adesh nodded.

"Yes, I know it was one-thirty because a young woman was coming out as they were going in, and she asked Lee the time. I remember distinctly, because what happened was rather odd. Both

Lee and his friend glanced at their wrists, but only Lee told the lady the time. His friend, Jake, whipped off his wristwatch and tucked it inside the pocket of his shorts."

Richard's brain was whirling. Scraps of information and images had been floating in a disordered and confused muddle in his mind, but suddenly they began to make sense.

"What did the watch look like?" he asked abruptly.

"Black, rather bulky. I can't think why he would have taken it off."

I can, thought Richard, triumphantly. He took it off because it wasn't a watch. Immediately, he realized why Lee Fairlie had been keeping a lookout from the deck of the pub and had hurried down to talk with the people who were hovering near the Zodiac. The last pieces of the puzzle were falling into place.

However, there was still one unanswered question. Lee might have been in a hurry to get hold of his inheritance, but why would Jake help him out? Why risk his own future to hurry things up for his friend? Unless....

Richard thought about the speculative look Lee had given him when he first entered the interview room, and he reflected on the argument that the redheaded boater had overheard in the marine park. He suspected he knew the answer to his question, but he needed confirmation.

He turned to Adesh and asked if he could speak to Nazeem again. Adesh looked surprised, but made no objection, and he ushered Richard back inside.

Nazeem was still in the living room, and she looked frightened when she saw Richard return with her father. Her eyes flashed anxiously when Richard asked if he could have a minute alone with her. Adesh looked as if he would refuse, but then, after a glance at his daughter, he nodded and slipped out.

Richard turned to Nazeem.

"I know this is upsetting for you," he said, "but there's a question that I have to ask. I'll make it as easy as I can. Just give me a truthful answer, a simple yes or no, and then I'll leave. Did you break up with Lee Fairlie because you discovered that he is gay?"

Nazeem went white below her beautiful golden skin. She bowed her head.

"Yes," she whispered. Then she began to cry as if her heart would break.

*   *   *

The case wrapped up quickly after Richard's visit to Nazeem's house. That evening, two constables, armed with photographs of Jake Seagrove and Lee Fairlie, were dispatched to the high-end gay bars of downtown Vancouver. By the following day, they were able to establish that both men were regular visitors to a particularly expensive club in the West End. Jake Seagrove was well known there as a bisexual opportunist who revelled in his power over the people who were unfortunate enough to fall for him. According to a young bartender who was one of Jake's discards, Lee had met Jake through the club and had fallen for him to the point of obsession. Jake, seeing Lee as his ticket to wealth and the easy life, had readily reciprocated and gone along when Lee set him up in a luxury apartment in English Bay.

Jake's ability to manipulate the various members of the Fairlie family had been masterful. Lee was convinced that Jake was going to marry him at some point in the future when circumstances allowed him to come out of the closet. He had even made a will naming Jake as his partner and heir. Delusional, sniffed the bartender. No one had ever pinned Jake Seagrove down.

"No wonder they had to get rid of Mother," said Klein, when he called Richard the following week. "While she lived, there was a constant danger that Lee's lifestyle would be exposed and he would lose his inheritance."

"That'll be why they both made such a public pursuit of the women in their circle," said Richard. "The men in Judith Fairlie's life were expected to be red-blooded heterosexuals. Not that Seagrove had any difficulty that way. I suspect Lee would have been the next one to go. A neat little accident for him, and the path would be clear for Seagrove to marry Robin as planned. Half the Fairlie fortune in two fell swoops. I bet Seagrove started planning Judith's death as soon as he hitched up with Lee."

"Probably," said Klein, "but Lee was just as guilty. They'll both stand trial for the murder. Seagrove may have handled the spear gun, but Lee Fairlie helped him carry out the plan."

"They might have got away with it, too," said Richard, "if I hadn't been at the marine park and seen Jordan Fairlie's underwater compass. I didn't even know there were such things, but once Nazeem's father described Jake Seagrove's watch, I realized the truth. He not only swam between the two coves of the marine park; he also swam across the bay to the pub. It was less than half a mile—nothing for a powerful and experienced swimmer wearing fins and an oxygen tank. No wonder he was there in twenty minutes. That gave him fifteen minutes to dump the gear back in the Zodiac, swim across to the bushes below the trail and dry off for ten minutes before walking out into the parking lot."

"Which was why Lee Fairlie went down to the docks and distracted the people standing near his Zodiac. Seagrove had to slip his scuba gear over the side of the boat unobserved. Everything was bone dry when our officers inspected the boat, but given the heat, it was a given that there'd be no evidence that it had just been used."

"Lethal plan," said Richard, "and it almost worked."

"Nasty pair. Those two deserve everything they get."

"How are the other members of the family coping?"

"Godfrey Spence has been released, of course. Christine Spence and Brian Maltravers are in the clear, too. They were on board the *Seagull* the entire time."

"What's the situation with her and her husband now?"

"Godfrey Spence has agreed to a divorce. I think the shock of being pulled in for murder gave him the reality check he needed to smarten up and let her go. I suspect Christine Spence will be Christine Maltravers by this time next year. There's a lot of love and history holding those two together. They'll be okay."

"I feel sorry for the young women," said Richard, "especially Robin Fairlie. What a rollercoaster ride that poor kid's been on. She must be pretty cut up. Nazeem has a loving family to help her get over her disappointment and humiliation, but Robin has a much harder row to hoe. She's lost her mother, and her brother, too."

Klein chuckled.

"Actually, she's recovering remarkably well," he said. "She's lost a mother but gained a father."

"What?"

"That's part of the history I was telling you about. Maltravers was the widow's toy-boy for the cruise of 1992, so it's easy to figure it out if you do the math. Maltravers actually started to tell me, but then he clammed up. But I winkled it out of Christine later. Not that I really needed to. The resemblance was obvious the moment he walked into my office. If you'd been there, you'd have seen it too."

Richard slapped his free hand to the side of his head.

"I did see him," he cried, "just as I was leaving. It was driving me crazy, thinking I'd met him somewhere before, but now it makes sense. Robin Fairlie looks just like him. She's Maltravers' daughter."

"A good ending, isn't it?" Klein's voice bubbled with bonhomie on the other end of the line. "Robin is going to move to the Island and live with her sister and Maltravers. You know," he added cheerfully, "we on the Coast have seen a lot of the Fairlies over the years—all those family cruises where kinship was only held together through duty and money. I like to think that some love is now going to enter the equation."

Richard smiled as he ended the call. Klein was a softy under that tough exterior. But then, as Richard had always said: They were a different breed on the Sunshine Coast.

Journeys End
in Lovers Meeting

September 2010

On the Bay of Fundy, standing as proud and distinctive as the monolithic heads of Easter Island, the Hopewell Rocks rise from the sands. Formed over millions of years, these dreamscape figures of conglomerate rock and sandstone lure visitors to walk below them at low tide or explore them in kayaks when the water rushes in. However, only the hardier tourists venture down to the beach, for the ninety-five steps between the sands and the cliff top are daunting, especially when it comes time for the return climb.

From the top of the stairway, an elderly woman stared down at the bizarre configurations below. It was easy to understand why the Mi'kmaq had created legends to explain the existence of the rocks, she thought, especially as some were adorned with scrub spruce and vegetation that reinforced the illusion of faces carved out of the cliff.

She could easily believe that the rocks were the natives' ancestors, who had escaped from the whales that enslaved them, only to be recaptured and turned into stone.

In the afternoon light, the gravelly sand gleamed with a pink incandescent quality, and seen from the lookout, the strand had the appearance of glossy compacted mud. Carefully, the woman started down the stairway. Her daughter and son-in-law had gone on ahead and were already taking photographs of the striking formations, but Thelma Trent was not as agile as she used to be, so she was content to proceed slowly and pause to admire the view from each level as new hollows and arches materialized in front of her eyes.

The scene was not the spectacular seascape she had expected from the Bay of Fundy. Adjacent to the beach was a thin blue strip of water, and the ocean beyond was a mud-coloured expanse, matching the sands and stretching across to another thin aquamarine line on the far side of the bay. Thelma was a little apprehensive, having heard that it was imperative to get off the sands before the tide came in. She had read that the tides in the Bay of Fundy were some of the highest in the world. People had been trapped on these beaches, not realizing the speed with which the water could surge forward as the tide neared its peak. The black shadows cast on the sides of the rocks gave the cove a sinister air, and Thelma shivered in spite of the heat of the day.

When she reached the bottom, she moved onto the sand and was almost blown over by a gust of wind. Her hat lifted on her head, and slapping it back into place, she put up her hood to anchor it down. She saw her daughter and son-in-law standing by a hollowed-out rock, one side of which resembled an elephant's foot. They were talking with another couple. The man was fair, blue-eyed, and darkly tanned. A peacock, thought Thelma, noting his long, curly mane, low-slung chinos and brightly coloured shirt that hung open to reveal a great deal of his muscular physique. The woman with him was tiny, a scantily clad brunette, with long hair dancing in the wind. She was giggling at whatever Thelma's son-in-law was saying. Carl appeared to be enjoying the exchange, but Doreen looked strained.

"There you are, Mom," she said. Her voice sounded shrill over the whistle of the wind. "Come and get a picture of me and Carl by this rock."

She thrust her camera towards Thelma, but before her mother could take the photograph, the fair man in the chinos stepped forward. "Here. Let me. I'll take a picture of the three of you."

He took the camera, lined up the trio in front of the rock, and, with professional élan, took the shot. His companion held out her camera to Thelma.

"Now you take one of us," she demanded. "We should have a honeymoon shot. Come on, darling. Under the elephant."

With a high-pitched shriek of laughter, she dragged the blonde man into the hollow and, pulling his arms around her, posed for the shot. But as Thelma raised the camera, she saw that the battery had died. She returned the camera and shook her head apologetically.

Carl took Doreen's camera.

"Not a problem," he said. "I'll take one with our camera and email it to you."

The fair man started, as if momentarily taken aback. Then he shrugged and nodded. He posed for the photograph, then pulled his wallet from his pocket, extracted a business card and handed it to Carl.

"Here," said Thelma, pulling a card from the pocket of her Tilley pants and handing it to the brunette, who was still clinging to her husband's arm. "This is our email. We run a B&B in Charlottetown. It's called The Captain's Corner. It's a wonderful place to stay if you're ever visiting Prince Edward Island."

"Sweet," said the girl. Her eyes started to slide off into the distance and, absently, she fingered the pendant that was hanging around her neck. It was an ornate piece with colourful stones mounted on a gilded base.

"That's beautiful," said Thelma. "Is it an antique?"

The girl sniggered. "I'll say," she said. "It belonged to Roger's mother. It has an inscription from Shakespeare on the back. Probably one of her contemporaries."

Roger did not take umbrage at the slur on his maternal parent.

"My parents met during a production of *Twelfth Night*," he explained. "My father had the pendant inscribed for their first anniversary. Come on," he added, taking his companion's arm. "We'd better get moving if we want to explore the rest of the beach. The tide's on its way in."

"I know what you want to explore," giggled the girl. She smirked at Carl. "We found a kissing bridge on the way here. Now we have to find a kissing cavern." She pulled her arm free and grabbed the fair man's hand. Dragging him along behind her, she carolled, "'Trip no further, pretty sweeting. Journeys end in lovers meeting.'"

"The inscription, I presume," said Doreen, after the couple was out of earshot. "What a performance!"

"She does seem rather excitable," acknowledged Thelma.

Doreen stared at her mother with exasperated affection.

"Mum! Don't you get it? She was on something. I hate to think what would happen if the police checked her fanny pack."

"Oh," said Thelma.

"Lucky Roger Sutherland," said Carl, reading the name on the business card. "Whatever she's on, Hopewell is definitely going to rock for him. What did she mean by kissing bridges?" he added curiously.

"Covered bridges," said Thelma. She might have been born too long ago to be conversant with the effects of drug use, but her knowledge of Canadian history was impressive.

"Did you have to go on about the B&B?" Doreen complained. "It's bad enough that our lives are tied up running it most of the year, but the last thing we need is that ditzy pothead on the premises."

"I'm sure you don't have to worry," Carl pointed out. "They didn't exactly strike me as bed-and-breakfast clientele. Those inadequate bits of clothing they were almost wearing had designer labels. Now stop griping and let's tour this beach before the tide comes in. I want to find the ET rock, and we have to get a picture of me and Mom by the mother-in-law rock." He beckoned to Thelma, took Doreen's hand, and set off across the sands.

Thelma followed Carl and Doreen as they explored the rocks. As the sun alternately hid behind clouds or emerged in full glory, the beach was transformed into an enchanted place with roaring dinosaurs, stranded whales, sleeping dragons and giant turtles, but whenever Thelma glimpsed a grotto hollowed out in the cliff face, the image of the girl with the antique pendant flashed into her mind.

When they'd seen all there was to see, they climbed back up the steps, proceeding slowly for Thelma's sake, and then strolled back along the trail. Thelma was relieved to be out of the wind and in the shelter of the trees. The woods were cool, with wide paths shaded by spruce, birch and pine, and the verges were dotted with wildflowers and patches of Indian paintbrush, giving cheerful splashes of colour amid the greens of the trees and ferns.

Seeing that her mother was tired, Doreen insisted that they stop for lunch in the coffee shop, but once they had eaten, they went back to the top of the cliff to have one last look at the view. The wind hit hard again as they stood in the lookout, and Thelma zipped up her jacket and anchored her hat. She glanced down and saw that the beach had narrowed considerably in the time they had been away.

The pink and purple expanse of the ocean was broader. It was eerily awe-inspiring in the glittering light.

The tide was coming in fast now, and a ranger was walking back and forth, keeping a lookout for stragglers. Thelma noticed uneasily that the section of beach around the elephant's foot was now surrounded by water. She hoped the ranger had rounded up the couple from their cavern. She wondered if she should tell someone about the two people who had wandered up the beach, but then she told herself not to be foolish. However silly the girl was, her companion seemed sober and reliable. He wouldn't let his wife come to harm.

But all the way home, the inscription on the pendant kept obtruding into Thelma's thoughts. *Journeys end in lovers meeting...lovers meeting...journeys end.*

*   *   *

June 2012

Philippa had enjoyed her week in Halifax—her cousins had proved as much fun as she remembered from their visit to Vancouver ten years earlier—but she was glad to be moving on, for she was anxious about her upcoming engagement. This was the first time she had been hired to perform with a company outside British Columbia. The sooner she tackled the challenge, the better she would feel.

She left Halifax early, hoping to avoid heavy traffic as she was driving an unfamiliar vehicle. Therefore, by seven o'clock, she was already speeding along the highway in a morning mist that brought to mind the Scottish Highlands, until the sun poked through and revealed the flat terrain that bordered the road. She detoured into Truro to look for a coffee shop and to see the strange statues that, according to her guidebook, were carved from dying trees. She found a café at the end of the high street, and armed with a latte-to-go, she set off for the drive to the Strait of Northumberland. From there, the Caribou ferry would take her to Prince Edward Island.

The ferry turned out to be an old tub—definitely not up to the standard of the newer B.C. Ferries—but the genial people who inhabited it enlivened the voyage. Eager to make the most of the crossing, Philippa went out onto the deck. A series of picnic tables, their seats and tops painted bright green, were arranged around a small concourse that was enclosed between two stairways to the upper deck. Philippa climbed to the top and huddled in the shelter of a lifeboat that was hanging from davits at the side of the ship.

The ocean was a smooth sheet of cobalt blue, stretching for miles beneath a white sky, which was streaked with patches of turquoise in the few spots where the clouds had parted. The sheer magnitude of the vast open space lulled Philippa into a pensive mood. So many opportunities might be opening up as a result of her role in Charlottetown. For years, she had longed to become a performer on the national scene, and now the dream was becoming a reality. So why did she have a curiously hollow feeling in the pit of her stomach? She was reluctant to acknowledge the cause of her depression, but deep down, she knew what was keeping her spirits low. There had been no word from Bob Miller since she left Vancouver. She was out of sight, and she feared she was out of mind, too.

Her deliberations were interrupted by the murmur of voices. A man and two women had climbed to the upper deck. The older woman was grey-haired and had a comfortable, motherly appearance. When she caught sight of Philippa, her eyes widened. She continued to stare as the trio moved to the railing. Then, realizing that her behaviour must be disconcerting, she stepped towards Philippa, smiled and apologized.

"I'm sorry to be so rude," she said, "but I'm sure I've seen your photograph. It was in the festival brochure. Aren't you the new girl playing Anne of Green Gables?"

Philippa blinked, surprised. If this was a taste of stardom on Prince Edward Island, she was going to have a very social summer.

"Don't mind my mom," laughed the younger woman. "We all get to be expert at Anne-spotting on the Island. You look so much the part, even if we hadn't recently seen your picture."

"Philippa Beary, right?" said the older woman suddenly.

Philippa nodded.

"I'm Thelma Trent," the woman said, "and this is my daughter, Doreen, and her husband, Carl. We run a B&B on the Island."

Philippa's attention was caught.

"Do you? Are you in town? I need something near the theatre, and a B&B might be ideal for me—except that I don't want to have to eat in restaurants all the time. Do you provide any other meals or let guests use the cooking facilities?"

"We have a heritage home a few blocks from the Confederation Centre," said Thelma. "It's walking distance, though you'd want to drive at night. And we do provide dinners for long-term guests. We're halfway between a B&B and a boarding house. We have wireless Internet too," she added. "All the mod-cons."

She took out a card and handed it to Philippa.

"Our house is called The Captain's Corner. It's almost as old as Beaconsfield House and every bit as luxurious."

"Thank you," said Philippa. "I'm booked in at the Best Western for now, but I'll get in touch once I've got my bearings. I expect you get very busy in the summer season."

"Yes," said Thelma. "The Festival brings us a lot of business."

"That it does," echoed Doreen. "All season, we're in bondage to ornate moldings, quaint furniture and pictures rails, and unlike the

Victorians, we don't have servants to dust them." She spoke in mock exasperation, but the underlying edge to her voice intimated that her words were in earnest. "That's what we get for being an old Island family. Too bad there aren't more of us left to share the load."

"I guess it's a lot of work for three people," Philippa said diplomatically.

"Five, actually," corrected Thelma. "I have a cleaner in twice a month for the heavy work, and my nephew lends a hand too. He's the caretaker in The Old Protestant Cemetery, but he pops by to help Carl with the grounds."

"Once a year when the pruning has to be done," muttered Doreen. "Honestly, it's heaven when we get away, though that only happens in the off season when we can budge Mum and persuade her to leave her beloved house."

"You know you love our home," said Thelma, "and I'm not unwilling to leave. I'm always happy to take our annual holiday." She turned to Philippa. "We go on a driving trip every spring," she said. "This year, we went all around the Maritimes."

"How lovely," said Philippa. "I'm going to try to do some sightseeing while I'm here. My cousins gave me a list of things I should see, and not just on the Island. They said I should drive over to New Brunswick to see the Reversing Falls at St. John. They said the Hopewell Rocks are worth a visit, too."

Thelma nodded.

"We were at the Hopewell Rocks the year before last. They're quite spectacular, but whatever you do, pay attention to the signs telling you when to get off the beach. A woman drowned the day we were there. The tide comes in really fast."

"What happened? Surely she could see the water coming up."

"She was on drugs," Doreen said shortly. "We met her. Spinny as a merry-go-round stuck in high gear."

"She was pretty far gone," Carl agreed. "She and her husband were honeymooners, and they made no secret of the fact that they were heading up the beach to find a cavern where they could have a bit of nooky. They got trapped in the cove."

"How did the husband get out?"

"We only know what we read in the paper," said Thelma. "We didn't actually see what happened because we left before the tide came all the way in." A shadow crossed the kindly woman's face. Thelma felt guilty every time she cast her mind back to that fateful day and recalled how they had left without speaking to the ranger. "They drifted off to sleep. The water lapping around their legs brought them to," she finished sadly.

"Brought *him* to," corrected Carl. "The newspaper article said that he had trouble rousing his wife, but he got her on her feet and did his best to bring her out. He yelled for help, but then he realized that no one could get them up the cliff in time, so he decided to swim for it."

Philippa was horrified.

"Leaving his wife there?"

"Oh, no," said Thelma. "He tried to rescue her."

"It sounds like it was a pretty spectacular attempt," said Carl. "He was a champion swimmer and his wife was tiny. He got her to put her arms round his neck and he strapped her to his back with his belt."

"It was so sad," sighed Thelma. "He swam all the way round the point and was heading in, but the belt gave way and the current swept her away. He went after her and eventually managed to pull her in, but it was too late. He couldn't revive her."

"Come on, Mum," said Doreen, cutting her mother's account short. "We're getting close. Better come back to the car. You need to take your time on the stairs."

Thelma said goodbye to Philippa and followed her daughter and son-in-law down the steps. Philippa turned back for one last look at the view. The ferry was close enough to the Island that she could see a long breakwater. At its end stood a white lighthouse and a whitewashed house with a red roof—a perfect calendar photograph of the East Coast.

As Philippa stood admiring the scene, her cellphone beeped. A text message had come in. It was from Bob Miller.

Miss you already. Hope the trip is going well. Look forward to hearing every detail when you return.

A warm glow spread through Philippa's body, and the hollow feeling she had felt earlier evaporated. Her sense of adventure returned, and she regarded the Island's welcoming coastline with a heart that was light and a spirit that felt restored.

*   *   *

The forty-minute drive to Charlottetown was another charming succession of calendar pictures. The road wound through corn and potato fields, interspersed with hedgerows, groves of trees, and picturesque houses. Philippa felt intoxicated by the beauty of the scenery and the thrill of exploring new territory. She stopped at a fruit store to sample the local wares, then drove on to the tiny waterfront town of Stratford. Charlottetown could be seen directly across the water. In the harbour, a cruise ship gleamed white in the afternoon sun. Philippa drove across the bridge and, seeing an info-centre sign at Founders Hall, she pulled into the parking lot.

The first thing she saw as she entered the building was the Starbucks logo, but the name over the coffee shop was Mavor's. While she stood puzzling over the sign, a guide in period costume greeted her and explained: Mavor Moore was an initiator of the *Anne of Green Gables* musical, and consequently, all Starbucks outlets in the town were named after him. Once the guide had helped her find town maps and brochures, Philippa entered the coffee shop. Suddenly hungry, she ordered a panini as well as her usual latte. A tall, darkly attractive man stood at the end of the counter waiting to pick up his order. He eyed Philippa curiously.

"Anne of Green Gables?" he inquired.

"It's uncanny," said Philippa. "Is this going to happen everywhere I go?"

The man laughed.

"Probably," he said, and pointed at the rack of local papers in front of the counter. Philippa glanced down and saw her own face staring back at her from the front page.

"Are you coming to see the show?" Philippa asked.

"Not possible, I'm afraid. We're off the cruise ship, so we only have a couple of days for a quick tour of the sights and then we're leaving again." The barista put two drinks on the counter and the man picked them up. "But good luck all the same," he said. He sauntered to a table by the window where a blonde woman in a floral dress was seated. Philippa could only see the back of the woman's head, but her silvery hairstyle had the casually wind-tossed look that only came with expensive hairdressing. As the man sat down, she reached out with her arm and took his hand. They leaned in towards each other and exchanged a lingering kiss.

Cruise-ship honeymooners, thought Philippa, with a pang of envy. Her order appeared on the counter, so she picked up the local paper and took it to a table, along with her lunch, and browsed through the articles while she ate.

By the time she had finished her panini, the couple from the cruise ship had gone. Philippa left the building, and with the help of the city map, found her way to the Best Western. It seemed to be the season for honeymooners, for she found herself waiting patiently while the receptionist dealt with a couple who had mistakenly not been booked into the bridal suite. Philippa watched the pair curiously. They were a fascinating study in contrasts. The bride was a petite brunette with a frail and unassuming air, whereas her mate was a muscular, hirsute redhead who exuded power and rugged determination. The woman clearly did not want to make a fuss, and she flushed with embarrassment at her husband's unequivocal refusal to settle for alternative arrangements. Philippa was not surprised when the receptionist called the manager to sort out the mess. She wouldn't have wanted to deal with him either. Finally, after a tedious wait, she was able to sign in and take her things to her room.

It was still early in the afternoon, and with her encounter on the ferry still fresh in her mind, Philippa decided not to unpack. She phoned her parents to let them know she had arrived safely. Then she put on her runners, tucked the bed-and-breakfast card into her fanny pack, and went down to the lobby. After getting directions from the concierge, she walked to the bank and replenished her supply of cash from the ATM.

On her way back, she spotted a graveyard on the far side of the road. It was The Old Protestant Cemetery Ground. The sign by the gate indicated that it dated back to 1784.

A caretaker was attending the grounds. Wondering if this was the relative her new acquaintances had mentioned, Philippa crossed over and walked through the open gateway. As she entered the grounds, she saw that the caretaker had company. A black cat was prowling around a strange green shrub that resembled a pixie's hat, its cap of down-turned leaves topped with a cluster of spindly, antenna-like stems. Philippa strolled up the path. The cat padded over to her and rubbed around her legs. The grounds-man glanced up and gave a brief nod to acknowledge her presence.

"I think I met some of your relatives on the ferry," said Philippa. "A couple with a very nice older lady named Thelma who runs a bed and breakfast at The Captain's Corner?"

"That would be my aunt with her daughter and son-in-law. They must have been returning from their annual vacation. Where would you be from?"

"Vancouver."

"Ah, other side of the country. One of our townsfolk is buried out west. A sad tale. You'll hear it if you visit Beaconsfield House. Shipbuilding family lost their fortune and was forced to sell their dream home. The father ended up working in a saloon in Vancouver and living in poverty until he died. Big country, Canada, but not so big that you'll not find connections everywhere you go."

Philippa eyed the rows of gravestones. She asked, "Are there any famous historical figures buried here?"

The caretaker gave a grim smile.

"The victim of the last public hanging in Canada is tucked over there in the corner."

Philippa examined a grave marker to her right. Curiously she asked, "Why does Henry Picton have *The Captain* inscribed after his name? He wouldn't by any chance be the captain of The Captain's Corner?"

"He would," said the caretaker. "He was another shipbuilder, but he held on to what he earned. A good businessman and a fine citizen. Well loved by all. Rather like Thelma. She's his great-great-niece, you know. She has a good head on her shoulders. Even though her father frittered away most of the family fortune, she's held onto her home and made it pay."

"So you'd recommend her house as a good place to stay?"

"Absolutely, young lady. If she has a spot for you."

"Is it that busy?"

"Yes, though it's early in the season, so you can probably get in there if you don't leave it too long. She may even give you a special deal as you're going to be here a while."

Philippa raised her eyebrows.

"How do you know I'm going to be here a while?" she demanded.

"You're the new Anne, aren't you?" said the caretaker, and turned back to his digging.

Philippa said goodbye to the cat and walked back into the main part of town. She located the Arts Centre, but did not go inside the building. Today was for exploration. However, before she could leave, an angular girl with unruly brown hair came out through the main entrance. When she saw Philippa, she stopped and beamed with delight.

"Well, look who's here," she cried. "Anne in the living flesh! Love the hair and the freckles. You've got to be Philippa."

Philippa nodded. She resolved to wear a hat when she went out in future.

"I'm Poppy," the girl announced. "Your ASM. Welcome to Charlottetown. A lot different from the West Coast, I bet."

"A bit," Philippa admitted. "Horizontal traffic lights, lobster subs and no mountains. But the general seaside atmosphere is the same."

"Doing some sightseeing before going into bondage?" asked Poppy.

"Yes. I just arrived today. Is anyone else here yet?"

"Just the locals. Mind you, most of the cast has been here before. You and the girl playing Josie are the only newcomers. We'll fit you in in no time. Playing Anne is like being a cog in a well-oiled machine."

"So I gathered when I read my contract. It's a pretty short rehearsal period. No wonder we're expected to come with our parts down pat."

"It'll be a breeze. Everyone will help you."

"I've never seen the show," Philippa admitted. "What are the regulars like?"

"The old-timers are great," said Poppy. "Winston Greene and June Laidlaw are darlings," she declared, naming two familiar figures on the Canadian theatre scene. "They play Matthew and Marilla, but back in the early days, they did several seasons as Anne and Gilbert." Poppy made a face. "Too bad Winston is past playing juvenile leads," she added. "Your current Gilbert is a pain."

"Oh?" Philippa hated being saddled with difficult leading men. "In what way?"

Poppy grinned.

"Well, put it this way, Tommy Broderick's from New Brunswick and he lives up to the name of his home town."

"Where would that be?"

"Athole."

Philippa laughed in spite of herself.

"Thanks for the warning," she said. "What's our director like?"

"Great." Poppy glanced at her watch. "Look, I have to run. I'll see you on Friday. Enjoy your days of freedom." She began to move on, then turned back. "Are you okay with your lodgings? You have somewhere to stay?"

Philippa nodded.

"I'm booked into the Best Western, but I'm going to check out the bed-and-breakfast situation. I hear The Captain's Corner is highly recommended. Do you know it?"

Poppy nodded vigorously.

"A gem," she stated. "The landlady is an absolute sweetie. I can't say the same for her daughter and son-in-law, but Thelma is the best. She'll spoil you rotten. It's only a few blocks from here. You could pop up now and check it out. Ciao!"

Poppy hurried off down the sidewalk, then turned to wave cheerily at Philippa before disappearing around the corner.

Still smiling from her encounter with the ebullient ASM, Philippa headed over to see the Confederation Building. Afterwards, she wandered through town, browsing in leisurely fashion through the tourist-trap gift shops. The souvenirs were tempting, and she bought an *Anne of Green Gables* doll for Chelsea and some boxes of locally-made chocolates for the other nieces and nephews. Satisfied with her purchases, she continued on, and soon she found herself in a charming residential district where rows of majestic, late Victorian houses bordered squares with neatly trimmed hedges and colourful flowerbeds. Then, using her map, she found the address on the card that Thelma had given her.

The house stood at the end of a block of historic residences. It was a stately mansion, surrounded by a well-maintained lawn. A white pergola, intertwined with wisteria, arched over the path to the front door, and a grove of red oaks, their roots dotted with lady's slippers, provided shade at the corner of the garden.   Beds of snapdragons and nasturtiums bordered the edge of the house, which sported yellow wooden siding and maroon and white window frames as cheerful as the flowers themselves. Three dormer windows jutted out from the high mansard roof, and a carriage house was visible on the far side of the building. Philippa was charmed. She peered at the hand-painted sign by the wrought-iron gate: *The Captain's Corner*. Somehow she knew that this would be her home away from home.

*   *   *

Thelma was delighted to see Philippa. She welcomed her into a high entrance hall where the scent of polish mingled with the mouth-watering smell of freshly baked bread. The foyer was a magnificent example of New World Victoriana. The red floral wallpaper was topped with a frieze of pink oysters that ran below the crown moldings, and the parquet floor, patterned in diamonds of brown and gold, gleamed in the light from a wrought-iron chandelier. An imposing mahogany hallstand and two ornately carved wooden chairs stood against the walls, while a golden statue of Aphrodite graced the foot of the steep oak stairway. The stair-runner's oriental design should have clashed with all the other patterns in the hall, but in fact, the overall effect was warm and pleasing.

Thelma assured Philippa that she would be able to make room for her. She chattered volubly as she took Philippa upstairs, proudly pointing out the distinguishing features of the home she loved. Philippa was particularly taken with the stained-glass window in the upper stairwell, with its rim of white maple leaves set on a semi-circle of royal blue that, in turn, framed an intricate golden insignia. However, she was surprised at the low height of the railing around the stairwell. It would never pass code today, she reflected, noticing uneasily how it only came up to the lower part of her thigh.

The floral wallpaper and oyster friezes were repeated on the upper floor, but here, paintings of seascapes and clipper ships adorned the walls. Thelma led Philippa down the hall and ushered her into the room at the end. Whereas the hall had been dark, the room was airy and bright, with pale pink walls and a stamped white ceiling, framed in a smooth cove molding that ran the circumference of the room. Green and lilac area rugs were spread around the hardwood floor, and watercolours of seabirds hung on chains from the picture rails. The sturdy double bed sported a cotton spread with a delicate pattern of pink roses, but at the foot of the bed was a cedar chest piled with folded blankets to augment the lightweight coverlet. On the opposite wall, a walnut dressing table and matching wardrobe stood on either side of a tall double-hung window that revealed a glistening strip of blue ocean in the distance. The third wall was dominated by a fireplace with a wooden mantel that held a carriage clock and a row of china dogs, all neatly duplicated in the gilt-framed mirror on the wall above. The fourth wall contained an oriel window overlooking the garden. A well-stuffed armchair was tucked in the alcove. Beside the window was a small writing desk, the perfect size for Philippa's laptop.

Philippa peeked into the bathroom. To her delight, there was a small anteroom with a marble-topped counter containing a coffee maker, kettle and microwave. The bathroom beyond was a bright confection of yellow and white, with a frieze of daisies bordering the wainscoting.

"It's lovely," pronounced Philippa. "I hope you have monthly rates, because I'm here all summer."

Thelma smiled. "We can work something out. Come down to the kitchen and I'll make you a cup of tea."

After half an hour in Thelma's kitchen, Philippa had not only arranged her accommodation, but had also agreed to a sightseeing trip to the north end of the island the following day. By the time she left, it was late afternoon, so she stopped for dinner at an enticing seafood restaurant with an enormous orange lobster on the marquee. Then she made her way back to the hotel. As she entered the foyer, her cellphone rang. It was Bob Miller.

"How are you doing?" he asked.

"Great," said Philippa, truthfully, for her spirits had soared the moment she heard his voice. "I'm in Charlottetown and I've just lined myself up with a home-away-from-home in a stately Victorian mansion."

"Sounds very grand. When do you start rehearsals?"

"Friday. I have one day off to enjoy the Island."

"Too bad I can't be there to sightsee with you."

Philippa agreed with the sentiment, but still maintaining a degree of dignified reserve, she said, "I have the next best thing. I get a personal guided tour tomorrow, which includes a visit to the fabled Green Gables."

"That should get you in the mood for your part. Who's your guide?" Miller added suspiciously.

Philippa laughed.

"An eighty-plus elderly woman—my new landlady. She knows the history of the Island inside out. I was excited just hearing her describe the Atlantic views—sapphire sea, red chalk cliffs, white sand—she gets quite poetic on the subject. She also mentioned a seafood restaurant to die for that we're going to visit after the tour. Can't wait to see it all."

"Well, don't wear her out."

"I won't. I still have my rental car, so I'm going to drive and she's going to be the guide. And I'm going to treat her to lunch, too, though she doesn't know it. She's a very generous soul. She's bending over backwards to give me a deal because she says having 'Anne' staying at her B&B is great publicity. I think I'm going to be in good hands."

"Well, have fun." Miller sounded wistful. "But don't get to like it so much that you don't want to come back. I miss you."

Philippa relented.

"I miss you too," she said.

She rang off and went up to her room. Feeling very contented, she settled herself in the armchair by the window, diligently reviewed her lines for an hour, and then read the rest of the evening away.

Since Thelma had insisted on giving her the first week free of charge, Philippa forfeited her pre-payment to the Best Western and checked out the following morning. She left early, giving herself time to settle her things in her new abode; then, recalling the barrage of personal comments the day before, she put on a sunhat that concealed her hair, and set off with Thelma for Green Gables.

The site had only just opened when they arrived, so Philippa and Thelma were all by themselves as they watched the film in the information centre. However, by the time they had ambled through the barn and reached the pretty white house with its famous green trim, a smattering of tourists had appeared. The house tour was short, since they were only allowed on the main floor, so they followed the ropes through the rooms and soon came out into the grounds.

"That's it?" said Philippa. She had anticipated something much more thrilling.

"No," said Thelma. "Now come and see what really inspired Lucy Maud Montgomery." She pointed to a path that cut across the grass and disappeared into the woods.

Philippa had no idea how long a walk was in the offing, but sensibly, she decided that a quick trip to the washroom was in order before setting off.

"I'll wait over there," said Thelma, "and keep that old man company." She pointed to a row of golden sunflowers that trailed over the white picket fence. A sprucely dressed man sporting a golfing shirt and Bermuda shorts was sitting at the picnic table in front of the sun-drenched flowers.

Philippa smiled inwardly. Thelma was probably more than a decade older than the man on the bench, but she obviously did not consider herself over the hill. Philippa watched as her friend parked herself on the bench and struck up a conversation with the man. Judging by the way Thelma was gesticulating, she was telling her new friend all about The Captain's Corner and its famous new occupant. The man turned and stared at Philippa, then broke into a big smile.

Feeling like a celebrity, Philippa hurried back to the information centre. When she entered the washroom, she noticed a woman standing at the mirror. Philippa's eyes were drawn immediately to an ornate pendant around the woman's neck. It was antique gold, set with vividly coloured stones.

"That's gorgeous," she said, unable to resist commenting.

The woman looked pleased. She was a very pretty blonde, though most of her hair was concealed under a broad straw hat.

"Isn't it?" she agreed. "It has an inscription from *Twelfth Night* on the back. 'Come and kiss me, pretty sweeting...'"

"'Journeys end in lovers meeting,'" finished Philippa. "That's so romantic."

"It is," agreed the woman with a soft smile. She fingered the pendant lovingly. "It's from my other half." She laughed suddenly, the dreamy expression fading from her wide blue eyes. "Sorry, you must excuse me being so ridiculously sentimental. I'm on a honeymoon cruise."

The woman slipped a jacket over her sun-top and zipped it up to her neck.

"Such a shame to cover it," she said, "but I'm sun-sensitive. Enjoy the tour."

With that, she left. By the time Philippa walked back to the house, the woman was nowhere in sight. Thelma's gentleman friend had also gone and been replaced by a young mother with a toddler and a babe-in-arms. Predictably, Thelma was chattering as happily to the newcomers as she had been with the man who had occupied the bench before. However, as soon as she saw Philippa approach, Thelma stood up to resume their tour.

Eager to explore the shadowy wood on the other side of the meadow, Philippa followed Thelma along the worn path in the grass. Once across the field, they came to a creek that was overhung with ferns and spruce branches. Trees rose eerily out of the water in places where the bank had been flooded. A bridge crossed the creek and led to a network of twisting, turning trails where, one moment, stunted birch trees stood like armed sentries amid the debris of fallen branches and the next, arches of maples formed delicate leafy tunnels. Philippa was enchanted.

"It's the haunted wood!" she cried. "The Birch Path and Lover's Lane! Look at those Snow White trees waiting to clutch at our sleeves as we pass by. No wonder Anne was scared to go through at night."

Thelma was delighted at her charge's enthusiasm. She was very proud of the Island history. She was starting to feel tired, though, and when the trail came out onto the road, she paused.

"If you cross over," she told Philippa, "you can follow that path and it will take you to Lucy Maud Montgomery's house. Only the foundation is left, but you can see the view and the grounds where she lived. It's very lovely, and not far. I'll wait for you here. I'm going to perch on this fence and take the weight off my feet."

Philippa crossed the road, glanced back to check that her friend was all right, and then set off along the other trail. The distance was short, for soon the woods thinned and she found herself amid masses of bright blooms in an overgrown garden surrounded by fields full of clover. She continued until she reached the grey stone pit that formed the original foundation of the house; then turned back, not wanting to leave Thelma for too long. She checked her watch. She had only been gone five minutes, but suddenly uneasy, she increased her pace and hurried down the rest of the path.

As she came out onto the road, her heart did a strange flip-flop. The street was deserted. Thelma was nowhere in sight.

Feeling a surge of panic, which she knew was utterly disproportionate in the circumstances, Philippa ran across the road and peered up the birch-lined trail. Then, with a wave of relief, she spied Thelma standing at the first bend in the path. She was staring at something further up the trail. Chiding herself for her irrational fears, Philippa hurried to join her. Hearing her footsteps, Thelma turned back. Her eyes seemed glazed, and she was squinting as if she was in pain.

Philippa gently placed a hand on her shoulder.

"Thelma, what's wrong? Are you all right?" she asked.

"What? Oh, yes. I'm fine. Just a bit puzzled. That's all."

"What happened?"

"I met someone I thought I knew. There was a couple, and the man looked so familiar, and even though he insisted we'd never met, I had such an uncanny feeling that he recognized me—but, of course, it couldn't be him. The hair was all wrong, and he had a moustache—and he'd never been to the Bay of Fundy. No, I'm just being silly."

Philippa felt relieved. She had been afraid the elderly woman was ill. Curiously, she urged Thelma to elaborate, but no matter how hard she pressed, no more information was forthcoming. Dismissing the incident as unimportant, Thelma insisted she had made a mistake. Still, throughout the rest of the day, Philippa had the sense that her new friend was miles away. Something was definitely on her mind.

*   *   *

"Your Dad called last night," said Doreen, as she served Philippa breakfast the following morning. "He sounds a sweetheart. He and your mum are booked in for a week, starting on your opening night."

"Excellent," said Philippa. "I gave him your number because I knew he'd love it here. How's your mother, by the way? Did she enjoy our day out?"

"Yes," said Doreen. "You must have put her in a holiday mood. She spent the evening on the computer pulling up our old trip photos."

"That's good. I was worried that I'd overdone things. She was rather withdrawn during the afternoon."

"Well, now you mention it, she does seem a bit distracted. Not on top of things in her usual way. I had to rescue your toast or it would have been charcoal. She's probably just tired."

Doreen plopped a coffee pot on the table and hurried back to the kitchen. As she poured herself a mug of coffee, Philippa heard a phone ringing in the hall. After two rings, the noise ceased, and then she heard a man's voice speaking quietly. A moment later, Doreen came back through the swing door.

"Do you have everything you need?" she asked.

Philippa nodded.

The voice in the hall stopped and Carl popped his head into the dining room.

"Where's Mum?" he said. "There's a man wanting to come and check out the place today. He and his wife need a room for the weekend."

"She's in the kitchen. You go get her. I'm busy. I have to go out this morning."

"So do I," said Carl calmly. He disappeared back into the hall.

"Just leave your dishes when you're finished," said Doreen to Philippa. "I'll get them when I come down. I have to prepare a guest room. Got to hustle. I have an appointment in town."

She darted away, looking harried. Philippa wondered if she should deliver Carl's message to her landlady, but a moment later, she heard Thelma's voice in the hall. Carl must have gone into the kitchen by the other door. Philippa put the interruption out of her mind, finished her breakfast, then went up to her room to get ready to leave.

By the end of the morning, the trials and tribulations of her hosts had receded from her consciousness, for she was totally immersed in the task of making *Anne of Green Gables* come to life. The cast and production team, with one notable exception, had made her feel welcome, but Poppy had been right about the juvenile leading man. Juvenile, Philippa concluded acerbically, was the right word to describe him. Having hit on her with all the subtlety of an elephant hunter, he morphed into pure acid once he had determined that Philippa was impervious to his self-perceived charm.

Poppy was sympathetic. She accompanied Philippa to the café and kept her company over lunch.

"What a bloody nerve." Poppy's eyes bulged. "Bit long in the tooth to play a little girl, indeed! Lots of actresses your age have played the part. After all, Anne has to grow up over the course of the show. Don't pay any attention to him."

"I won't." Philippa feigned indifference, although she was more nettled than she let on. She had not reacted to the comments on her age, but the addendum to Tommy's remark had stung. Philippa was well aware that her voice was light. Its ethereally bright quality would actually help her sustain the illusion of youth, but her co-star's snide concluding comment had really needled her.

Poppy read her mind.

"'*If* you manage to be heard beyond the first couple of rows.' What a nasty thing to say. Hasn't he heard of projection?"

"Obviously not," said Philippa.

"You'll get even when the reviews come out. I expect your voice carries beautifully."

"So I've been told."

"He's such an …"

"Athole. Right. Well, you warned me. Let's forget about him and enjoy lunch."

To Philippa's relief, on their return, her leading man was more subdued, and although he was not overly friendly, he refrained from making any more comments about her performance. Matthew and Marilla both wore grim smiles, which made Philippa believe that the senior members of the company had taken the male lead to task. Whatever the reason, she was glad to be able to concentrate on her part without distractions. Five o'clock came quickly, and she felt a sense of accomplishment as she packed away her script and prepared to walk home to The Captain's Corner. She resolved to spend the evening reviewing her notes and assimilating all that she had learned throughout the day.

But once on the street, her rehearsal mindset evaporated. The festive holiday atmosphere of Charlottetown was infectious. The sun was still warm, and tourists in gaily patterned summer wear paraded along the sidewalks and frequented the cafés. Flowers bloomed in window boxes, and as Philippa crossed the grassy square to the street where her new home was situated, her fatigue from the day's exertions melted away. Her thoughts drifted onto Bob Miller and she wondered if he would call her every day. And then, as if cued by a prompter, or maybe by telepathy, her phone rang. It was Miller.

"How did it go?" he asked.

"Fine. It's a huge part, though. I'm going to be working hard this summer."

"Good. That means you'll be too busy to fall in love with your leading man."

"No danger of that," laughed Philippa. "He's from Athole."

There was a brief silence at the other end.

"Is that a place?" Miller said finally.

"Yes, in New Brunswick. But it also describes him to a tee."

"Well, this all sounds quite satisfactory," said Miller complacently. "A geriatric landlady and a leading man whom you detest. I can breathe easy and not worry about what you're getting up to on the other side of the country."

Philippa had continued walking as she talked to Miller, but when The Captain's Corner came into view, she stopped in her tracks. Two police cars were parked at the end of the block. She hurried forward, and as she neared the house, she saw a burly uniformed constable standing on the front path. With a flutter of apprehension, she noticed a ribbon of yellow police tape cordoning off the property.

"Oh, my God!" she said. "Something's happened. I have to go."

"Wait a minute," interjected Miller. "What's going on?"

"I don't know. There are police cars outside the B&B. There's tape, and a constable on guard."

"Okay, calm down. Go and tell him who you are. Ask him what's happened. I'm going to stay on the line. If he gets chippy with you, tell him who you're talking to."

Philippa hurried down the block. As she turned to enter the garden, the constable came forward to stop her, but upon hearing that she was a resident in the building, he instructed her to come inside. Philippa had completely forgotten that Miller was on the line, but a few minutes later her cellphone rang again.

"You forgot me," he said. "What's going on?"

"It's absolutely horrible," said Philippa. "I wish you were here."

"Thanks for the postcard endorsement. I wish I were there too. Someone's been hurt?"

"Yes, Thelma. My landlady. It's serious. She's been taken to hospital, but no one's holding out a lot of hope for her."

"What happened to her?"

"She fell over the stairwell," said Philippa. "But there's more to it than that. I can tell by the way the police are behaving. Bob, I think she was pushed."

*   *   *

Thelma was still in hospital a week later. She had not regained consciousness after surgery and the doctors were keeping her under heavy sedation in the hope that her internal injuries would heal. Philippa had been forced to retreat to the Best Western while the police investigated the accident scene, but the following week, Doreen and Carl were allowed to reopen the guesthouse. Philippa was glad to get back to her room at the B&B, not just because it was so much more comfortable than the hotel, but also because she wanted to hear what was happening.

She returned to The Captain's Corner after her Wednesday rehearsal. As yet, no one else was booked in, and when Philippa arrived, Doreen was putting the finishing touches on the lemon sole she had prepared for dinner. Philippa joined her in the kitchen, insisting that the dining room did not have to be opened up for one guest. She observed her hostess closely. Doreen's face was pinched and white. The strain of the past few days had added more than ten years to her appearance. However, she was anxious to talk.

"We think Mom was given a violent shove and pushed over the balcony," she said bleakly. "There are bruises on her chest—at that age, people mark so easily. My mother would turn black and blue from something as simple as bumping into the counter, but the police say these marks were made by someone's hands."

"What are her chances of coming through?"

"She may never recover." Doreen caught her breath. "I thought she was dead. She was lying there so still. I couldn't believe it when the paramedics said she was still alive. But what sort of life will it be if she's so crippled up that she can't do anything? Oh, damn this place," she burst out. "She should have packed it in years ago."

"You don't really mean that," said Philippa gently. "I had the impression that this beautiful heritage house was what motivated her to keep going."

Doreen sighed.

"Yes, you're right, of course. Carl and I were the ones who wanted out. We just kept on because it meant so much to her. But what a sorry way for it to end."

"What will you do if Thelma doesn't recover?"

"Sell up, I suppose. But for now, we'll forge on. Mom would expect us to. Though I had to cancel all the bookings scheduled for this week. I didn't know how long the police would keep us out. Still, I have a new batch arriving next weekend, so I have my work cut out for me. The police were all over the house."

"Have they any idea at all who was responsible? Was there a break in? Was anything stolen?"

Doreen bit her lip.

"No. That's what's so strange. If it hadn't been for those bruises— and they said something about the angle of the fall, too—it would have looked like an accident. That railing was far too low. I always told Mum it was dangerous. If only she hadn't been there on her own."

"Did none of the neighbours see anyone arriving or leaving?"

"No. Mrs. Jacks next door was in her garden when Carl and I left in the morning, but she was inside when I came home, and of course, Carl didn't get back until much later."

"Who was the person who came to inquire about rooms? Have the police traced him?"

"No," said Doreen. "He didn't show up. He left a message on the answering machine to say he'd booked in somewhere else. So nobody came to the house. The police have no suspects. Now..." Doreen's voice tailed off and she dropped her eyes. Then she looked up again and stared frantically at Philippa. "Oh, Philippa, what am I going to do? If Mom dies, I'm the one who inherits the place. They're going to think I pushed her."

"There has to be something they've missed," said Philippa.

"Like what? There's just no reason for the attack."

"Was there some ancient family feud that could have caused your mother to have enemies? Try to think."

"Everyone loved Mom," insisted Doreen.

Philippa frowned.

"You said she was distracted that morning. Remember. You told me she didn't seem to be on top of things the way she normally was. Was she worried about something?"

"Possibly."

"This is pure speculation," said Philippa, "but there was an odd little incident at Green Gables. Thelma said there was nothing to it, but I could tell it had bothered her. She thought she recognized a man she ran into on the trail, but he insisted they'd never met. Did she say anything to you about it?"

Doreen shook her head.

"No, but that might explain why she pulled up the photo files from our Maritime holiday. I wish I knew which ones she was studying. What did the man look like?"

"I don't know. I didn't meet him. Thelma told me about the incident afterwards. I'd walked on to the Montgomery house and your mom waited for me by the road. She said a couple had stopped to talk with her, and the man seemed familiar, except that his hair was wrong. Wait. She said something about him never having been at the Bay of Fundy. Isn't that where you met that couple who were trapped on the sands?"

"At the Hopewell Rocks. Yes. That's right."

"And the woman drowned?"

"Yes. But that was an accident. The husband did everything he could to rescue his wife."

Philippa shook her head.

"It would be pretty easy to drown someone while pretending to rescue them," she pointed out. "I wonder if we could find an old newspaper clipping with the man's photograph."

"It's more likely you'd get the woman's picture," said Doreen. "But," she added jubilantly, "*we* have a picture of him. We took a photo for them because their camera battery died. We'll even have the man's email somewhere. Come on. It'll be in the computer too."

She swept out of the kitchen and Philippa hurried after her. Doreen led her into a private room at the back of the house. It was a snug, book-lined study with French doors opening onto a small brick patio. A computer desk took up the end wall.

Doreen clicked on a folder, and another series of folders popped into view. Clicking on one entitled *The Hopewell Rocks,* she scrolled along the series of pictures until she came to the end. Then she wrinkled her brow, and, looking perplexed, reversed the process.

"I don't understand," she said at last. "The picture is gone."

"Check the deleted file," said Philippa.

Doreen complied.

"Empty," she said.

"And I suppose it's long gone from the camera?"

"Yes."

"What about the email address? Is that there?"

Doreen logged onto her email and scrolled down through the address file.

"No, it's gone too."

"We have to tell the police," said Philippa. "There has to be a connection."

"But even if it was the same man, why would he feel threatened by Thelma?"

"If he'd changed his name and altered his hairstyle, there has to be a reason. People don't get new identities because they're bored with their appearance. He's obviously married again. Maybe he's planning to do a repeat on wife-number-two. But what I can't figure out is how would he have known where to find Thelma?"

Doreen shook her head sadly.

"Mum made it easy for him," she sighed. "She was always so ready to hand out cards for the B&B. She gave him one when we talked on the beach. It was just before he went off with his wife. That poor crazy girl was so enamored of him, for all her chemically enhanced state. She went off waving her pendant and quoting Shakespeare."

"What!" exclaimed Philippa.

Doreen stared at her, bewildered.

"Sorry?"

"Did you say she had a pendant?"

"Yes. A gorgeous thing. Intricate gilt filigree with lots of coloured gems. I'm not sure what they were, but the centre one was blood red and there were sparkly pale blue stones around the rim. There was a quote from Shakespeare on the back."

"It was from *Twelfth Night*, wasn't it? 'Journeys end in lovers meeting'?"

"Yes, that's right."

Philippa felt sick. She turned and stared intently at Doreen.

"I met the wife . . . the new wife. She was in the washroom. She was wearing that pendant. And she told me she was on her honeymoon. They're on the cruise ship. What a perfect setting for another accident."

"What are we going to do?" whispered Doreen.

"I'm not going to go through a pile of red tape with a bunch of policemen who have to be convinced we're not crackpots. I'll call my brother. He's RCMP. He can move mountains."

"Wait," said Doreen suddenly. "I've just remembered. We *do* have the man's email, assuming he hasn't changed it. Carl copied our email list into his laptop because he wanted access to our address list when he was away. I bet it's still there."

She bent down and pulled a computer case from below the shelf. Opening it, she drew out the laptop and switched it on. A moment later, triumphantly, she pointed at the screen.

"There you are. Rogersutherland@hotmail.com."

Philippa jotted down the address on a slip of paper. "It may be defunct," she said, "but on the other hand, Roger Sutherland might be adept at keeping both of his identities alive. I'll pass this on to Richard. I'll call him from my room. Try not to worry, Doreen."

Philippa left the study and went upstairs. She punched in Richard's cell number, but only reached his voicemail, so leaving him a message telling him the call was urgent, she sat down by the window and restlessly drummed her fingers on the arm of the chair. Five minutes later, Richard still had not returned the call. Eyeing her laptop on the desk beside her, an idea occurred to Philippa. She opened the AnneGG@hotmail.com email she had created for non-personal contacts during her stay on PEI and clicked on a new message.

She entered the address she had copied from Carl's computer. Then she rapidly typed a message and pressed _send_. Just then, her phone rang. It was Richard. Quickly she explained what was going on. Richard was a good listener, and he waited patiently while she related the whole story as she knew it. When she concluded, somewhat apologetically, by telling him about the message she had sent, the reaction at the other end was predictable.

Richard was annoyed.

"Do you think that was smart?"

"Probably not, but if he knows that someone has guessed what he's up to, he's less likely to drop the second wife overboard. For all we know," Philippa added, trying to detour her brother from the lecture that she knew was coming, "he could be one of those serial killers who makes a habit of marrying women and popping them off."

"That may be," said Richard, "but now I'm going to have to alert the local police to keep an eye on you as well as your landlady in hospital. If the man is a killer, he won't want to leave anyone around who knows what he's up to."

"He's on a cruise ship," said Philippa. "He can hardly do me or Thelma any harm out there. It's his wife you have to worry about. What you need to do is keep a watch on him and catch him when he makes another attempt. There was only one cruise boat in the harbour that day, so you should easily be able to get the name of the ship."

"As you yourself pointed out," said Richard acidly, "he probably won't do anything to his wife if he gets your message, at least not on this trip, but he might well try to track you down once he's off the boat. Have you checked to see if the message has bounced back as undeliverable?"

"Yes. Nothing as yet. I think it's gone through."

"You've no idea what his name is now?"

"No, and I can't describe him, except that he has a moustache. He probably has short, dark hair, because Thelma said the hair was different, and according to Doreen, Roger Sutherland had tawny blonde hair that was quite long. But I did see his new wife. She's blonde, and very svelte. Sweet face. Big blue eyes. About five-six, I'd say, because she was a fair bit taller than me."

"Everyone's taller than you."

"Never mind the put-downs," said Philippa. "Find the woman. No one else will have a pendant like the one she's wearing. I'm quite sure you'll be able to identify them from that. Let me know what happens."

"I will," said Richard grimly. "And for heaven's sake, concentrate on your part and stay out of trouble. Whatever you do, don't yap about this to anyone else."

"I won't, but is it okay if I call Bob and tell him what's going on?"

"Sure. He'll be as annoyed with you as I am. Maybe he'll have more luck impressing on you what an idiot you are."

"Well, thanks a lot," said Philippa, but she was talking to the air. Richard had rung off. She shrugged, and started to dial Miller's number, but then she wavered. Richard was right. She had been reckless, and Bob would be furious with her. He'd also be frantic with worry, and there wasn't anything he could do to help. Richard was RCMP and had the connections to deal with an East Coast incident. She would leave things to him and not involve her VPD friend. Sighing, she put her phone away. Anne of Green Gables, she reflected, had no idea of the drama that had evolved out of her beautiful haunted wood.

*   *   *

Richard had no difficulty finding the name of the cruise ship that had visited Charlottetown on the day in question, but even with first-class cooperation from the captain and his crew, the couple Philippa had described proved elusive. There were more than a dozen honeymooning couples on board the *Gloriana*, but none of them fit the profile provided by the RCMP. Furthermore, none of the women were sporting the distinctive pendant. Several of the husbands had the muscular physique that Doreen had mentioned, but none of their wives were blue-eyed blondes, and the only bride whose description matched the pretty lady that Philippa had met at Green Gables was the trophy wife of a portly middle-aged businessman with a heart condition—a gentleman who, the captain reported cynically, had ditched his wife of forty years in a wild endeavour to recapture his youth, and was now suffering the consequences of attempting to keep up with a woman less than half his age. More fool him, thought Richard, unsympathetically.

Grimly, Richard realized that Philippa's email might have frightened Sutherland into changing his plans and that the couple could be anywhere on the East Coast by now. However, the police could not afford to make that assumption. It was more likely that Sutherland had chosen to keep a low profile by persuading his wife to keep secret the fact that they were honeymooners—and with that eventuality, every married couple on board would have to be vetted.

Therefore, when the ship docked at Halifax, it acquired another honeymoon couple in the form of two undercover detective constables who were delighted with their new assignment. Sharing a cabin with a colleague of the opposite sex was a small price to pay for a luxurious voyage where every meal, drink and cruise-line service was gratis. But three days into their voyage, they had drawn a blank. The pair they were searching for did not appear to be on board.

The RCMP were also unsuccessful in tracking Roger Sutherland, but what history they did unearth served to accentuate the doubts that Philippa had raised. Sutherland, they discovered, had dual citizenship, having been born in Montana to an American father and a Canadian mother, both of whom had died when he was young. Sutherland was an only child and a bit of a loner. He had lived in both countries, but had settled in Montana in 2000. In 2008, he had married a Canadian woman named Anna Paget. Six months after the marriage, they had sold their home and moved to Calgary—at least, that was what investigators were told by their neighbours in Montana—but north of the border was a different story. Sutherland had arrived in Calgary on his own, and within a year, was courting a local girl by the name of Cindy Bauer, who later died during their honeymoon at the Hopewell Rocks. After the death of Cindy Bauer, Sutherland had returned to Calgary and arranged for Cindy to be buried there. No one had any idea what had happened to the wife he married in Montana, and no one had any idea where Roger Sutherland was now. After his wife's funeral, he had sold the house that they had planned to live in together and moved away from Calgary. He left no forwarding address. His bank accounts were still open, but had been gradually emptied over a three-month period, and there had been no activity on his credit cards since the end of 2010. Sutherland had vanished as completely as Anna Paget and Cindy Bauer. But there was one thing all the characters in this strange drama had in common. They were all alone in the world, without parents or siblings who could help to track them down.

"Sounds like there's a body of another woman dumped somewhere in the Rockies," said Sergeant Martin. "I think your sister's right. We have a serial wife-killer on our hands. How are they doing at the PEI end? Any progress there?"

"Nothing," said Richard. "They're checking on the background of any man on board who even remotely fits the description, but the reality is, none of them are married to the woman Philippa met. The man who most closely fits the profile of the swimmer at the Hopewell Rocks is a brawny redhead with a moustache, but his wife is a tiny brunette. Mind you, she does have big blue eyes, so we sent Philippa her photo, just in case some trick of the light in the washroom at Green Gables had altered her hair colour."

Sergeant Martin was sceptical.

"Light couldn't change a brunette into a blonde."

"Not as a rule, but the woman in the washroom was wearing a sunhat, so most of her hair was hidden. Anyway, it was worth a try, but when Philippa studied the picture, she was quite definite that it wasn't the person she'd met at Green Gables. Funnily enough, she did recognize the woman in the photo. She'd seen her at the Best Western the night she arrived. Evidently, the husband had been raising hell about not being booked into the honeymoon suite. He made such a fuss, the manager said they could have it for a full week free of charge after they returned from the cruise. Philippa says his wife seemed mortified."

"Could your sister have been mistaken? She only saw these women very briefly."

"No, I trust Philippa on that. She's very observant. Besides, to be absolutely sure, we checked on the man's whereabouts on the day Thelma Trent was attacked. There was no way he was anywhere near the place. He spent most of the day holed up with the hotel travel guide setting up the tours he and his wife were going to take after the cruise."

"Are there no other leads?"

"There were two no-shows, but they were dead ends, too. One couple phoned later to say they'd missed their connection to Charlottetown. The other was more promising. A couple by the name of John and Jackie Lee didn't return to the ship after their day ashore. They fit the description quite well, but they were tracked down in the same hospital where Thelma Trent is laid up. The wife had ended up with sunstroke and was quite sick. By the time the police found them, they'd already called the cruise line to say they'd be renting a car to drive over to Halifax and pick up the ship again there."

"Did you send Philippa a picture of Jackie Lee? Maybe her husband put something in her afternoon tea to give them an excuse to stay in town."

"Philippa didn't think it was the same woman. The photo wasn't that good, so she couldn't be positive. But the Lees have rejoined the ship now, so they'll be watched just like the other couples. Somehow,

I don't believe John Lee is our man. His background is impeccable. Too much history to be a stolen identity. But we'll see. It's only a matter of time. We'll get him, even if we have to put a tail on every married man on the whole blessed ship. Something will crack open somewhere."

"What about the pendant? Any joy there?"

"None of the jewellers or engravers in Alberta have any recollection of such an item. We're checking in Montana, too, but we may have to go nationwide with the search. He could have had it made anywhere."

"Where is the cruise ship now?" asked Sergeant Martin.

"Somewhere off Florida. It's heading back up the coast now. In fact, it'll arrive in Charlottetown the day of my sister's opening night, which is four days from now. Good job she's going to be at the theatre surrounded by a big cast and an enthusiastic audience. That'll keep her safe and out of trouble. Nobody's likely to try to pop off Anne of Green Gables, but the locals are going to have someone in the theatre anyway, just as a precaution—and there will be a watch on Thelma Trent at the hospital, too. The duty constables are being given photographs of all the possible suspects, so they'll be able to pick out any one of them who shows up either at the hospital or the theatre. And," added Richard with satisfaction, "Bob Miller is flying out with my parents. He'll be celebrating with Philippa after the final curtain, and you can bet your boots, he won't let her out of his sight."

"Well," said Martin philosophically, "that should help the romance along. Maybe *their* journey will end with lovers meeting. At least old Will Shakespeare would approve that match."

*   *   *

Four days later, Air Canada flight AC884 from Vancouver to Charlottetown, via Montreal, was soaring across Manitoba. Although it was only just past noon, Bertram Beary was already in need of a refill. The early hour did not stir any qualms in his conscience, since he considered air travel the equivalent of an extended cocktail hour. When his mood was beatific, Beary tended to wax poetic.

"We are heading for the Home of Confederation," he crooned. "The commencement of our magnificent country as a nation. I've always wanted to visit PEI." He hailed the flight attendant and waved his mini-Glenlivet bottle. "This little guy is lonely," he said breezily. "He needs a twin to keep him company."

"No, he doesn't," snapped Edwina. She waved the attendant away. "Philippa won't appreciate you arriving for her opening night half-cut," she added acerbically, "and if you wanted to visit PEI, we should have taken the extra time to go to the coast on our last motor-home trip. Then we could have detoured to Halifax and visited your uncle and cousins as well."

"I don't like visiting people when I travel," said Beary mulishly. "I want to see the sights, not a passel of relatives who, however politely they receive us, will breathe a sigh of relief when we vacate their premises. Charlottetown will be enjoyable because we're booked into Philippa's B&B. Comfort and independence. The woman I spoke to was very accommodating, and I swore her to secrecy over the fact that we have someone else with us." He swivelled in his seat and called across the aisle. "Hey, Bob! Stop working and relax. You're on holiday."

Miller looked up from his laptop.

"Policemen are never on holiday," he said. "You should know that with a son in the RCMP. But you're right. I should make the most of my leave. I just hope Philippa isn't annoyed that I've come with you."

"Of course she won't be annoyed. She'll be delighted. Why should you imagine she'd mind?"

"Because I raised the idea with her when she first broke the news that she had the part, and she didn't exactly jump for joy."

"But why not?" asked Edwina.

Miller gave a rueful smile.

"She said that playing Anne was a good career opportunity, but not her idea of the perfect role. Her exact words were, 'Why would I want you to see me play the role of a precocious little girl? It'll just make you think you can treat me like your kid sister.' Mind you," he added wryly, "given the casual way she treats me, it would serve her right if I did."

Beary leaned across the aisle and whispered something so that Edwina could not hear. Miller grinned.

Edwina pursed her lips irritably.

"What was that you just said?" she demanded.

"Just a little fatherly advice," said Beary smoothly. "And I really do need that second glass of Scotch."

With a seraphic smile, and ignoring Edwina's scowl of displeasure, he waved to the flight attendant and ordered his refill.

*   *   *

Sergeant Martin found Richard reading an email that he had pulled up on the screen of his computer.

"Anything new and exciting?" he asked. "Bodies in the bilge? Corpses in the Caribbean?"

"Believe it or not, they *have* had a corpse on board," Richard replied, "but it's not the one we're seeking. The old geezer with the trophy wife had a heart attack, surprise, surprise, and the ship's doctor made no bones about the fact that it was induced by his determination to keep up—or, as he more specifically put it, keep *it* up—with spouse-number-two. But there's been nothing as yet to identify Roger Sutherland, or tell us if he's actually on board the ship. However," Richard added, "another report has come in from Montana."

"Anything interesting?"

"Not so far—" Richard stopped abruptly. "Wait a minute! Yes, here it is. This is the clincher. Roger Sutherland couldn't swim."

"Then our man isn't Sutherland," said Martin. "He's just nicked his identity."

"Yes, maybe. But in that case, where is Sutherland? Our information is quite clear on one point. Roger Sutherland may have been a loner, but not so much that the long-time residents didn't know who he was. It was definitely Sutherland who married Anna Paget in Montana."

Martin's eyes bulged.

"And turned up alone in Calgary? That mean there could be two bodies buried in the Rockies. The jerk must have killed both of them."

The door opened and Constable Jean Howe hurried into the room. Her eyes sparkled with excitement.

"We've tracked down the jeweller, sir," she announced. "Scarborough, Ontario. It's a popular local establishment that's been in business for ages, luckily for us, because the pendants were made in the late sixties."

"Pendants?"

"Yes. There were two. Gilded bronze with a fire opal surrounded by zircons. Not seriously expensive, but not junk either. They were crafted for a husband and wife acting team who were playing Viola and Sebastian in a production of *Twelfth Night* at Stratford. Their names were Edward and Jennifer Seeger. The jeweller remembers them very well because they were so much in love, and he always used to say they should be playing the lovers, not the brother and sister."

Richard felt a surge of excitement.

"If Edward Seeger was playing Sebastian in the sixties, he's much too old for our man, but if he had a son, that would fit perfectly. Maybe the man on the beach was telling the truth when he said the pendant had belonged to his mother. We're getting close to him. We just need a name and a face, and we'll nail the bastard."

"We're working on it, sir," said Jean. "I should have the answer fairly soon."

"I want it sooner than soon," stated Richard. "That ship will be coming back into Charlottetown two hours from now. If we haven't zeroed in on him by the time the ship docks, I'm going to ask the team back east to put a tail on every one of our possible suspects if they go ashore. They can watch every bloody one of them until further notice."

*   *   *

By seven o'clock that evening, the theatre was humming with activity. The Bearys picked up their tickets from the box office and wove their way through the milling crowds. Suddenly, Edwina stopped and pointed to the centre of the foyer.

"Look!" she cried. "It's Green Gables."

A group of people had gathered around a glass case, which contained a model of a white house with green gables, roof and shutters. The house was surrounded by flowerbeds edged with green leaves, and beside it stood an apple tree loaded with blossoms. The miniature garden was bisected by an path that led to the front door. A tiny figure stood in front of the house. It was Anne, in her yellow pinafore and straw hat. The entire thing was made out of sugar.

"Trust the Japanese," grunted Beary, noting the label.

"I believe Anne is very big in Japan."

"So is Godzilla," muttered Beary. He eyed the model in the case. "They obviously shrunk her down to bring her over."

"Don't be silly," retorted Edwina. "Come on, we'd better get to our seats."

"We don't have to go in yet." Beary had caught sight of the concessions. "I have time for a drink."

"No, you don't. I hope Philippa received the flowers we sent round."

"She did," said Miller. "I checked with the usher. She said Philippa was thrilled." He furrowed his brow. "I hope my plan doesn't backfire on me. I left my flowers in the office so I could take them round after the show. But what if she's upset, thinking I haven't sent any. That won't throw her, will it?"

"Probably be a benefit," Beary reassured him. "She might be slightly nettled, but that'll focus her. If she had a bouquet from you, she might go all dewy-eyed and lose her concentration. We want her attention focussed on her performance, not her private life. Let her wait."

"That's rather brutal," said Miller.

"The arts are brutal," said Beary. "Every bit as cutthroat as crime. Your world and her world have a lot in common. So sit tight, and as soon as the show is over, you can retrieve your flowers from the office and hustle backstage."

"Don't hustle too much," Edwina advised. "There's an opening night reception, so she won't be waiting around to receive people in costume. She'll be rushing to take off her makeup and change into a dress, and she won't thank you for seeing her covered in face-cream. I'd give her a good fifteen minutes to make herself presentable. Now, come on. Let's go in."

Edwina motioned them towards a group of Japanese tourists who were chatting noisily while they waited in line behind a soignée blonde who was receiving directions from the usher. Beary shuffled into the queue, eyed the blonde, positioned himself with his back to Edwina and mouthed, "Ooh-la-la!" at Miller. The blonde threw them a sidelong glance and smiled as she took her program and moved on. The tourists surged forward, leaving their tour leader to hand in their tickets, and in no time at all, the Bearys were shepherded inside.

The auditorium was large and exceptionally wide, so Beary was relieved to find that their seats were on the aisle and reasonably central. The house was full, which was not surprising since it was the opening show of the season. The air of anticipation was high. When the lights went down, there was an expectant hush. The conductor raised his baton, the orchestra swung into the overture and the show began.

It was a lively production, sleek and effervescent, with a young, enthusiastic cast. Beary was charmed to see his daughter as a young girl again, though the imaginative and emotional Anne was hardly the embodiment of Philippa in her early years. Philippa had been a solemn, highly focussed little girl, with impressive powers of observation and sparks of impish humour that demonstrated that her father's sense of fun lurked inside the grave exterior. But the more he watched, the less he saw Philippa. There was something tantalizingly familiar about her performance, although he couldn't place what it was.

Edwina identified it first.

"She's playing Janie Crittenden," she whispered, naming one of Philippa's livelier childhood companions. "She has her spot on."

Beary chuckled.

"You've got it," he said. "Clever little minx, our daughter."

As the lights came up at the intermission, Miller regarded Beary inquisitively.

"What was so amusing?" he asked.

"Philippa nailing one of her childhood friends," said Beary. "Her Anne was the spitting image of a girl that she went to school with. If I hadn't known it was Philippa on that stage, I don't think I would have recognized her."

"I hardly recognized her," said Miller. "She's a very good actress, isn't she? She's even made herself look different. She'd make a fantastic undercover cop."

"Don't ever tell her that," Edwina said firmly. She stood up and stepped out into the aisle. "I'm going to pop up to the gift shop and pick up some postcards," she announced. "I won't be long," she added, with a warning stare at her husband.

Miller was still pondering Philippa's performance.

"It just goes to show," he philosophized, "how easy it is for people to change their identities. Leaving aside the tricks for altering one's appearance, just a few different mannerisms will create a whole new persona. It's only when some hint of the former character slips through, or when a habit or skill gives the person away, that anyone can identify the individual under the disguise."

"On that note," said Beary, seeing that Edwina was out of earshot, "this individual is going to be true to character and go out to the lobby for a drink. Come on, let's go fortify ourselves for the second act."

*   *   *

As the Bearys were enjoying the last act of *Anne of Green Gables*, Richard was standing by Jean Howe's desk, listening intently to the results of her research.

"There was a son, sir," she said. "Two children actually. We managed to get hold of one of their former high-school teachers and she was a mine of information. It's not a happy story." She shook her head solemnly. "Sounds like the parents should never have had children."

"Go on."

"Evidently, the Seegers were very successful on the Canadian theatre scene, particularly with the Shakespearean festivals. However, during their tenth season at Stratford, Mrs. Seeger had to withdraw as she was pregnant. Appropriately, since Viola and Sebastian were the Seegers' greatest roles, Jennifer Seeger produced twins, a boy and a girl, who naturally, were named after the characters in the play. The children should have been the crowning glory for the Seegers, but the reality was, the parents were too much focussed on each other and their careers, and the twins were left to fend for themselves. They became unmanageable, and there were a lot of problems at school. The two of them were inseparable. They did everything as a team."

"What sort of things?"

"Getting one-up on other kids. Scoring off teachers. And their high-school counsellor was convinced that the relationship between the twins was not a healthy one, so we can guess what that was supposed to mean."

"Young Sebastian was a little too interested in his sister?"

"Exactly. Anyway, in 1992, when the twins were fourteen, their parents finally acknowledged that something had to be done. They resolved to split the twins up and send them to boarding schools in separate provinces."

"Did they follow through and actually do it?"

Jean's expression became grim.

"They never had the chance to," she said. "They died in a boating accident in the summer of that year. Sebastian was with them, but unlike his parents who were not good swimmers, he had competed in several swim meets and had completed his lifeguard training. We're told he made a valiant attempt to rescue them, but in the end, he had to give up and swim to shore."

"We've got him," said Richard.

"I should say so," agreed Jean. "Sebastian Seeger, born in 1978, which means he's thirty-four now."

"Do we know where he was between losing his parents and turning up at the Bay of Fundy?"

"No. He and his sister moved away after they graduated from high school and no one heard of them after that. They just quietly vanished."

"Are there any photographs of him?"

"I've requested his high-school picture," replied Jean. "There's no other source, but that should be coming in any minute. Wait a mo," she added, hearing a ping from her computer. "This could be it now."

Jean flicked the mouse and clicked on the message that had just come through. A photograph was attached. It showed a square-jawed, handsome youth, with shoulder-length fair hair and startling light blue eyes.

"Good-looking little swine," commented Sergeant Martin.

Richard's eyes narrowed.

"Bring up the photo of that muscle-bound redhead with the moustache," he ordered. "The one with the tiny brunette wife."

Jean went into her files and found the picture that her boss wanted. She gave a sharp intake of breath.

"It's him, isn't it?"

Richard nodded grimly and picked up the phone on her desk.

"I'd say so. I'll get onto the PEI team. They can pull him in and find out what the hell is going on."

*   *   *

The opening-night audience loved the play. After three curtain calls to thunderous applause from the partisan crowd, the lights in the auditorium came up and the theater-goers began to filter out to the lobby. Miller fought his way over to the office to pick up his flowers. He was not the only person retrieving bouquets. As he entered the cubicle, the alluring blonde whom he and Beary had admired earlier was coming out carrying a luxuriant arrangement of carnations, lilies and daisies. As she swept by, he caught a whiff of what he imagined was a very expensive perfume. He didn't think the scent was coming from the flowers. An oblong beaded evening bag hung from a gold chain over the woman's shoulder, and its variegated colours of purple and pink matched her stylish evening suit. Definitely an eyeful, thought Miller, as he picked out his long-stemmed red roses from the remaining bouquets. Having found his flowers, he asked the usher for directions to the backstage dressing rooms.

As he came back into the lobby, he spied Edwina hovering near the gift shop. She was already holding a wine glass. He made his way over to join her and tapped his watch.

"What do you think? Will she have had time to change by now?"

"Probably," said Edwina. "Go ahead. Bertram is in the washroom. I'm going to pop in once he gets back. Then we'll come round. We'll see you in Philippa's dressing room in a minute."

"I can wait if you like," said Miller.

"Nonsense," interjected Beary, bobbing up behind them. "Off you go. Hey," he added indignantly to Edwina, "that was my glass of wine you just drank."

"I was thirsty," Edwina retorted.

Miller grinned and set off across the lobby, clutching his roses firmly in his right hand.

Beary watched him go.

"So obviously a cop," he observed. "Anyone would think he was holding a truncheon."

"Well," said Edwina serenely, "Perhaps he's preparing to do battle with the Athole."

She set the wine glass firmly on the gift-shop counter and sailed off in the direction of the washrooms.

I must be slipping, Beary thought mutinously. Now she's even stealing my lines.

*   *   *

Richard put the phone back down. He looked puzzled.

"Sebastian Seeger is still on board the *Gloriana*. He hadn't gone ashore. They're going to move in on him now."

"So we've nailed him."

"Yes." Richard frowned.

"It is a bit odd," commented Jean. "Why would he still be waiting around on board the ship? Why not go to his hotel? Didn't you say he was booked into the bridal suite at the Best Western after the cruise?"

"Yes," said Richard thoughtfully. "Jean, get back to the high school and ask them to send a picture of the sister. I want to see what Viola Seeger looks like."

Jean nodded and picked up the phone. Richard beckoned to Martin to follow and headed back to his office.

"What are you thinking?" Martin asked curiously, once they were inside.

"I'm not sure what I'm thinking. Yes, I am. I'm thinking about two blue-eyed blondes who didn't want to be separated—who have spent their entire lives working as a team—and that would mean

Sebastian Seeger wasn't the only one who spent time in Montana."
Richard crossed his arms decisively. "I'm willing to bet," he stated,
"that there *is* only one body in the Rockies after all."

"And it isn't Anna Paget?"

"Exactly."

"You think it's Roger Sutherland?"

"Yes. Somewhere along the way, the twins disposed of him.
They're in it together."

"But if Anna Paget was Viola Seeger, why didn't she just go along
with her brother and pose as his wife?" Martin looked perplexed.
"After all, Seeger took over Roger Sutherland's identity. Why arrive
in Calgary as a single man?"

"To leave him free to pick his next victim," Richard said tersely,
"and to leave her free to help him find another mark. What a
pernicious pair they are. I—"

Richard stopped abruptly and went pale.

"Oh, my god!" he said. "Two pendants! We've been assuming
that the woman Philippa met at Green Gables was the next victim,
because she was on her honeymoon and she had the gilded pendant.
But what if she isn't a victim? What if she's the sister? What if she's
Viola Seeger?"

Martin's eyes almost bulged out of his forehead.

"They must be working separately! We've got two killers. Two
pendants, and two murderers. We should be looking for two
different couples, not one. No wonder we couldn't make them
match."

"We can now," said Richard. "The woman that Philippa saw is
the one who fits the description of the trophy wife on board the
Gloriana."

"The wife of the heart-attack victim?"

"Yes. Let's hope they didn't perform a burial at sea."

Richard picked up the phone and punched in a number. He turned to Martin as he waited for the call to go through.

"With any luck, I'll be able to get the businessman's body brought back to shore and delivered to the morgue," he said. "In my opinion, an autopsy is in order. That heart attack could have been induced by more than an extra-vigorous piece of tail."

Richard got through and spoke rapidly for a few minutes, but as he listened to the response from the other end, his lips compressed into a tight line. After a moment, he paused and shook his head at Martin.

"Viola Seeger was allowed to bring the body ashore," he muttered. "It's at a funeral home in the middle of town. They're calling the parlour right now. I'm on hold."

"When did she leave the ship?"

"Soon after it docked. Hopefully, she's still at the funeral parlour." He stopped speaking as someone came back on the line. Richard listened briefly, then hung up.

"Damn," he said to Martin. "She's already left. She said she'd be back in the morning, but she only left her home address and a cell number. The mortuary receptionist doesn't know where she's staying in town."

"That's a bugger," grunted Martin. "If she gets wind of her brother's arrest, she'll slip out of our hands again."

Richard nodded.

"Yes," he said grimly. "And I'm willing to bet she's every bit as cunning and vicious as he is."

"No wonder Seeger had an unbreakable alibi for the day that Thelma Trent was attacked," said Martin. "He made the appointment to view the room, but Viola Seeger was the one who went to the house."

Suddenly Richard froze and his face went pale.

"Oh, my god," he said quietly. "That's why Seeger is still on board the *Gloriana*. He's making sure he has an alibi. They're planning another murder."

"Well then," Martin pointed out, "it's a good job that they have a guard on Thelma Trent at the hospital."

"Yes," said Richard, "but none of the team at the theatre know to watch out for a woman. What about my sister!"

*   *   *

Philippa had just finished taking off her makeup when she heard a knock at her dressing-room door. Assuming it was her parents, she was about to invite them in, when the door opened and a familiar face peered round. It was the blue-eyed blonde whom she had met at Green Gables. The visitor held a huge bouquet of carnations, lilies and daisies.

Philippa's eyes widened.

"It's you. My goodness, I'm glad to see you. You're all right. You've no idea how worried I was."

The woman in the doorway arched her eyebrows quizzically.

"Worried about me?"

"You don't know why? Then why are you here?"

The woman glanced around the room, and seeing Philippa was alone, she stepped inside and closed the door. "I just wanted to meet you and talk with you. You see, I read your message. I had to know what it meant."

"How did you know it came from me?"

"It wasn't that hard to figure out, especially as my husband met your landlady in the Birch Wood at Green Gables. She told him that the girl playing Anne was staying with her, so I knew I'd find you here."

"Did your husband see the message I sent?"

"No. Only I read it, but I wanted to know what was so important. That's why I came." The woman gave a shy smile. "I loved your performance, by the way."

Philippa stood up. Nervously, she kept her eye on the door.

"Where's your husband right now?"

The woman did not reply right away. When at last she responded, there was a strange quiver in her voice.

"My husband? Don't you know? He's dead."

Philippa was stunned.

"Dead? How?"

"He died of a heart attack three nights ago. It happened on the cruise ship. It was very sudden, but he's been ill for some time so it wasn't unexpected. All the same, I really need to find out what you thought he'd done. You made it sound as if he were guilty of something terrible. Please tell me. It's bad enough that I've lost him, but I need to know."

Philippa hesitated, wondering how much she should say. If Roger Sutherland was dead, then the woman was safe, and it seemed unnecessarily cruel to shock her with the news that the man she loved had killed his first wife. She bit her lip.

The blonde woman looked pleadingly at Philippa.

"Please," she said.

Philippa felt sympathetic, but she was still reluctant to tell what she knew.

"Honestly, it wasn't anything that you'd want to know. I think it should go to the grave along with your husband. It really is better that way."

"But if other people know what he did, it could still cause me grief. Who else knows what you found out?"

Philippa ignored her conscience and decided to lie.

"No one," she said. "I didn't tell anybody else."

Philippa had difficulty later in recollecting the series of events that followed. She recalled that the blonde woman seemed to transform before her eyes, and the face that had radiated sweetness and concern took on the appearance of a feral, predatory tiger. The blue eyes turned black, and instinct made Philippa recoil and step back as the woman tilted the bouquet and thrust it towards her.

From the corner of her eye, Philippa sensed movement in the doorway.

Then, unaccountably, the blonde careened forward, propelled by some inexplicable force, and crashed into the makeup mirror. From there, she bounced down against the counter. Then she slid back and collapsed motionless onto the floor. With amazement, Philippa saw that a second bouquet of glorious red roses had magically materialized and was crushed around the immobile woman's neck.

Philippa looked up. She saw that someone stood by the door. His back was turned to her, but she could hear him rapidly firing instructions into a cellphone. The man ended the call quickly and then turned to face her.

It was Bob Miller. With a sob that combined bewilderment, relief and utter joy, Philippa threw herself into his arms.

*   *   *

Beary and Edwina were in perfect agreement over the fact that they should give Bob Miller a few minutes with Philippa before they went in to congratulate her. Glowing with pride, for all the way backstage they had been regaled with compliments about their daughter's performance, they found their way to the corridor where Philippa's dressing room was located.

Noticing that the door was ajar, Beary stepped forward, but then, having caught a glimpse of what was happening inside the room, he drew back. Stealthily, he pulled the door closed. He took Edwina's arm and steered her back down the corridor.

"What's the matter?" asked Edwina. "Can't we go in and give her a hug now? If we wait until the reception, she'll be inundated with a mob of admiring strangers."

"Not a good idea to disturb her at the moment," Beary informed his wife. "Young Miller is following some advice I gave him during our flight."

To Beary's surprise, Edwina smiled.

"Oh," she said. "That advice."

"What do you mean, *that advice*?"

"The advice you gave him on the plane."

"And how would you know what advice I gave him?" demanded Beary.

"I asked the steward," Edwina said blithely. "He was serving the person in the seat behind, and I could see from the smile on his face that he'd overheard what you'd said. He considered it very amusing that you'd told Bob just to grab Philippa and give her a great big kiss. I must say, I approve. It's about time those two stopped dragging their feet."

Beary breathed a sigh of relief. The steward had obviously not related the sentence that had followed, which had been something to the effect that Edwina had taken advantage of his youth and innocence and landed him in a similar fashion. Basking in rare approval from his wife, he followed her back to the lobby and indulged in yet another glass of wine.

*   *   *

Later that evening, Philippa handed her car keys to her father and gave him the directions to The Captain's Corner. Then she and Bob Miller strolled back together.

"Sorry about your flowers," said Miller.

"Don't apologize. It was the best bouquet I've ever had."

"I didn't have time to put it down, but it's a good job I didn't hesitate. The blade she had tucked in her carnations was eight inches long."

"How did you know I was in danger?"

"I didn't," said Miller. "Not until I opened the door—and then my policeman's instinct just kicked in. We have a nose for danger. Your face looked horrified, and her body language was unmistakable. She was about to assault you."

Philippa giggled.

"What if it had only been a bouquet of carnations? She could have been a jealous actress who was ticked off because she'd been turned down for my part. You might have ended up facing an assault charge."

"It would have been worth it," said Miller, and ended the conversation with a kiss.

The lights were on in the front rooms when they reached The Captain's Corner. They went up the steps, and as they reached the porch, the front door opened. Doreen stood in the doorway. Behind her, in the lighted hall, Philippa could see her parents standing with Doreen's husband, Carl. All three were beaming.

Doreen stepped forward and engulfed Philippa in a hug.

"Mum's come round," she said joyfully. "She's okay. She's going to recover."

She stepped back and shook Miller's hand.

"Welcome to The Captain's Corner," she said. "Come and join us. We're celebrating with a glass of champagne."

Philippa glanced at her watch. It was almost midnight. She sighed. Anne of Green Gables was going to have the challenge of her life to be vivacious at the matinee the next day, but somehow, she didn't care a bit. She followed Miller inside, watching how easily he greeted her parents and joined in the happy celebration in the living room of The Captain's Corner.

All at once, the inscription on the jewelled pendants came drifting into her mind: *Journeys end in lovers meeting.*

With a delicious sense of adventure, she knew that her journey with Miller was just beginning.

Author's Note

I first read Daphne du Maurier's *Rebecca* when I was fourteen and was so enthralled by the book that I continued reading long into the night. I would never have thought of basing a story on the novel's theme, but there is a stretch of road on the Sunshine Coast that evokes the description of the approach to Manderley and the power of suggestion has been at work every time we have driven that route. Since the Coast is the place where I do most of my writing, it was inevitable that a story on the *Rebecca* theme would ensue one day.

The third story in the collection, "Mimi's Farewell", was inspired by Puccini's *La Bohème*. I was in the chorus of a Vancouver Opera production back in the seventies, and still remember the atmosphere in that wintry Act III scene as I stepped on stage with my basket of bread. The turbulent emotions of the operatic characters in *Bohème* lend themselves so well to a mystery story, especially when one looks closely at the words in the libretto. The quotations in the story were taken from Peggy Cochrane's translation of Giuseppe Giacosa and Luigi Illica's opera libretto and from Henry Mürger's *Scènes de la vie de Bohème*.

All the stories in the book have roots in settings that are familiar to me. I spent several years as a Pets and Friends visitor at the George Derby War Veterans' Hospital and have many happy memories of the people I met there. I also taught in British Columbia high schools, sang in the Vancouver Opera Chorus, and, less enjoyably, was involved in a lengthy case at the Vancouver Courthouse. A trip to PEI and the Charlottetown Festival inspired "Journeys End in Lovers Meeting" and "The Camera Lies" was prompted by the periodic visits of movie crews to Robert Burnaby Park.

A note about the dedication of this book: Jacqollyne Keath is a friend who has been wonderfully supportive with my arts projects. Jacqollyne, who is a classically trained singer, has performed voiceovers for my marionette musicals; she has produced for, acted in, and worked on sound for my various plays; and she is always one of the first people to buy my books when they come out. Such support is wonderful, and I take great pleasure in dedicating this book to her. It is especially appropriate, because Jacqollyne played the role of Beatrice in Vagabond Players production of *Rebecca* several years ago, and our friendship started soon *after Rebecca*! Thank you, Jacqollyne, for all your unwavering support.

Thanks go to my editor, Lorraine Meltzer, for her careful review of my manuscript; also to fellow puppeteer and publisher, Luman Coad and to tech-consultant, Lucky Saini, both of whom helped me navigate a variety of computer-related issues; and last, but definitely not least, to my husband, Hugh, without whom I would never have ventured on writing a series at all.

Elizabeth Elwood is the author of five previous books of mystery stories featuring the lively members of the Beary Family. She is also a playwright whose plays have entertained audiences across Canada and in the United States. Born in England, Elizabeth lives with her husband in Vancouver, British Columbia. Visit her website at www.elihuentertainment.com.

Mystery Stories

To Catch an Actress and Other Mystery Stories
A Black Tie Affair and Other Mystery Stories
The Beacon and Other Mystery Stories
The Agatha Principle and Other Mystery Stories
The Devil gets his Due and Other Mystery Stories

Plays

Casting for Murder
Renovations
Shadow of Murder
Body and Soul